Praise for the Novels of James Conroyd Martin

Push Not the River

"As intriguing and engrossing as its title."
—*Harvard University Quarterly*

Push Not the River contains all the sweep and romance of the classic romantic epics such as *Gone with the Wind* and *Doctor Zhivago,* with a heroine who remains strong in the face of both personal and political tragedy. An enthralling tale of courage, survival, and hope, Anna Maria's story is at once timeless and timely."
—India Edghill, author of *Queenmaker*

"James Conroyd Martin's vivid historical novel captivates the reader with its sweeping depiction of a bygone society on the cusp of violent change. Combining politics with intrigue and romance, **Push Not the River** gives us a glimpse into the turbulent era of late eighteenth century Poland and its people.

Aristocrats and peasants, patriots and traitors come alive in this story, and the Polish soul is beautifully illuminated through ancient myths, folkways, and wisdoms. With his juxtaposition of the personal and political, Martin weaves a compelling tale of transformation—both of a remarkable young woman and her remarkable nation."
—Jennifer Donnelly, author of *The Tea Rose*

"Enthralling. **Push Not the River** is a wonderful epic historical saga in the grand romantic style. The plot never lets up; it gallops at breakneck speed through a vividly portrayed historical landscape."
—Jane Feather, author of *Kissed by Shadows*

Against a Crimson Sky

"Entertaining...fans of historical romance will find much to enjoy in this sprawling epic."
—*Publishers Weekly*

"With Napoleon Bonaparte's ill-fated campaign to conquer Russia as a backdrop, **Against a Crimson Sky** manages to turn the wily emperor's exploitation of Polish patriotism into a classic read that lovers of *Push Not the River* will devour. James Conroyd Martin brings back the characters that made his first novel so compelling, deftly weaving their daily lives into the panorama of war and turmoil that consumed Poland in the early nineteenth century. He portrays a world of hardship and heart in marvelously rendered 'little pieces of happiness stolen from a tapestry of turmoil, war, and separation'."

—Leonard Kniffel, Editor-in-chief of *American Libraries*

"Readers will revel in this engrossing tale of courage, family loyalty, and the Polish nation."

—*Historical Novels Review*

"I was both enthralled and educated by this story of a changing family in a changing Poland. You don't have to have read *Push Not the River* to get the most from this sequel, but after finishing **Against a Crimson Sky** you'll want to—just as you'll be rooting for another book from James Conroyd Martin."

—Suzanne Strempek Shea, author of *Hoopi Shoopi Donna*

"**Against a Crimson Sky** continues the saga of Anna Berezowska and her family as Poland is caught in a deadly vise from its more powerful neighbors. The story line provides a feel for the history, but is more a historical romance spanning over two decades of two people (Jan and Anna) trying to do what they feel is right for their country yet also keep their loved ones safe. In many devious ways Zofia is the star of the tale as a Lady Macbeth plotting at the cost of others (collateral damage) to achieve her goal. . . . [A] fine sequel."

—Harriet Klausner, Amazon's Hall of Fame #1 Reviewer

The Warsaw Conspiracy

With **The Warsaw Conspiracy**, James Conroyd Martin concludes his sweeping trilogy of Poland in the 18th and 19th centuries in grand style. Blending memorable characters from *Push Not the River* and *Against a Crimson Sky* with fascinating new arrivals, Martin's masterful story-telling is at its best. We are instantly thrust into the action as impetuous young military cadets conspire to overthrow the Russian oppressor and regain Poland's freedom. While the ultimate outcome may be pre-ordained, the story unfolds with all the intrigue of an espionage thriller and the gripping tension of a heartfelt love story. This one is not to be missed.

—Douglas W. Jacobson, author of *Night of Flames* and *The Katyn Order*

If you thought the first two installments of James Conroyd Martin's historical trilogy were enthralling, wait until you read the third. More than a simple adventure or romance, **The Warsaw Conspiracy** is a heartstopping journey through post-Napoleon Poland as another generation of freedom-loving Poles resists the domination of a hostile neighbor. Martin's uncanny insight into the Polish national psyche and his vigorous prose make this a compelling page-turner as we learn the fate of our heroines Anna and Zofia and their family. Historical facts and details of daily life combine to keep you riveted to the page.

—Leonard Kniffel, former *American Libraries* Editor-in-Chief; author of *Reading with the Stars: A Celebration of Books and Libraries* and *A Polish Son in the Motherland*

Martin's passionate saga of Poland and its long struggle for autonomy continues in **The Warsaw Conspiracy**. Here he examines the dreams and heartbreak of a brave insurrection against the Russian czars and the rise of Jósef Steinicki, one of those thrilling military warriors, uniquely Polish, called hussars.

—Karleen Koen, New York Times bestselling author of *Through a Glass Darkly: A Novel* and *Before Versailles*

THE WARSAW CONSPIRACY

JAMES CONROYD MARTIN

HUSSAR
QUILL PRESS

CHICAGO

While some characters are based on real people as described in the diary that
inspired *Push Not the River* and other characters are historical personages, this is
a work of fiction.

Also by James Conroyd Martin

Push Not the River
Against a Crimson Sky

Acknowledgments

Among the many deserving of my deepest appreciation are Greg Bimm, Frances Drwal, Judith Sowiński Free, Linda Hansen, Ken Mitchell, Mary Rita Perkins Mitchell, Faye Predny, Sean Scanlon, Pam Sourelis, John Stelnicki, as well as Craig Hansen and Glendon and Tabatha Haddix of Streetlight Graphics.

For Mary Rita Perkins Mitchell
~compatriot on my journey~
With love and thanks

Pronunciation Key

Czartoryski = Char-ta-RIZ-key
Jan = Yahn
Jósef = Yu-zef
Jerzy = Ye-zhĭ
Halicz = Hah-leech
kasza = kasha
Kościuszko = Kawsh-chew-shkaw
Kraków = Krah-kooff
Michał = Mee-how
Paweł = Pah-vel
Sochaczew = Saw-hah-cheff
Stanisław = Stah-neess-wahf
szlachta = shlack-ta

Congress Kingdom of Poland
1815–1831

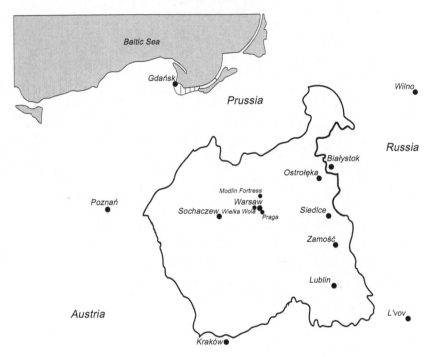

Prologue

Birth is Much
But Breeding is More
—POLISH PROVERB

November 1813, Warsaw

ANNA WAS EASING HERSELF OUT of the blue brocaded high-back chair when her water broke. "Sweet Jesus," she cried in a half-whisper, falling back into the cushions and staring down in disbelief as she watched the pale green of her gown darken.

Her pulse quickened with panic and a flushed heat ran like a river through her veins. Labor would start at any moment. What to do?

Her hands went to her unbraided hair, her fingers frenetically pulling and tugging at the long chestnut brown strands, her mind insensate to the pain. It was a habit that dated to childhood and one that she employed at moments of intense unease or pain, a habit dormant for years, until now.

She fought off fear and willed herself calm. The experience of birth was not new to her—she had already borne three children. But this was the first time she would give birth away from home, away from experienced women, away from a capable midwife.

How could this be? She had thought the half-day carriage ride from the Sochaczew estate to Warsaw to be safe, short, and smooth enough for a woman eight months pregnant. Now she became convinced her judgment was flawed. Had it been the bumps and lurches the carriage and she had weathered? There was no counting the holes and ruts left in the unmended roads as tokens of a government usurped by foreigners. Damn the Russians! Or—was she closer to full term than she had supposed? These were moot questions now and she would spare them no time. For the safety of the baby's delivery, she took a moment to catch her breath and to pray. Early babies meant complications. Early babies often meant . . .

"Anna! What is it?"

The voice drew her back. Jan stood at the entrance to the reception room of the town house, his handsome face paling as his blue eyes moved from her face to the wet folds of her gown.

Anna swallowed hard. "It's time, Jan. It's time." She managed a smile.

"Oh, my God," he mumbled.

Anna watched her husband—a Polish lancer who had fought Prussians, Austrians, and Russians, a man who had endured capture by Cossacks, a man who had sustained sword and bullet wounds—stand mute and motionless at the sight of a woman about to birth.

At last he moved slowly toward her. "Oh, Anna," he breathed, "what are we to do?"

Anna knew her own sense of composure was all important now. She contrived a little laugh. "Do? It's a safe wager we won't get back to Sochaczew. The path is set, husband."

He sat on the edge of the chair at the bedside and took her hand in his. "You said you had time. You said the journey—"

Anna put a finger to his lips. Her laugh this time was gently mocking. "And you have never been wrong in your life, Jan Stelnicki?"

"Not in such matters," he said.

"To be certain. Such matters are not men's matters." Anna took the measure of her husband's knitted brow beneath the silvering blond hair. "Now, we must both be calm. We will weather this. . . . Where's Zofia?"

Jan shrugged. "She went out earlier. By the look of your cousin's attire and the scent of her French perfume, she'll not return home any time soon."

"Mary, Help of Christians!" Anna blurted. She took a breath then, fending off the return of her own panic. "You'll have to find someone here in the capital, Jan. Someone who can deliver our child. The servants are scarcely more than children themselves. Zofia herself would have been worthless, but she would have known of someone."

His eyes widened. "Find someone? Who, Anna? Where?"

"That is for you to determine, Major Stelnicki. Surely all the doctors didn't follow Napoleon. And if they did, one or two must have survived the Moscow retreat. Go, now. Soldiers are good at foraging. Their lives depend upon it. You told me so yourself. Now go forage me a midwife at the least." Anna's hand moved to the contour of her belly. "This life depends upon it."

Jan stood. "We should get you to bed first."

"No, the girls here can tend to that much." Anna pulled the rope that would ring the bell in the kitchen. "You must go now. Hurry! Unless you wish to play doctor yourself."

Jan's chiseled face bled to white, a stark contrast

to the cobalt eyes and dark blue of his short, tailored coat. He bent to kiss her on the cheek and rushed from the room, nearly colliding in the doorway with the young servant girl, Jolanta.

Anna had been unable to take more than one flight of stairs, and so had been placed in Zofia's bedchamber on the first level. Oblivious to the luxuriousness of the huge bed, its crimson hangings and down-stuffed mattress and pillows, she lay staring at the ceiling. She was alone when the pains took on an increasing regularity, just an hour after Jan had left the town house.

Coming to Warsaw had been a gamble, one she had lost. That much was clear. She had wanted to attend the funeral of Anusia Potocka's mother. Anusia had been a good and dear friend to her in the old days, and despite Jan's cautions, Anna was not to be kept away. Of course, as it turned out he had been right to urge prudence. However, Anna was thankful for the small blessing that before embarking on his search for a doctor or midwife, Jan had not chided her for her stubbornness. His fears for her and for their child prevailed.

She *had* been foolish to attempt the journey and could only blame herself. There was nothing left to do now but pray. For someone to help. For a safe delivery. For a healthy baby.

And for a girl. She would offer up no more boys to war. She had lost one to the war machine. Dear, sweet Tadeusz, lost on the death march from Moscow. Yes, she would have a girl, a sister for Jan Michał and Barbara. It must be a girl!

The pains were sharper now and becoming more frequent. Where was Jan? Why hadn't he returned?

Jan. Her love for him had not diminished over time despite the fact that the military had taken him away for more years than he had spent with her.

Their marriage had not been what she had imagined, what she had expected. And yet she did not begrudge him his years with Kościuszko or his time with Napoleon. They were years spent for Poland. Always for Poland. On that they had held the same dream, one first given life by Tadeusz Kościuszko, a dream that they would keep an independent Poland. And when it was lost, how they had hoped that with Napoleon they would regain it. While his promise to restore freedom to Poland had been more implicit than explicit, the majority of the country had bought his bill of goods. What was it the little corporal called himself? *A dealer in hope*, that was it. Well, he had been that. He had given them hope and taken so many thousands of young men to their deaths on the steppes of Russia, moving toward Moscow, and then away—in winter.

A pain tore through her like a gutting knife, and she called out to be attended.

This would be her last child. Somehow she knew that. And it would be a girl. No more sacrificial boys, no matter how worthy the cause. The independent Commonwealth of Poland and Lithuania had vanished. Might it ever be pieced back together in her lifetime? Not likely.

Looking back even further was no easy thing. By seventeen she had lost her parents and infant brother, all untimely deaths.

But she had her own family now. She had that, no little thing. What was it Aunt Stella had said about family? The words came back to her now: *Before there are nations, there are families.*

Anna pulled the bell rope near the bed. Where were those girls? And Jan—what in God's name was keeping him?

The pains seemed somehow different this time. What was it? Were they coming quicker? Sharper? More intense?

Until now she had been blessed in giving birth. Not so her mother, who had had notions of filling the house with sons after Anna's birth. Anna had always sensed that her own birth—the birth of a daughter— had been a disappointment to her mother. There was aloofness in her mother's demeanor toward her, a coldness even, one that contrasted sharply with the sun-kissed love emanating from her father. Countess Teresa Berezowska steadfastly pursued her goal of bearing myriad sons, and there were multiple pregnancies, too, but only one that came to term. Anna closed her eyes, the thought of her infant brother bringing on the blur of tragedies that took him and her parents from her.

Anna pulled herself up against the goose down pillows. She would weather this, she told herself. She would have her family. Poland would go on, with or without its title or borders, with or without her. She would have her Jan and her children, all but one.

The door opened. Wanda and Jolanta crept in like mice. "Madame?" Jolanta asked, crossing half way to the bed. Wanda hung back near the door.

Anna cradled her belly with her hands. "My time is close. Is there no sign of my husband?"

Jolanta shook her head.

"Have you tended a birthing before?"

"No, Madame," Jolanta said. She addressed Anna in the French fashion in which Zofia had coached her, but these were not the sophisticated French maids Zofia had employed in the years before the nation's dissolution. These were country girls, no more than thirteen or fourteen, wide-eyed, fidgeting, and fully frightened at the prospect of delivering a child.

"Well, you are about to manage your first. Come here. Wanda, come away from the door. You will both earn your wages today and see life brought into the world."

Anna gave them their orders now, telling them exactly what would be needed. She spoke in plain terms and without visible panic. She had to keep her head if they were to keep theirs.

They scurried from the room then, still like frightened mice, but mice on a mission.

"Oh, Lutisha," Anna said aloud, "if only you were here." The old and trusted servant had already claimed her eternal reward for a simple life lived well. She had seen Anna through her three previous births, starting with that of Jan Michał, a child born out of rape. But she would not be here this time, with her large, capable hands. Dear, superstitious Lutisha! She would not be here to tie around the infant's wrist a little piece of red yarn to ward away the evil eye.

What seemed a long while passed.

"Wanda!" Anna called out. "Jolanta! Do hurry!"

Anna pushed the pillows out from under her head, shoving them down to lend support to her legs.

Anna called again. This baby was not to be put off.

Just then she heard a commotion on the stairs. The girls had left open the bedchamber door. A man's voice now. Jan's? Yes, she became certain that it was indeed his and her heart lifted. Then came the high-pitched panic of the mice in return. And now a fourth voice, mature and masculine, but strange and gravel-like. A man's voice, surely.

"Anna!" Jan came rushing into the room some minutes later. "I've brought help."

"Where?"

"In the kitchen with the girls."

"Thank God. A doctor. Oh, thank God."

'Not a doctor, dearest. None to be found."

"No? A midwife, then?"

Jan came to the side of the bed. He took Anna's hand. "Well, yes, she says she has assisted."

"What do you mean—" Anna stopped mid-sentence, her eyes widening as the door opened.

A woman clad in a gray and grimy dress came into the room then, hissing in a husky sort of way and prodding ahead of her the maids with their burdens. She was short of stature but large in presence. "You," she told Jolanta, "put the ewer on that table. And you," she said nodding to Wanda, "put the pan and towels there, too. Then wait outside the door until I call for you both. Stay at hand, do you hear?"

Anna thought the puzzlement on the maids' faces as they left could only be mirrors to her own.

"Now, let's have a look at you," the woman said, adjusting the red kerchief that covered thin, graying hair. She approached the side of the bed.

Jan, who had been shifting from one foot to the other, had to drop Anna's hand and step back to allow the woman access. "This is Mira, Anna." And then to the woman: "This is the Lady Stelnicka."

The woman said nothing.

Anna looked up at the dark and serious face coming near her, the hooded eyes like ebony stones above a sharp nose peering down at her as if she were a curiosity. Her hand went to Anna's forehead. "You . . . you have experience?" Anna asked.

"You need not worry, milady," the woman said, her tone anything but deferential. "How long have the pains been coming?"

It was the first of several questions, and as Anna answered them she tried to decipher the look on Jan's face. He no doubt felt the awkwardness of a man caught up in women's business, but she sensed he was closely watching her reactions, too, as if to determine whether the results of his quest met with her approval.

Anna's dizzying thoughts for a short while superseded the pains. A gypsy! He had brought a gypsy into the house to birth their child. Oh, she had nothing against gypsies—on feast days she had never failed to send food to the little colony that collected at the cemetery—but were there no doctors, no mid-wives in all of Warsaw? How had Jan come upon her—this

Mira? Did she truly have experience or had she seen in Jan's desperation her own fortune? A way to gain entrance to a noble's home? A noble's munificence?

But there was no time for further thought. Anna, her face bleeding perspiration, became consumed with the ever-increasing pains, and her body unwillingly writhed now as if below a hot spring were building, as if the greatest hurt of her life were imminent. Had she forgotten her other pregnancies, the price of motherhood? No, she had not. This time was different, she was certain, more difficult than before, more difficult than she could have imagined. And more dangerous.

What was the woman doing now? The activity around her played like a visual and auditory blur. Moment by moment the effort siphoned her strength, leaving a mist of confusion and weakness.

Her mind snapped to attention then as she heard the gypsy dismissing Jan from the room. No! she wanted to call out but found no reservoir of energy to manage a sound. Suddenly she felt his hand holding hers, squeezing it tightly, as if to transfer hope into it.

Before her eyes could focus, before she could even return the pressure, she heard Mira's sharp and mannish voice again, driving Jan from the room and calling in the servant girls. Now came the sound of his boot heels retreating over the wooden floor. Anna lifted her hand—the hand he had held—to her lips, praying she would see Jan again, bask again in the cobalt blue of his eyes.

She heard Jolanta and Wanda come in, heard their gasps at the sight of her. Jan's departure crushed her calm. Fear ratcheted upward. Would she survive this? Would the child survive?

The woman drew aside the sheet and lifted Anna's gown. Anna felt her legs pushed toward her and apart, knees toward the ceiling. The woman's roughened hands moved over Anna's belly and below.

A minute later she felt a tug beneath her left arm. "You will sit back against the headboard," the woman said, instructing Jolanta to help in the lifting from the other side.

"No!" Anna fought against the two. She had never heard of such a thing. But she was no match for the strength of the two at either side. Pain ripped through her as they pulled her as if tugging at a sack of grain.

"Is good. Is good for the delivery." The woman shoved a pillow behind Anna's back. "I birthed three sons with my back against a tree. Is good."

The woman's recollection had no effect on Anna, who tried to stifle her screams as the contractions came, the attempts sometimes failing. The scalding spring below was moving now. The baby was coming. Did this woman know what she was doing? If only Lutisha were here. She would console her, reassure her, give her something to hold on to.

Something to hold on to . . . Anna began to mutter. Mira ignored her at first, but as Anna persisted, the woman asked Wanda what it was she was mumbling. When the maid leaned close to Anna's mouth, Anna managed to whisper, "My rosary, Wanda, please, my rosary. Upstairs."

The girl relayed the message to Mira and—God

bless her!—hurried from the chamber without waiting for the woman's approval.

Time and pain seemed to draw Anna into some dark and fearsome labyrinth. The gypsy plied her with a foul-tasting herbal brew. The room swam about her. Anna attempted to lie down but was held firmly in place against the oak headboard.

"Listen to me!" The woman grasped Anna's upper shoulders, her fingers pinching like pincers. "The baby will come easier this way."

The pain had reached its zenith when she felt someone take her hand.

"Here it is, Lady Anna," Wanda whispered. "Your rosary."

Anna felt the beads in her hand, fingered them. Managing to lift her hand, she peered at them through wet-stained eyes. These were not her usual coral beads. These were amber beads from Lithuania, sent back to her—in the care of Michał—from a dying Tadeusz. A final gift from her son—hers and Jan's.

Later, she would be tempted to tell Jan that the spirit of their son filled the room at that moment, that the pain drained away, as did uncertainty. Strength seeped back into her body, and she knew everything would be all right. *Tadek is here*, she would remember thinking. *Tadek is here.*

And yet what seemed like hours passed—and with it, hope—the contractions and wrenching pain continuing in rises and cadences without end. Her confidence and strength all but gone, Anna became convinced she would not survive and could only pray that her little daughter would.

"The head is coming," the gypsy said, matter-of-factly, as if to say *someone is at the door.* "Push!" she barked. "Lean forward! Push now!"

Anna obeyed. The pain heightened. Anna called out as she was urged to push yet again. She closed her eyes against the hurt, but the salvo of white heat invaded her entire being, body and mind. She screamed like a hag on All Hallows.

"It is here," the woman said.

The pain suddenly ebbed and Anna fell back against the headboard, her head striking it, her heart thumping crazily. She closed her eyes against the spinning of the room, listening for the sound of the baby that had been taken from her.

The room had gone silent. Neither the servant girls nor the gypsy offered a word.

Something was wrong. Her daughter had not survived. Was it stillborn, like several of her mother's babes?

A coldness, like a hand made of ice, clutched her heart and she was about to call out when the noise came. The baby was being slapped. Hard. Once, then a second time.

Then, loud and lusty, a cry from the little lungs filled the room.

"Listen to its strong cry," the gypsy announced. "It is the cry of a strong boy."

With slaps like that, Anna wanted to say, any baby would let go a great wail. Instead, she asked for her baby. The insufferable woman was wrong, she told herself. It could not be a boy. She was certain.

"In good time," Mira said. "In good time. You both

need to be tended to first." Mira worked at tending Anna while Wanda and Jolanta, bubbling with youthful wonder, bathed the baby in the porcelain wash basin.

Then, when Anna finally held the naked little creature in the crux of her arm, she had to face the truth. It was indeed a boy and the fears of bringing another boy into the world resurfaced. Tears formed at once, blurring and stinging her eyes.

Lutisha would have consoled her, would have wiped away her trepidation with the tears. The bleary gray figure hovering over her did neither.

Jan entered the chamber now, smiling despite his fragile state of nerves. His smile soured quickly when he saw her expression. "What is it, Anna? The baby—is— ?"

"The baby is fine, milord," Mira said. "Is a fine boy."

"Then what is it?" Jan pressed. "Anna?"

Anna held back her tears, but she could not reply.

"The mother is fine," Mira blurted. "Sometimes it is this way with the mother. After the birth." She was washing her hands in preparation to leave. "It will pass."

Had she washed her hands before tending her? Anna wondered. She could not recall.

Where were the emotional and physical relief and the joy that had come with the three previous births? Would this darkness pass? Turning her head to the wall, she listened to the final exchange between her husband and the midwife, the tinkling sounds of coins being passed along with whispered words, and then the door's closing behind the woman.

"Now, what's wrong, Anna?" Jan came and sat at her bedside. "Mira says the baby is healthy."

Anna turned toward him, simultaneously cradling the baby tightly against her side. "I won't have it," she spat out. "I won't!"

"What, Anna? What?"

Jolanta and Wanda were gathering things together. Anna waited for them to leave the bedchamber, then said, "I won't lose another son to the military. I won't!"

"Ah! Is that it?" he soothed. "Such a worry. He is but a baby, Anna."

"Yes, and so was Tadeusz! Dear sweet Tadek, left frozen now on the tundra in Napoleon's wake. You must promise me, Jan. You must. Poland or no Poland—I will not lose another!"

"Very well. I will offer no encouragement."

"No, Jan, if necessary you will prevent him. You know as well as I that children are what you make them. It's more than just a saying."

Jan smiled down at her, a bit solicitously she thought. For a moment she was tempted to tell him about Tadek's rosary and the little miracle it had worked, but he was kneeling at the bedside now, taken up with the pink little bundle that was their son. And he might, she thought, think it merely a woman's silly notion.

"Mira didn't do so badly by you, I see," he said.

Anna nodded, wordlessly conceding agreement. "But she doesn't have Lutisha's loving manner, I can tell you that."

"Still, she managed everything just as efficiently?"

Anna seized on one difference: "Everything but

the little red yarn Lutisha would have tied about his wrist to ward off the evil eye."

"What's this, then?" Jan asked, lifting the baby's little leg to reveal a red string tied at the ankle.

Anna gave a half-smile, but the amazement faded quickly. She took and held her husband's gaze with her own. "Jan, what did that woman say to you just now?"

Jan's smile seemed to go false. "Why, she—she merely named her price."

"There was more said than that."

"A bit of bargaining, that's all."

Anna knew this was untrue. She was certain her husband would never bargain for the birth of his son. "You are a poor liar, Jan. We have kept secrets from one another in the past, but we've not lied to one another—or am I mistaken?"

"No, Anna, you are not mistaken."

"Then I ask you again: What did the gypsy say to you?"

Jan swallowed hard and took good time to divest himself of the words. "She said, 'The boy will one day bait the Russian bear'."

Anna sank back into her pillows. Even as her eyes grew large, they lost focus. Jan and the details of her surroundings blurred, receded. Her heart began to race. She immediately thought of how, upon the very day of the late King Stanisław's birth, an astrologer announced to a disbelieving Poniatowski family with no claim to the throne: "Hail to you, Your Majesty, King of Poland!" Some thirty-two years later, aided by his lover Empress Catherine and her Russian troops, the astrologer's prediction was vindicated when Stanisław Poniatowski was elected King of Poland.

Many believed it was no story, no legend. Anna herself believed there was truth in such augury. After all, a friend of Anusia Potecka's family was in the room for the event. Was her son, she wondered, heart quickening, not yet an hour old, fated to go against the imperialist enemy to the East? She had already lost so much to the Russians. Was he, like his father and brothers, to be bred for the military? It was her greatest fear. No! Not while her body was home to breath.

"I'm thinking," Jan said, "we should call him Józef. After Prince Józef Poniatowski, the nephew of the last King of Poland."

Anna bristled. "After a soldier? A man who died in battle?"

Jan nodded. "After a prince, a general, and a hero, Anna."

Anna did not respond.

Jan whispered close to her ear now: "You're thinking of Mira's words. They are merely words, Ania." No one since her father's death had spoken her diminutive with such tenderness. "They are words from an old woman who imagines herself to have special powers." He continued in soothing tones, attempting to assuage her fears, but the only words she heard now were the gypsy's: "The boy will one day bait the Russian bear."

Part One

You cannot Escape
Your Fate
—POLISH PROVERB

I

3 May 1830, Sochaczew

ON THIS MONDAY, THE THIRTY-NINTH anniversary of
a day Poles were forbidden to remember, the
Stelnicki family gathered at Topolostan, their
estate in Sochaczew, west of Warsaw, under the guise
of celebrating Michał's thirty-eighth birthday.

As the family began to assemble in the dining hall
of the manor home, Michał, body rigid and eyes alert,
stood alone at the window of the reception room,
peering out at the long avenue that curved down
from the main road. He shaded his eyes against the
afternoon sun that glinted through the bordering
poplars and sent reflections shimmering off the twin
ponds situated on either side of the avenue.

The message had arrived that morning and Michał,
seldom prescient, could not put to rest the thought
that his life was about to change. Interpreting the
presentiment as wholly unfounded and unwelcome,
he tried to shake it. Nonetheless, his fingers drummed
the window sill.

"Michał," his mother called, "come in to dinner."

At that moment he caught sight of movement in the distance, a rolling cloud of dust coming closer, closer, passing now into the estate's avenue. He watched as the vehicle came into view. It was a sleek black carriage drawn by four white stallions, a fitting conveyance for Prince Adam Czartoryski.

Michał moved quickly out of the reception room.

"I wondered where you had gone," Anna said, standing at the doorway to the dining hall. "Come in, Michał."

"Mother, I have a guest arriving. I'll join you in a little while."

"A guest? Now?"

Michał nodded.

"A friend? Then bring him in. I'll have an extra place set."

"No," Michał said, providing a swift kiss on the cheek. A whisper now at her ear: "Please don't ask questions. We'll talk later."

"A mystery?" The amber flecks in her green eyes sparkled with amusement.

Michał's eyes went to his sister Barbara, younger by five years, and her husband as they assisted seating their two-year-old twin boys. He allowed no time for his fierce emotions regarding his sister's marriage to surface. Instead, he smiled at his mother. "Later, when everyone's gone home."

Before she could respond, he shooed her into the dining hall and pushed closed the mullioned French doors. Behind the glass now, in colorful finery, the diners seemed to him like tropical fish.

Michał hurried to the front portico, hospitality

symbol for every Polish manor house, thinking that perhaps he and the prince should converse outside, but he rejected the idea as unworthy of a host welcoming a man of such stature, a statesman and one of Poland's wealthiest magnates. Later, when he had learned the full details of the prince's visit and witnessed the curiosity the visitant aroused among the guests, he would regret the decision.

Prince Adam Czartoryski gave him a smile—sincere yet serious—as he climbed the three steps to the portico's platform. Introductions were formal. The prince was a generation older and had known Michał's stepfather Jan, but this was Michał's first meeting with him. All the more reason for the mystery of the occasion. Why had he come?

Michał ushered him into the house, hurrying him past the dining hall, hoping that those seated at table would not happen to glance through the glassed doors and wonder at the guest. They moved into the reception room and, once they were inside the commodious chamber, Michał made quick work of pulling closed the oak doors. Here they would have privacy.

"Please be seated, your grace," Michał said, already setting up two crystal glasses. "Vodka?"

"Yes, thank you." The prince would not offend his host with a refusal. He remained standing. "I came at a bad time, I see. You're entertaining, it seems. A celebration of the Third of May Constitution, no doubt."

Michał grimaced. "It was to have been, but that was before we knew my brother-in-law was coming.

So now, for the sake of appearances we are celebrating my birthday."

The prince gave a quizzical look. He had an unusually long face, distinctive features, and small, piercing eyes, more gray than blue. Michał took him for sixty, but a handsome man, just the same.

"My sister Barbara married a Russian, you see." Michał passed a glass to the prince, then held his gaze in a meaningful way, brown on blue. "A civil servant in Warsaw, no less."

"Ah, I see. Discretion is the best policy. . . . And you were born on the third of May? Truly?"

"Yes, 1792, a year after the Constitution."

"Those were heady times."

"And all but gone, Constitution and independence— before I was even three." Michał took up his own glass. "Regrettable. A national tragedy."

The prince let out a poignant sigh. "Ah, it does seem as if the Russian interlopers have been with us always."

But not always at our tables, Michał thought.

The prince raised his glass. "To the Constitution!" The glasses were properly emptied. Michał and the prince seated themselves across from one another. Each took turns at small talk about the weather and the spring planting. When it was played out, a silence ensued.

At last, the prince gave the slightest shake of his head. "I've been caught up in politics all of my life, my boy. I still am and it's politics that brings me to Sochaczew. I've come to enlist your aid."

"My aid?" Michał was thunderstruck. The thought

that such a great man had come to see him was more
than a mystery. It was a wonder, as was the thought
that he could be of some help to the prince. "I just
cannot imagine what you could want with me, your
grace. I haven't been involved in the military, if one
even calls that politics, since Waterloo."

"You were there—with his Polish lancers, I know.
That Napoleon had chosen Polish lancers for his
Imperial Guard speaks volumes. And as doomed as
his grand plan was, his Polish Lancers did us proud.
I congratulate you."

"No need. I was one of the few to survive. And I've
given all that up. I don't think militarily anymore. I
manage my mother's estate here. I avoid politics. I
even avoid going to the capital as much as possible."

"Out of sight, out of mind?"

Michał forced a smile.

"Lady Stelnicka, your mother, how is she?"

"She puts on a strong front. She misses Father
terribly." A shudder ran through Michał as he
recalled his father's arrest in '26 for his membership
in the Patriotic Society. How they had tried him and
others of the club for being sympathizers with the
1825 Decembrists' plot in Russia against the new
tsar, Nicholas, who was so much more the severe
autocrat than his predecessor, Tsar Aleksander. How
ignominiously his father had been bound and taken
from his home and beloved Poland. "It's as if Russia
swallowed him whole."

"Has there been no word, Michał?"

"None," Michał said, shaking his head. "If he's
alive, he is most likely in some godforsaken camp

in Siberia."

"What about you, are you . . . content here? After having led a soldier's life for so long? You had gone to Moscow with the little Corsican, too, yes? And lived to tell about *that!*"

"I did," Michał said. He found himself blinking back tears that sprang spontaneously. "But my brother Tadeusz did not."

"I'm sorry for that, Michał. . . . Forgive me, I am a clumsy conversationalist today to remind you of so much sadness. Perhaps I shouldn't keep you in the dark any longer about my . . . visit. And . . . what shall I call it?—a *mission,* pehaps."

"Mission?"

The prince nodded. "First, a few facts. But before that, I think we should have another vodka. What say you?" He managed a laugh. "The road to Sochaczew is dry and dusty."

And, Michał thought, the road to the prince's purpose is circuitous. "Of course, your grace." Michał went to the table by the window and returned with the decanter. "Good Polish stuff!"

The prince stood to make the toast. "Sto Lat!"

"Ah!" Michał intoned at the birthday toast that called for a century of living. "I appreciate the sentiment, your grace, but I can't say I wish to live a hundred years."

"At least not under Russian rule, yes? Your Polish blood is true, young Michał. Well, then, to what shall we toast?" The prince paused only a moment. "I have it. To a brighter tomorrow, free of foreigners' rule!"

"Now that I'll drink to!"

The two drank down the vodka at once, in the Polish fashion.

As the prince settled back into the high-winged chair, his expression went dark. "Times have become very dangerous in Warsaw. Dangerous for Poland. While we have been given more freedom than we might have expected under Russian rule—we've kept the Sejm and a Polish military—there are always those who yearn for the days of the Constitution and independence, those who wish to throw off Tsar Nicholas' yoke altogether. I can empathize with such feelings but having seen what I've seen, I've become a cautious man. Things carelessly done can create havoc."

Michał sat now. "Like interminable winter marches to Moscow?"

"Exactly. Although the Prussians, Austrians, and Russians have claimed so much of our former nation, we still have this shrunken entity called the Congress Kingdom of Poland, this by the so-called good graces of the Congress of Vienna. It is a ghost of its former self, and insult to injury is suffering a Russian tsar as our king. Ah, but despite these things, Poland remains. It endures. Why, even beyond the new boundaries our people retain our language, our faith, and our heritage."

"That's all very well," Michał said, leaning forward, "but what freedom do we really have? You mentioned the Sejm and the military. You know as well as I that the men making laws in the Sejm are answerable to the Grand Duke Konstantin who is, himself, Commander of the Polish Army."

"You're right, of course," the prince said, one eyebrow lifting slightly.

"And forgive me, your grace, but isn't it true that old General Zajączek, having been raised to Prince and named Viceroy of Warsaw, has become but a tool of Konstantin? In fact, would I be mischaracterizing things if I were to say that true patriots in all branches of government have been supplanted by Poles who are nothing more than Russian sycophants?"

The prince's gray-blue eyes seemed to simmer. "You would not."

"You asked if I'm content here. I was a soldier, bred to the bone, as you correctly implied. I stayed with Napoleon through to the end. He said his Polish Imperial Guard was the best in the world. When I came back from Waterloo, I continued on in my service in Warsaw. But under Konstantin, the army—Polish or no—became a blood brother to the government in its movement to rid our country of any sense of nationalism and make us thralls of Russia. The liberty of the press was denied. Freemasonry was forbidden. Under Tsar Aleksander things had been somewhat tolerable, but when Nicholas succeeded him and the Grand Duke Konstantin—his brother, and Grand Tyrant, I say—arrived in Warsaw, I asked to be dismissed. I found it preferable to the degradation and depression so many other soldiers endured. They say half of the officers and generals asked for dismissal. Many others, among both officers and enlisted men, committed suicide. So, you see, my *contentment* here matters little. Family is here. The old ways are here. I'm needed."

The prince sighed. A little nod seemed to validate Michał's speech. "Allow me to present my case, Jan Michał." That he employed Michał's full Christian name presaged a serious turn in the prince's mood. "It's our own military that concerns me. You see, there are two young officers at the Officer Cadets School whose careers are stalled. They have become bored with a sedentary military life and—"

"Wait a moment, your grace. Does your visit have something to do with my brother Józef? He's a cadet there. Of course, you must know that."

The prince's eyes held Michał's. "I do know that." He smiled tightly. "Please allow me to go on."

Michał nodded. The mystery was unfolding too slowly—and he was beginning to like none of it.

"The two firebrands I'm speaking of are burning with romantic dreams of personal heroism and patriotic notions of national independence."

"Typical, yes? The relentless Polish dream of glory?"

"True, Michał, and all too often a false dream. I can tell you that these two have wrongfully fired up the young cadets with their zeal."

"Like my brother?"

The prince nodded. "Most likely. And it is a dangerous zeal."

"I don't think we should allow that dream of independence to die. With all due respect, Lord Czartoryski, are you not aligned with Russia?"

"Touché. If I were you I would be questioning my motives, as well. It is true that as a young man I was a great friend to Tsar Nicholas' brother. But Tsar

Aleksander was a cut of a different cloth. A much finer cloth."

"You were in his cabinet."

"Ah, yes. Oh, Aleksander had great plans for Poland in the early days. He was very liberal in his thinking. He agreed with me that an independent Poland, one serving as a barrier to Prussian aggression, was to Russia's advantage."

"What happened?"

"Aleksander vacillated. He couldn't come to decisive action regarding our independence. And then events took over, Napoleon being one of them."

Michał stared into his empty glass. "And now we're left with Tsar Nicholas as King of our shrunken kingdom and his brother Konstantin ensconced in Warsaw as Imperial Commissioner and Commander of the Army."

"Indeed. And although the Grand Duke Konstantin claims to be more Pole than Russian because he has married Lady Joanna Grudzińska and calls himself Polish, you can be sure he is true to Mother Russia. He has a volatile temperament and if given the opportunity, he would walk over his mother's grave to pluck a candy from a child's hand."

"As would Tsar Nicholas—"

"Ah, there is much to fear with *him*—and in the arm of the secret police here in Warsaw."

"The Third Department?" Michał asked.

"Yes, overseen by the Imperial Commissioner, General Nikolai Novosiltsev. He and I were two of Aleksander's three most trusted advisers in the old days. And Nikolai was a friend to me. But the years have corrupted him and turned his thoughts dark against Poland."

Michał nodded. "They're known to torture prisoners."

"Hah! If that were only all."

"And he has wind of the cadets' dissension?"

"I'm certain he does."

"Who are the two you spoke of? The firebrands, as you call them."

"A second lieutenant named Wysocki and a Colonel Zaliwski. They are putting together a plot, Michał. No doubt a very dangerous plot. They're too young to know the hardships that came with the dismemberment of the Republic in '95, too young to know that the battlefield affords little lasting glory, as you and I know. It affords more blood, bashing of brains, missing limbs, and death than anything. They don't understand how hard we've worked to carve out this Congress Kingdom of Poland, albeit under the aegis of Russia and the eye of Nicholas' brother. Men such as Wysocki and Zaliwski could lose it all for us."

"Is it so serious?" Michał asked. "Can two dreamers really do anything? Perhaps they've read too much nationalistic poetry, my lord, too many verses from Adam Mickiewicz."

"It's not to be made light of, Michał." The prince leaned forward. "The cadets alone may or may not do any real damage, but their instigation of some big event could muster the voices and arms of the many who have suffered decades of a poorly masked tyranny."

"What plot, my lord?"

"That's just the thing, Michał. We don't know."

"And—I?" Michał asked although he was certain he had already divined the direction of the prince's thoughts.

"Józef is your brother. If he is one of the insurgents—or if he merely knows one of the insurgents—he can provide us with needed information."

"So I'm to be a spy then—on my young brother?"

"There is much at stake here, Michał."

Michał attempted a smile. "I'm sorry you have come all this way, your grace. Certainly there are others in Warsaw who can infiltrate the Cadets Academy."

"None that can be trusted." The prince's eyes narrowed. "None I can count on."

"Why me?"

"I know your family by the sacrifices you've made. I knew—I know—your father." He paused, as if he had just played his best card, then continued: "My friends at the capital and I am watched day and night by the Russian secret police. It took no little doing for my driver to shake off a Russian detail following us today. We had to exit the back door of an inn to make our escape. In short, Michał, the fact that you are removed from the activities in Warsaw means that you would not arouse suspicion."

"Still, your grace, I do have my duties here. And I have no wish to interfere in Józef"'s life."

"In his *interest*, Michał."

"Shhh! Did you hear that?" Michał whispered.

The prince shrugged. "It escaped me. I heard nothing."

With a finger to his mouth, Michał motioned. "Outside the door," he mouthed. "The floorboards."

The prince rose and stood silently while Michał made for the door, pulling it open at once. Nothing. The hallway was empty.

He stepped out, turning just in time to see the dining hall doors being pulled closed.

Someone had been in the hall. The question was, had he—or she—heard anything of his conversation with the prince?

Michał stepped back into the reception room. "Nothing," he said, shrugging, attempting to ignore a knotting of uneasiness in his stomach.

"I should go. I've overstayed my welcome." The prince retrieved his hat from the table. "It's probably just a matter of time before the Russian detail ferrets me out even though we took well-travelled roads so as not to leave tracks leading to your door. . . . Michał, I do hope you don't doubt my motives because of my past associations with Russia. I am thinking only of Poland."

""I do not doubt that, your grace." Michał spoke the truth.

"Ah, well, I've made my case, but it was not my intention in coming here to pressure you in any way. You needn't decide now." The prince smiled. "I'm certain your judgment is equal to your hearing. Contact me in the capital should you wish to help. Discreetly, of course. I am closely watched."

Michał nodded. His mind was in a ferment.

"You know my residence?"

"Yes," Michał replied, suppressing a laugh. Everyone

knew the very impressive Czartoryski mansion.

"I'm sure you're of good use here, Jan Michał, but you may have a higher calling." The prince shook Michał's hand, the earnest gray-blue eyes piercing Michał. "A fine man, your father. How proud Jan must be of you, Michał. I'll shake a few trees. I'll see what I can find out about his whereabouts."

"Would you, your grace? My mother and I would be so grateful."

"No promises, my boy."

"No, no, of course not. Now if you don't mind, your grace, please allow me to show you out through the rear of the house." Michał forced a little laugh. "Forgive me, but discretion starts at home."

Michał had played the hospitable role expected at the home of the szlachta, the minor nobility, but he was greatly relieved to see the roiling dust from the black carriage of a magnate moving down the estate's avenue, heading for the main road that would take the prince and his "mission" back to Warsaw. Good riddance, he thought. Prince or no, statesman or no, what nerve had he to arrive on short notice with such a request? Aside from not wishing to interfere in young Józef's life at the Cadets Academy, Michał had no intention of getting caught up in the old dreams, the old fire of independence, the old disappointments. He had lost too many years in the efforts, in the pains. He turned to go back into the house. Gone were the days of the enemies at the gates—the Swedes, Austrians, Turks, Prussians, Cossacks, Russians. No, the enemy was within now. The man who dared call himself King of Poland was the Russian tsar. Poland, it seemed, would always serve the wishes and whims of others. What was there that *he* could do about it? He resented the prince's visit and the tacit sense of patriotism and responsibility it was meant to incite. Hadn't he done enough for his nation, a nation that, in truth, was no more than a ghost of its former self?

Entering the house, Michał impulsively moved to the reception room where he drank down another vodka. His thoughts stayed with a particular facet of the exchange he had just experienced: namely, the intimation that the prince might be able to find something out about his father's whereabouts in Russia. *How that would please Mother! Might he also be able to do something about freeing her husband? Or—is this a masterful play to engage me in the "mission"?*

Torn by the emotion of the moment, he sent his vodka glass crashing into the fireplace. The sheer volume of the explosion startled him enough to clear his mind for the moment. He went directly to the dining hall.

"Michał," Anna said, watching him enter, "you've missed dinner. We're having our pudding."

"So I see. Cranberry kissel!" he exclaimed, affecting a festiveness he did not feel. "It's my favorite. And it's not even Christmas Eve!"

"Cranberries are plentiful this year," Anna said. "You'll have it on Christmas Eve, too, as ever."

"A great relief," Michał joked, settling himself across from his sister's family, in the chair next to Zofia, who was attired in a revealing rose satin gown. "I apologize to you, Mother, and to everyone for my tardiness."

Anna directed Marcelina to prepare a plate for Michał.

"Was it an important guest?" Zofia asked. In a side glance, Michał saw her wink at Anna, her black eyes glittering. "A woman, perhaps?"

"Would that it were, Cousin Zofia. But, alas, I was not so lucky." Michał hoped she would drop the subject, but he suspected his mother's cousin was not about to let it go. Inwardly, he sighed in relief that she evidently had not seen the prince pass the dining hall's mullioned doors.

"Well, who was it, Michał?" Zofia pressed.

Michał felt his mouth tighten. He stared across the table at the two-year-old twins, bookended by their parents. Handsome little boys. One had been given a Polish name, Konrad; the other, Russian, Dimitri. Which was which?

"Zofia," Anna asked, "will you have some more pudding?"

"No, Anna, my stomach has been well sated, thank you. It's my curiosity that has not been satisfied." She turned back to Michał. "Tell me, Michał. Whisper it in my ear if you must."

Michał was making much of taking a plate from the servant, attempting to feign composure. "I assure you, Cousin Zofia, it was no one of any importance."

"No one of any importance?" The irony in the deep male voice rang like an abbey's bell.

Michał slowly lifted his eyes to the speaker directly

across from him, his brother-in-law Viktor, whose comment commanded the attention of everyone at the table. The Russian's eyes were pale blue, cold, self-assured. The coldness penetrated Michał's heart. He knew at once that the prince's visit had not escaped *everyone's* notice. He returned Viktor's stare. "That is correct," Michał said, his voice flat. "No one of any importance."

"Perhaps no longer," Viktor said, "but in his day he carried some weight."

So the prince had been seen *and* recognized. Michał dared a fixed look at Viktor. Had he been the one outside the reception room door? Had he heard any of the conversation? Michał said nothing, took a fork, and started to poke at the venison stew Marcelina had laid before him.

"So *you* know!" Zofia cried, directing herself to Viktor, oblivious to Michał's discomfiture. "You'll tell us then, Viktor."

Viktor smiled. He paused, allowing for the suspense to take hold.

"Well?" Barbara asked, turning to her husband.

Viktor kept his eyes trained on Michał. "It was Prince Adam Czartoryski." There was smugness in his voice as well as in his unwavering gaze across the table. "His importance may have waned with the years, brother Michał, but I would not say he's of no importance."

Brother! Michał fumed at the sarcastic familial term. With just his peripheral vision he sensed his mother was closely watching him with concern that he might create a scene. He felt himself paling.

He would not be the cause of ruining his mother's celebratory meal. His attention was quickly claimed by Zofia.

"Lord Adam Czartoryski!" Zofia cried. "Adam! And he didn't have the politeness to give greeting?"

Michał turned to her. "It was politeness that kept him from doing so, Cousin Zofia. He didn't want to disturb our meal which was just starting."

"You are acquainted with the prince in question?" Viktor asked Zofia.

Zofia was flushing—with what emotion Michał could not decipher.

"He was more than an acquaintance, I daresay." Zofia said, the slitted black eyes wide now and glinting. "Why, I—I nearly married Adam Czartoryski! It was a few years ago, of course."

"A few?" Anna chided.

"Why didn't you, cousin?" Barbara asked.

Zofia needed no further prompting. "You see, the prince had been a close friend and confidant of Tsar Aleksander, and he was completely besotted by the tsar's wife, Elizabeth. It had been a marriage of convenience, of course, and Aleksander actually sanctioned the budding romance between Adam and the tsarina. Can you imagine! The times we live in! How the gossips wagged about that. Ah, but when Adam suggested his friend divorce her, well, that's where it ended. A royal divorce, if you please? Not a chance in hell. No, it was Adam's relationship with Aleksander's wife that ended—and quite abruptly."

"As it should have," Viktor said, his voice almost harsh.

"Does my story of your past tsar offend?" Zofia asked. "I can assure you it's quite true. And that it broke poor Adam's heart."

"But what about you and the prince, Cousin Zofia?" Barbara asked.

"Ah, it would have been a fine match, don't you think, Basia? Just fine. A magnate like that. But, young as I was, I could tell he was on the rebound, as they say. He was interested, I can tell you, but I chose to put him off until such a time as he would forget his simpering little Tsarina Elizabeth and be prepared for a woman."

"You," Anna teased, only to be rewarded with a raised and well-drawn eyebrow.

"And?" Barbara asked.

Zofia shrugged, and though she had finished her cranberry kissel, she made a show of bringing a thimbleful to her reddened lips. "It was a lethal misjudgment on my part, my dear. While I dithered, a ruthless old woman pushed her daughter on to him when my back was turned, and before I knew it his attention had been claimed. Not that he married her, mind you. Then, years later, he did marry. Would you believe it, a child bride twenty years his junior! Once, not so long ago when I met him at a ball, he told me that letting me go was the biggest mistake of his life. Well," she sighed dramatically, "he lives with his regrets now."

With that, one of the twins began to make a fuss—Dimitri, Michał thought—and the subject mercifully came to an end.

Michał sat alone at the table. The dishes and silver had been cleared. Nearby he could hear the sounds of the servants going about their kitchen tasks. From outside came the cheerfully excited voices of the twins and the muted goodbyes of adults being made. He had refused to see his sister's family off. Oh, he had been prepared to bite his tongue and attempt a smile in order to play the polite brother-in-law, but that was before Viktor fired his parting shot. He could feel blood rising into his face anew at the thought. He would never—could never—accept Viktor Baklanov as a member of the family. The thought disgusted him. In the future, he decided, he would avoid him at all costs, even if it meant foregoing family events. He abhorred hypocrisy.

He was still at the dining table brooding and peering into his coffee cup when Anna returned from seeing Barbara and her family to their carriage for the return trip to Warsaw.

"Did Cousin Zofia go with them?" Michał asked.

"She did. And she said you should come for a visit—that it would do Izabel a world of good."

"Why didn't she come with her mother?"

Anna seated herself across the table from Michał. Although her auburn hair had silvered of late, her smooth complexion and the amber coruscation in the emerald eyes lent her youth. "According to Zofia, her years in the convent have made her terribly shy."

"But she's been out for a year."

"Still, I think it's difficult for her to move in Zofia's sphere."

Michał emitted a sarcastic laugh. "I can

believe that. Did you note her dress? Zofia must be—what? Sixty?"

"Sweet Jesus," Anna said, her voice a low hiss, "don't let her hear you say that! She's fifty-seven and be careful not to slip on your own doorstep, Michał, for I'm but a year behind her."

"But she still thinks she's quite the ingénue. What with that rose gown and lime green bonnet, she resembles a great tropical bird."

Anna laughed, too. "A rare one at that. A bird of paradise, perhaps. And she will be thinking she's the ingénue well into her dotage, I'm afraid. That is my dear cousin. Quite the coquette. You know that story about the prince?"

"Yes? A fabrication, I presume?"'

"Oh, the facts about the younger Adam's infatuation with the tsarina were true enough, but he had not courted Zofia. On the contrary, he is one of the country's many magnates on whom she has set her bonnet—lime green and every other color— over the years. She had done everything to gain the prince's attention except hit him with a mallet—all to no avail." Anna laughed. "Isn't it amazing that one can lie with honeyed lips even while knowing that someone at table had been witness to the real history? But that is my dear cousin."

"Do you mean puddinged lips?" Michał asked with a laugh. "Sometimes I think we humans start to believe the history we spin out of our imagination. True history or no, she's an excellent raconteur. I give her credit for that." Michał was silent for a moment, then turned to his mother, a new heat coming into his face. "Did you hear what *he* said when he left?"

"Viktor?" his mother asked." Yes, dear, I heard."

Michał sat forward, one hand pushing aside the cup and saucer. "Instead of wishing me well on my birthday, he said, 'Happy Constitution Day, Michał.' The ass! He knew all along what we were truly celebrating."

"I know. It would seem so. He was in his cups by then."

"And, as they say, wine makes a person transparent. So it was all a sham, Mother, this birthday business. He knows as well as anyone we celebrate my name day and not my birthday."

"I wouldn't worry about it, Michał. Barbara probably let it slip. You know she does that sometimes."

"It's not that that galls me, Mother. It's that he openly mocks our short-lived constitution and our attachment to it. His comment was an insult to every Pole."

"I understand your anger, Michał, but—"

"Damn it! Don't go making excuses for him. He's Russian to the core—in our house, eating our food, and finding faults. It's maddening! And what is this civil service job he has? Does anyone know? Does even Barbara know? My God, how I hate the man."

"There, there. Michał. It makes little difference now. He's in the family."

"Are you taking his side, for God's sake? This arrogant interloper! Has he won you over? Has his gimpy leg worked on your sympathy?"

"No, Michał. And to give him his due, he tries to disguise it as much as possible."

"Still, you forbade Barbara to marry him. You forbade her to ever bring him here. And yet she defied you on both counts. Admit it, Mother. You hate him as much as I!"

"Ah, Michał. Russians have always brought trouble. But Barbara Anna did marry him. She did bring him into the family. Their children are my grandchildren. Am I to deny them, too? My blood runs through their veins."

"And so does Father's blood. Your husband, who sits rotting in some Russian camp!

"Michał!"

Michał drew in a deep breath, at once regretting his words. "I'm so sorry, Mother. Really. That was thoughtless." He longed to take her hands in his, but the width of the table precluded the gesture. "I guess Barbara isn't the only one to let things slip. It must be a Stelnicki trait."

His mother chuckled. "Well, you were tightlipped enough about the prince's visit. Are you going to tell me what brought him here?"

"Politics. Just politics."

"An offer of some kind—a position in the capital?"

"Something like that."

"You're not going to tell me, are you?"

"Not now."

"Very well, I'll respect that. But Michał, perhaps you should visit Zofia and her daugther for a week or so. Longer, if you wish. You know we can get on here just fine."

"Ah ha! You're thinking I'll find a place socially. You're thinking—"

"Michał, you're thirty-eight. You should be thinking of starting a family. And sequestered here on the estate you're not about to find someone."

"I hope you haven't plotted with Zofia for her to play matchmaker."

His mother's smile was indecipherable. "I would not go so far."

"Indeed? Well, what if I don't marry? I was off soldiering when men of my generation were finding wives. Look, you have two grandchildren, Mother. Don't be greedy."

"Yes, and I love them dearly, but I want some grandchildren who will carry a *Polish* surname! The Stelnicki name."

"Well, don't hate me if I am unable to deliver— or rather that some future bride of mine is long in the tooth and beyond child-bearing! Remember, you always have another bird in the hand. You always have—" Michał stopped mid-sentence.

"Józef? You were going to say 'Józef,' yes?" A shadow flickered momentarily across his mother's face, a darkening that reflected pain and hurt.

"What? Oh, yes—Józef. I'm sorry, I lost my train of thought." The truth of the matter was that he had no wish to worry his mother about the prince's speculation concerning Józef. And no wish to remind her further that Józef had defied her by joining the military. Michał bent to kiss Anna. "Mother, I told the stablemaster I'd discuss something with him after our meal. We'll talk later." As he proceeded to make his retreat, his memory checked him and he pivoted toward Anna. "Mother, while I was shut up in the reception room with Prince Czartoryski, someone left the dining hall. Do you recall who it was?"

"Of course, dear, Viktor left for a short while. Now do think about taking Zofia up on her invitation! Warsaw will do you a world of good!"

Princess Anna Maria Stelnicka stayed at her place in the dining hall. All traces of the celebratory meal had been removed from the table, as well as from her thoughts which had turned to her son Józef. If only Michał would visit Warsaw, she thought, he could look in on her youngest at the academy.

Despite her resolve to cultivate Józef's interest in music and steer him away from the paths of her husband and two older sons, the military had, like some mythical siren, managed to seduce her youngest. She had yet to come to terms with her defeat. Only God knew what dangers he would face as a soldier.

Anna wished Jan were here to lend support. But would he—with his own military ways—have supported her, or Józef? And when she thought of Jan her serious thoughts turned darker.

Anna thought back to the day they came to take her husband away. Oh, she had known he had become active in the Patriotic Society, but who could have imagined that its members would be accused of complicity in a Russian plot to assassinate the tsar in faraway Moscow? *Had* the Society been involved? Jan had told her that he had not taken part in the conspiracy in any way, and she believed him. But

the Third Department—the Russian secret police—
cared little for the truth. They were interested only
in making examples of men like Count Jan Stelnicki,
former military heroes, men of stature and respect.
Men of the nobility. He and two others had been
sentenced to exile somewhere in the Russian Northern
hinterlands. Anna's heart constricted as she recalled
the day the three had been sent off. The families were
allowed their goodbyes in the Castle Square prior
to witnessing their loved ones' being hurried into
the coach that would take them away. Because no
one could recall any convict returning from Russia,
such sentences usually meant severing ties forever.
Russian soldiers linked hands, holding back a large
crowd of Polish well-wishers, many weeping openly.
Such a public spectacle for the last memory of her
husband. It was the Russian way of making examples.
It was their way to continue suppression.

Jan's hands were bound and hidden beneath the
grubby greatcoat he wore so that it was she who had
to embrace him. And it was only as Jan turned away
and grasped hold of the carriage, pulling himself up
into the coach, that she noticed that one of those
hands was bandaged. "Sweet Jesus!" she called out.
"What have they done to you, Jan?"

Jan turned and gifted her with a smile that said,
It's nothing, dearest. Just a scratch. It was his way.

And then the carriage was wheeling away, taking
the man she had thought vain, superficial, mocking—
and handsome—so many years before when he had
boldly approached her in a summer meadow in
Halicz, the man whose character she had foolishly

questioned, the man who waited for the duration of her arranged marriage, the man who had married her and become a devoted stepfather to Jan Michał and father to Tadeusz, Barbara Anna, and Józef.

They had had their separations, some lasting years while he fought side by side with Kościuszko and after that with the French in Italy and finally with Napoleon himself on the Eastern steppes. But he had come back. Like the faithful storks returning to their nests in the spring, he had come back. At that moment, though, watching that carriage move through Castle Square and descend toward the River Vistula and the Praga Bridge that would take them east, Anna had not managed to conjure the thinnest thread of hope that she would ever see her Jan again. This time she could not bring herself to believe that he would come back.

Pain had overcome her there in the square, thrumming through her body, her pulse gone wild. This she could not, would not, endure. It was too much for one heart. While she was able to fend off tears, the old habit of tearing at her hair overcame her—until Michał took her hands away from her head. She thought she would pass out. The ground moved beneath her. She wished only for her life to end.

But when she turned to her children—the grown Michał, the nearly grown Barbara, and little Józef— three hearts huddled together, faces streaming tears, she drew herself up, kissed each on the forehead, and said, "Let's go home. God's teeth! We'll not give the cursed Russians any further satisfaction."

How ironic, Anna thought now, that today she

should have to temper Michał's anger at Viktor and his hatred of Russians. But who could have guessed that Barbara would fall in love with a Russian? Who can ever guess where the heart will lead? What would Jan think—if he has survived the brutal Russian wilds—to know he has half-Russian grandchildren?

Anna's thoughts reluctantly came back to Józef—her last born—and the searing words of a gypsy woman she had often failed to keep in abeyance for the past seventeen years.

Warsaw

IZABEL GRONSKA SAT IN THE reception room near the window watching a purplish dusk descend on the capital. The Third of May celebrations in the city were small and secreted behind closed doors, but occasionally a bit of rebellious—and no doubt innocent—gunfire could be heard.

She had sat here as a child in this very spot, even into her twenties, those years before cloistered life. Growing up she had watched the outside world from this vantage point, wondering about, anticipating, and if she was honest, fearing the time when she would venture forth and grasp hold of life. So many things had changed, and yet her feelings at this moment were not much different. She was as unsettled now as she had been then, and it gave her pause.

Elzbieta knocked at the open double doors. "Would

Mademoiselle wish something?"

Iza turned and smiled. "No, thank you, Elzbieta."

"The carriage will likely arrive soon. A light supper has been prepared for the travelers, as Lady Gronska ordered."

Iza nodded and the servant retreated to the recess of the town house. Elzbieta was the daughter of Wanda, who—aside from a few years prior to being widowed—had been in Zofia's service many years. She was sincere and attentive, but after doing for herself and others for years, Iza found it odd being waited on once again.

How like her mother to have ordered a little late supper in advance. She had probably given explicit menu requests. Iza turned back to the darkening street outside. The day had dragged on tediously. Interminably. Perhaps she should have gone to Sochaczew with the others. After all, she had made numerous visits to Topolostan—Poplar Estate—as a child, when it was owned by Anna's parents, the Berezowskis. Her mother had expected as much and kept it no secret how disappointed she was that Iza chose to stay home. Her mother seldom minced words. Iza supposed now she should have gone if only to keep peace in the family.

It had been the thought of a journey in a crowded carriage that put her off: three adults, not counting her, plus the twins, who could be a handful in such close quarters. She had not forgotten what it was to go on an enjoyable outing, but she was certain this one would not measure up. Oh, she could have tolerated the children—and even her mother—and would have most enjoyed the time spent with Barbara, her childhood friend and confidante. Since leaving the convent, Iza had spent too little time with Barbara, who now had the added responsibilities of a husband and twin boys. She thought of Viktor now. He seemed an odd sort for Barbara. A Russian government worker and all that. She resolved to be fair, though, telling herself she had had too few interactions with him to set a judgment in stone.

It was just that back in their years together at convent school, Barbara had always seemed so lively and independent, much more so than she. Marrying Viktor seemed to go against the grain. He seemed to lack—what? Warmth? Spontaneity? Iza could not put her finger on it. But something about him had won Barbara over. What was it? She could only trust that her dearest friend had made a wise decision.

Iza had to admit she was curious about the Princess Anna. It would have been good to see her. How had she weathered the last few years? Had she aged? How was her spirit, considering her youngest had gone into the military against her wishes—and her husband Jan had been bound and packed off to Russia on trumped up charges? And Jan Michał, the countess' eldest. What was he like? Try as she might, Iza could not imagine Michał, as he was called so as not to confuse him with his father Jan. Was he still handsome after all these years—and out of uniform? An image of him at nearly forty was hard to conjure. After their youth, it seemed he was always on campaign, and then, of course, it was she who staged a disappearance, not in some remote and romantic place, but within the environs of Warsaw, behind the high convent walls on Wolska Street. Another world, it was.

Yes, she was curious about the princess and Michał, but she also had to admit, if only to herself, that it was more than a crowded carriage that held her back from making the journey to an estate that offered happy childhood memories of summer visits. She had to concede the truth to herself—and a heated blush to her cheeks confirmed it—that she was afraid to be caught on a social occasion with so many people. Afraid. The thought disturbed her, but she did doubt her capacity for conversation, her ability to sustain the interest of others. Or she herself might be *too much* of interest. Having left the convent, she would be the object of others' curiosity. Sometimes she felt she had *become* a curiosity. And, family or no, there would be queries—subtle, polite, and even the unspoken kind that arise in conversation lulls. Others might be brutally direct. If provoked, she might say the wrong thing. When the waters were stirred, she might speak on impulse, as she had on occasion in the convent—to the dismay of her superiors. It was a failing she was attempting to rectify. There might be other guests, too, at the Sochaczew estate. There was that possibility. Strangers. It was too much to imagine. Too much to leave to chance. She had made the right decision in staying home.

Movement outside caught Iza's eye. She noticed several groups of people walking toward Saint Martin's Church, which was situated across Piwna Street, just down a bit from the town house. She glanced at the mantel clock. It was time for Vespers.

On Wolska Street, too, the sisters would be leaving their cells and going to chapel. Some of them, Iza knew, would be passing her cell, now bare and empty. Would they think of her, these friends, companions, and sisters of the past few years? Or was memory of her already fading, like the light outside? Perhaps some young postulant had been admitted and assigned her cell. Surely that would facilitate forgetfulness, much as the River Lethe purged the past.

She should have stayed, Iza thought now. She had been content on Wolska Street. She should have stayed. But it had been taken out of her hands. A mere week away from the final vows—when she would change the white veil for the black—came a seemingly innocuous summons to Abbess Teodora's office that changed everything. Everything.

Now a bustling in the nearby dining hall and muted clamor in the kitchen drew Iza's attention. The carriage bringing her mother, Barbara, Viktor, and the twins was arriving at the stable to the rear of the town house.

Like quicksilver Iza stood and hurried to the dining hall where Elzbieta was laying the table. "Elzbieta, be so good as to tell my mother I have retired for the night with a headache." She did not wait for a reply and made for the stairway.

As she climbed the stairs to her rooms on the first floor, she thought—with humor and truth—*Look at me, returned to the world, and already telling lies.*

Sochaczew

MAY AND JUNE GAVE WAY to July and an unusually hot summer with Michał's thinking very little about Prince Czartoryski's suggestion. However, a day didn't go by that he wasn't reminded in some way that he was not of any real help in the day-to-day operation of the estate. He had been less than truthful to the prince on that subject: he was no estate manager, not really. The Jewish manager, Jacob Szraber, though gaining in years, was fastidious in his dealings with workers and tenants. His longtime loyalty to the family had been proven time and again. Thus, Michał spent much of his days reading, riding, hunting—all the while shutting out memory of the prince's visit, having assured himself he had answered the call of patriotism in his early years, and that now others must come forward. And the prince made no further overture to involve him in affairs at the Officer Cadets School. Michał's mother, on the other hand, had begun to make the carriage trip to Warsaw once a month to visit with Józef at the academy. While Michał saw to it that she was well accompanied by a splendid driver, he himself declined to go.

He thought that in some vague way his not going reaffirmed his stance with the prince. He would have nothing to do with the cadets, nothing. Something else kept him at Topolostan, too: his relationship to his half-brother. He recognized this summer that he felt at his core a distance from and even resentment of Józef, younger by so many years. But he was disinclined to plumb the source of his feelings.

August and September—Harvest Home notwith-standing—passed with painful slowness. The winter months loomed: dark, long, uneventful.

In late October, Michał was returning from a ride when he hailed his mother, who had just returned from her monthly visit to Warsaw and was ascending the stairs of the portico. Lady Anna Stelnicka turned about at his call. As Michał drew his horse closer, he saw that she was visibly shaken. "What is it Mother?"

"It's Józef, Michał. He's different. He's changed." The lively green eyes had dulled, darkened.

"Is that all? He's become a soldier, I suspect. That's the change. He's grown. He's become a man."

The countess waved her hand dismissively. "No. Of course, I can see those changes. Any mother would. But there's something about him now. Something I've noted more and more with every visit. Something secret."

"What about that girl you thought he was smitten with? Perhaps it's not working out?"

"The Chopin girl? Yes, he had been quite infatuated by her. Come to think of it, he hasn't mentioned her of late. But—"

"There's something more?"

"I'm sure of it."

"Something dark?"

"Not necessarily. But something passionate, something like . . ."

"Mother?"

His mother sighed. "Something like I saw in you and Tadeusz when you both knew you were to follow Napoleon to Moscow. That kind of excitement. That kind of passion. There isn't another war afoot, is there, Michał?"

"No, of course not."

Anna attempted a smile and turned to enter the house.

Michał wheeled his stallion about in the other direction but gave it no signal to proceed. His eyes mindlessly scanned the River Vistula tributary not far away. The setting sun reddened the water like a thousand votives dancing and sparkling within St. Martin's Church, which sat on Piwna Street, just across from Zofia's town house.

Was Józef involved in the type of movement the prince had spoken of? A little ways off he spied a heron wading in the shallows on her long spindle-shanks, beak poised to collect supper for her fledglings. She would do well, for the water was tranquil today, very unlike Michał's eddying emotions.

Part Two

The Wolf may lose his Teeth
But not his Disposition
—POLISH PROVERB

2

5 November 1830, Warsaw

I'M GOING TO BE LATE again, Viktor Baklanov thought, watching himself in the mirror as he finished with his tan cravat. He buttoned his gray double-breasted waistcoat, then pulled on his black frock coat. He had yet to grow accustomed to Polish tailoring.

"Viktor!" Barbara called, even as her husband hurried into the commodious dining room of their apartment.

"I'm here," Viktor said, adjusting his white shirt cuffs, "but I'm afraid I'm running late—no time for breakfast."

"You will take time. Ewa will be quick about it." Barbara called the maid and directed her to prepare a plate at the sideboard.

Viktor sighed, bent over his wife, and as she lifted her head in expectation of a kiss, he pinched her upper arm.

"Ouch!"

"It's your fault I'm running late nearly every

morning." He moved past Dimitri's chair, patting his blond head as he went. Both of the twins were giving full attention to their cinnamon-drenched kasza. Barbara had discovered that the cinnamon made the buckwheat porridge quickly disappear. Viktor quickly removed his coat, and as he sat at the head of the table, he saw that Barbara was blushing, holding her tongue until Ewa had set a plate before Viktor and retreated into the kitchen.

"Oh?" Barbara chided. "It's not I who is so, shall we say, *stirred*, in the mornings?"

Viktor harrumphed, produced a wicked smile, and started to eat his portion of French omelette. She was right, of course. To his mind there was no better way to begin the day than with lovemaking, and as important as punctuality in relation to his position in the department was to him, he had been late before, would be again.

He watched Barbara as she finished her meal, talking with great animation all the while of some acquaintance who had just returned from Paris. "Oh, I should very much like to see Paris," she said. "Mother calls it the City of Light."

The boys had finished and were becoming restless, so she assisted Ewa in releasing them from confinement. Polish to the bone, the matronly Ewa seldom glanced at Viktor. Her aversion to all things Russian was not an uncommon one in Warsaw. He endured the sometimes less than subtle condescension on the part of a servant because she was so well loved by the twins and appreciated by Barbara.

Viktor watched as Barbara swept back the curtain of blond hair that had fallen forward in her movements. What had attracted him to this young Polish woman? Oh, he had had several dalliances with Polish ladies upon being assigned to Warsaw, but he never imagined he might one day marry a Pole, and one of the nobility—albeit the szlachta, the minor nobility. To watch her provided his answer. There was a certain glittering ebullience about Barbara. She was so full of life, he decided, so genuine that at times people wondered if she thought long about things before giving them voice. And if at times she was inappropriate, her manner charmed everyone.

Viktor had found his wife irresistibly beautiful on that day he pretended to meet her for the first time. He never told her the circumstances of his initial attraction when he had watched from a distance, like a voyeur, and for the sake of their marriage, he would never tell her.

The omelette finished, he drank down his coffee.

With the twins off to play with their wooden soldiers, Barbara moved near to Viktor, sidling into Konrad's chair and shoving to the floor the cushions that allowed the child to reach the table. She smiled at Viktor as she covered his hand with hers.

The desire in Viktor at her gaze, her touch, leaped like a flame. Barbara was no shrinking violet. Her direct and ingenuous manner was the reason he had married her.

He knew he could not delay his departure, however, and so withdrew his hand, managing a kiss on the back of hers in the process. "Ah, temptress

Basia," he said, "you know I must hurry."

"That is nothing new, husband. But I—I wish to ask if you have seen the Imperial Commissioner in recent days?"

A dread descended on Viktor, fully dampening the desire that she had aroused. This subject yet again. "Now, Barbara, you know I'm just a lowly bureaucrat in his little government here, one of hundreds. Of course, I do see him from afar now and then, but I have no entrée to his office. I can't suddenly broach him with the subject of your father's status in Russia."

"Why not?"

"I just can't. To General Novosiltsev, I am a mere cog in one of his many wheels of government. I might as well be invisible. I'm certain that I am, in fact."

Barbara considered this and said, "If you are such a valueless member of his staff, how is it you have been given this excellent apartment in the heart of the city and on one of the best streets?" She reached over and lightly fingered the fine cotton of his white shirt. "And how is it you can afford the finest shirtmaker in the capital? The cloth—French, isn't it?"

Viktor shrugged, anger rising when no answer would present itself.

"I tell you, Viktor Baklanov, given the chance *I* will certainly broach the man. He is merely a man, after all. I will go into his office and I—"

Viktor rose at once. He felt his face flushing as the anger took hold. "You will do nothing of the kind, Barbara. Not ever! I forbid it! Do you understand me?"

"You forbid it?" Barbara stood, her mouth agape, green eyes flashing. "Why must it be so? If it were *your* father in some rat-hole of a prison or work camp, you would not rest a moment, I trust."

"You're wrong about that," Viktor countered, even as his anger bled away, assuaged by the fire of her passionate nature. "There was no great love between my father and me."

"I'm sorry for that. Then you can hardly empathize with me."

"I can and I do, Barbara. Now I must go."

"Tell me then that you'll do something . . . you'll watch for an opening. Maybe you know someone at the Commissioner's headquarters—or even someone in the Third Department who can find out—"

"That's enough, Barbara. I know of no one in the Third Department. I can promise nothing." He thrust his arms into his frock coat, pulling it on in a frenetic manner. "It's best you forget this notion." He made for the door.

"I do not forget, Viktor," Barbara shouted at his retreating form. "Neither does my mother! Nor my brother Michał! He's coming to visit Cousin Zofia tomorrow. Perhaps *he'll* manage to do something. We Stelnickis remember!"

Opening the front door, he found himself calling back, "But you are a Baklanov now, Barbara!" He had been caught off guard and immediately regretted the parry.

The door had scarcely closed behind him when he heard a crash against it and the sound of shattering glass. He took the few steps to the street, colliding head-on with a street vendor pushing her cart toward Market Square. He gave no acknowledgement to the startled old woman who cursed him. Viktor steadied himself. His lameness had made him a master at staying upright in such circumstances. The woman had gone down, and a passerby was helping her up now. Viktor took his bearings and began making his way to his office.

Good god, he thought, how had the morning come to this? He moved slowly, not because of his disability but because his mind was in a ferment. It had been a while since he had thought of his own father, and Barbara's mere mention of him roiled what had been placid waters. On several occasions Barbara had asked about his life at home in Russia, but he had always put her off. How could she—with her ideal family, one so full of ideals—understand? When he did think of his father these days, it was with no feelings of longing or sweetness. Mikhail Baklanov had been a low-level bureaucrat in Moscow, one who—to hear him tell it—had never received his due. And he had taken his bitterness out on his wife and one of his two sons in such abusive ways Viktor could still cringe at the violence he had witnessed growing up. Viktor and his mother took the brunt of Mikhail Balkanov's anger and frustration, his inexplicably favored elder brother, Fyodor, usually fully escaping any verbal or physical affronts. While his brother's name meant "God's gift," at the earliest of ages, four or five, Viktor instinctively perceived that his club foot made himself the easiest target. Even in siring his children Mikhail—to his mind—had been proven imperfect. Viktor thought now how he had come to hate his father, more for the harm done to his stoic and saint-like mother than that done to him. In time, however, after his mother's early death and his father's dismissal from state service—with the meagerest pension—and descent into a drunken retirement, he came to feel pity for the man and his failure at life. Viktor could admit to himself now that he had, at first, obtained his position in the government as a revenge quest. He was determined to show his father how to rise within the ranks. He would succeed and finally be noticed by his father. How he would enjoy that! Fyodor had, after all, become a ne'er-do-well caught up in a distillery business.

Viktor's hate had yielded to pity for his father, and now he realized for the first time that beneath the overlay of hatred and pity lay the ruins of—what? Affection? Love? Was it possible? No, it could not be that. Anything but that for the man who had reigned over an unspeakable domestic nightmare, the husband who had regularly blackened his wife's eyes for a supper that didn't meet satisfaction or wasn't produced on time, the father who had dragged his lame son down the street by his ear for his lack of celerity.

Viktor would be everything that his father aspired to—and more. He would succeed where his father had failed. Doing so had consumed his life, and only his marriage to Barbara and the birth of their twins held any meaning commensurate in any way to his desire for position and power. Thoughts of his family made him realize, too, that he wished to succeed in the domestic area of his life.

Oh, he could tell Barbara the unhappy details

of his life, and she would attempt to empathize—and perhaps she truly could understand—but, he thought, a heat rising into his face, doing so would shame him. He could not bear that, nor sympathy from anyone for his club foot.

As he turned the corner, ignoring the beggars outside a church, he remembered Barbara's own imagined meeting with the Imperial Commissioner. She wouldn't dare, would she? Doing so would likely bring down a house of cards, destroying both his professional and personal lives in one swoop. It was a far-fetched idea, one that he forced out of mind. But more threatening was this visit from his brother-in-law. What did it portend? Was it merely social—or would the meddlesome Zofia or Barbara set Michał Stelnicki to investigate the whereabouts of his father? Perhaps he had his own notion to do so? His brother-in-law's arrival in Warsaw could spell nothing but trouble.

Viktor despised Michał and knew the feeling was mutual. Damn, he thought, how he would like one day to show him just what he thought of him, his disdain for Russia, his status as minor nobility, his damned peacock strutting. How he wished he could hint, merely hint, at the power he himself had at his beck and call. That would take him down to size.

Having taken a circuitous route to his place of work, Viktor was nearing Kanonia Square, where an unmarked, five-storied building, once used by the clergy of the nearby St. Jan's Cathedral, now housed the offices of General Nikolai Novosiltsev, the Imperial Commissioner, second in power in Warsaw only to the Grand Duke Konstantin. Viktor's office was small, but it was at the rear and had the enviable advantage of two square windows. The other offices and interrogation rooms of the Third Department were secreted in the cellar.

Following his custom of avoiding the front entrance, he entered the alleyway that led to an unimposing back entrance. Here there was no one to notice the care he had to take in managing the stairs. He had no sooner entered the building than he heard a muffled commotion below. Instead of proceeding to his office, he picked his way down stone steps into the cellar and pushed back a heavy iron door.

Upon the door's closing, the cellar became very dark. It stank of mold, urine, sweat and fear. Several of the cells were occupied. As he walked the long, narrow hallway that ran down the cellar's middle, he could hear one detainee pacing, another coughing, another whispering—no, praying. Here the Third Department detained suspects and conducted interviews. Viktor picked up his pace, passing, on each side, cubicles once used by the clergy for their monastic-like retreats. More masochistic than monastic, he thought. He had converted from Russian Orthodoxy to Roman Catholicism as a requirement to marry Barbara, but he had little use for any church, and after his wedding ceremony never again accompanied Barbara to Mass at Saint Martin's.

He moved toward the light emanating from the little window-like opening of one of the cells. He could hear the questioning more clearly now, sense the fear in the trembling tenor voice answering his inquisitors.

At the window now, once used by servant nuns to pass meager meals to the clerics, he peered through the lacework curtain that had been hung there so that he might watch without having those being interrogated see him, recognize him as an officer in the Third Department, the secret police. His anonymity in connection to the Third Department made for a distinct advantage. And his marriage had made it an absolute necessity.

His argument with Barbara that morning disturbed him, and like a wound that refused to heal, an old, festering regret opened. If only he had thought to rig the lacework years before, he would feel more secure now in his position, in his marriage. But standing in that very spot four years ago, he could not have guessed that revealing his face to a prisoner—a particular prisoner—would later haunt him and threaten his position—and his marriage. The memory chilled him. Neither Barbara nor any of the Stelnickis must ever know of his position in the Third Department.

Two of Viktor's lieutenants, Sergei and Luka, were questioning the young, pitifully pale cadet. Strapped into a straight back chair and streaming tears, the boy was answering in short, staccato sentences. The cadet's right hand was held in place by a cuff fastened to the table. Entwined about the base of his fingers were thin leather straps that could be tightened by the turn of a knob. The straps were taut, the fingers bluish. Sergei looked toward the window and caught the motioning signal from Viktor. Momentarily he turned the questioning over to the hulking Luka and left the cell. Luka started right in on the boy. "What of this plan do you know?" he demanded. His Polish was as crude as his demeanor was imposing. With luck both would work the will of the Third Department.

"Well?" Viktor whispered even before Sergei could close the door behind him.

The thin Sergei gave a sheepish roll of his dark eyes and a shrug.

"You mean you have nothing to report?"

"The boy says he has heard of nothing, that he knows nothing."

"And you believe him?"

"He's a frightened child, sir. If he knows anything of value, I think he would have broken by now."

"You've been too easy on him."

As if on cue, the boy cried out as the device was tightened. Luka's threatening voice made up in volume and gruffness for what it lacked in vocabulary.

"Of course, sir, you may try your hand."

"Watch it, Sergei, or you'll find yourself doing guard duty in Siberia."

"Yes, sir," Sergei responded, properly chastened.

Viktor let out a sigh. "If he doesn't *know* anything, that does not preclude his *learning* something in the future, does it, lieutenant?"

"No sir."

Viktor thought for a moment, then said, "Take off his finger."

"Sir?

"His index finger—take it off. If he is right-handed, take that one off."

"But, sir—"

Viktor had only to issue a signal with his eyes for Sergei to realize he was serious. "If doing so offends your sensibilities, Sergei," he said with sarcasm, "have Luka do it. I'm certain he can make a good job of it."

Sergei swallowed hard. "Shall I warn him? Shall I give him one more chance to speak?"

"No," Viktor spat. "Just do it, and tell him, my friend, that unless he comes back with real information, with having heard something substantive, next time it will be his ear."

Viktor turned and retraced his way the length of the hallway, moving toward the steps. He had hoped to have the heavy iron door closed behind him before the shrill scream could follow him. His foot had slowed him down just enough, however, and he paused at the door, momentarily closing his eyes at the animal-like cry.

Viktor slowly climbed the steps and made his way to his office.

"Good morning," Anzhela said as he entered the outer office.

He replied in kind, wondering if there wasn't something different in her lifeless monotone this morning, something ominous. His secretary was at least fifty, unnaturally thin with sharp features exaggerated by her dark dress, and a sour disposition, all descriptors that belied her name: she bore no relation to an angel.

He had just reached for the door handle to the inner office when she spoke up, as if just remembering something. "The general sent for you a while ago."

"Did he?" Viktor asked before turning back to her.

"He did." Anzhela glanced up from a neat pile of papers and nodded, her lips so thin as to be invisible, her eyes an indecipherable cypress green.

Viktor turned his back to her and entered his office. Damn the woman, he cursed. Was there more here today than her usual cloying taciturnity? He moved past the desk and stood in front of the mirror, smoothing his straw-colored hair and adjusting his tall standing collar and wide tan cravat.

He left the office then, silently passing Anzhela and making for the staircase. Imperial Commissioner Nikolai Novosiltsev had his offices at the top of the building. Four flights, Viktor cursed. What was wrong with the man? God rot him! He must be nearly seventy and yet he seemed to enjoy taking the stairs. Viktor wondered if perhaps he most enjoyed wearing out his visitors before they came before him. It would be just like him. There was a strategic advantage in such a staging. It was the equivalent of standing over someone being interrogated. Viktor knew that technique well enough.

For Viktor the stairs were a real hardship. He held to the railing on the right, painstakingly lifting his right foot from one step to the next, drawing up the lame leg behind, all the while listening for the sounds of others so that he could steel himself against the humiliation of having others see him, of having others pity him. Today he was thankful he had the staircase to himself.

On the fifth level he stood outside the office many

minutes, catching his breath, straightening his coat and cravat, collecting his thoughts. What did the man want so early in the day? Then, again, Viktor had come late. Had Novosiltsev noticed? Was he petty enough to mention it? No, his was a sly pettiness. The general's having him sent up the moment he came in *was* his way of mentioning it.

When he entered the outer office, Larissa glanced up at him, her gray eyes tightening, but she said nothing and went back to the business of sorting through some papers on her desk. Color had come up into her cheeks. She was beautiful as ever.

"The general wanted to see me."

She did not afford him even a glance. "Still does, I imagine. You're late. Go on in."

Viktor moved toward the door. Her indifference was feigned, the tension in the room palpable. Larissa had not forgiven him and although he couldn't blame her, it was nonetheless annoying as hell.

He gave a light knock at the door and upon hearing the general's response, pushed it open.

"Ah, Viktor," General Nikolai Novosiltsev said, looking up from his desk, "at last." He remained seated. The Imperial Commissioner's office was situated at the front of the building so that the four large windows on the wall behind his great desk—two on either side of a massive mirror—allowed for the unusually bright November sun to spill into the room, the coruscating light momentarily blinding Viktor. Another disadvantage for someone being summoned.

Viktor moved toward the desk, stopped, bowed.

"Sit down, Viktor. Sit down."

Viktor obeyed, sitting in a hard, uncushioned chair positioned in front of the desk. It seemed a bit low so that he had to peer up at his superior.

The gray-haired general folded his hands together on the desktop, his milky blue eyes set deep in a puffy face like robins' eggs in a nest.

Viktor took in the situation. To see the general's demeanor, one would think him Viktor's spiritual advisor who was about to impart some profound advice. And sometimes the general did presume that stance. But not today. No cleverly polite observations or little jokes today. Something was amiss. The hackles at the nape of Viktor's neck rose. He waited.

"How goes the investigation into the academy?"

"Nothing to report of any importance, sir. But we're not wasting time, you can be sure."

"Meaning what, Viktor? Be specific, man."

"One of the cadets has aligned himself with us." Viktor hoped the exaggeration sounded genuine. "We hope to get a break soon." He could only pray that the cadet below would not make a liar of him. God help him if he did not provide the break.

"Good. You've put pressure on him? There's *something* afoot and we may not have a lot of time."

"I know, sir. I can assure you that he does indeed know we mean business."

"As do your men?"

"Yes, sir."

Viktor breathed a little inward sigh of relief, thinking his presentiment of something more serious was groundless. He was certain that he was about to be dismissed when Novosiltsev rose instead and turned away, facing the nearest window.

His body silhouetted against the invading sunlight, Novosiltsev peered out the fifth level window for a long minute, looking down on the square. "Your brother-in-law, Michał Stelnicki."

It was not a full thought and yet it seemed to take Viktor by the throat. What was this about? "Michał Stelnicki," Viktor parroted.

Novosilsov swung around, his eyes honing in on Viktor. "How devoted of a brother-in-law are you, Viktor?"

An easy answer here. "There is no love between us, sir."

"None?"

"None, sir. No kinship of any kind other than accidental."

"You would not protect him?"

"Sir, with a clean conscience I could send him off to Siberia."

Novosiltsev smiled neatly. "You've already done something of the kind, haven't you?"

Viktor's stomach tightened at the allusion. He did not respond.

Nikolai Novosiltsev came around the desk and stood over Viktor. "Tell me, did you know of your brother-in-law's arrival in Warsaw?"

Viktor looked up, noting the sallow complexion and loose skin at the neck. "Only this morning, sir," he said, taking in the smell of old pipe tobacco on the commissioner's clothing, alcohol on his breath. "Barbara told me he's due tomorrow. I'll have him watched, you can be sure."

"You're tardy to the battlefield, Viktor," Novosiltsev snapped. "That won't do."

"Sir?"

"The fact is, Jan Michał Stelnicki arrived yesterday."

The general seemed to be checking Viktor's facial reaction. Viktor's surprise was sincere and too sudden to be masked.

"Do you remember last May when Prince Czartoryski visited the Stelnicki estate?" Novosiltsev asked.

"Yes, sir."

"Then you remember how his visit raised questions. And suspicions. You yourself observed the prince in consultation with your brother-in-law. The prince has been at the top of our watch list for some time. We wondered at the visit and whether the prince wasn't trying to enlist him in some intrigue. Something we should be on guard about. I recall that you said you heard a few key words while listening at the door to the room where they had sequestered themselves. Words like *plot* and *insurgents*, Viktor. *Highly suspicious*, you said, and going forward, your department was to keep an eye on the situation. Is this the case or not, Viktor?"

"Of course, I remember. We did keep an eye. We did and nothing arose. For months there wasn't even innocent correspondence between the two. I'm certain—"

"Just *when* did you take your eye off your brother-in-law, Viktor?"

"We've been hard-pressed here, sir. We have only so much manpower, as you know. The cells are nearly full."

"When, Viktor? When?"

"Toward the end of the summer, I think, sir."

"Ah, and now he's here."

"He's to stay at my wife's cousin's town house, close by. It will be easy to keep him under surveillance."

"Ah, my dear boy," Novosiltsev said, as if bringing down a hammer, "he has already met again with the prince."

Viktor took in a sharp breath and struggled to keep his composure. He was not so worried about anything of real import Michał could be up to, but he was concerned that Novosiltsev was pointing out a failure in the department, which was to say, a failing in Viktor.

The Imperial Commissioner commenced on a long, cynical diatribe, measured and circuitous, concerning loyalty among family, how it was only natural, but that there were greater loyalties to be held to, namely loyalty to the Emperor and loyalty in descending fashion to the Grand Duke Konstantin, to the Imperial Commissioner Nikolai Novosiltsev himself, and ultimately to the Third Department. Somehow Viktor interpreted that any disloyalty to the Imperial Commissioner was the most reprehensible of all. Anyone displaying such disloyalty, Viktor knew, would be crushed.

Viktor sat, watching the general pace about, his words, like his gait, both slow and precise but nonetheless blurring in Viktor's mind, which was wandering. The man was a bit of a mystery. He had once been one of three great friends to advise Aleksander, the late Russian tsar. Prince Adam

Czartoryski had been one, as well. It was well known that Novosiltsev and Tsar Aleksander had once shared liberal attitudes in regard to Poland, attitudes that influenced the former tsar in no small ways. But times had changed with Tsar Nicholas. Novosiltsev had become rabidly conservative politically and anti-Polish, resulting in his relationship with Czartoryski disintegrating to the point at which the Polish patriot was an enemy worthy of being watched. And discovered—at what? Was this distrust of Prince Czartoryski valid—or a product of Novosiltsev's personal feelings and delusions?

As the general droned on about fealty, Viktor wondered at the irony of the lost comradeship between Novosiltsev and Czartoryski.

At last the general brought his lesson on loyalty to a conclusion and turned on Viktor. "I'll tell you this: if something does happen, if something significant slips past us, Viktor Baklanov, the Grand Duke will have both of our goddamned heads!" The general leaned over Viktor, his expression menacing, his breath sour. "And you can be certain, my friend, that yours will go first."

Viktor was dismissed and as he passed through the outer office, Larissa avoided his eyes. At the door, however, he felt her gaze upon him and swung quickly around. She looked away, but she had been watching him with those steel gray eyes and the oddest hint of a smile. With what intent? What emotion?

He said nothing, closed the door behind him, and began maneuvering his way down the four flights.

Viktor sat for some minutes at his desk thinking

about his meeting with Novosiltsev. The man was insufferable, despicable. It grated on Viktor that he was answerable to him, that he was fully dependent on him for his job and for any hope of advancement. He grudgingly admired—and aspired to—the Imperial Commissioner's innate intelligence, administrative acumen, and political cunning. And Viktor felt his own blind ambition equaled that of his superior's. But Nikollai Novosiltsev's dissipation, alcoholism, and pathological cynicism were intolerable.

Viktor had considered the possibility of attaining a transfer. But his marriage to Barbara complicated notions of leaving Warsaw. That Novosiltsev would be transferred was a preferred scenario but unlikely: the man was entrenched in Polish affairs, having represented the Russian Empire in Poland since 1815. Retirement was more likely, for Novosiltsev was old. Still, it might be years before he relinquished power. Old men died hard. Old powerful men died hardest.

His mind came back to Larissa. The image of her expression as he left the office stayed with him. There had been a haughty smugness in the lines of a half-smile that chilled him. He had wanted to slap her. Had she known of the substance of the interview? It occurred to him then that it might have been she who brought the information about Michał Stelnicki to Novosiltsev.

At once he discredited that notion. It was impossible. What was more credible was the notion that Novosiltsev had confided in her. Had this old man taken her as his confidante? Or worse, as his lover? Like himself, Larissa was ambitious.

Viktor chided himself for his imagination. Novosiltsev and Larissa? It was too repellent a thought. Besides, Novosiltsev was known to anyone worth his salt in the Third Department for his predilection not for pretty secretaries but for prostitutes.

Or, if Larissa did indeed have knowledge of the meeting's content, it was more than possible that she had listened at the door. She was capable of doing so.

Another thought. It chilled Viktor to think Novosiltsev received classified information from sources other than the Third Department, but he was notorious for working one branch of the Russian bureaucracy against another. Viktor had no illusions that the Third Department was the sole purveyor in clandestine activity. Competition abounded.

ß

"Y OUR BAG ARRIVED EARLIER THIS morning, milord."
Michał thanked the Gronska stable boy, affecting a smile as he dismounted.

"I'll take good care of this fine stallion, sir."

"Do that. His name is Bonaparte." This drew a smile from the boy. "But he's not French or Corsican," Michał continued. "He's a Polish Arabian."

"I saw that, milord. Smaller than an average stallion—more adaptable in battle."

"Indeed. What's your name, lad?" Michał took him

for eighteen or nineteen.

"Kasper, milord."

"Ah, keeper of the treasure, is it? Most appropriate."

"Milord?"

"Your name, Kasper, that's what it means."

"Oh."

"I'm going to take a turn about the city before I go in to see the Countess Gronska—should anyone ask."

Michał left the carriage house, moving down the alleyway toward the street. The sick feeling at the pit of his stomach had not abated. The late night meeting with Prince Adam Czartoryski had not gone well. Not well at all. The prince had fumed with anger, fired stern questions at him. How had he presumed to just show up at the prince's residence unannounced, under cover of night notwithstanding? Didn't he realize the mansion would be under surveillance day and night? Hadn't the prince told him back in May that his moves were watched? Didn't he realize the danger, the need for absolute secrecy?

Michał had reacted with the obsequiousness due the statesman but thought him a bit overwrought, a bit overly suspicious. However, as he rode away from the prince's city mansion before dawn, his keen ears picked up the sound of another horse's clip-clopping some distance behind, and when he alternated speeds between a walk and a trot, so too did the other rider. His arrival in Warsaw and his visit with the prince were no secret, it seemed. He was being followed. Coming to the Market Square, he dismounted and led the chestnut Arabian in among the crush of shops, stalls, vendors, and early shoppers. In time he looked back but saw no one trailing him. At least not a rider. However, the person following him might easily have given his horse over to someone, and with no image of a face to go by, Michał knew he might be any one of the faces in the market. His eyes on alert, he had briskly led his chestnut past admiring or curious eyes to the opening of a side street and remounted, taking a roundabout route through various narrow streets, then doubling back to Piwna Street and the Gronska town house.

Now, his horse safely stowed with Kasper, he strode along the alley abutting Zofia's town house, coming out at Piwna Street. To his left and across the street, the narrow lane was dominated by Saint Martin's Church. Farther down, it emptied out into the Castle Square. He turned right, his mind still burning with the knowledge that his nighttime visit to the prince had been noted and recorded. The prince had had every right to be angry. He had been foolish. Stupid. He, like the prince himself, would be under suspicion now, under watch by the government. It suddenly occurred to him that the person tailing him had been obvious—too obvious. Was someone deliberately trying to intimidate him?

Impulsively, Michał stopped, turned back, retraced his steps, crossed the street, and entered Saint Martin's Church, slipping into a back pew. The church was empty, but for a handful of veiled women lighting candles at Mary's statue. The quietude welcomed him. The coolness of the marble, the scents of the yellow and white crysthanthemums and beeswax candles coalesced to calm him.

He knelt for no longer than a minute before sitting back. The kneeling was a perfunctory action. It was expected and so he complied. Not many years before, he had come to realize his attitude toward religion was much like that of his stepfather's. On one occasion, they had been hunting and had brought down a deer. The death scene, strangely echoing in some small way the many battles in which Michał had taken part, prompted him to ask Jan whether he believed in God.

"I do," Jan said. A long pause ensued and Michał somehow knew to wait. "I will say," Jan continued at last, 'that I don't believe God has chosen any one church or any one religion in which to dwell."

"But you go to church."

"More for your mother than for me or my God."

"Your God?"

"Yes, Michał. Look at the trees here in the forest, their height, their strength and majesty. Look at the light coming from the bluest of skies and slanting through the treetops and falling through a mist to the ground. Take in the earthy smells about us. Listen to the songs of the birds above, the rabbits rustling in the briar below. My God is here." Jan pointed to the lifeless stag. "Even in this gift there. He has sent it."

"Have you spoken of this to Mother?"

"Once, in a meadow, many years ago."

"Did she understand?

"I think so. Oh, I'm not saying I don't believe in the God of her church, Michał. What I'm saying is that I believe in the God of all the churches, synagogues, and temples where people believe him to dwell.

How could it be otherwise? He was in that long-ago meadow and he's here today."

Sitting now in Saint Martin's, Michał could not help but hope—and pray—for guidance. Rankling thoughts of his blundering visit to Prince Czartoryski persisted. He put down his recklessness to too many years on the estate, away from wars, away from soldiering, away from politics and intrigue. He had not grown fat, but he had grown comfortable. They were good years, those, he thought, and the temptation to return to Sochaczew as soon as possible arose now, beckoning. As the minutes passed, and as Michał sorted out his thoughts within the cocoon of the church, he confronted the temptation and put it to rest, admitting now that those had been bland and colorless years. Just the mere acceleration of his pulse at the thought of his being followed underscored the lack of excitement in his life at Sochaczew. The years in the military—long, lonely, grueling, and bloody as they were—had provided intermittent adventure, a dark war joy, and, more importantly, a hard and fast purpose. A noble purpose. And now, as he thought back on the real meat of his tête à tête with the prince, the real danger to Poland, he came to realize in his heart of hearts, that the recent years of inactivity, however comfortable, were over.

As a young man—boy, in truth—he had joined the cavalry. He had done his duty. Now, at thirty-eight, his duty had come to him, a duty not to be taken lightly, for Poland herself hung in the balance.

"Welcome to Warsaw, Michał!" Zofia chimed.

Michał had been admiring a painted porcelain clock on the mantle, and he turned to see her gliding across the well-appointed reception room, toward him. "Thank you, Cousin Zofia," he said, meeting her half way and kissing her on either cheek, ever so lightly for they were powdered. She wore a scent of roses.

"Sit down, sit down. I've ordered afternoon tea for us. Now, you must tell me how the summer was passed at Sochaczew. And how is my cousin?"

Michał sat in a French styled tub chair, too low to the tiled floor for his long legs. "Mother is well and as for—"

"Do you know, Michał," Zofia asked, settling into a high-backed wing chair, "there was a time I dreaded the summers in the country? No parties, no opera, no theater. But now, from time to time, I do long for the slower months. The peace, you know. The returning storks tending their new little ones in their nests next to our chimneys, the scent of fresh-cut wheat and rye at Harvest Home. The sense that time will go on. Oh, I could do without the deafening sounds of the cicadas." With much animation Zofia launched into the telling of one summer invasion of cicadas in Halicz during her girlhood at Hawthorn House, the Gronski family estate in Southern Poland, long sequestered now by the Russians. The bringing of a tea tray by a young maid and the serving of tea did not slow the tale.

Michał sipped at his tea, marveling at this woman's verve and great beauty. She was nearing sixty and yet her her face was unlined and her high, ornately arranged hair was still as black as her eyes. Oh, he knew she bathed her face in a yogurt concoction with some regularity, but what kept the silver from her hair he could not fathom. She wore a shimmering gray day dress, high-waisted with straight lines and daringly low-cut in what he thought must be the most recent style. Beneath her hem the silver buckles of her matching slippers glinted in the light given off by the fire in the grate.

In time Zofia did allow Michał to manage a short account of a reasonably successful harvest home, a minor roof collapse of the barn, and other mundane doings at Topolostan.

"How very interesting," Zofia said, with more politeness than interest, "however, I have an afternoon engagement and I should get about my toilette." She set down the cup of tea that had gone cold during her conversation. "Your portmanteau arrived this morning. You'll find it and everything you'll need in the front suite on the second floor." She started to rise.

"Thank you so much, but I wanted to ask about Iza." Michał thought it strange that Zofia had failed to mention her.

"Oh, Izabel!" Zofia said in a breathy exclamation, falling back into the well-cushioned chair. "I'd quite forgotten. I'm so glad you're here, Michał. I hope you can engage her in some activity. She may have left the convent, but the convent has not left her, I must say." Zofia produced her plinking little laugh. "I'm at my wit's end with her. She keeps to her room, sometimes even for meals, and lord knows, she refuses to attend any social function. What's to become of her? She's many years past her girlhood and the ideal marrying age, but there are some men in the circles in which I travel—older men, you know, widowers and the like—who might take an interest, but she refuses an outing of any kind."

"It must be hard, Cousin Zofia, coming back into the world out of a cloistered convent. Did she not seem happy there—on your visits?"

Michał thought Zofia's face colored slightly. "Well, truth be told, Michał, I didn't often visit."

"Oh."

"Now don't think too harshly of me. I seldom hold a grudge, but I must admit to one in this regard. I hadn't wanted her to enter the convent in the first place. We had many strong words about it. I had had plans for my only daughter. My only child. Grand plans! Why, in *my* youth I always said my years were golden ducats to be spent and enjoyed. And what does *she* do with hers but throw them away—like so many worthless pebbles down a well!"

Michał affected a laugh. "Why, Iza is younger than I by three years, I think, and I'm not yet wrinkled and arthritic, cousin, so she's not so very old."

Zofia shrugged and got to her feet. "Time is more heartless with women, I'm afraid." She sighed, a stage sigh, Michał thought. "You know, she is nothing like me. I could swear she's a changeling. Maybe you can breathe some life into her, Michał." She held her hand out for Michał to kiss. "I shall be hopeful for that. Now I must fly."

"Is she in her room? Will she come down to supper?"

Zofia turned and made for the doorway, speaking as she did so. "Oh, I did manage to get her to go out. It took some doing. She's selecting materials for dresses, and if I hadn't lied and said I had made an appointment for her, she wouldn't have felt compelled to go. She's the type that wouldn't want to disappoint even a shopkeeper, you see. Catholic guilt, I suppose. It plagued Mother, too, rest her soul." Her laughter poured out like tinkling coins. "I guess it skipped a generation." At the door now, Zofia turned, her lips a reddened gash beneath a perfect nose, the comedy gone. "I suppose she made a fine nun, Michał. And yet to me she has been a disappointment. A great disappointment."

Michał found his quarters to be a two-room affair: a small sitting room leading to a larger bedchamber, the two windows of which fronted the street. The sitting room had a small sofa, writing desk and caned chair; the bedchamber a wide, comfortable-appearing bed embraced by blue velvet hangings, table nearby, capacious armoire, reading chair by the windows. After unpacking his portmanteau and storing it atop the armoire, Michał ventured out into the hallway and started down the stairs. Upon reaching the first floor landing, he heard light footsteps coming up the carpeted staircase from the ground floor. Since Zofia had gone out and the maids exclusively used the rear stairwell, he at once guessed the identity of the person ascending the stairs. He waited.

As the woman reached the first floor landing, her eyes were cast downward, one hand clutching a package, the other carefully tending the folds of her dark dress.

"Iza," Michał said in a cautionary whisper, realizing they were about to collide.

"Oh!" the woman cried, for she had neither heard nor noticed him.

Their first meeting in years seemed almost a tableau in some drama.

Even in the shadowy light her face blanched noticeably, the expression reminding Michał of a startled bird's. "Forgive me, I didn't mean to frighten you." At once he doubted himself as to her identity, for this woman seemed younger than thirty-five. "It is Iza?"

She nodded. "No need to apologize," she stammered. "My thoughts were elsewhere.—Jan Michał, is it *you*? Really you?"

"My lady." Michał gave a little bow.

She gave a hint of a giggle. "I see that it is, indeed. It's been a very long time."

"I'm sure I look very different."

"Well—of course. You've grown up. You've had adventures. You've—you've become a man, Jan Michał."

"I'm simply called *Michał* now."

"And why is that?"

"It's just something that evolved out of deference to my mother so that the name *Jan* would not be a constant reminder of her missing husband."

Iza nodded in understanding.

"I see that time has been gracious to you, Iza. May you have adventures, too, now—"

"That I've left the convent? I can assure you I'm not seeking adventures. I'm content with my own chamber, a fire in winter, and a good book."

Michał laughed. "They may find you in any case. Adventures, I mean."

"Only if Mother sends them my way." Iza seemed to immediately regret her lightly sarcastic words and her body tensed, her arms pulling the package to her bosom. It was wrapped in brown paper and tied with string.

"Material?" Michał asked.

Iza nodded, her honest face reflecting the realization that her mother had spoken of her errand. She was at a loss for words. That her mother had been speaking of her seemed to cause her to draw back, as a deer might at the sight of a yeoman. Iza nodded uncertainly and shifted from one foot to the other.

Michał had not meant to embarrass her. He wished to engage her in conversation, but calculating that Iza intended to take flight, he excused himself instead, saying he would see her at supper. She gave him an indecipherable smile. As he moved down the stairs, he heard her footfalls on the Persian runner softly moving away. For all the lost years, the little reunion on the landing had been brief. Strangely awkward, too, he thought. Perhaps she was as unsure of his disposition as he was of hers. Life had taken them on very separate paths. He had thought little about her over those years, so the fact that he found himself somehow intrigued now came with a little jolt.

It wasn't until after he reached the ground floor that he heard the distant echo of her door closing on the first level. This delay gave him pause: Had she taken the time to peer over the railing, watching him as he descended? What had she thought of him?

"Fish for supper?" Zofia cried. "Again? And for the main course!"

Michał looked from the scowling Zofia, at the head of the table, to Iza, who sat directly across from him. Iza was casting a covert smile at Elzbieta, Wanda's pretty twelve-year-old daughter, who was collecting the soup bowls in advance of Wanda's laying down of the fish and potato course—and who, out of the ways of servitude or out of fear of Zofia, knew not to return an overt smile.

Iza's mother was not to be ignored. "I take it this was your request, Izabel? Is this Lent? Is this Friday? Am I suddenly in the poorhouse? Or have you made an unholy alliance with a fishmonger?"

Michał suppressed a laugh out of concern for Iza.

Iza, however, did smile and allowed a light laugh. "This is a different kind of fish than what we ate yesterday, Mother. This is—"

"Fish is fish, Izabel. One smells as much as the next and they all stare up at you with the blankest expression. It really puts me off my appetite quite completely."

"I'm sorry. We could arrange to have them beheaded in the kitchen."

Michał's eyes honed in on Iza, expecting to see

what he had not detected in her tone: sarcasm. But her face seemed relaxed, her eyes as honest as the blue sky. She was the quintessence of innocence.

Zofia ignored Iza, turning to Michał. "It seems the good Carmelite sisters ruined my daughter's taste for animal flesh." Her disapproving eyes went to her daughter. "Don't they eat any kind of animal, Izabel?"

"They do on occasion, Mother, but—"

"But what?"

"Well, in my first year as part of my kitchen duties, I had to kill the chickens. It's one thing to have a fish on your plate and quite another to put a poor chicken's head on the block and lift the axe."

Zofia gave this brief consideration. "You needn't be faint-hearted. There are others here to lift the axe."

"And then," Iza continued, "if you don't get it into the pail immediately the headless creature will run about with blood spouting into the air until it drops. It's quite horrible."

The image had little effect on Zofia. "Your ghoulish description merely reminds me that I have a taste for *czarnina*. I'll tell Wanda directly."

"Duck's blood soup? Mother, really!"

"And I want a full week without fish, do you hear? If you must putter in the kitchen, getting in the way of staff, you are not to alter the menu."

Michał chuckled. "Do you putter in the kitchen, Iza?"

Iza's eyes were cast down upon her fork as she poked delicately at her fish. "I keep a winter herb garden there, near the big windows. I enjoy experimenting with herbs. Maintaining a garden was my task at the convent, outside in the summer, of course, and inside during the winter months."

"I see," Michał said. "The food must have been rich in flavor."

"They say that hunger makes the best sauce," Zofia piped.

Iza ignored her mother's quip. "Oh, I also worked with herbal medicines. I confess that I would be found with Brunfels' *Herbarum Vivae Eicones* in hand when I should have been reading the Holy Book."

"Truly?" Izabel Gronska was, he decided, quite charming in a guileless, retiring sort of way. She wore a simple gown of dark blue that covered her arms and neckline, and with no jewelry to set it off, she should have looked like a spinster, but the effect actually made her look almost girlish. Like her mother, she had the dark hair credited to the Tatar bloodlines so prevalent in Southeastern Poland where Zofia was born, but unlike Zofia's olive complexion, her skin was porcelain white. And her eyes were round rather than almond shaped and a vivid cornflower blue instead of black. The effect of the light eyes and visage framed by the black hair proved startlingly attractive.

"It's an occupation she should have left behind, Michał," Zofia was saying.

"But I enjoy it, Mother."

Zofia pushed her plate away. "Just leave the maids to do what they're paid to do. Lord knows, there are more entertaining things to do this side of cloister walls."

"The fish has been well prepared," Michał offered. "They say that to taste good, fish must swim three times."

Iza immediately laughed while Zofia shot Michał a quizzical look.

"They swim in water, Cousin Zofia," Michał explained, "then in butter—and finally in wine."

"Ah," Zofia said, all but ignoring Michał's attempt to meliorate the tension and changing the subject. "We have an invitation to a concert and ball at the Belweder Palace, Michał, and she doesn't wish to go."

"Given by the Grand Duke Konstantin, I assume?" Michał asked. It pained him to think that one of the residences of Poland's last king was home to Russian royalty. That Tsar Nicholas called himself King of Poland brooked no respect from most Poles. No, the last true king of the one-time Commonwealth of Poland and Lithuania had been the weak but well-meaning Stanisław.

"Of course," Zofia was saying, "The young Fryderyk Chopin everyone is talking about is set to play some of his own compositions."

Michał's silence—or perhaps expression—was not lost on Zofia.

"You don't approve?"

Michał shrugged. "Of Chopin, I have no opinion although my brother Józef was tutored by Chopin's father at piano prior to his electing to go into the academy. But of Konstantin? No, I don't approve. Commoner or Grand Duke, one Russian in Warsaw is one too many."

"Michał," Zofia said solicitously, "be careful in saying such things now that you are here in the capital. This is a far cry from provincial Sochaczew.

The Russians are here and they have the power. One must dance with the devil or—"

"Not dance at all," Iza blurted.

Zofia's gaze shot to her daughter. "It's the dancing that must put you off, Izabel, isn't it? Not the politics. What can you know about politics, having been shut away as you have?"

Zofia's caution had caught Michał's attention. "Are the politics," he questioned, "such that we can't speak our minds in our own homes?"

"Perhaps one may dare to do so, Michał," Zofia replied, "but it is best not to be too open about one's more liberal opinions. They say the secret police are plentiful as blades of grass these days." She fell silent and gave a tight smile as Wanda reentered the dining hall with an apple cake. It was only after the cake had been cut and Wanda had retreated to the kitchen that Zofia finished her thought. "So it's best to be cautious, Michał."

Michał nodded and did not answer. As a guest in Zofia's home, he would not venture further into the political realm where he was certain he and Zofia clearly differed.

Zofia spoke after a while, shifting to a thread of thought Michał had initiated. "Michał, why did Józef give up his piano lessons? Why, we might be going to see *him* perform had he persevered!"

"I don't know why he lost interest. But I do know his going into the military broke my mother's heart."

"Indeed," Zofia said. "Losing one son is more than enough. It was thoughtless of young Józef to go against Anna's wishes."

"Well, I think," Iza offered, "that he had his own path to take."

Zofia shot a hard look at Iza, her dark, slivered eyes narrowing further. It was not lost on her—or Michał—that Iza intended the comment as an indictment against her own mother. Michał noted Zofia's sharp displeasure at her thirty-five-year-old daughter's little mutiny and could only imagine to what extent she had attempted to control Iza's life—before Iza took refuge in a convent.

Iza was working at her cake and did not notice—or chose not to notice—her mother's displeasure at being contradicted.

Zofia refused the apple cake and excused herself, begging off to go to her room and prepare to attend the opera. "I don't need any more apple cake. Eventually a woman ends up wearing her desserts in the most inappropriate places." The dark eyes flashed toward Iza. "You don't have that awful religious garb anymore to cover up your cakes and dumplings, Izabel. Something to think about."

In Zofia's wake, Iza calmly applied her fork to her cake. Michał saw no change in her visage. She was unperturbed. However, Wanda, who had returned to collect dirty dishes and who well knew Zofia's barbs, looked up from her tray as she retreated to the kitchen, her eyes widening slightly and her mouth forming a subtle but perfect little o.

The dining chamber remained awkwardly quiet as the two maids returned to collect the plates and utensils from the evening meal, making several trips through the swinging door leading into the kitchen.

Finally, Michał and Iza sat alone at table. "I must congratulate you, Iza."

"Me?" She looked up, her alabaster skin coloring slightly. "Why?"

"For the way you respond to your mother."

"Oh."

"You exhibit such patience. She doesn't irritate you?"

Iza smiled. "Oh, yes, a great deal."

"But you're an adult now. And she treats you— well, you're very patient."

"I have a great deal of patience—up to a point."

"And then— ?"

"Then something happens and—and I snap." On her last word, Iza brought her fork forcefully crashing down on her dessert plate, the porcelain intact but ringing out its hurt.

Caught unaware, Michał blinked at the clanging. A moment later the kitchen door swung open just enough for Elzbieta to poke her head in, her blond braids falling forward.

"It's nothing," Iza said, waving her away, the blue of her eyes at once innocent and clever, "my fork slipped."

Michał laughed once the wide-eyed servant's face vanished. "Well, it's good to know you have a flashpoint. Although you do have a sneaky little parry when it's least expected.—Did you *snap* in the convent?"

"I'm afraid so. Not regularly, but there were occasions."

"Is that why you left?"

"No, not at all."

"I see."

After a moment of silence, Iza asked, "You're wondering why I did leave. Everyone does."

Michał shrugged, unable to deny it. "It's none of my business, Iza."

"I was asked to leave, Michał. That's the truth of it. You see, I never took my final vows. I was timid about doing so, had been for years. And then, when I thought I was ready—well, it's complicated. In the end, Mother Abbess insisted my vocation was a delusion."

"And was it?"

Iza released a long, sad sigh. "Oh, I loved the life, Michał, the quiet, the meditation, the isolation. And the work in the kitchen, too! Kitchen chores are so simple, honorable, and rewarding. My herb garden was everything to me!"

"Then why— ?"

"Didn't I take my vows? I finally had to face the truth that I didn't have a true vocation. I was there under false pretenses and the abbess at last pressed me on it."

"I don't understand."

"I was running away, Michał. My mother had her mind set on marrying me off to someone of *her* choosing. I'm not at all like her—and she doesn't understand that. And I don't think she'll ever really forgive me for entering the convent."

"She didn't visit often, I know, but surely—"

"*Often*?" Iza said, her finely shaped mouth falling slack. "Is that what she told you?"

Michał nodded.

"Michał, relatives are allowed only one visit a year."

"I see."

"No, you don't," Iza countered, and for a moment the subject hung fire. "Michał, Mother *never* visited me—not once in those seven years!"

Michał had no reason to doubt her, but the knowledge that Zofia had effectively written off her daughter for years on end left him stunned. And now he noticed the tears brimming in Iza's eyes. "Iza, I'm so sorry—"

"Oh, I'm fine. Mother and I will never see eye to eye, and I've finally resigned myself to that.—Now, what plans do you have for your visit?"

Her interest at once pleased Michał and diverted the subject of her relationship with her mother. "I'm here to see how young Józef is making out at the academy. And I've already met with Prince Czartoryski on some political matters. I'll have to see him again."

Iza was taken by surprise. "Prince Adam Czartoryski?"

"Yes. Oh, your mother had a fine story for us when she visited Topolostan back in June. She said he had proposed to her some years ago, but his offer came just after he had had an unhappy romance with the tsarina of Russia, and she did not wish to accept him on the rebound."

Iza began to laugh and Michał marveled at the transformation in her visage. He thought her quite beautiful, charmingly so.

"I hope you took the story with a grain of salt, Michał."

Michał hesitated, then said, "I have to tell you my mother said it was probably Zofia who proposed."

At that precise moment Zofia appeared in the doorway, sending a shock through Michał and a rush of blood to his face. He prayed she hadn't heard his comment.

"I'm off to the opera," Zofia announced, "though I daresay I shall be bored to death. I live for the intermissions. They're the true entertainments."

Iza laughed all the harder. No blushing on her part.

"What are you two talking about? It's good to see you laugh, Izabel."

"It was nothing, Mother. Just silliness. You have a good time."

Zofia smiled uncertainly, as if she knew a secret was being kept from her. She cast a glance at Michał, one that seemed to commend him for being a good influence on her daughter. She flashed one last puzzled look at her daughter, turned and left.

The two waited until Zofia was out of earshot. "I suspect *your* mother's version is the true historical story," Iza said, still laughing, "but you won't believe the addendum I have to add to the Prince Adam Czartoryski epic!"

"And what is that?"

It took some effort for Iza to calm herself. "Before I entered the convent Mother had her heart set on my marrying a wealthy magnate. They came through this house like a circus parade. Why, I remember one whose face resembled the backside of a boar. But at the end of the parade, it was the Prince Adam Czartoryski on whom she had set her sights *for me!*"

"Good God! He was still unmarried all those years later?"

"Yes—and old enough to be my father! I did my best to keep distance and appear unattractive—and he eventually found another."

"His present wife?"

"Yes, and what truly angered Mother was that his wife was even younger than I!" Iza covered her mouth as mirth overtook her yet again. "Oh, I do hope it worked out well for both of them."

Michał joined Iza in her laugh at Zofia's expense.

Michał sat alone sipping at a brandy in the reception room. A small fire flickered in the grate. He had asked Iza to join him, but once they had had their little laugh at table, she had reverted to her serious mien. Michał put it down to her lack of social interaction behind cloistered walls. There seemed to be a dichotomy in her character: she could display playfulness, wit, and—in light of her admitting that she could "snap"—a healthy impatience; and yet she appeared quiet, retiring, and perhaps even fearful at times. Michał sensed that it would take her a while to feel more comfortable in company. It occurred to him then that perhaps she had never been comfortable in company. What if—her mother's meddling notwithstanding—her lack of social skills had led her to the convent? When he had met her on the stairway landing earlier, her eyes had been veiled and colorless, but as the supper played out her eyes seemed less and less like those of a cloistered nun. At table she had displayed innocence, reserve, sagacity, patience, humor, and hurt. And those eyes—they coruscated blue cleverness. She was a mystery, a very pretty mystery.

The delicious supper and the brandy lulled Michał into sleep as he sat in the deeply cushioned chair before the fire. He dreamed. It was a haunting, terror-filled dream he had had nearly every night for years, but he had not experienced it for many months.

It was the winter of 1812, a brutal one he had relived in and out of dreams numberless times. He and his brother Tadeusz had followed Napoleon's Grand Armée in the interminable and agonizing retreat from Moscow. Michał had been twenty; Tadeusz, seventeen. As part of the Polish Young Guard, they had been ordered to stay behind in order to destroy Moscow's artillery supplies, and so when they had completed the task and caught up to the Old Guard and multi-national main forces at Maloyaroslavets, it was to a grisly post-battle sight. They regretted their tardiness. Five thousand of their own—French, Polish, and men of a dozen other allied nationalities—lay dead, side by side with almost as many of the Russian enemy.

From there the starving and desperate ragtag army pushed west—toward home—attempting to second-guess the several Russian units seeking them, all the while fighting off Cossacks and peasant bandits who victimized with the cruelest of violence those many stragglers who could not keep up even the snail's pace and fell to the wayside. Then to the steppes came winter—"General Winter," in the words of Napoléon Bonaparte—and he began to claim as many souls as those who died in battle.

Michał had been determined to see that he brought his younger brother safely home, but that quest grew more difficult when in a great Russian assault Tadeusz took a shot to his leg. The medic on the field warned them that he had not gotten all of the ball out and that they should find a surgeon as soon as possible. The slow, plodding journey to find a town or city with a physician began, and it was at this point that the recurring nightmares picked up. General Winter raged on with temperatures not rising above zero, day or night. Tadeusz became numb from the cold and insensate from the infection that had set in from his open and festering wound, but Michał was alert enough to push on, encouraging Tadeusz, both brothers bearing witness to frozen corpses at the sides of the road and the pitiful calls from French soldiers who were dying and wished to be finished off before falling victim to Cossacks or ruthless peasants. When Michał's starving horse fell dead, Michał worked feverishly, hacking away at the animal's emaciated haunches and carving out slender steaks that could feed them and be used as barter in villages ahead. He caught what blood he could in his regulation saucepan, and once the cutting was done, he managed to nurse a fire to life, which was more than he could do for the frozen French corpses encircling it. The flames warmed their blood-and-horseflesh soup.

They were still only half way to Wilno, the Lithuanian capital and the promise of a good doctor, when they stayed the night in the cottage of an old couple. It was there that their other horse was stolen and they were forced to travel on foot. Tadeusz was so ill with fever and dazed by this time that Michał carried him on his back, insisting that they sing so that Tadeusz would not lapse into a fatal unconsciousness. Michał vowed not to return home without his brother. Hour by hour, they pressed on, singing in weak voices:

Darling war, darling war,
What a lady you must be
For all the handsome boys
To follow you like this.

Michał came awake now in the Gronska reception room, his lips still mouthing the song, still shivering with cold from the wind off the steppes. The fire had died and the room was chilled, the last two candles slowly guttering. The house was utterly silent.

Tadeusz, he thought. *Forgive me.* He recalled that their family friend and military mentor Pawel—Zofia's one-time love—had found them and taken them to a man who knew something of rudimentary medicine and surgery. But he was no doctor; he was, in fact, a bear tamer. While the man seemed fully capable, it was too late for Tadeusz, little Tadek. The poisons had run their course through his system. In the end, Michał had to return to Warsaw, to his parents, without his brother. It had been the worst day of his life.

While his parents had not held him responsible in

any way, and he knew at his core that he had done everything possible to protect and bring his brother safely home, he was haunted by guilt, guilt that he had survived while Tadek had not.

Michał thought of his youngest brother now. Józef was nearly seventeen, the same age Tadeusz had been. Against their mother's wishes, he had taken up a military career. And only the night before, Prince Czartoryski had warned him of the dangerous plans escalating within the Officer Cadets School. Was Józef mixed up in a scheme of some kind? A military coup against the Russians? Was Józef foolishly and unnecessarily placing himself in danger?

When Michał had left Sochaczew for Warsaw, his mother had made him promise to look in on Józef, to make sure he was doing well at the academy, to make sure he was happy. He had humored her, saying he would follow her directive and he certainly did intend to see his little brother, but truth be told, he had thought little of her request. She was merely being a concerned mother. However, the old nightmare—and the facts laid out by Czartoryski the night before— fired real concern for Józef, as well as real fear.

And giving him pause now, too, was that strange thing his mother told him about some gypsy who had been present at Józef's birth. The self-proclaimed seer had said, "The boy will one day bait the Russian bear."

Michał found himself fully chilled with a cold that arose from within. He would see Józef as soon as possible.

4

ZOFIA STOOD FIRM: NO REFUSAL to attend the Saturday concert was acceptable. Iza stepped into the silk-covered slippers that matched her emerald gown, one that draped in straight lines and was set off with a tied sash just below her bosom, in the French style she had come to appreciate. Women's fashions were so much simpler than those prior to her entering the convent. She faced the long mirror, admiring the upsweep of her black hair and the emerald studded pins that held it. Wiola, Zofia's personal maid whose work this was, stood to the side.

"Turn around, Izabel."

Iza flinched. She had not heard her mother enter the dressing area of the bedchamber. She turned about. Her arms that had been lifted to discipline a stray lock of hair slowly dropped to her side. She could sense the corpulent Wiola tensing beside her. The woman was nearing fifty, Iza guessed, and had been Zofia's lady's maid for some years. She knew to tread lightly.

"The color is a bit dark for a young lady, Izabel, and the cut is less than revealing in front. Are the other dress designs you are now choosing like this in shade?"

"I'll be certain to order several lighter colors, Mother."

"Make at least two of them white. And I hope some are a bit more—revealing. Remember, you're not in the convent anymore."

Iza bit at her lower lip. "If the dressmaker suggests—"

"No, no, you are in the wrong, sweet. *You* are the one to suggest—or rather *order*. Never mind, I'll send her a message tomorrow with some directives. Now, your hair is fine, but Wiola needs to get busy with your makeup. We need to leave within the quarter hour."

"Oh, I'm quite ready now, Mother. My makeup is finished."

Zofia's eyes widened and she stared for a long beat, then took two steps forward, her black eyes fastening hard. "Why it's scarcely noticeable!" She looked from Iza to Wiola, then back again.

Exactly, Iza thought. "At my suggestion," she said, attempting to avoid smugness. She heard Wiola draw in a deep breath as if bracing for Zofia's fury. Servants knew not to cross her. "I'm very happy with Wiola's craft."

Zofia's expression folded into a false smile. Iza guessed she was considering ordering Wiola to thicken the cheek and lip rouge, so she quickly drew up her black evening cape, an item borrowed from her mother. Turning her back to her mother, she handed it to the nervous Wiola, indicating her desire for help in draping it from the shoulders. As Iza stood before the mirror, clipping it at her throat with the silver lover's knot, she saw her mother, clearly ruffled, turn and leave the room, her steps heavier than usual.

The November night had darkened when the carriage drew up in front of Belweder Palace, an impressive white edifice with an imposing portico and columns. It was situated on a hill just above the massive grounds of Łazienki Park. Iza followed her mother, stepping down on the stool the footman provided. The building was as Iza remembered, but this would be the first time she would step inside, and to her surprise a little thrill ran through her.

She followed her mother into the crush of people entering the palace. They passed Russian sentries, numbering so few as to be merely ceremonial. The Grand Duke Konstantin is trusting, she thought. The wide halls glowed with brightly lighted sconces and sounded with the low but excited voices of the rich, the powerful, and the intelligentsia. Leaving their capes at an attendant's station, they proceeded to the great rectangular Blue Hall, named for the hanging Lyon fabrics adorned with arabesques. Here, rows and rows of blue velvet upholstered chairs spanned the length of three walls, cascading toward the middle of the long inside wall, where a black lacquered piano sat embraced in a modest niche, like a corpulent nun. Its bench was empty. Three massive chandeliers gave light to the colorfully dressed crowd now claiming their seats.

"Look, Mother, there are seats just two rows from where the pianist will sit."

"Come with me, Izabel," Zofia said, taking Iza by the hand and drawing her across the room to seats in the second-to-last row. "This is much better,

Izabel. From here we can see just about everything and everybody."

"But, Mother—"

Zofia raised a gloved hand to shush her daughter. "I did not come for Fryderyk Chopin. I did come to be entertained, but not by Monsieur Chopin—and I hope perhaps to do *you* some good. Now, stay here and keep this aisle seat for me. I shall return before the start."

Iza settled into the comfortable cushioned chair, perfectly content to sit by herself and watch the sophisticated circus unfold before her, its bouquet of players fanning themselves, talking, laughing, moving, motioning. It was a sight so unlike any she had seen in what seemed a decade. Fascinating as it was, crowds made her nervous. She didn't know why.

Her eyes fastened on her mother who stood bending over an acquaintance on the other side of the room. Even at this distance the décolletage of the fuchsia gown was apparent. Her mother's face and figure, and especially her sprightly mien, belied her age. Iza could remember the earlier years and what a beauty she had been. Her earliest memories of her mother were images of a beautiful woman who stopped in momentarily at the third floor classroom to give instructions to the governess. On occasion Iza was allowed to kiss her lightly on the cheek, but whenever her mother appeared like a vision of the Madonna in the doorway of Iza's adjacent bedchamber—prior to going out in the evening—no kisses were allowed for fear damage would be done to the makeup or gown.

The music room began to fill and two women Iza

guessed to be in their fifties moved up the aisle to the row abutting the back wall, seating themselves directly behind Iza. Even while watching the animated tapestry around her, Iza could not help but be distracted by the conversation of the two women. After complaining about how far away from the pianist their seats were, a complaint Iza silently shared, they commented on the recent rehabilitation of the palace.

"You do know," one intoned in an annoyingly high-pitched voice, "that King Stanisław resided at the Royal Castle and he had the temerity to use this lovely estate as a porcelain factory?"

"I didn't know," her friend answered. Her low, measured voice reflected muted shock. "What an utter shame."

"Indeed! Oh, look, Nina, at the woman in red!"

"Where?"

"There! Follow my finger!"

"Oh, her? That's hardly red."

Iza started to get a sick feeling in her stomach. She was certain they were talking about her mother.

"Well, it's as if someone set fire to red. I'll not argue the color. That's that Gronska woman! Can you imagine dressing like that? At her age?"

Iza sat paralyzed in her chair.

"I don't know, Olga—if either of us had the figure—"

"Nina, just look at that neckline!"

"I am, as is the gentleman she's talking to. Ha ha."

"She's a disgrace! You know she signed the Confederacy of Targowica years ago, inviting Russia in?"

"As did many of the nobility," Nina said, shifting into the role of apologist.

"Oh? Did your husband—Ah, I see. Perhaps he had his reasons. But let me tell you, she *entertained* Russians in her own mother's house across the river, in Praga."

"Do you mean— ?"

"Yes!" Olga hissed. "She had her finger in the wind even then. Well, she disappeared just after the fall of Warsaw in 1794. Rumor had it that a Russian had taken her atop his horse in the meleé. Then, if you can believe it, she turned up months later, and in no time her belly was big as a house."

"I had heard that," Nina answered, "and that she had once had an affair with King Stanisław."

"She did, but that's not the half of it! When that Corsican rascal came calling, she entrapped him as well!"

"Napoleon Bonaparte!"

"Indeed. That was before he became so taken by Maria Walewska."

"Was there a child, Olga?"

"If you mean by Maria Walewska, yes, a boy. If you mean by the Gronska woman, yes again, a girl. No one knows who the father was. In fact, I don't know what's become of the child." Olga snickered. "Maybe she's put her away—or had her drowned like a kitten!"

"Goodness!" Nina feigned shock. "But to think that one woman managed to attract a king, as well as the little emperor!"

"Goodness, nothing—the woman's a *witch*!"

For Iza, the other sounds of the crowded room had fallen away and she heard only the chatter of the women. She thought she would pass out even as the two harpies pursued other gossip now. She sat still as a stone, watching her mother with new eyes. She didn't want to believe what she heard. Yet her mother was indeed an iconoclast, often striking out at society's norms. Iza had always known her mother was no saint. But were *these things* true? And if they were, what was she to think about her father? To hear these women talk, her father might be a Russian. The thought chilled her to the marrow. Her mother had told her a very different story.

Slowly, slowly, Iza became aware that many of the tapers were being extinguished and that a hush was falling on the audience. She looked up to see her mother, a vision in fuchsia, gliding up the aisle toward her, her head held high, the diamond pins glinting in her dark hair. Iza heard a spate of whispering in the seats behind her sputter and then go silent.

What was she to do? Allow these women their nasty gossip? Pretend she hadn't heard? She had told Michał that there are occasions when she snaps. *You're irascible, Sister Izabel!* the abbess had said, more than once. *I call it peevish,* Sister Iwona, the novice mistress, had declared, *and most unbecoming.* Whether it was irascibility or peevishness, Iza felt her emotions rising now to a fever pitch.

She stood as her mother arrived at their row. Before Zofia could take her seat, Iza took her hand and pivoted both of them toward the row behind theirs. They now faced the two crones.

The women, Olga and Nina, sat stunned, their tart tongues at rest, mouths gaping like gargoyles.

Iza allowed a long moment to pass. "These lovely ladies, *Mother*," she said at last, "were just going on and on about how *bewitching* you look. Isn't that right, Ladies Olga and Nina?" Iza's eyes moved from Olga to Nina as she spoke, for she had been careful to identify each by their voices and seating placement behind her.

The pair might have been stones they were so motionless.

"Oh, how generous of you both!" Zofia exclaimed.

The one who had been more listener than informer—Nina—attempted to apply a false smile to her crimson face.

Just then, the audience burst into applause at the arrival of Fryderyk Chopin. Iza and Zofia turned about and took their seats, cutting short Iza's clever inquisition. She had hoped for a longer moment of exultation, but was cheered nonetheless. She looked forward to the intermission when she might address them again. They were not to be acquitted so easily.

It was a measure of Chopin's talent that Iza eventually put away thoughts of the gossips and became enraptured in the magical strains of a nocturne. She closed her eyes and imagined with great vividness that she was again behind cloistered walls, away from society and the likes of Olga and Nina, with only her simple chores and an herb garden to think about. Anyone around her might think she had dozed off, but she cared not what they thought. She did very much wish herself away from this place—but only if the enchanting music would accompany her.

Iza lost all notion of time so that before she knew it the audience was applauding and her mother was nudging her. "Come, let's claim a glass of wine."

"No, I'd rather wait for you, Mother."

"Very well." Zofia stood. "I do hope he plays something livelier next." She turned now to the row behind as if seeking agreement. Iza's head turned simultaneously.

The women were gone.

Zofia cast Iza a puzzled look, then gave a little shrug of dismissal and went off to slake her thirst.

For his final set, Fryderyk Chopin did play livelier compositions, wonderful mazurkas of his own creation. These, however, did not afford Iza the opportunity to dream. She found herself caught up in dark thoughts about her parentage. Her mother had told her years and years before that her father was a brave count who had died at the ramparts of Praga in late 1794, defending his city from the great onslaught of Russians. He died in what became known as a great massacre in Praga, the Warsaw suburb across the Vistula. What truth is there in this story? she asked herself. What if my father is one of the Russians with whom her mother associated? Her heart thumped. Dare she approach her mother about the matter? Odd as it was, she found it easier to confront two strangers than to challenge her own mother. Still, one way or another, she determined, *I must know. I must!*

It was not until the end of the concert that Zofia

told Iza there was to be dancing. It was a deliberate omission, Iza knew, but she was too upset about what she had overheard to care. As she accompanied her mother to the refreshment table and then to the Mirror Hall that was to serve as the ballroom, she made up her mind to confront her mother in the carriage on the way home.

The orchestra was already playing a polonaise as they entered the Mirror Hall. Zofia turned to Iza. "You will dance, won't you?"

Iza knew it was more a statement than a question. She drew herself up, managing a smile. "It's been too long, Mother, and I'm happy just to watch the spectacle and enjoy this little French cake and sparkling wine. And besides there are many young girls here who will be taking the available men."

"Don't worry, dearest. I'll find you a partner." Zofia was moving away, into the crowd, even as she finished the sentence.

Iza stood alone, her stomach tightening. Her mother issued no idle threats. She thought of relocating herself but knew her mother would search her out with some stuffy gentleman she had cajoled into asking her spinster daughter to dance. How humiliating! How much more she would rather be home reading *Delphine*, a novel by Anne Louise Germaine de Staël that addressed the freedom of women in a patriotic society. A good little while passed and hope took seed that her mother would have no luck finding her a partner when someone tugged at her sleeve. Her heart dropped.

Iza turned to find not some old widower, but a

familiar face. "Why, Viktor, you surprised me!"

Viktor gave a little laugh. "You look more like I terrified you."

"Oh," Iza laughed. "I cannot deny the terror. But then I was overwhelmed with relief to see it's you. You see, Mother promised to find me a partner—so I turned expecting to find a cadaver at my side."

"I'm tired, but not that far gone," Viktor said, laughing.

"Is Barbara here—oh, I should love to see her!"

"No, I came alone as a favor to my superior. Barbara is at home with the twins."

"A good place to be. This place is so—so swamped with people."

"Don't look now but it looks as if your cadaver still has the ability to perambulate. As I speak he is approaching us as if on a mission."

"Oh, no!" Through the tall mirror nearby she saw that Viktor was exactly right.

A mazurka was just starting.

"Ahem! May I have this dance, young Izabel?" Iza turned around. "General Kozlowski at your service, Mademoiselle."

No time had been given for a battle plan. Iza observed the bargain her mother had made. The general had brought his heels together and was now bowing before her. When he looked up, she saw that he was neither as old nor as weather-worn as she had expected . . . late forties, perhaps. And while he wasn't ugly or uncouth, the increase in her heart rate was not the result of attraction. Still, she felt as if she had to allow him one dance.

But fate in the personification of Viktor intervened. "I'm afraid, my good General," Viktor announced, "that the young lady has pledged this dance to me."

"I see," the general said. "To the victor the spoils, heh?" He punctuated his comment with a hiccup of a laugh. "Perhaps the next one, then?"

"No," Viktor said before Iza could reply. "All of the lady's dances are pledged."

The general's head went back in surprise. "Indeed?" He harrumphed and his face ran scarlet. His gaze moved from Viktor to Iza.

"Don't look to her, General," Viktor said in a kind of growl, "I suggest you take my word for it."

The general's surprised gaze went back to Viktor. "Another time, then," he said, giving a perfunctory bow to Iza and skittering away.

"Now you've done it! You've broken a heart, Izabel."

"*I?* You were mean to him," Iza said. "That was not necessary."

"I suppose that I was. Meanness works, however, as I just demonstrated. Should I apologize, Izabel?"

"No, that would further humiliate him. Oh, I see you're merely being flippant and have no intention of apologizing."

"Oh, Izabel—"

"Please call me Iza. Only Mother calls me Izabel. And I must confess I had to stifle a laugh when he used that dull cliché about victors and spoils. What irony—he couldn't have known your *name* is Viktor, could he?"

Viktor shook his head, laughing as his cool, pale blue eyes spilled over her. "Spoils indeed. I don't think it will be very long."

"Before what?"

"Before you do break hearts."

Viktor's abruptly rude manner toward the general had taken her by surprise. She was not the only one who could be snappish. And now his gaze, voice, and words unnerved her. She certainly had not meant to invite such familiarity. He seemed to be flirting with her. Out of want to say something, she suggested they be true to the excuse given the general—and dance.

"I'm afraid not," Viktor said, his eyes moving down momentarily and with purpose toward the floor, to his feet.

Iza immediately remembered his lameness. "Oh, I am sorry, Viktor."

"Don't give it a thought," he said, although his face had darkened. "No harm done. What say you to going into the Portrait Room where it is less crowded?"

Iza nodded agreement, more out of embarrassment over her faux pas than any notion that his suggestion was appropriate. *Was* it appropriate? Oh, he was handsome enough with his fine Russian features beneath thick blond hair. But he was, after all, the husband of Barbara, her dearest friend from childhood.

Viktor took the lead in conversation and in the path to the Portrait Room. "And what is new in the Gronska household?" They walked slowly enough that Viktor's limp was scarcely noticeable.

"Nothing at all, really," Iza said. "Oh! I should say that we have a guest."

"Oh?" They stopped in front of a painting of King

Stanisław and Viktor turned to her.

"Yes, Michał has come in from Sochaczew."

"Has he? I saw him there last May. It was quite a festive occasion. Ostensibly it was for his birthday, but between you and me, I think they were actually celebrating the Third of May Constitution. You Poles can be sly, you know."

Iza shot him a fiery glance in lieu of unkind words about Russians.

Viktor ignored it. "Probably thought I would be offended."

"Would you have been?"

"Not at all. What's offensive about a constitution that exists only in the past, only in the memory of Poles?"

Iza bristled at his arrogance and condescension. She glanced up at the image of King Stanisław, recalling that he had ushered in the Constitution— and had lost the throne for doing so. "It exists in our hearts, Viktor."

"Indeed. Ah well, anyway, Barbara and I thought you would be accompanying your mother to Sochaczew. She had been looking forward to seeing you."

"No, I—I wasn't quite ready for such an adventure."

"What brings Michał Stelnicki to the capital?"

"Why, I don't know. A change of scenery, perhaps."

"To see someone?"

"I told you, Viktor, that I don't know." She took several paces toward the portrait of Queen Jadwiga.

"Perhaps," he suggested, catching up to her, his eyes—shadowy blue in the candlelight—laughing, "he has come to see you."

Iza felt heat rising to her face. "No more than to see my mother. Viktor Baklanov, you are testing me!"

"Teasing a little, maybe, not testing. But if he hasn't come to see you—"

"Oh!"

"What?

"I forgot—he's going to see his little brother Józef. At the Officer Cadets School."

"Why do you suppose he is doing that?"

"Why?" What an odd question, Iza thought. "Why *not*? Michał promised his mother to check up on her youngest. That's all."

"I see." They silently looked at another portrait, that of King Jan Sobieski, the man who—with his winged hussars—had led an army of allies and saved Europe and Christendom from the Turks in 1683. It was he who had ennobled Iza's grandfather for his service at the Battle of Vienna. She demurred mentioning these things and instead retraced in her mind the conversation about Michał. Had she said something out of turn? There was something odd about Viktor's questioning, as well as a sudden intensity he tried unsuccessfully to mask. Or was her imagination at work? They moved along, making small talk and giving cursory attention to the portraits. When they moved from one portrait to the next, Iza felt his hand on her waist as if he was directing her. The sensation was not a welcome one; her reaction was to step ahead in a livelier fashion so that his hand would fall away. At the final portrait Viktor turned to her. "I must beg off, Iza. Time to get home to my responsibilities. I'll return you to your mother."

"No, no, I'm just fine in here for a while," Iza said, realizing she felt a cool surge of relief. "You go ahead and do give Basia and the boys my love."

Viktor nodded, bowed from the waist, and moved away rather quickly, heedless that his limp caused one woman to turn and stare through her lorgnette.

Viktor was her closest friend's husband, but in her few meetings with him Iza had yet to warm to him. Now she felt a stinging complicity in the way he had treated General Kozlowski. She thought it odd, too, that he referred to his family as *responsibilities*. Was there a message in that? And the way he had appraised her, the way he had touched her, gave her pause. In the future she would have to be careful in his company.

Her eyes alert so that she might avoid the general Viktor had crushed, Iza returned to the Mirror Hall in search of her mother.

She was making her way through a throng of people when a hand clamped on to her shoulder and spun her around. "Where have you been, Izabel?" The dark eyes sizzled with anger and the reddish incandescence in her face was no reflection of the fuchsia gown.

"In the Portrait Room, Mother."

"To what purpose?"

"I was speaking with Viktor Baklanov."

"He's here? A lot of good he can do you. What in God's name did you say to General Kozlowski? The man seemed humiliated and he's a very eligible widower."

"I'm afraid Viktor said something discourteous."

"Oh, but you are the one who declined to dance, yes?"

Rather than further indict Viktor, Iza remained silent.

"I have another gentleman in mind, so you are to wait here and—"

"Mother, I wish to go home."

"It's out of the question," Zofia whispered. "Invitations like this do not come every day."

Iza put on her sternest face. "Still, I wish to go home."

"I have no intention of leaving."

"That's fine, Mother. I'll take the carriage home and send it back for you."

"You're to stay, do you hear?"

"I'm not about to dance with anyone."

Her mother went silent and Iza prepared for a storm. But she saw now that her mother's eyes had fastened on the Grand Duke Konstantin, who had just left his dance partner and was crossing the chamber. Zofia's interest in her daughter was snuffed out at once, like a candle in a downpour. "Very well, go if you must," Zofia hissed and gave a dismissive wave of her hand.

Fate had won the match for Iza, who watched her mother moving quickly to put herself in the path of the Grand Duke, a man with a myriad of medals on a military coat and the face of an aging shoemaker.

In no time Iza was crossing the drive in front of Belweder Palace, her eyes searching the line of vehicles for the Gronska carriage, her mind attempting to compute the distance back to the city center.

She had to call up to Kasper—the stable boy and occasional driver—to jar him into consciousness. The boy jumped down immediately, his eyes downcast in embarrassment. "So sorry, milady, I—"

"My mother is staying a while longer, Kasper. You're to wait for her. Tell her I've gone on ahead."

"But, beggin' pardon, milady. How— ?"

"How am I to go? Why on the two feet God gave me, that's how."

Kasper's deep blue eyes loomed large. "But—it's late and dark. And the city is no place for a lady alone."

"I'll be fine."

"I can take you, milady, and still get back well in time."

"I realize that, Kasper, but I have not had a good look at the city at night in years. And I wish to have a gander."

"It's best you take the scenery in from the carriage window, milady."

Iza smiled tightly. "Just tell my mother I found my own way home, will you?" Iza turned about, effectively closing the subject, and made for Avenue Ujazdowskie.

Her mother would be livid, she knew, but didn't care. And she didn't care about scenery. She needed time to reflect on what she had heard tonight about her mother, about herself.

Here, so close to Belweder Palace, Avenue Ujazdowskie ran through parkland, trees, and thickets to the immediate right and shadowy, darkened buildings to the left, across the street. An occasional street lantern pointed the way north, but the avenue was dark and all but deserted. Iza pulled the black satin evening cloak closed. It was light, made for dress attire, not for warmth, and it was no match for the cold November night. She moved quickly, rejecting the idea of surrender to the chill—or to the stableboy's warning.

Her thoughts became caught up on the enigma that was her mother. Were the things those women had said about her true? Or were they but malicious gossip and exaggerations that arose from jealousy or some other motivation? She wanted to believe the latter. It was much easier to do so. The largeness of her mother's personality, she thought, invited legend and legend thrived on fiction. Everyone knew that the barest facts grew, over years, into fantastical legend.

And yet, there was that question that had doggedly haunted her since childhood. Just who was her father? Was he a Polish lord who had died bravely fighting the Russians at Warsaw's ramparts? The details had always been terse and when pressed further, her mother became morosely dark, and Iza could not determine whether it was anger at her daughter's insistence or sadness about a lost, long-ago love.

What kept her mother so taciturn about this matter and so loquatious about others? Iza ruled out shame at having a child out of wedlock. Not her mother. She could boldly face down an army. Iza tried to imagine her mother in love. Knowing how her mother looked with a critical and even designing eye upon courting and matches and marriages today, she found it difficult to imagine her fully entranced by a man. But if she had been in love, with whom?

Her mother had never provided Iza with a name for her father. Why? Had she consorted with Russians as that wretched Olga had said? Or perhaps she had *loved* a Russian. That was reason enough to avoid his name. Iza stopped in mid-step. The thought that she might be half Russian pierced like a lance to her heart.

A cold wind came against her, making her shiver and push on. She put her head down and hurried along, determined to avoid thoughts of her mother.

Suddenly a distinct cracking sound broke the frigid quiet. Iza stopped and turned around. It had sounded like the breaking of a twig underfoot, but the street was empty of people. Neither were any vehicles within sight. She looked to the shrubbery and trees that flanked the avenue to her right. The bare branches stirred slightly, but she caught no sight of any living thing. Even Warsaw's legendary red squirrels knew enough to avoid the cold night. She had the oddest sensation that she was a lone figure in some artist's eerie landscape—and that she was not truly alone.

Iza looked ahead to see where the park gave way to the capital's political and diplomatic district and hastened her steps, her ears alerted to the slightest sound. She sensed that someone was nearby, that she was being observed. The trees certainly afforded cover for anyone following her. Her heart quickened. If only a carriage-for-hire would come by . . .

When she came at last to the end of the parkland where both sides of the avenue boasted mansions of aristocrats and wealthy merchants alongside of the official edifices, she slowed just a bit, breathing more normally. A private carriage passed by, the coachman gawking at the sight of her.

While far from bright, the area was better lighted and here and there two or three souls were moving quickly about their nighttime missions. She pressed on. With each intersection Iza relaxed a little, and when she came to Saint Aleksander's Church she crossed herself. She arrived then at Three Crosses Square, where nine streets meet. Allowing but a cursory look at the three gold-covered crosses that stood like black shadowy sentinels against the starless sky, she navigated the wide Avenue Jerozolimskie, passing into Nowy Świat, a fashionable street of palaces, town houses, a market, and a park. Here people were on the street, and Iza was relieved to see it well lighted. However, when she passed Świętokrzyska and Nowy Świat led into Avenue Krakowskie Przedmieście, posted lanterns became scarce—as did people on the street—and poorly tended this night. Iza's shoes echoed eerily on the bricks. Caution caught her up again when she heard the echo of a man's boot steps at some distance behind her. She did not, could not, turn around. Had the sounds been forthright and distinctive, she would have paid them no mind, but these came slower and softer, as if someone meant to muffle his footfalls. Iza picked up her pace, and so too did her heart.

There was a disturbance ahead, very near Warsaw University, she realized, and was glad for it. In another instance she would have crossed the street to avoid it, but she now moved toward it, figuring there was safety in numbers. And perhaps protection. As she drew near to a group of young students it became clear they were well intoxicated. One was relieving himself in the gutter. Abandoning a plan to draw them into conversation while she scanned the street behind her, she passed through the middle of them. Two or three of the young men shot lewd comments—like verbal arrows—in her wake. She dared not turn around.

She had gone some little distance when she heard loud and aggressive comments of a different sort from the drunken students. She knew these were directed at the man with the muted boot steps, who no doubt was passing through their midst. She didn't have to turn around to know that he was following her. *Christ the Savior protect me*, she prayed.

Iza still had a ways to go. Ahead, there was no one in sight. She moved on a full block, then paused, her ears pricked. At first she heard the steps, but then they stopped. Had the man turned the corner? She prayed that he had.

Her prayer went unheard, for the same scenario played out at Karowa Street and yet again at Bednarska Street. Despite the cold wind coming off the river, beads of perspiration had formed on her upper lip, forehead, and back of the neck. Her heart raced. How had she been so foolish as to place herself in this situation? She scolded herself more severely than would her mother on the morrow.

At long last she came into Castle Square. The castle wasn't even visible so thick was the fog that rose up from the River Vistula. She moved in what she sensed was the direction of her street, Piwna Street, stumbling and nearly falling over a drunken man laid out on the cobblestones. Fear propelled her forward. She was very close to home now. Her hands reached out like those of a blind person, finding in good time the stone surface of the building sitting on the square at Piwna Street.

Iza paused before continuing. She dared to turn around but could see nothing more than a few paces into the fog. She listened. A horn sounded from off the river. A dog across the square barked. And then came the too familiar boot steps.

Iza pivoted and ran up Piwna street. She came to St. Martin's Church, where she had worshiped as a child. Her first impulse was to climb the few steps and find sanctuary. But what if the doors were locked? Or worse, what if the church was empty? She would be trapped.

She ran now, cutting a diagonal path across the street, putting the church behind her as if it housed the devil himself. It was not far now to the Gronska town house. Here she knew the buildings by heart so that the fog was little hindrance to her.

In moments she was climbing the steps to the front door of the town house, fumbling for the pocket of her cloak and praying the key had not fallen out.

Even as her hand clasped the key she heard him on the other side of the street. Her throat constricted and she froze for a moment, certain he would make a dash toward her. The noise that took her out of the momentary trance was the metallic ting of the key hitting the top step. She had dropped it.

Iza bent, retrieved the key, stood, and found

the lock. It turned smoothly within the well-oiled mechanism. She pushed the heavy door inward, stepped in, closed it behind her, latched it and drove the extra bolt home. She turned around and fell back against the door, breathing now a great sigh of relief.

A full minute must have passed. Everything was silence, within the house—and without. Collecting herself she went to a hall table where a single candle had been left guttering. She extinguished it and returned to the door. She listened. Nothing. Had he gone on? Had he been merely making sport of her? Well, she had learned her lesson.

Slowly, slowly she moved toward the tall, narrow window at the side of the door. She pushed back the lace curtain and peered out, half afraid she would see some awful face staring back at her.

No one was there, however. The little portico seemed quite empty. No one was in front of the house, either. She stared into the fog attempting to make out the outlines of St. Martin's and the other buildings across the way.

And then her eye was caught by an almost indiscernable reddish glow. Directly across the street, in a little alleyway, someone had just lighted what seemed a pipe. Was it the man who had been—or so it seemed—following her? Iza waited many minutes, and when she became convinced it had been a mere passerby who must have moved off into the fog, she saw the glow again, as he he drew in on his pipe. Iza's heart pounded.

The man was watching the house.

5

J ózef Stelnicki sat alone in the music room of the Officer Cadets School. At a small desk he worked over the notes of the final movement of a symphony he had been laboring on for three months, crossing notes out and replacing them with others provided by the music in his head. It was the counterpoint—multiple, independent, and simultaneous melodies—that had been giving him difficulty. He let out a sigh that reflected neither dismay nor hope.

Pulling the composition from the desk and going directly to the great piano, Józef seated himself and positioned the rumpled and nearly illegible music sheets. Drawing in a long breath as if his instrument were not a piano but a flute that required breath control, he started to play, his fingers nimbly working over the black and ivory keys. He began where he had begun at least a hundred times: at the opening and he deemed it worthy. The middle movements of the piece pleased him as well. As he started to play the final movement he was cheered by the changes he had made. He had found the right formula, it seemed, and felt himself lifted, as if he had infused the instrument with new life. It was the elixir, the euphoria, that creativity brought with it.

But just as quickly, during the final swelling and fading, the crescendo and diminuendo, he recognized a redundancy between the newly added melody and the final movement in a work he had created earlier in the year. He was merely repeating himself. The realization drove the blood from his heart.

He halted his playing immediately and with violence brought his fists crashing down upon the keys. The wildly discordant result reverberated throughout the room. Józef felt hot tears begin to build, but crying was no outlet for a man in the military. Instead he took hold of the music sheets and drew them closer. But concentration came hard. Did Fryderyk Chopin have moments such as these? He thought not, but the question put his mind on a tangential path. He wondered now how the Chopin concert had been received at the Belweder Palace the night before. He would have given his cadet's czapka and gone bareheaded to have snared an invitation, but he knew the event for him would have proven more bitter than sweet. Years before, Józef's mother, intent on a musical career for her youngest born— rather than a military one—had secured a tutor in their home town of Sochaczew. Józef took to music and the piano with great fervor, and his talents were so well mined that his teacher told the Stelnickis that young Józef had outgrown his tutor's potential and that of any local musician. Subsequently, at the age of twelve Józef was sent to study at the Warsaw Lyceum and Fryderyk Chopin's tutor, Józef Elsner, the German director of the Warsaw Conservatory, was engaged to tutor him in composition and harmony.

Chopin's parents, Mikołaj and Justyna, had established an expensive student residence for out-of-town boarders at Kazimierz Palace on the Avenue Krakowskie Przedmieście, and it was there that Józef went to live and study. His mother could not have foreseen the irony, but it was that decision that led to her son's relinquishing his musical career in favor of a military one.

Józef Stelnicki's close proximity to Fryderyk Chopin became the musical boon and bane of his ambition. Fryderyk— or Frycek, the diminutive by which he allowed Józef to call him—was three years older than Józef and occasionally mentored him in his musical studies. Chopin had already been deemed a prodigy, and over time Józef came to the unhappy conclusion that he himself indeed had talent and desire for composing and playing, but that Frycek possessed an unparalleled and godlike genius. While Józef had mastered the mechanics of harmony and the rudiments of creating new melodies, Frycek's unusually complex piano fingering and creative mastery of counterpoint were astounding. Mesmerising. That Józef would never be another Chopin crushed his hopes and, for a time, his spirit. He decided, much to his mother's consternation, that instead of going on to a three-year curriculum at the Central Music School, also at the Warsaw Conservatory and supervised by Elsner, he would enter the Officer Cadets School.

Only much later would he realize that the disappointment he felt regarding his musical potential led to an inner turmoil and anger, resulting in rebellion, a youthful rebellion against everyone's expectations of him. Why not a career in the military? His mother would rebound. His father had led the way, after all, followed by his two much older brothers. Later, too, he would recognize his own ego in his adamant belief that he had been born to do something important. If not in music, what other than the military would provide ample opportunity to rise?

Despite quitting his lessons, however, he often found himself—like now—sitting in the academy's music room agonizing over a new musical piece, underscoring the fact that music ran through his blood.

Others knew to find him here, as well. The door abruptly opened inward now. Józef looked up to see Marcin, his roommate.

"Did I interrupt a piece?" Marcin asked uncertainly. "I know how you hate that. I listened outside the door, but I didn't hear anything."

"It's all right, Marcin. Don't worry. Come in. What's the matter? You look so serious."

"It's Gustaw. He showed up a little while ago." Marcin moved toward the piano.

"Where has he been for the past two days?"

"At his family's farm, so he says."

"Absent without leave—to go home?" Józef questioned. "Who would do that?"

Józef thought Marcin would laugh, but instead he was all seriousness. "That's not all. He's had an accident. He's got a finger missing—says he was careless with some farm implement."

"Good god!" Józef cried, standing and pushing back the piano bench. "That's awful!—Wait, you think that unlikely?"

"Don't you?"

"Yes, I guess I do, given the fact that I doubt he really went all the way home. Near Poznań, isn't it?"

"Yeah, good and far, maybe too far to go, get injured at some farm task, and make it back, all in two days. What do you suppose is the real story, Józef?"

"Why would someone lose a finger, Marcin, barring stupidity while using a scythe or something? And everything to be reaped has been reaped by now, yes?"

Marcin agreed.

A long moment ensued—until Józef's gaze locked onto Marcin's serious blue eyes. It was as if he could read them. "Torture?" Józef whispered.

Marcin shrugged at first, then nodded.

Józef was about to scoff at the notion, but a moment's pause provided a second thought. He had to nod in tentative agreement. "A way to get someone to talk, to reveal information. And who in Warsaw is known for such methods and worse?"

"The secret police." Marcin's voice was less than a whisper now. "But—but what knowledge would Gustaw have that would be valuable? You know what a queer duck he is."

"He wouldn't be the first innocent to be victimized by the Third Department. Maybe he knows something, maybe not. Where is he now?"

Marcin maintained his hushed tone: "He was taken in hand by Wysocki and Zaliwski as soon as he returned."

"Mmmm, maybe he *does* know something about what they're planning."

"About Project C?" Marcin asked. "Come on, we don't know anything about the event we're training for. It's something very big, and that's why only Wysocki and Zaliwski know the plans. We're but pawns."

"Don't undervalue a pawn, Marcin. They can be tortured and pressured into revealing things. And I have no doubt the police are very interested in what goes on here."

"Wait a minute! Suppose it's not torture. Suppose it's a threat. You know, to keep him silent about something."

Józef was taken aback. "You mean by our superiors? My god, you may have something, Marcin. The question is, would Wysocki and Zaliwski resort to such a threat to keep their—our—plans from falling into the wrong hands? It seems a bit overt, even for them."

"You know as well as I, Józef, that if Project C is an anti-Russian one—and no doubt it is—the two of them would cut the privates from a private to keep knowledge of it in house."

Józef gave a little laugh. "Perhaps. But I think it unlikely. We'll have to keep an eye on our friend Gustaw. Maybe he'll let something slip."

"He's a strange one, that's for certain.—Are you coming up to the room?"

"Not just yet." Józef sat again, splaying his fingers in preparation to play.

"Józef, *you* don't know, do you? About Project C?"

"I wish I did," Józef said. "I wish I did."

Marcin turned and moved toward the door.

"Marcin," Józef called. "Gustaw's finger—which one is it?"

"On his right hand—the index finger."

When the door closed behind Marcin, Józef sat staring at his long slender fingers against the black and white of the keys. Lifting the index finger, he attempted to play an old familiar piece without it. The results brought only a half-voiced curse.

It was a dark thought this, losing his ability to play. Inexplicably, it occurred to Józef that had he lost a finger, he would at least be able to put before his mother a valid reason for giving up a career in music. How he loved her, and how it stung each time he saw her to know that he had added ache to a heart already broken by the arrest of his father. But he would prove to her one day that he could—would!—become someone of importance. Perhaps some day he would search out his father across the Russian steppes. Perhaps . . .

Before going up to his room, Józef took from his pocket an object d'art wrapped in a thinning piece of blue velvet, something he had never shown Marcin. He had his own heartbreak, one Marcin would not understand. No one would. He folded back the velvet, revealing the miniature portrait on ivory of a pretty, black-haired girl, the love of his young life. Even after quitting his musical lessons and giving up his rented room, he had still visited the Chopins at Kazimierz

Palace on the Avenue Krakowskie Przedmieście. He
went with regularity to see their young daughter,
Emilia, with whom he was very much in love.

They were scarcely into their teens, but they were
in love. No one understood, truly understood. Only
later would he remember and see in a different light
the little cough she would give out. For the longest
time it was barely noticeable. Then, he had thought it
a nervous reaction on the part of a shy girl. Perhaps
even an affectation. Whichever, he had thought it
charming. But the cough was no innocent thing.
Word of her death had come to the academy in a
black-bordered note. It was April, a time of daffodils
and daisies, he remembered now, and Emilia Chopin
had yet to turn fifteen. That was three years ago,
he realized. Already three years! And in springtime.
"Emilia," he whispered. "Emilia." And the tears that
he had shut away earlier were dormant no more.

As planned, Michał attended Sunday services at
St. Jan's Cathedral, having begged off attending
Mass at St. Martin's with Iza. Zofia, it seemed, was
not in the habit of attending Sunday Mass. While
St. Martin's Church was across the street from
the Gronska town house, St. Jan's Cathedral, the
church of kings, was not much farther, situated on
the parallel Świetojańska Street. Despite the number
of churches in the city center and the number of
Sunday services, this final Mass of the day was
nonetheless packed with people. The bishop himself,
several concelebrant priests, and half a dozen altar

boys filled the sanctuary.

Michał entered just at the start of the service and made his way to the front. When he spied Prince Adam Czartoryski in the middle of the third pew on the left, he genuflected and indicated to an old lady on the aisle of the fourth pew that he wished her to make room for him. She did so, slowly and grudgingly.

At no time during the Mass did Michał notice the prince turn to take notice of his presence. When the service ended, Michał stepped outside the pew to allow the stern old lady and the other occupants to exit. Within fifteen minutes the sanctuary was empty and dark and the cathedral had cleared of all but a few lingering worshippers. Michał looked about him and when he saw they were women of varying ages, all veiled, he moved toward the middle of his pew and knelt, behind and a little to the right of the prince.

Prince Adam Czartoryski, who must have been aware of Michał's presence all the while, sat back in the pew so that his ear was very close to Michał's mouth. "I must apologize, Michał," he whispered. "I was too harsh at our last meeting."

"No need, your grace. I was in the wrong. It was foolish to just show up at your home without taking precautions."

"The city is full of spies, my friend. You must be careful. I am very glad to have your help. It can be invaluable. Now, when do you see your brother?"

"I plan to go on Tuesday."

"Go on Monday. The situation is worsening." The prince fell silent as a woman moved away from the statue of Mary where she had lighted one of the hundreds of cascading votives in ruby glass holders that winked and flickered. She turned and proceeded down the main aisle, toward the entrance, her veiled face seeming to turn toward the prince and Michał as she passed.

When Michał heard the echo of the heavy door closing behind her, he ventured a furtive glance about. Just two others left now in the back pews, widows he thought. He waited for the prince to speak.

"The stakes are rising, Michał," Czartoryski said. "I have it from a respected source that Tsar Nicholas is pressuring his brother to shore up the Dutch who are, as I'm sure you know, trying to hold on to their control of Belgium."

Michał had heard of the Belgians' quest for independence and an overthrow of Dutch control. "But how does that—" he began.

"Raise the stakes? According to my source, Nicholas has asked Konstantin to send not only his Russian troops but our Polish contingent, as well. And our cadets, already infused with notions of our independence, will resist fighting against others who are seeking theirs. It spells trouble right here."

"So you're thinking whatever the cadets' plan is, it will likely be executed prematurely."

"Exactly. As soon as the cadets catch wind of their marching orders. God made time, but man made haste."

"I see. My father always said one should hasten slowly."

"An excellent proverb that, but not one Zaliwski and Wysocki are likely to abide by. Michał, this little

Congress Kingdom of Poland, as they call us now, may seem a shadow of what we once were, but we could lose even this, my boy, even this. Whatever thoughtless and ill-conceived coup against the Russians those two have contrived will bring ruin to Poland. It will bring the end."

Michał was about to respond, about to say he would contact Józef on the morrow when he heard a noise some little distance in front of them—in the sanctuary, he thought. Someone had dropped something or perhaps kicked the wooden stalls meant for dignitaries. The noise rippled into a soft but distinct echoing within the empty and cavernous cathedral.

Prince Czartoryski's spine had stiffened at the noise. "Tuesday," he said, clipping his words. "Morning Mass. Six o'clock." He rose then, exiting the pew on the outer aisle and moving toward the street entrance.

Michał scanned the sanctuary left to right and back again, thinking perhaps the bishop, one of the attending priests, or an altar boy had come from the sacristy to retrieve something. But no one was in evidence in the sanctuary. The sound had died away. Michał stood and moved to the middle aisle of the nave. He took no time to genuflect before making his way to the sanctuary and vaulting over the communion rail. He paused, listening. He had the uncanny sense that someone had been present there, close enough to Michał and the prince to hear their conversation. In buildings like this, he knew, sounds could carry unusual distances. What one whispered behind a clustered column might be heard clear as a bell in the balcony. Was his meeting with the prince being documented by someone? By a spy for the Third Department?

Michał moved forward cautiously, his eyes honing in on the heavy oak door that led to the sacristy. Even as he walked, doubt challenged him, chastizing him for an overactive imagination. What if the bishop were to suddenly open the door? What could he say to him? He would look a fool and perhaps even be arrested. Nonetheless, he pressed an ear to the door and listened. Nothing. The celebrants had probably already changed and gone their various ways. The bishop would no doubt find an ample breakfast in the rectory.

Michał put his hand on the polished brass door handle. Dare he go in? He was debating this thought when there came another noise, this time a wood against stone scraping, slight but close by. It was not within the sacristy, but somewhere within the sanctuary.

Michał pivoted, his eyes flying at once to the dignitary stalls across the way, on the western side of the sanctuary. They each had a prie-dieu with armrests upholstered in crimson, and they had exceedingly high backs and fronted a little gallery that could easily have hidden the perpetrator of the noise.

Michał's heart thumped and raced. He moved toward the gallery.

He hurried now, certain he was going to find someone hiding there—but nervous and uncertain as to what would happen next. In moments the rear of the stalls came into view. The diffused prism of light from small transept windows played beautifully on the space there. It was empty.

Vaulting into the gallery attached to the wall, Michał was at once disappointed and relieved not to have found out a member of the secret police. It was at that moment that he heard the faintest squeek of a hinge and a click that could be nothing other than a door closing. He spun around, his eyes taking in the panelled gallery wall. No door was in evidence. He remembered now the footbridge. In the 1620s after a failed attempt to assassinate King Zygmunt III in front of the cathedral, a long elevated corridor had been built, attaching Saint Jan's to the Royal Castle. In Zygmunt's and succeeding reigns, kings and queens had used it to access the gallery for Mass, a safe and convenient way to take their places next to the main altar.

Michał went to the wall and examined it closely. Knowing what he was looking for, he discovered the well camouflaged door, its seams scarcely noticeable in the richly carved panelling.

Today, Michał thought, it may very well have provided an avenue of escape for whoever had been spying on him and the prince. He looked at once for a door knob or handle. Not finding one, he put his ear to the door and strained to hear. Was there a slight movement on the other side? He thought so. By accident—or Providence, he allowed himself the momentary thought—his hand came to rest on a small piece of the wood relief that moved slightly. The hidden handle.

But before he could push down on it, there came the unmistakeable sound of a bolt being driven home. The handle moved now, responding to his pressure, but the door stood firm.

He placed his ear to the door again—and heard faint footsteps falling away into the distance.

Michał was absorbed in thought as he walked the short distance back to the Gronska town house. Upon entering the front door, he came upon Iza sitting in a hallway chair. "Waiting for me?" he joked.

Iza looked up without a hint of a smile. He noticed that she was dressed to go out.

"What is it, Iza?"

"What . . . oh, nothing. I was just about to go out, to see a friend at the convent."

"Not planning to re-enlist, are you? Besides, I thought visitors were a once-a-year phenomenon."

Still no expression from her. Michał noticed now how pale she was.

Iza stood and made for the door. "I'll be home for supper if Mother is interested."

Michał reached out to detain her, his hand lightly clasping her upper arm. While she turned, momentarily startled, the sensation that ran like a current between them was, to him, of a different nature. "Something is wrong, Iza. What is it?"

"I—I did a foolish thing last night, Michał. I walked home from the Belweder Palace."

"You did what?" Michał cried.

"Shhh! I walked home."

"And?"

"And I was followed."

"Followed!"

"Shhh! I don't want Mother to know. She's angry enough as it is about my leaving the palace."

"Sit down then, Iza, and tell me about it."

Iza obeyed and Michał pulled up a chair for himself. Iza's story of the man in the shadows poured out with specificity in regard to the weather, streets she had taken, the university students encountered, the lighting of the stalker's pipe across from the town house—but with no details about the man's appearance.

"You think I'm mistaken, Michał," she said upon finishing. "You think it my imagination. Anyone would. Mother says I read too much."

"I don't think it's your imagination, Iza." Michał gently touched the hand that gripped the arm of her chair. "Believe me, I don't."

Iza looked up at him as if to assess his sincerity, her azure eyes disarmingly vivid and beautiful against porcelain skin and lustrously black hair.

A long moment passed.

"And so" Michał said, "just now you were cautious about going out today. It's only natural."

She shyly slipped her hand away and stood. "Foolishly so, I suppose. But I feel better now. Thank you for listening."

"You still don't intend to go out?"

"I do indeed. Will I see you at supper?"

"You will."

Iza nodded. Was there the hint of a smile on her

face? "You will be staying for a while, yes? Business here in Warsaw?"

"My business is with young Józef."

"What is it, Michał? Something serious?"

"I don't know. He may be involved in something at the academy—something dangerous. A plot of some kind."

"A plot?"

"By the cadets to incite rebellion." Michał realized he was saying too much. What prompted him to so easily confide in Iza? A fine spy he would make. "Anyway, it's important that I see him at once. I intend to go to the academy tomorrow." His eyes held hers. "And it's also important that you do not leave the house alone. It may be nothing, but we'll put the servants on alert, keep the house like a citadel. And you are not to go out unaccompanied."

"Michał, I appreciate your concern, more than you know, but I didn't leave my cloistered life in the convent to lead a cloistered life here. I do promise to be careful, especially at night." Iza moved toward the door.

Michał followed. "In that case I intend to play chaperone. At least today you will *know* the person following you about."

Iza turned back to him. "Really, Michał, they won't allow you into the convent. And there's no need for this."

"Perhaps not. Let's call it a pleasure then, milady," Michał said, making a mock-bow. "I'll wait patiently outside."

Iza rewarded him with one of her rare full smiles.

Fortune was with Michał when Czartoryski had suggested visiting Józef on Monday, for things had changed since the days of his own military training, Monday was now the only designated visiting day. The change had to be very recent because he was certain that only that summer his mother had visited on days other than Mondays. Something important was definitely in the wind. Well, he had been lucky. Had he waited until Tuesday, he would have been put off for another week. The dormitory, however, had changed little, he thought, as he followed a young cadet who led him to the top floor and then halfway down the hall.

Józef answered the knock. "Jan Michał!" he cried.

"Thank you," Michał said to the retreating cadet and moved into the small room. Michał returned Józef's smile. They stood looking at one another for an awkward moment. A brotherly hug seemed to be in order and it was performed with a modicum of enthusiasm. The siblings were separated by some twenty years. As the family's youngest, Józef had been doted on by his mother and sister, but Michał had—for reasons he had not quite plumbed—remained aloof from his half-brother. Just the same, having experienced the darkest aspects of war, he, like his mother, had been sad to see Józef give up his music for the military. "You look good, Józef!"

"Come to check up on me, have you? Sit down, Michał. Here, you take Marcin's desk chair. He's gone off somewhere."

The brothers sat and they exchanged pleasantries,

Michał providing details about family and life at Topolostan, the estate at Sochaczew, Józef going on in good humor about classes and conditions in a military institution.

It was Józef who turned serious, turquoise eyes darkening. "Has there been any word of Father?"

Michał shook his head.

"Not what prison? Or camp?"

"No. Mother writes, tries all the appropriate channels."

"Do we know if he's alive?"

"Mother is convinced that he is."

"And you?"

"I won't think otherwise."

"She's often right about things," Józef said. "Pray God, that stays true."

"She wasn't right about you."

"You mean the music?"

"You have talent."

Józef shrugged. "I catch on to things quickly."

"Don't berate yourself."

"Oh, I still play and compose a bit."

"I'm glad to hear that! Whatever was it that loosened your confidence?"

Józef abruptly stood and went to the window.

Michał looked about the quarters, keenly aware of Józef's shift in mood. He took a light tone. "You know, I had the room three doors down, Tadek and I."

"Tadek?" Józef returned to his desk chair and sat facing Michał. "I can imagine you here, Michał, but it is hard to imagine a brother I never knew, a brother who died before I was born."

Michał felt himself tearing up. The memories of the years at the academy with Tadeusz came back in a rush, inexorably leading to their time in the Young Guard, accompanying Napoleon to Moscow, battle by battle. And then the fateful retreat across the frozen steppes. . . . Michał had to take a swipe at his eyes. "I'm sorry, Józef, this place and talking about Tadek brings me back."

"Is that why," Józef asked, "you would never tell me about your time with Emperor Bonaparte in Moscow and at Waterloo, no matter how I begged?"

Michał forced a smile. "You did beg, too, didn't you? But my memory of Tadek wasn't the only reason. Mother didn't want you romanticizing my experiences."

"I think I did, even without the details. Perhaps more so."

"Józef, what's going on here?" Michał could think of no convenient way to ease into his little interrogation.

"Going on? What do you mean?"

"Word has it that there's something afoot. Something anti-Russian. Something violent."

"It's news that *you've* brought, Michał. I haven't heard of anything. Where did you get wind of such a thing?"

"From an excellent source. What do you know?"

"Nothing, really." Józef looked innocent enough.

"Swear it."

"Michał, I'm a lowly cadet. I'm not likely to be let in on anything of that sort."

"Józef," Michał whispered, "if we test relations with Russia without having made the necessary preparations, we can lose everything we have! The Polish military would be disbanded, this building crushed to rubble."

"We haven't independence. We haven't a country named Poland. Not really."

"There will be time for that. Patience, Józef. Now, have you heard anything? Anything at all?"

"There are always rumors flying about. Independence—isn't that why you and Tadek followed Napoleon? You and he thought the little emperor would restore our sovereignty?"

"What kind of rumors?"

"Nothing specific. Like you said, something big. Listen, Michał, I have to get to a fencing practice. I'll be missed and it will go against me."

"Can I come again?"

Józef shrugged. "Next Monday?"

"No, sooner! I know the new rules, but there must be a way."

"Perhaps—"

"I'll tell you whatever you want to know about the campaigns with Napoleon—and about our brother."

"You will? Promise?"

"I promise—if you will keep your ear to the ground about—about whatever it is Wysocki and Zaliwski are up to."

Józef blinked at the names, and for Michał this was an admission he knew *something*.

"A brotherly quid pro quo," Józef said, recovering. "I do have a way for you come back, a secret way."

"Fine!" Michał replied, mollified for the moment.

6

O N TUESDAY NOON, WEARING A full length dark gray cloak and matching bonnet, Iza left the town house, moving in the direction of the Market Square. The day was cold but crisp and bright. The scent of snow was in the air, and she felt exhilarated as she slowly made the full turn of the market, surveying the shop windows of the four and five story buildings bordering the square. Michał had been at the afternoon meal, but she avoided mentioning the little sojourn she had planned. Oh, she had enjoyed his company on her trip to the convent and had come to know him better, but she doubted that perusing shop windows would elicit his interest and she would not be rushed. They did have a brief exchange at table before her mother joined them. Iza had asked him how his meeting with Józef had gone. There was too little time for him to explain to her in private, but his expression and clipped statement that it went well told her that the meeting had yielded little or nothing. Just what was he trying to learn from Józef? What might the boy be involved in?

Her thoughts went back to Michał. He had the same olive skin tones as did her mother; his eyes were similar, too, in their almond shape—Tatar-like—but more brown than black, more sanguine than critical. No, he was not the young and dashing soldier any longer. His features had evolved into those of a man—a handsome man, but one who had seen much, experienced much. And it seemed he had, in short order, become a kind of beacon of good humor in the Gronska household.

Upon finishing the tour of shop windows, Iza ventured in among the stalls, tents, and carts crushed closely together throughout the square. Most of the tradesmen maintained small fires to fend off the cold. She felt for these poor peddlers who defied the elements in order to feed their families. How they managed to do it, day after day, she couldn't imagine. It was the rugged Polish spirit, she guessed, the spirit that kept a country alive for peasant and nobleman alike, even when borders had been erased as if written in lime and washed by rain, even when mention of the Third of May Constitution had been all but forbidden.

Iza stopped to buy a little bag of roasted pine nuts, pausing a few minutes to warm her hands over the old farmer's fire. Suddenly the sensation that she was being watched came over her like an ill wind. She looked about, at first putting the feeling down as a silly notion. Surely it was merely the fact that not a few minutes before she had been recalling her unease the previous day—and the safety that Jan Michał provided. Such was the power of suggestion. Or—perhaps it was Michał, come to search her out. The thought gave her pleasure.

It was then that she saw him. Across the square, nearly obscured by the various booths and meandering shoppers, a man in a gray greatcoat and a wide-brimmed leather hat stood looking her way. Staring.

Iza felt a fluttering at the pit of her stomach. The visage was no more than a shadow under the hat, but she knew it was not Michał. She tucked the bag of pine nuts into a pocket, spilling some in the process, and started to walk along the row of stalls. When she turned her head, she saw that he was walking in parallel fashion, three rows away. Iza stopped, as did he. Heart quickening, her first impulse was to run for home, run from this person as fast as possible. Was this the man who had followed her home? *Who is he? What does he want?* She needed to know these things.

He was still watching her. Did he think she did not notice?

Another impulse. She took in a breath and turned in his direction, making her way through a pass between two abutting stalls to the next row over. When he realized that the hunter was about to be confronted by the game, he stiffened, watched another few moments—perhaps in disbelief—as she came yet another row closer, and made his move. Away from her and with some speed.

Iza followed. Even at that moment she knew it was foolish, but she was brazened by daylight, the number of people in the square, her curiosity—and indignation that someone might mean to frighten her. And she would not allow someone to so intimidate her that she would be afraid to leave the house. She would confront him here in the public square. Where better? What overt move could he make? And even if the man remained mute, she would at least have had a good look at him.

He moved quickly but with some effort. He was older than Iza would have imagined. Using her method, he ducked between two stalls, moving to the outer row that faced the storefronts. Iza followed. Head down, the man exited the Market Square, going up Krzywe Kolo, turning briefly to look back before following the street's sharp turn. Iza pursued. He turned right at Nowomiejska and seemed to be heading for the city walls. Iza's pace slackened in conjunction with doubts that shot like darts from that part of her where suspicion and sense prevailed. She had thought she had turned the tables, but he was taking her into a less populated part of town. There were lonely paths and dark alcoves there. Vulnerable places. Would any passerby or beggar at the wall pay her any mind if she were placed in danger? What was she doing? Risk now outweighed curiosity, anger, and the need to know.

Iza stopped. Taking a moment to catch her breath and then her bearings, she turned about and walked away. She had gone but a hundred yards when the temptation to look back became too much to resist.

He was there, standing at the wall, the shadow of the wide-brimmed hat still sheltering his visage. What expression was he wearing? Was it one of relief? Mockery? Amusement? Disappointment?

The voice within that had cautioned her settled on the last possibility.

Iza was too disturbed to go home. She walked and walked. Miles, it seemed, her mind consumed not with the current streets and boulevards but with the path her life had taken after leaving the order. Suddenly she realized she was in Łazienki Park. Taking care to stay on well-populated paths, she lost a good hour. She looked about, noticing now the great hulk of a building on the edge of the park. It was the Officer Cadets School.

Józef was there, somewhere behind that great façade. What if she were to go in to see him? Michał had been so serious about learning of some political plan. Might she be able to coax information from him? It was unlikely—she hadn't seen him in years—since he was a child. And yet, she had often been able to charm the most difficult children. Are seventeen-year-olds so very different? She was here, standing in front of the academy. It was worth the try.

Called again to meet with Nikolai Novosiltsev, Viktor laboriously climbed the four flights to the fifth level, cursing the man, not for any of his many failings but for the placement of his office. In the outer office Larissa nodded dispassionately at Viktor to go in to his superior's inner sanctum. Viktor knocked and entered.

"Sit down, Viktor," Novosiltsev said, his emotions clearly roiling and near the surface. His face was red as rouge, the tiny purple veins in his nose apparent.

Viktor obeyed.

"Why is it, Viktor, that important information

comes to me from sources other than my Third Department?"

"I'm sorry, sir. If you would just tell me—"

"I'll tell you on what pike at the city's walls I would like your head placed if this happens again. That's what I will tell you."

Viktor thought it best not to respond.

"Perhaps you're losing your enthusiasm for Russian interests. Perhaps a Polish wife has recalibrated your world view. They can do that, you know. These Polish sirens."

Viktor's fingers curled, his nails digging into his legs. But he knew that—beyond insult to him—this was a scarcely masked indictment against the Grand Duke Konstantin, who had taken a Polish wife—Countess Joanna Grudzińska—and had come to profess an unusual affinity for Polish culture. It was an unfiltered and loose remark leading Viktor to assume Novosiltsev had had his morning quotient of vodka. But it was also a measure of Novosiltsev's contempt for the Grand Duke—and a quote worth jotting down when he would return to his office. Who knew when it might come in handy, when it might rid him of this man and push himself up a rung? "My views remain Russian, sir."

"Indeed. Well, Viktor, are you aware that your brother-in-law has been to the Officer Cadets School?"

Viktor swallowed hard. A lie would be too easily found out. "No, sir,"

"And why not?"

"I've had a man on him." *Damn! How could he know this?* "He must have lost him. I'll find out, sir."

"Do that, will you?"

Christ! Viktor cursed to himself. It was no secret that Novosiltsev had other sources doing the work of the secret police—but to think others were monitoring the Third Department came as an unexpected slap.

"I do not think any of this is coincidental," Novosiltsev said. "First, Prince Czartoryski's visit to Michał Stelnicki, then Stelnicki's nighttime return visit to the prince—and now, your brother-law's visit to the Officer Cadets School, the very place where the pot is boiling, but no one seems to know what kind of rancid stew it is they are making!" He was shouting now. "Is everyone aware of the secret goings-on but me?"

"Sir, Michał's brother is a cadet there. He might be merely checking up on his well-being."

"So," Novosiltsev bellowed, "you think it is unconnected with Stelnicki's alliance with the prince? You're a fool, Viktor—or is it that you think me one? Either Michał Stelnicki is involved or he is seeking involvement. And it's likely that the young Stelnicki cadet is privy to important information. You're to find out what little scheme those damn cadets are up to. And find out who the hell they are!"

"Sir, if I may . . ."

"What?"

"I suggest another possibility. What if the prince is urging Michał to somehow douse whatever plan may be in the works? He's a realist and he's not known to be a war-monger. He knows that, ultimately, the Poles cannot stand up to us. David and Goliath is a Biblical fable, sir."

The general thought for a long moment. "Ah, Viktor, you know a bit of politics. There *is* something holding those ears together. I'm impressed. What you say is a possibility, I admit. He may be trying to tamp down their insurgency. If that is the case, we need to know it. We need to know everything!"

"Yes, sir, of course."

"You're in a difficult spot, having married into that family. I thought you a fool for doing so, but perhaps your position will prove a catbird's seat, after all. You need to keep your occupation in the Third Department secret. That is, if you wish to keep your position."

"I do."

"Your wife is still unaware of your duties in the Third Department?"

"She is."

"I wish we could bring in the boy, your brother . . . what's his name?"

"Józef."

"Yes, well, whatever may happen in reference to the Stelnickis or, for that matter, to Prince Czartoryski in the unfolding days, the Third Department must appear free of any involvement. Do you understand?"

Viktor nodded. The Polish nobility still carried considerable weight at Belweder Palace—too much in Novosiltsev's view. On more than one occasion Viktor had heard the general curse the Grand Duke's Polish associations, and he understood that should something untoward happen to any Pole of significance, Novosiltsev himself meant to appear free of any involvement. Self-preservation. No doubt, too, the general thought he was protecting his own reputation as friend to the Poles, a reputation as inflated as his ego—and false.

The conference came to an end and Viktor forgot for once the pain and humiliation of the slow, jolting movements down the stairs so absorbed was he in wondering at the innuendo that something sinister may befall the Stelnickis. As for the fate of Prince Adam Czartoryski, he cared nothing.

Coming into the Castle Square, Iza sighed heavily. Her feet hurt. She could not remember ever having walked so much. She was close to home now, but she was in no hurry. Her little scheme had failed. She had tried several different approaches to the stern official at the academy, to no avail. *It is not visiting day, Mademoiselle*, she was told and no words or pleasant expressions could make the officious gatekeeper see her way.

And how she had imagined bringing news to Michał of some romantic plot of a group of young idealistic cadets! How she longed to see his face light. He could then move forward with his plan to dissuade them. Peace would be maintained. "Christ's wounds," she whispered to herself, "so much for that."

She thought that if she ever attempted entry to the academy again, she would wear her brown Carmelite habit. It would open doors for her, quite literally. The Russian beast would at least honor her once-upon vocation. She had kept both her everyday habit and the new one used at celebratory services. They hung unhappily at the back of her wardrobe. Her final act at the convent had been a sinful one: she had kept them both, including the black veil that was to take the place of the white, had she stayed and professed her final vows.

What she hadn't kept—never possessed, in fact—was her vocation.

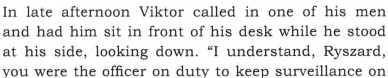

In late afternoon Viktor called in one of his men and had him sit in front of his desk while he stood at his side, looking down. "I understand, Ryszard, you were the officer on duty to keep surveillance on the Gronska home and to monitor the comings and goings of Lord Jan Michał Stelnicki."

"Yes, sir."

Much better, this position, Viktor thought, realizing he was playing Novosiltsev's role. The shoe felt best on this foot. "What went wrong?"

"I did follow Lord Stelnicki yesterday. I did. He didn't know, I'm sure. He went into a tavern down at the river. I waited outside."

"And?" Viktor didn't care for this pup's lack of seriousness.

"And he didn't come out. Ever. Must have gone out the back."

"You said he didn't know he was being tailed."

Ryszard merely shrugged. No, *yes sir*, no *no sir*. Viktor struck him hard across the face. "You'll learn proper Third Department respect, Ryszard, or you'll wind up in climes so cold your most private parts will fall off. Understand?"

"Yes sir, I understand."

"Get out."

Ten minutes later, Viktor descended the cellar stone steps to inquire about the status of their mole in the academy.

"Nothing new, sir," Sergei answered. "It's not been long since we took the finger. I expect he'll bring us some news, though."

"He'd better have something. Novosiltsev is losing patience. I'm losing patience. What did you promise young Gustaw if he failed us again?"

Sergei smiled. "Oh, the promise came from Luka and he believed it, I can tell you. Luka's most convincing.

"I asked you what it was!"

The glint in Sergei's dark eyes failed. "That he will lose an ear, sir, as you ordered."

"Not good enough. We'll waste no more time on him. We'll have to try a different tactic. We must send a message."

"Yes, sir."

Viktor turned, heading for the stairs to his office. "If he's useless, kill him," he called back, "Kill him and be quick about it. And quiet!"

The heavy metal door to the stairway closed behind him, cutting him off from any response Sergei might have made.

Perhaps the disappearance of one of their own would rattle the cage of the cadets and bring their plans to light.

7

ICHAŁ ARRIVED AT THE GRONSKA town house an hour before suppertime, his mood grim, for he had been able to report nothing of substance to Prince Czartoryski that morning at Mass, and the day had wound down slowly in anticipation of his secret meeting with Józef which would—if all went well—take place the next day. He strode into the reception room to find Zofia entertaining an unexpected guest, one that brightened his mood.

"Mother!"

"Hello, Michałek," Anna said, standing to receive kisses on either cheek. She wore a dark blue traveling dress.

"What are you doing here? This is so unexpected—not to say it it isn't very fine indeed."

"I've come on a little business."

"You will both excuse me," Zofia said, "I'm going to change for supper. Isn't this lovely, Michał, having my favorite cousin here?"

"Your only cousin," Anna said with a laugh.

"Favorite nonetheless, Princess. I've invited Barbara and her husband for supper, Michał. We're to make a party of it—and why not, I want to know?" With that Zofia swept from the room.

Michał turned to his mother. "Did I detect a note of sarcasm in her address to you?"

"That's Zofia. I'll be glad to see Barbara and the boys."

"Why sarcasm, Mother?" Michał asked, pressing the issue. "Was she mocking your title?"

"Oh, it's just her way."

"Mother?"

"Never mind."

It took some persistence on Michał's part before Anna gave way. She sighed. "Oh, I guess you're more than old enough to know some things."

"I should hope so, for God's sake. Come sit down." Michał led Anna over to the fireplace and to chairs that faced each other.

"Years ago," Anna began, settling into the thick cushion, "not long before King Stanisław was forced to abdicate and live under a kind of exclusive house arrest in Russia, he gave me the appellation of princess."

"Because you brought him news of an impending uprising here in Warsaw, one that was premature and doomed to fail." As he spoke it came home to Michał how similar was the situation in which he now found himself. He, too, was attempting to preempt a foolishly planned and executed coup.

"My patriot friends and I thought the king would step in, see it aborted, and then—when Kosciuśzko arrived—we could successfully expel both Russian and Prussian troops without a great deal of bloodshed.

My pleading didn't convince the King to take action, but he was impressed enough to award me the title. From countess to princess in one swoop. I never cared the price of an apple for it because, as you know, the Polish Sejm does not bequeath titles of any kind in the interest of democracy, so my title came through King Stanisław's influence with Russia's Catherine."

"His old flame."

"And the person who saw to his election years ago, but she is no friend to the Poles."

"And Cousin Zofia?" Michał whispered.

"Zofia did care," Anna said in even a softer whisper. "She had a difficult time. You see, she had known King Stanisław long before I met him. She had some—how should I say—history with the king."

"Ah! This is the part I never knew. You mean she had been *intimate* with him!"

"Hush, Michałek! Hush."

"God's bones!—or should I say, the King's bones!"

"Michał!"

"And she became jealous that he gave you the title."

Anna gave a little wave. "Human nature, I imagine."

"You never told me this."

"And I expect it is indiscreet of me to do so . . . Now I want to know about Józef. Have you seen him?"

"Yes, and he seems fine. You'll be glad to know he still plays the piano."

"Does he? Composes, too, I hope. That is encouraging. And is he still enthralled with the military life?"

"He seems to be, although my visit was short. He won't be able to see you until next Monday, visitors' day."

"Oh, that's a change! So strict now, I wonder why? I'm not sure I'll be staying that long."

"Mother, just what is this 'little business'?"

Anna's expression darkened, signaling a resolve Michał had seen many times before. "I plan to see whomever it takes to get some answer out of these Russians as to where your father is. I've written to everyone I could think of only to receive precious little in return."

"I told you that I spoke to Prince Czartoryski about him last May at Sochaczew, and he's been doing what he can to elicit information."

"Ah! But Adam is no longer currying favor with the Russians. Not like in the old days when he was advisor to Aleksander. No, if I must cozy up to the Russians for your father, I will. I'll find my way to the Grand Duke if necessary. I mean it, but I plan to start with the Imperial Commissioner."

"Novosiltsev? Really? That's not starting at the bottom, to be certain. But he's a difficult nut to crack, I hear.—You do know Viktor works under the commissioner?"

"I do—do you know in what capacity?"

"He's been rather vague about that, purposely so, I'll wager. You'll have to ask Barbara."

"It doesn't matter. Don't think I'm going to ask *him* for any help."

Michał was relieved. He would not wish to find himself beholden to Viktor Baklanov. He was caught up in a second thought, however. Might his mother be humoring him, knowing his hatred of Viktor?

After all, she would go to any length to search out her husband. He could not blame her for that.

A few minutes later the door knocker sounded. Presently the Baklanov twins came toddling and whooping into the reception room, behind them a maid ushering in Barbara and Viktor Baklanov.

The meal started out peacefully. Wanda and her daughter Elzbieta had engineered a celebratory meal of wine soup with spices, pork roast with caraway, slivered beets, and mushroom cutlets.

"Mother, it's so wonderful to see you," Barbara said after Zofia and her guests were well settled at their places, the twins sitting at the table on huge books for height. "What are your plans? To see Józef, of course?"

"Yes, Basia, that was part of my plan, but Michałek here tells me that visiting days are Mondays now, and strictly so. Why, back when he and . . . Tadek were at the academy, I could almost come and go as I wished, and even this past summer they had no such rule in effect."

Michał noticed the tremor in her voice when she mentioned her son lost to to the French winter march on Moscow, what she often called *Napoleon's folly*. "But Józef is doing well," Michał said, speaking to the table at large, "as I was telling Mother. He's continuing with the piano, too!" Michał went on, providing what little knowledge he had about Józef's life at the academy, hoping to keep his mother from mentioning her real reason for coming to Warsaw. He didn't want her speaking of his father's incarceration in Russia. Not in front of Viktor. It was none of his business and he was, after all, Russian.

"You saw your brother Monday, then?" Viktor asked. "On visiting day?"

Michał nodded, stared at Viktor, whose face pleaded polite interest only. He returned the expression in kind. What was his game? That he worked within the Imperial Commissioner's office was enough to give pause.

Anna laid down her fork. "I'm determined," she said, her emerald eyes focused on Barbara, "to find someone in this city who can at least find out where your father is. Siberia is no small place."

Barbara's eyes widened. "Oh, Mother, if only you could.—Perhaps Viktor knows someone."

Viktor colored slightly and gave a little shrug. "As I have told your daughter, Lady Stelnicka, I haven't much influence. I wish I had."

A clumsy but convenient way to deny assistance, Michał thought. He sensed a tension between Barbara and her husband on the subject. He watched his sister now, wondering what it was she had seen in him other than his good looks. He took in her fashionable silver gown and sapphire necklace. She lacked for nothing, it seemed, and on a minor bureaucrat's income, a bureaucrat who had no influence? It was a mystery.

"Oh, if only we could turn back time," Zofia was saying. "Just the other night when Izabel and I attended the Chopin concert at the Belweder, I had one dance with the Grand Duke Konstantin. It was a polonaise, one of Chopin's in the new livelier mode, you know? Anyway, had I known you were coming with this quest of yours in mind, I might have said something about Jan."

Anna's eyes registered hurt at the lost moment, an expression lost on Zofia.

"You know me, Anna, I'm not shy," Zofia said.

Anna forced a laugh. "Quite the contrary, cousin." Here, Michał noticed in his mother's comment a certain sarcasm but of a lighter tone than Zofia had shown with her *princess* comment. He knew that many fences had been mended between the cousins, and yet a rivalry, not unlike those of siblings, remained. Over the years he had fitted together, like pieces of a puzzle, the causes of the discord between them: how his mother had been raped by Zofia's adopted brother Walter; how Zofia had used the situation to foist upon her the man her parents had arranged for *her* to marry; how that man, Antoni, had attempted to murder Anna—his own wife—for her money and estate; and, most especially, how Zofia's scheme succeeded in keeping his mother from Jan, her true love, for years. These were bittersweet thoughts that touched Michał: bitter because he was the result of that rape by Walter; sweet because when his mother was at last able to marry Jan Stelnicki, a bond of love as strong as any grew up between Michał and his stepfather.

Michał noticed now that his mother's green eyes were fastened on Iza. "My dear, you look divine. You have been missed all these years. Not that being a nun is not a wonderful calling. But the world is happy to welcome you back."

"Thank you, Cousin Anna. I can tell you it is a different Europe I see now. So little peace, what with new revolutions in Belgium and in the German and Italian states."

"And in France all over again," Zofia piped. "Can you imagine? Hadn't they had enough? I may never realize my dream to visit Paris, City of Light!"

"I hear, too," Barbara said, "that even the Papal States are rising up. It's like a disease sweeping Europe."

Viktor harrumphed. "But Russia is free of this disease, my love. People in my country know their place."

"I beg to differ, Basia," Michał said, ignoring Viktor's comment, yet at the same time striking a discordant tone because of it. "Not a disease, hardly that." He felt all eyes come to him. "It's a desire, Basia, nothing so negative as a disease. People want little. They want their *freedom*. They want to live like men and like women. Like human beings." Michał's gaze at his sister across the table moved away, taking on a challenging intensity and becoming fixed now on Viktor. "One day it will happen in Russia, too."

The barb hit home like an arrow flying true. Viktor's features seemed to tighten in a face gone red. "Are you a prognosticator, Michał?" he asked, shifting in his chair. "Should we mark your words? Perhaps you can divine what will happen in these places, yes? France? Belgium? Italy? Germany? The Papal States?"

Michał smiled to himself at his brother-in-law's bluster. "I can say only that people will strive to be free. Always."

"Ah! I see. And what about the Congress Kingdom, my brother? What do you forecast here?"

"The Congress Kingdom of *Poland*," Michał corrected, bristling not at the retort, but at being called his brother. "There was a time when the saying went, 'In Russia do as one must; in Poland as one will.' One day it will be true again."

Zofia's fork came down, ringing hard against porcelain. When Michał glanced at her, she shot him a cautionary message. *Avoid politics.*

"You're alluding to the days of your constitution, I suppose," Viktor said. You must come to terms with the fact that you have another constitution, another name, another king—Tsar Nicholas." Viktor's ice-blue eyes flashed. "It is a dangerous thing to always side with insurgents."

Michał had more to say in rebuttal but knew he was being baited now and would not give Viktor satisfaction. Neither did he wish to spoil his hostess' little supper, so when Zofia announced that the maids were bringing in a special dessert—waffles with poppy seed—he let the subject lapse.

When the meal ended, the little company adjourned to the music room, where Anna would keep a promise to the twins to play something for them on the piano.

Pretending to nurse his coffee, Michał sat at the table a bit longer, lost in thought. He was still thunderstruck by Viktor Baklanov's use of the word *insurgents. It is a dangerous thing*, he had said, *to always side with insurgents.* Was this merely talk? Was it an accusation? Was it a warning? It almost seemed to Michał that his brother-in-law knew something of his mission here in Warsaw. Could that be possible? How? He knew he had said too much to Iza, but he was certain that she had no opportunity to speak to Viktor. Nor, he guessed, would she have the inclination, for as much as everyone loved Barbara, her husband Viktor remained an outsider to the family.

In exiting the dining hall, he noticed Iza near the front door. "You're not going out?" he asked.

"No," she said, her voice barely audible.

Michał walked over to her. "What is it? Something said at the table? I was too argumentative, I admit."

"No, Michał, it wasn't that had all. In fact, you voiced my thoughts."

"Then what is it?"

Her blue eyes, wide as moons, looked up into his. "As I came out into the hallway, I—I just had, I don't know, a premonition."

"Of what?"

"Something prompted me to look out the window . . . and—"

"And?"

"He's out there. Watching the house."

Michał moved quickly to the tall, narrow window to the left of the door. Pulling back the lace curtain, he peered out. Dusk had long since passed, but the full cover of night had yet to fall completely. Michał could make out a figure standing across the street in a very narrow gap between two town houses. His head seemed to lift slightly as if he was taking note of Michał. As if he *was* indeed watching the house!

"Stay put," he ordered Iza. "I'll see what this is all about."

Iza reached out, grasped his arm. "No," she pleaded, "it's not safe, Michał. Please don't go!"

"I'll be fine," he answered, lifting her hand from his arm and letting it fall, but not without a subtle squeeze. "I'll not have anyone threatening you or frightening you, do you hear? I won't!" With that Michał left, pulling the door closed behind him.

His eyes took a moment to adjust to the dark. The watcher had wasted no time in giving up his station and moving up the street, toward Market Square.

Michał followed. The man hastened his steps, as did Michał. And then they were running. The man led him up Piwna to Celna, through Market Square, where few seemed to notice the chase, and then toward the riverfront, Michał closing the gap, little by little.

They came upon a narrow, winding street perched on the bluff above the river. The modest shops were closed but ramshackle taverns didn't lack for customers. Michał clapped onto the man's shoulder, stopping his forward motion, and spinning him around. He was astonished to find him a man well into his fifties, albeit handsome and in good form, for he was no more breathless than was Michał.

"Who are you?" Michał demanded, having taken hold of the man's arms at the wrists. "Who?"

The man attempted to pull away. "Let me go!"

Michał held. "No! You were watching the Gronska house on Piwna Street—why? You will tell me." It occurred to Michał now that he had thought to give chase without a weapon. What if this man had one?

The man pulled one hand free and struck Michał hard upon the chest with enough power to propel him a foot or two and allow for his own escape. Michał caught his breath and flew at the man, bringing both of them to the hard graveled street, Michał atop the man's back, twisting his arm behind him.

The man seemed to accept defeat. "Look, I meant Izabel no harm."

"You know her name? How? What's your purpose? Who's put you up to it?" Michał shoved the man's arm high up on his back. Another inch and it would break like a twig.

The man grunted. "No one. Truly."

"You followed her the other night—gave her the fright of her life."

"No, not at night. In the square the other day when she turned the tables and came after me, but never at night."

"But what is your interest? Be truthful unless you wish your arm broken."

"I will tell you. You must care about Izabel. I will tell you. I suggest you release me. We can go into that tavern across the way. It will take some explaining."

"Why should I trust you? Don't play me for a fool."

"I will not fight you. You've outdone me there. Neither will I run. What I have to say is confusing— and surprising. And quite true."

In his years in uniform, Michał had learned a bit of human nature; he had learned when to trust a man—or not. Michał's gut feeling now was to believe the man. He released the arm, allowed him to stand,

and the two made their way toward a tavern called
The King's Ransom.

Iza sat in a chair near the door, away from the little
group surrounding Anna at the piano. Her fingers
drummed the arms of the chair. Where is Jan Michał?
He went tearing off on a dangerous chase, all because
of her. She wished she had kept silent. It was her
fault. She little doubted that he was in peril, that he
might be hurt. Perhaps he was hurt already, lying
prone on some deserted street. This was no game.
And for him to go off like that, taking after someone
who might be well-armed. She caught herself now,
realizing that Michał could not possibly be armed. He
had only just left the supper table when the trouble
arose. It was such an impulsive thing for him to do,
a thought that brought her up short, for only the day
before hadn't she done the very same thing?

Her heart and mind elsewhere, Iza vacantly
watched the Stelnicki family happily singing
along with Anna's playing, the twins laughing and
mimicking the adults. Then she saw Viktor, who sat
removed from the others. He had not attempted to
join in with the Polish or French songs. She doubted
that he would ever fit into the family. He was that
odd piece of sky that one could never find a place for
in a table puzzle. Iza brought her eyes into a keener
focus on him. Her heart lost a beat. He was staring
with the greatest intensity—at her.

8

HAVING LEFT THE MAN WHO called himself Jerzy to finish his beer, Michał exited The King's Ransom, his head swimming with what he had been told. He passed through the front door and out onto the darkened street. He did observe peripherally the two young men approaching the tavern but was too preoccupied to take real notice—until they were upon him and he felt the force of a mighty fist to his stomach. He bent over in pain, breath knocked out of him, but nonetheless attempting to stay upright. It was then that an upper cut to his jaw—from the other ruffian, he thought—propelled him backward. He fell into a sitting position. Not for long. Each assailant took an arm and heaved him to, allowing him to stand on his own. Only now, it seemed, were they ready to speak.

"Lord Stelnicki?" the thin wiry blond asked. When Michał didn't respond, he said, "It is our commission to respectfully suggest to you that it is best for you to return to Sochaczew."

A halfway intelligent ruffian, Michał thought.

"Respectfully? And only now do you check for my identity? And what if I am not the man in question?"

This response visibly rattled the thicker, slightly older fellow, whose wide brow furrowed. "You mean you're not Stelnicki?"

"Shut up!" his friend growled. "Don't be a fool. It's the count, all right, isn't it, milord?"

"It is!" cried Michał. "And here's a print of my signet ring to prove it." His arm moved in an arc toward the thin one, the clenched fist and signet coming into contact with the soft flesh of a beardless cheek. Later he would wonder at his impulsiveness, but for now his anger fed him.

From there things became a blur. The gullible one was upon him with punches to his side and then Michał's arms were pulled behind his back so that the elbows were nearly touching. With his head hanging down, his mind cloudy and his body wracked with pain, Michał caught in the diffused lighting from the tavern the glint of something.

A knife.

The wiry one, blood dripping from his cheek, held it menacingly, moving it closer, near to Michał's throat. "You can make us take the easy route to keep you from the academy, milord. In which case you won't have the option of returning home—or anywhere!"

At that moment someone came down hard on the thin assailant, who spun about, the knife moving away from Michał and toward the newcomer. Michał tapped all of his reserve and pulled his arms free, his captor likely distracted by his compatriot's struggle. He saw that the knife had changed hands. It was lifted into the air, swiftly coming down now, finding soft flesh amidst the ribs of the thin assailant.

By this time men were spilling out of the tavern to observe the fracas. Later Michał wondered whom they might have helped, or whether they themselves would have merely enjoyed giving vent to liquor-induced violence. But for now his assailants, the one helping the other, were hightailing it down the darkened street, no one giving chase.

Michał's dumb surprise must have passed over his face as he realized now that the man who had come to his defense was the man whom he had just left sitting in the tavern. He simply nodded his thanks in the way it was often done on the battlefield when one's life was saved by a compatriot. Stooping, he picked up the knife from the gravel. It was an ordinary sort. When he looked to his new friend and protector, Jerzy, he realized that the thin, wiry attacker had not been the only recipient of a wound.

It was a hellish task half carrying and half dragging Jerzy back to the Gronska town house. Finally, they stood waiting at the front door, Jerzy's arm around Michał's shoulders. "You see," Michał said, quite out of breath, "had you stayed in front of the house here, we could have avoided those other two."

"And miss the excitement?"

They were both laughing when Iza opened the door to Michał and the bleeding man. She was shocked into silence by their appearance and bizarre laughter so that she merely stepped aside as the two crossed the threshold.

Michał managed to get the wounded man to the hall chair, then straightened up to speak to Iza. "Look, he's bleeding badly at the shoulder. We need to get him upstairs to a bed. I can staunch the bleeding myself, but we'll need a doctor as soon as we can get one here." Michał had thought of having him tended to right there on the ground floor, but in less than a heartbeat realized the complications that would arise should Zofia come upon him.

Iza had yet to recover. "But he . . . he's—"

"Jerzy, the visitor to your garden at the convent, I know—as well as the one from yesterday in the Square." Michał went to place his hands on Iza's shoulders but thought better of it when he saw how bloodied they were. "Listen to me, Iza. I know who he is. There is nothing to fear. Trust me."

Iza looked hard into Michał's eyes for several beats, then her eyelids closed, as if to say, *I do.*

"I'll need help getting him up the stairs. Where is everybody?"

"Viktor and Barbara took the boys home, your mother's gone to bed, and mine has gone out. The servants are asleep. . . . I'll help you, Michał. There's a guest room on the third level."

The stairway was just wide enough for the three to painstakingly climb, step by step. On the second landing Jerzy turned to a silent Iza. "I'm sorry for all this, Sister Izabel," he said.

Iza remained silent for several seconds, her face paling before she brought herself to say, "You have more than this to be sorry for, I think. Is your name Jerzy—or is it Rafal?"

Michał witnessed some indecipherable current pass between them before the bleeding man answered, "Jerzy."

Michał first provided the patient with more than a dram of brandy, then staunched the wound with oil from the leaves of geraniums. Iza had brought the oil to the door. "It's from my herb garden," she said, before making a quick retreat. Suddenly Michał could imagine her as a nun on just such a mission of mercy, her face framed by wimple and veil. Upon arrival, the doctor, who lived right there on Piwna Street, complimented Michał for his preliminary work and went about the business of stitching up the wound. After seeing off the doctor, Michał sat for a short while with a well-bandaged Jerzy.

"Will she hate me, Michał? Jerzy asked, his head turning on the pillow toward Michał, the silvery blond hair shifting on his furrowed forehead. This seemed to be what concerned him, not the wound, not the pain.

"No, Jerzy, I don't think so. Not when she learns that which you've told me—"

"I don't know. I should have been honest from the start." Brooding, Jerzy turned his head away.

The ensuing silence became too much to bear, so Michał spoke: "Who do you think they were?" When Jerzy didn't respond, Michał said, "I thought at first they were military cadets, but they were not so young." It was his thought that the cadet leaders had learned of Michał's mission and his visit to Józef.

Perhaps even of his questioning of his brother. They would be intent on keeping Michał completely out of the picture. They would not want anyone or anything interfering with their grand plan, whatever it might be. "Could they be cadet superiors?"

"Hmmm," Jerzy droned.

"You don't think so?"

"I don't know. They're a little rough around the edges, more like me."

Of good peasant stock, he was implying. That Jerzy was of the peasant class was something Michał had already deduced at the table in The King's Ransom. He was well-dressed and well-spoken, but his quizzical reaction to an offhand comment Michał made in French gave him away. More than any other language, French was the language of the continental nobility. Oh, Jerzy was intelligent and gentle, but he had not been raised a gentleman and certainly had no title. He had told Michał he had come from Kosumce, a little village near the River Vistula.

"Their Polish was adequate," Jerzy said, "but not native."

Michał felt the heat of embarrassment warm his face. Of course, only now did he realize there was something about their dialect. Jerzy had it right: it was learned Polish. "Russian—of course! And *your* idea who they were?"

"Secret Police."

"Secret Police?" Michał echoed. "The Third Department?"

"Very possibly, but there are multiple branches of secret police. One distrusts and spies on the next."

The Third Department, Michał thought. It was a strong possibility. Had they gotten wind of his mission? How stupid he had been to march right up to the the Czartoryski Palace that first night in Warsaw. And upon leaving, he had been followed. Despite subsequent measures to operate under a guise, he may well have given himself away at the start.

"Lord Michał, let's be direct. You're trying to learn what mischief the cadet lads are up to, yes?"

Michał's mouth fell open.

"And you're trying to abort their mission once you find out."

Michał's breath was sucked from him, as if he had taken another punch to the gut. "How—how do you know . . . how could you know?" He felt hot blood swimming from his heart to his face. He had thought himself a good soldier in days gone by, but now in this matter of spies and intrigue he was at sixes and sevens. "You told me your interest in this house, in Iza. Now there's what—something else?"

"I can't blame you for being upset and confused, Lord Stelnicki. I will be forthright. I know these things because I come from my village to meetings here in the capital."

"Meetings? One of the secret clubs?"

"Yes, and I take advantage of these visits to try to catch sight of Izabel."

"So, in watching the house, was it *I* that you were interested in—or *Iza?*

Jerzy smiled. "Both."

"What club?"

"Now I put my life at risk in telling you. You have seen to my safe-being here once, I trust you will keep your silence if I tell you?"

This evening was all too much for Michał to digest. And it was not over. He looked into Jerzy's earnest bright blue eyes and nodded.

From the first landing, Michał heard Zofia's raised voice coming from the hallway below. Much softer and more meliorating were Iza's replies. He hurried down, having left Jerzy sleeping.

"What is this, Michał?" Zofia cried, turning from Iza to him. "Izabel tells me you've put up some stranger here in my home? That you don't even know the man! You know you are very welcome here anytime, but I am not running a pension."

"There are circumstances, Cousin Zofia. The man has been hurt. And . . ." But Michał couldn't reveal all that he knew just yet. Not until he spoke with Iza alone.

"And?" Zofia pressed. "And what? Izabel told me he's been hurt. I came in to find her wiping up blood from the stairs, for God's sake. If he needed care he should have been taken to a hospital.

"Please, Mother," Iza interceded. "Please let it go until morning. The doctor said he's to have complete bedrest."

"Indeed! In the morning we may find he's had the strength to make away with the silver." Her black eyes swept from Iza to Michał and back again. "All right, I won't fight you both. I'm going to bed. But in the morning other arrangements are to be made for this man." Zofia started for the stairs, had another thought and turned around. "I don't suppose this person has a family name I might recognize?"

Iza turned to Michał. Only he could appreciate the irony of the situation. Tomorrow they all would. He remained silent.

"I thought as much!" Zofia declared, turning and making her way toward her room on the ground floor. "A peasant in the guest room," she muttered. "What next?"

Neither Iza not Michał spoke until they heard the door of Zofia's bedchamber close with some finality.

"Oh, Michałek," Iza said, "I was so concerned for your safety."

Michał looked down into the sky-blue eyes, her violet scent redolent. "Were you?"

"Oh, yes," she whispered, a flame of color rising in her porcelain cheeks. "I don't know what I would do, had you been hurt."

Michał took her hands in his. "I was not hurt, Iza. I admit to having made better judgments in my day, but I have only a few bruises to remind me."

"You do?" Iza cried. "Where?"

"Upper torso. Nothing serious. He gave a little laugh. "Modesty prevents me from making a show."

"But you could have been hurt badly. You might have been stabbed! And I'm to blame. I—"

Michał raised his index finger and placed it over her lips. "Shush, Iza. Do you hear?"

She obeyed. The hand that was still held by his seemed to tremble, the fingers tightening almost imperceptibly.

In the dim light of guttering hall sconces, her

182   James Conroyd Martin

eyes flared as if through a blue haze, two pools that seemed to mesmerize. The moment hung fire.

At last, his hands moving to lightly grasp her upper arms, Michał bent to kiss her. Her lips were soft as satin, cool at first, then heat-filled. The act was done without the slightest premeditation. The moment lengthened.

Michał pulled back, his hands falling to his sides, too surprised at himself to decipher her reaction. "Forgive me."

Iza's eyes went round, perfect as saphires. She remained speechless.

Michał chose his words now with great care. "Iza, the man upstairs—"

Iza blinked, as if in quizzical response to his shift in thought. "He called himself Rafal when he visited me in the convent's garden."

"And he was the one at the Market Square, but he was not the one following you home from the Belweder Palace. He has confessed to me his interest in you."

"His interest?" Iza's voice was but a breath, her face pale and stricken. "I did think him innocent, as I told the abbess. To think he would stalk me—like an animal—"

Michał's gaze locked on to Iza's. His hands took hold of hers. "There is no need to fear him, Iza . . . and there are no easy words for this. . . ." Michał drew in breath. "Iza, the man upstairs—Jerzy Lesiak—is your father."

Iza lay in bed, her mind recalling in vivid detail one of her final days at the convent on Wolska Street. On that clear, bright morning when the garden was in full bloom, she was called in to speak to Abbess Teodora, little suspecting the outcome.

"Well, Sister Izabel," the abbess said, "the time has come."

"It has," Iza answered, still certain this was a routine interview before the formal reception of the black veil that symbolized her final vows.

"You're certain—this time?"

Iza felt her ears warm beneath her skull cap and white veil. "Mother Abbess, you're referring to my lack of certainty last year."

The lips of the plump abbess widened into the semblance of a smile. "I'm speaking of the year before that. You remember, when you couldn't bear to have your tresses cut back."

"That was hardly the reason for my asking for an extra year as a postulant."

"Oh?"

"I was—unsure of my vocation."

"And the second time? When you asked for yet another year."

Iza was certain her face was aflame by now. She drew in air. "The reason was the same, Mother Abbess." The terrible presentiment that she was to be asked to leave gripped her. Dismissal? It was not possible!

"How many entered as postulants with you, Sister Izabel?"

"Six others."

"That was eight years ago. How old were you?"

"Twenty-six."

"One of the six saw fit to leave us. The other five took their final vows, as prescribed, after their sixth year. They have been fully professed for two years, yes?"

"Yes," Iza conceded, the words now coming in a rush, "but, Mother Abbess, I don't see how that matters. Everyone is different. I'm certain one or two of them had doubts and—"

"Not everyone is different, Sister Izabel. You are different. It is you. It is eight years now since you came to us. You were the oldest of that group of seven, and I might add, your mother was set against your entering, yes? So much so that she refused to provide for your dowry. Has that played into your indecision in the past?"

Iza tried to read the abbess' intent but could not. "I am not undecided now. I have worked hard. My herb garden is the best in Warsaw, so I'm told. It provides a modest income. It seasons your food. My pestle and mortar helps to mend your colds."

"Don't be impertinent, Sister Izabel."

"I'm sorry, Mother Abbess."

"Tell me, Sister, did you lose your love to the Napoleon war machine?"

"No, I did not."

"So many men died in the effort to take Moscow that girls of your generation were left with few prospects for marriage. Is that what brought you to us?"

"No, Mother Abbess. I did have prospects." Iza immediately regretted the last statement. Pride had pushed her to say it. What woman wanted to admit she had no prospects? Her lips tightened now. She would say nothing about Armand.

"Oh? By way of your mother?"

Iza fell silent. Ah, here was a way to avoid mention of Armand. Gossip about her mother and her mother's many attempts to marry her off to a wealthy magnate had likely come to the attention of the abbess. Iza would allow her this thread of thought and so feigned shyness at returning the hard stare of the nun, steady as a sharpshooter.

"I see. So you have no doubts now about professing?" the abbess questioned. "Taking the black veil and adhering to the solemn perpetual vows?"

"No," Iza said, relief daring to seep into her. The abbess was merely testing her. This little interrogation would soon be over.

And yet the abbess had succeeded in bringing back to her the name of Armand. Armand Polcyński. Now, after a decade, days did go by without thinking of him. Thank God for that. She had fallen for him hard, this fair-haired young man from Gdansk who wrote poetry and who came on occasion to stay with his cousins in Warsaw. He had returned her love, too, she was certain of it. But her mother, thinking him too poor and untethered to any kind of power or influence, had done her best to scuttle the relationship. In the end, it was his parents who, having investigated and finding her of questionable parentage, designated her an untenable choice. They spirited Armand back to Gdansk to stay. Iza suspected that her mother herself had played the

missing father as her highest card. But she was not
certain. In any case, Armand did not try to return to
Warsaw and within a year the cousins informed her
that he had married.

Now, like a large, dark cloud, the abbess stood and
scudded around her great oak desk, passing where
Iza sat and moving behind her, her huge wooden
rosary beads rattling, the crucifix swinging like a
clock's pendulum. The abbess' next words came at
Iza from behind, whispering arrows from an unseen
source. "The novice mistress has her doubts about
you, Sister Izabel. And who would know better?"

Who, indeed, Iza thought, her heart tightening
as if in a vise. Sister Iwona, the novice mistress,
had been more than a teacher to the seven novices.
She had, Iza had thought, been her friend, teacher,
protector, and confidante. Iza tried to stave off
dizziness, a vortex that sought to draw her in. What
had she told the novice mistress? There had been
secrets shared. What could Sister Iwona have told
the abbess? The name Armand had not crossed
her lips. However, Iza recalled, spirit sinking, that
in confidence she had told Sister Iwona of second
thoughts. In confidence. When was that? A fortnight
before? A month? Time was an incalculable thing in
the convent. Iza was taking too long to collect her
thoughts, too long to respond. Silence stretched out
before her, like a chasm.

By now the abbess had completed her circle and
stood behind the desk, her eyes taking hostage those
of Iza. "And there is the other matter, Sister Izabel."

The gravity of the abbess' tone and unrelenting

bead of her dark eyes gave Iza a new fright. "Other matter?" Iza heard herself say.

Abbess Teodora leaned over her desk, her chubby hands placed flat on the waxed surface of the desk like the bases of two darkly-clothed columns that held up her considerable frame. Her brown scapular fell forward, freed from the rise of her considerable bosom. "The man, Sister Izabel, the man."

The fear and the dread vanished at once and Iza exploded with a laughter she had never dared behind convent walls, much less in the presence of the abbess.

Abbess Teodora came straight as a rod, her chin retreating into her turkey wattle. "You forget yourself, Sister Izabel."

Iza collected herself at once. "Yes, of course, you're right. I was taken by surprise. What—what man are you speaking of?"

The abbess' eyelids tightened and she spoke with a deliberate evenness. "The man in the garden."

The dread returned with an intensity and suddenness that took Iza's breath away.

"You're turning as white as your veil, Sister Izabel. You don't mean to deny it? That you've seen a man on occasion in your garden?—In *our* garden!"

Iza pushed a tongue around a mouth that had gone dry. "I don't, Mother Abbess. But you can't think—"

"Who is he?"

"Rafal."

"How many times has he been here?"

"I don't recall. Four or five."

"You let him in? Each time?"

"Only the last couple of times. The other times he took advantage of those moments Sister Aldona leaves the gate open while she goes out to the street to buy from the farm wagoneer."

"These last times—you've struck up a romance of sorts."

"Oh, no, Mother Abbess!" Despite her situation, Iza struggled not to giggle. "Rafal must be twenty years older than I."

"I'm told he's handsome just the same."

"By whom?"

The abbess ignored the question. "If not romance, what was your interest in this—this Rafal?"

"We talked about my herb garden. He gave me hints how to make my plants thrive. He was very knowledgable. And sometimes we discussed the weather."

"And what of this man's interest? Do you think it is the weather or your herbs that he was about? Are you so naïve, Sister Izabel?"

"Rafal is a good man, I can tell you that. I think something drew him to me. I can't say what. I think he was lonely. Sometimes he spoke of Kosumce, his little village on the Vistula."

The abbess sat now, her round face beneath the black veil screwed into a scowl. "I cannot decide, Sister Izabel, whether you are as naïve as you would appear—or whether you are a master of words. Our convent's own storyteller."

"Oh, Mother Abbess, I can assure—"

A single forefinger, raised like a chalice at Mass, shushed Iza at once. "Whichever the case," the abbess continued, "vows have been broken, have they not?"

Iza thought. She had not been silent while at her work. She had not kept verbal communication within the community. She had accepted visitors. She had not reported a trespasser. So the tally came to silence and obedience. But certainly not chastity, not even chastity of spirit.

Iza looked into the face of the abbess and she knew—despite the admissions she might make, the defense she might mount—that her future was ordained, that an eight-year chapter of her life had closed.

The realization shook her. Anger quickly fueled her and the words leaped out of her mouth. "You mentioned my mother's refusal to pay the convent my dowry, Mother Abbess. No doubt you also remember that *I* paid it with monies and a French tract of land left to me by our family friend, the Princess Charlotte Sic. The value I'm certain exceeded the dowries of all the postulants entering with me. What becomes of that money and those lands now, Abbess Teodora? What?"

Even now as she lay trying to sleep, Iza was still able to feel her ears burn at the rudeness shown to the abbess. The initial anger had driven her. In the end, after she had come to accept the decision of the abbess as the right one, she left the convent without another mention of the dowry.

Iza rose from the bed, took the single guttering candle and went to her wardrobe. If she couldn't sleep, she would choose her gown for the morning. Her green day dress would be a suitable choice. In reaching for it in the dark, by chance she extracted one of the Carmelite robes she had purloined. She quickly replaced it and stood very still as her heart caught.

Not completely had her life closed with the shutting of the convent gate. Abbess Teodora, it seemed, had been correct: this man, Rafal, did have a special *interest* in her. Was it possible that he *was* her father? The thought, coupled and confused now with the vivid memory of Michał's sudden and sweet kiss, set her pulse thrumming at her temples, thus robbing her of a good night's sleep.

9

VIKTOR TURNED ON HIS SIDE, facing the bedchamber's windows. The gray light of day crept like a burglar through the heavy draperies. The apartment was quiet. No sounds from the boys. Opportunity, too often these days stymied by the rambunctious twins, beckoned now. Barbara lay with her back to him, the rise and fall of her breathing just audible. He rolled onto his other side, toward her, one arm sliding under her head where the pillow gave leeway, the other over the rise of her hips to her stomach and upward to the opening in the thin silk nightgown. He cupped one of her breasts.

Barbara came slowly awake. "What time is it?"

Viktor's mouth was at her ear. "Never mind." He gently shifted her to her back, his hand exploring.

"Viktor, the boys . . ."

"They're sleeping." He began working on her nightgown.

"Not for long. Is the door latched?"

He was laying kisses on her now. "I don't know. I don't much care. Hush, now and kiss me."

Barbara did not resist further—could not, he thought—and their early morning lovemaking commenced.

In the midst of their passion, there came rapping sounds from the main rooms of the apartment, sounds they attempted to ignore.

After a brief silence, the rapping came again. Barbara asked, "Is it the boys? They're hammering at something. Viktor, go see."

"Dog's blood!" Viktor cursed. He pulled away, rose from the bed and drew on a robe.

Coming into the hallway, he saw one of the twins—which one he would not remember later—exiting the boys' bedchamber. He was wiping at his eyes, clearly having just awakened. He looked up at his father, his precocious expression seeming to say, *What's this, now?*

The third rapping, louder, tore away at the mystery. Someone was knocking at the front door of their apartment. Ewa, their only servant, had not yet arrived. "It's probably just Ewa," Viktor said. "Probably forgot her back door key again."

He moved toward the door, attempting to put in check his fury. It would do no good to take it out

on the middle-aged woman. Her cleaning talents left
something to be desired and her patronizing attitude
toward him was galling, but she could cook the best
of Polish and Russian dishes. The boys loved her, too,
so he would have to smile at her, lest they lose her.

He pulled open the door and his feigned
smile vanished.

It was not Ewa. Standing before him was one of
his minions, Luka, thick in body and brain.

Luka took in Viktor's expression and manner of
dress and stuttered, "Milord . . .that is, sir . . ."

"What is it, Luka? Speak up."

"Things didn't go as planned, sir."

Viktor let go of his immediate displeasure, girding
for a new one, one he would dislike even more. He
turned, shooing the twin who had followed him to
the door off to the kitchen, where Ewa could be heard
now, making her appearance. The child resisted. "Go!"
Viktor said, the angry guttural order frightening the
boy into submission. Drawing the man in from the
hallway, he led him to a small reception room and
closed the door.

Luka's story came out in painful fits and starts.
He was sorry to have come to Viktor's residence, but
he knew how badly Viktor wanted to be made aware of
events before others were notified—Novosiltsev being
the primary "other" implied. As ordered, the night
before he and Sergei had been watching Lord Michał
Stelnicki's movements. Assuming he would remain
at home with the family gathering, he and Sergei had
left their post and continued their spying from the
removed site of a couple of riverfront taverns—Sergei's

idea, it was, Luka professed—before happening upon the Stelnicki fellow by chance. Sergei meant, as ordered, to deliver to Stelnicki the warning to leave the capital. They knew not to identify themselves as officers of the secret police. Then, against orders, the warning turned physical. A stranger interceded on Stelnicki's behalf and the fracas became an incident with witnesses. An incident with a knife. Sergei was wounded.

Viktor felt an intense heat rising into his face, anger that was not lost on the thick-headed Luka. Considering the setting, Viktor clenched his teeth, doing everything he could to harness his emotions.

"If only the stranger had not stepped in on the lord's behalf, sir—"

Taking a deep breath, Viktor raised a single finger and immediately silenced the man. "It's a damn lucky thing for you and Sergei that he did intercede, Luka. Had Stelnicki been injured—or worse—Novosiltsev would have your hides flayed." Viktor's voice dropped to an intense whisper: "And while I have no love for Stelnicki, he is my wife's brother. As a matter of honor I would personally do the skinning and it would be a slow process."

Luka had been paling by the moment. He opened his mouth but no words emerged.

"Sergei is in the hospital?"

Luka nodded.

"Better for him there than here at the moment, I think. You'll both be demoted, of course, if we don't ship you back to the motherland for detention. Here I'll find the most grueling jobs I can for the two of you. Far from the riverfront taverns. And you may tell Sergei that should he ever again disobey orders, a hospital will be of no use to him. Understood?"

"Yes, sir."

"Get out!"

Luka stumbled away, head hanging.

Viktor closed the door. He could hear both of his sons going about in search of him. He drew in breath, trying to maintain control. It occurred to him now that perhaps he had underrated Luka's mental capacity. Yes, he had told his men that he wanted important information like this immediately, but Luka's sense of self-preservation may have kicked in, too: the man knew that by delivering the bad news to Viktor at the family home—with wife and children closeby—he was less likely to suffer the violent brunt of anger for which Viktor was known. For now, at least.

Iza thought she was the first to settle in at the breakfast table but Wanda informed her that Michał had already left the house, alone. She had slept little. Could it possibly be true—that her father was alive and that he had searched her out? That this Rafel—Jerzy—was her father? Her memory scanned the fleeting images she had had of him. Did she resemble him in any way? She had her mother's dark hair, but her blue eyes and light complexion—could these be his?

Cousin Anna came to the table next, and it was all Iza could do to allow her to start her breakfast before plying her with questions. Even though Zofia often came down quite late, Iza worried that this morning might be the exception. She knew she would have to work fast if she was to ascertain the facts as Anna knew them before her mother might interrupt.

The two exchanged occasional pleasantries while Lady Anna took good time at her bowl of buckwheat kasza. When she moved on to shelling a soft boiled egg, Iza could wait no longer. "Cousin Anna, I am anxious to know about my father. He's been a mysterious figure to me all these years. Did you know him well?" She had blurted this out as a child might—and yet she didn't care.

Anna stopped her task, the widened eyes moving to Iza like emerald searchlights. She seemed at a loss for words. Iza had planned this as the best opening question; it left room for little waffling. She waited.

"No, Iza, I did not."

"You met him, of course?"

Now Lady Anna glanced down at her egg, but the hand holding the spoon remained motionless. A long moment passed.

"Cousin Anna? I'm sorry to interrupt your breakfast like this with annoying questions, but this is important to me."

Anna cleared her throat. "No, Iza, I never met the man."

Iza blinked in surprise. "Never?"

"What has your mother told you of your father?"

"I'll tell you, Cousin Anna. Only please tell me what you know first."

"It's not very much, child."

"Please."

Lady Anna lifted tiny spoonsful of her egg to her mouth, her mind clearly at work at something else—or perhaps in conflict. Iza suspected she was playing for time, hoping Zofia would make her appearance. Iza persisted, her gaze riveted on her mother's cousin.

At last Anna set down her spoon. "In November of 1794," she began, "the Russians invaded Warsaw, coming first to Praga, of course, where your mother and her parents had once had their city town house just above the River Vistula. Your mother and I were attempting to escape the invaders. We were among the thousands in Praga trying to get across the bridge to the safety of the capital's walls. Someone on the Warsaw side had already set fire to the bridge in order to take it down and keep the Russians at bay, so time was precious. Oh, Iza, the Russians were merciless to Praga citizens. We had the advantage of having a wagon, and just before we came to the bridge that would take us across and behind the Warsaw walls, a Russian soldier on horseback took hold of me and tried to lift me out of the vehicle. Zofia—your mother—seemed to know him by name and she offered herself in my place. He took her up onto his massive destrier. She then convinced the brute to help get the wagon onto the bridge. By nothing short of a miracle, I managed to get across to the capital just before the bridge collapsed into the Vistula, taking hundreds of innocents with it." Anna was clearly on the verge of tears. "It was an unspeakable sight, Iza. Unspeakable."

"And Mother?"

"I looked across and saw her atop the Russian's

horse near the broken bridge where people were still being herded off and into the cold river." Lady Anna's tears were streaming down her face now. "The Russian soldier could not control his horse in the meleé and . . . and the horse, the Russian, and Zofia toppled off and into the swiftly moving river."

Iza gasped. "She never told me these things."

"Your mother disappeared for months and we certainly thought her dead. In the meantime Jan and I married and started our life at Sochaczew. Then one day we got a letter saying she was alive and back in Warsaw. By the time I saw her, a few months later, she was well along with expecting you. My first thought was that Pawel Potecki was your father."

"Oh, I knew otherwise. Mother had me call him Paweł. Dear Paweł, how he loved Mother. He left her everything after he died at Waterloo, including this house. Mother says she would have married him, had he come home.

Anna nodded. "He was a good man."

"So—you don't know anything more?"

"No, except the timing does indicate she was pregnant before returning to Warsaw."

"That is something to go on."

Anna pressed her hand on Iza's. "I'm sorry. Now, what has your mother told you?"

"That he was a brave lord who died at the Praga ramparts on the very day you spoke of. That seems most unlikely now, doesn't it?

Anna managed a wan smile. She and her story had stood as witnesses against Zofia. They sat in awkward silence as Elzbieta came in to take away their dishes.

After a while Anna stood and prepared to leave. "I must go out, Iza.—You should ask your mother to be straightforward with you."

"Do you wish use of our carriage? It's at your disposal."

"No, my destination is nearby. I'm going to the office of the Imperial Commissioner."

"About Cousin Jan?—Oh, I hope you are successful!" Iza reached out for Anna's hand. She would not mention the man who lay upstairs. "It seems that we're both on searches."

"Indeed. While I have little chance of getting in to see him today, I hope to set up an appointment." Anna bent over to kiss Iza on the top of her head. "Good luck to you, dearest."

It was another half hour before an expressionless Zofia arrived in the dining room wearing a lime green satin day dress, its straight lines accenting her figure. "Is that man gone from the house, Iza?" she asked, taking her seat. "I cannot believe the nerve of Michał importuning us that way."

"I believe he is still with us, Mother."

"Well, he's to be gone today, you can be certain." Zofia tested her coffee. "Too much chickory," she concluded.

"Mother, the man's name is Jerzy."

Zofia was inspecting the plate just put before her by Wanda. "Yes? So?" she replied offhandedly.

Iza watched for a flicker of recognition but her

mother's face was a sculpture of detachment. "I think his surname is interesting, though," Iza continued. "It means *forest dweller*. At this, Zofia's head lifted a bit, her eyes widening, almost imperceptibly. The moment lengthened. Finally, Zofia said, "Well then, the man has a place to go back to."

"Jerzy Lesiak."

Zofia seemed not to hear.

"Mother, the man claims to be my father."

"Ridiculous!" Zofia spat, too quickly, Iza thought. "How could you fall for something like that? I've told you—"

"You've told me very little, Mother."

"What has *he* told you?"

"I have yet to speak to him about it."

This seemed to buoy Zofia. "It's second hand, then, from Michał? Do you know, Izabel, during the first French uprising hundreds of immigrants arrived in Warsaw claiming to be of noble birth who were not. Duke such-and-such, Princess so-and-so. Well, they were imposters, upstarts quick to impose on gullible Poles!"

"This man—Jerzy Lesiak—is from a little village near the Vistula, some twenty miles east. He makes no such claim."

Zofia became clearly vexed. She stood. "He's to go from this house today. Is that clear, Izabel? Please make it known to our thoughtless guest, Michał, who brought him here. I'll be out all day."

Iza stood. "Mother, I have more questions."

"You're my daughter, Izabel, not my inquisitor!" Zofia tossed her napkin on the table and exited in a swishing of green satin.

Iza wondered if other parents were so hesitant to relinquish their parental roles when their children became adults. She sat again for a couple of minutes, coming to realize that her questions *had* been answered well enough in what her mother did not—would not—say.

She heard then a faint sound in the hallway. How odd, she thought, then she realized she could not recollect having heard her mother's steps recede.

Careful to make no noise, Iza pushed her chair from the table, rose, went to the open double doors. Slowly she peered around the door frame and saw her mother, who stood studying herself in the hall mirror. It may have been fantasy, but it occurred to Iza from her mother's expression that she was looking back in time to her younger self—and finding her current reflection too much of a contrast. Was it possible she was thinking of her days with Jerzy?

But then, again, Iza thought: *I don't know this woman at all.*

Iza waited for her mother to leave the house before she went upstairs to the bedchamber where Jerzy Lesiak had been placed. She knocked. When no answer came, she deduced he was sleeping, yet she could not resist taking a look. She entered, walked over to the bed, and gently pulled back the bed hangings.

The bed was empty and neatly made up. Jerzy Lesiak was gone, as if he had never come into her life.

Iza's hand went to her heart. Might the mystery of her birth never be solved? Now she spied on the bedside table a closed note. She stepped forward with some little hope that it held an explanation.

The sealed missive was for Michał.

At mid-morning Viktor Baklanov sat in a café on the fashionable Nowy Świat drinking French coffee at a small table by the window. He stared vacantly as a well-dressed matron outside abandoned her formal composure to comically chase down her bonnet that a blustery wind had commandeered. She went quickly out of view. Viktor didn't give her another thought. He was pondering his next move. Michał Stelnicki was up to no good. Was he part of the rumored conspiracy, or *attempting* to become part of it? Perhaps his young brother had drawn him in. As one of Napoleon's Polish Young Guard who had blown up the ammunition warehouses in Moscow in 1812, he would be a welcome conspirator to the cadets. Or was he trying to halt or postpone the execution of the plot? Viktor had to know. His own position with Novosiltsev hung in the balance. It would be useless to question him casually—even if they had liked one another. Viktor could not risk exposing his own position in the Third Department. He would be ruined professionally and personally. The secret would be revealed to Barbara.

There was one person in the Stelnicki family, however, who would supply answers—if Viktor was clever enough.

IO

IN LATE MORNING MICHAŁ SAT alone on the low
retaining wall of Castle Square, staring out over
the Vistula. White cumulous clouds hung in the
bright blue background of Praga, Warsaw's suburb
across the river, a river that flowed silently today, its
subtle ripples giving motion to the sun's reflection.
And for the moment Michał wished himself back
home at Sochaczew, sitting—without cares—at the
branch that flowed past Topolostan—Poplar Estate.
At this time of year—Autumn—he relished sitting on a
bench in the orchard, the extreme quiet occasionally
interrupted by the lazy buzz of insects and thuds and
plops of ripe fruit falling to the ground.

If Jerzy was correct, Michał's presence had drawn
the attention of the Third Department. His continued
presence might very well put others of the Gronska
household at risk. Who had been following Iza home
the night of the concert at Belweder Palace? Had
she been in grave danger because of him and his
stupidity? He had been trained as a soldier, not as a
spy. He had no business meddling with the notorious
Third Department.

Michał craned his neck to look up at the top of

Zygmunt's Column, situated in the middle of the square. The statue of the long dead king held a cross in one hand, a sword in the other. The juxtaposition seemed to wordlessly tell the story of Poland. Faith and independence.

So much for what he would like and where he would prefer to be. Prince Adam Czartoryski had drafted him for this task and—who knew?—its implementation just might bring some little importance to the modest existence of the Congress Kingdom of Poland, a reduced and pale reflection of what was once The Commonwealth of Poland and Lithuania. He had to stay in Warsaw for that. And for Józef. What part, if any, did his brother have in this rumored insurgency? Their mother would be devastated should something happen to the youngest. And Michał's memories of Tadeusz were etched in his mind, evidence of guilt that *he* had survived the trek back from Moscow while young Tadek had been left, buried in frozen foreign ground. Michał had been unable to save him from tragedy, but he might do better by Józef. He must!

Michał thought about Iza, too. About her gentle manner that could—according to her—sometimes be stirred the way a breeze could be provoked into a mighty force. He thought about the exquisite, uncannily blue eyes beneath black hair, eyes that would sometimes dance in collusion with the corners of her mouth, allowing—only once in a while—a full smile warm as the sun. And that kiss, that impulsive kiss. He could not help but think it had changed things completely. He did not for a moment regret it.

No, Michał would not be leaving Warsaw any time

soon. He set off now in the direction of Łazienki Park.

Arriving at the Officer Cadets School at the prescribed hour—noon—he went to the side of the building, found the garden door in the stone fence separating the academy grounds from the park, and knocked lightly. Seconds later came three light taps. He tapped in return. The door opened and Michał slipped in.

Silently Michał followed Józef through neatly manicured grounds toward the cover of a forested area, where leafless trees were thick enough to obscure them from the many windows of the academy. Józef in the lead, they talked now, walking along a path well known to cadets, as well as to Michał from his days at the academy.

Michał knew he had to create a sense of camaraderie in order to gain Józef's confidence so that he would feel encouraged to provide the kind of information needed. He thought it prudent to start with his own—and Tadeusz'—life at the academy. He did this in short order with anecdotes—funny and not—about eccentric teachers, outlandish cadets, typical high jinks, the breaking of rules, and the like. Sometimes Józef would enthusiastically interrupt with a similar tale. As this went on, their exchange took on a natural tenor, and Michał realized that they were connecting in a way they had never done, that for too long he had remained distant—willingly so—from Józef even though a number of their years at Topolostan coincided. There was the age difference; Józef was young enough to be his son. While Michał knew the ways of the military and estate management, Józef seemed to take to the artistic and musical avenues upon which their mother—so afraid of raising another soldier—had marshaled him. But Michał knew there were more than these things that set them apart. The truth was that after losing Tadeusz, Michał would not invest heart and soul in another brother. When he was younger, too, he even held the birth of Józef against his parents. Did they think they could replace Tadeusz? Was Tadek a puppy to be replaced by another puppy? That resentment—illogical as it was—too often made Józef a target for Michał's aloofness and resentment.

Well into the park, they came to a bench and sat. Michał spoke of the youthful idealism he and Tadeusz had shared, the desire to be tested, the longing for glory, the quest for a Poland independent of Austria, Prussia, and Russia, neighbors that had effectively erased their nation from the map in 1795. "When the little Corsican came with his talk of independence, Józef, we saw it as our main chance."

"I've taken a class on Napoleonic strategy," Józef chimed. "He seemed invincible."

"His victories were astonishing, but the blunders were even more so. Tadeusz was lost to the Moscow debacle. Napoleon should have had less ego and better sense than to have crossed the Russian steppes just prior to winter." Sparing nothing, Michał related the long treks, the battles, the gore of guns, swords, and lances cutting through flesh, sinew, and bone; battlefields littered with bodies stacked two and three high in places, as at Borodino; farmers' fields stretching for miles crimson with blood and reeking with the stench of death, the only life present the whirr of wide kite wings. And the cold—always the frigid cold and North wind bearing mercilessly down on man and beast. More of Napoleon's men were lost to the cold than to battle—left like fallen white statues in the snow, men who could not help but give themselves over to a numbing and endless sleep. "I can tell you, Józef, war is not like you or the other cadets here might imagine."

"But we have the desire to test ourselves, just as you and Tadeusz did. And the right, yes?"

Michał could not answer. Józef was more adult than he had imagined. "Tell me, Józef, why did you give up your music?"

"I still play."

"You know what I mean—as an occupation. As a vocation! I'm no judge but others more qualified said you could have a career at it. You had—have—a passion for it."

"I made the mistake of boarding at the Chopins' and encountering Fryderyk Chopin. Michał, I realized in short order I could never be that."

"So? Listen to me. In the military you're not likely achieve the station and glory of General Józef Poniatowski, either. For whom you were named, I might add."

"Who's to say? In music I had discovered my place and, Michał, it was not to my liking. Here, I have yet to make that discovery."

Michał was taken aback by the neat logic but would not acknowledge it. "Well, what about the Chopin daughter—what is her name?"

Józef's face lost its expression, then its color, and when he spoke it was with little more than a whisper, reverent as a prayer: "Emilia."

"Yes, Emilia Chopin. Are you to leave her behind, like Mother was left behind so many times? Or are you no longer sweet on her?"

Józef turned away and Michał could see the tears gathering in the blue-green eyes, the color—sometimes a striking turquoise—a perfect meshing of their mother's green and father's blue.

The romance must have come to an end, Michał realized. "I'm sorry, Józef. I spoke out of turn. I thought—"

Józef drew in a long breath. "Emilia's dead, Michał."

"Forgive me—how—"

"Consumption, a couple of years ago."

"Years! I didn't know."

"I didn't even tell Mother. I was . . ."

Michał put his hand on his brother's shoulder. Neither spoke for some minutes. Józef's shoulders shook with slight tremors, as if he were cold.

Slowly, very slowly, as if in indecision, Józef moved his hand into his cadet jacket's inner pocket. He withdrew a blue velvet pouch and opening the drawstrings, he removed an item and passed it to Michał. It was a miniature portrait, painted on ivory. The subject was a young girl with dark curls and startling, sparkling eyes.

"She's beautiful, Józef." His hand gently pressed Józef's shoulder before he let if fall away. "Beautiful."

"She *was*," Józef replied, the correction scarcely audible.

Michał passed the portrait back to Józef, who received it and coaxed it into the pouch with the sancrosanctity of a priest caring for his chalice.

Another short silence ensued. Michał volunteered something then he had never shared with anyone but Tadeusz—and only him because he had been present. "I loved a girl once. One I hadn't left behind at home. I found her in Russia. She was a Polish girl with a boy's name—Metody—married to a Russian soldier who had not returned in some time. He was probably dead. Tadeusz and I were bivouacked in a little peasant's cottage when we arrived at a tiny hamlet outside Moscow. She and her baby were hiding in the attic. At first I just pitied her. She hadn't left with the other villagers when they fled our forces because she was Polish and as an outsider she feared them more than Napoleon's men. But Metody cooked for us, washed our shirts, and ate with us. And when I was wounded in the chest, she nursed me through it. I would have gotten myself up and about without allowing the thing to heal, but she was adamant about my recovery being a proper one. Sometimes when she did chores outside, I took the baby into bed. He was . . ." The memories, revisited so many years later, proved more vivid than Michał might have thought.

"What happened to them, Michał? Do you know?"

"I know. She wanted to return to Poland, and it took some doing, but we got clearance and she and her baby were placed in one of the camp followers' wagons. Camp followers trailed Napoleon's Grande Armée, like the tail of a large tortoise. Except it wasn't so grand anymore. And winter had set in. 'General

Winter,' Napoleon called it, for it had beat him more than once. When we arrived at Smolensk, I found Metody near death from frostbite, the baby in her arms, already gone. She lasted only a few hours. I saw to it that they were buried in a trench outside the city walls. It was a mass grave. Many soldiers had died of wounds, of course, but even more—women and children, too—were dying of hunger and exposure. I paid a man to cover them immediately so that the wolves would not get to them—and so they would not be cannibalized."

Another silence.

"She was your first love," Józef ventured.

"I guess you can say that."

"Then you don't forget."

"You don't forget, Józef, but you go on. . . . You will, too. You'll love again. The heart goes on."

"Did you love again? You never married. Have you never found someone else to care about?"

"Well, for many years I hadn't, but perhaps I have, just recently." This was all Michał intended to say on the subject. The time had come for Józef to keep his part of the bargain and tell what he might know about the insurgency planned by the cadets. But he looked up to see they were being joined by a third party, another cadet, quite out of breath.

Józef and Michał stood.

"Michał, this is my roommate, Marcin. He knew to find me here."

Marcin gave a little bow. "They're looking for you, Józef. I came as fast as I could."

"For what?"

"You have a visitor."

Józef sneered. "My visitor is here. An illegal one, as you can attest."

"Well, you have another and a relative, too, so he says. Why, he must have some influence beyond that to have been allowed a pass today. He thinks quite highly of himself, but I suspect it's the Russian accent he's affecting that got him past the gatekeeper."

Michał and Józef exchanged knowing looks.

"Does he walk with a limp?" Michał asked.

"Tries to disguise it, he does," Marcin said, "but I noticed it."

"The accent is no affectation," Józef said. "Marcin, you go on back and tell them I'm coming directly. Hurry."

After Marcin was out of earshot, Józef turned to Michał. "What do you suppose Viktor wants of me?"

"I can't say, Józef, but for the good of our country you must tell me what's happening here. You must confide in me."

"You're right to think something's afoot, but I can tell you I have no specifics."

"The goal?"

Józef shrugged. "Independence."

"Come on, Józef. Tell me *how!*"

"I don't know anything more than the fact there's talk and that they've doubled our practice maneuvers. Now come along, I need to get you out the garden door before they send someone else after me."

On a personal level, the meeting with Józef had begun

to bridge a great chasm allowing them a real sense of kinship. But Michał was no closer to learning how the insurgency was to go forward. In that respect, the meeting had been a failure; however, as he drew near to the Gronska townhouse, his thoughts became more focused on Viktor Baklanov than on Józef. Why was he visiting Józef? It certainly was not brother-in-law affection. And how had *he* been granted admittance to see Józef? To hear him tell it, he was little more than a secretary to a middle level attaché. But, come to think of it, Michał could not recall his ever mentioning the name of the attaché. What was his true role in the Imperial Commissioner's employ?

Iza met him at the door. "I've been waiting for you, Michał. I want to know what Jerzy Lesiak told you about—about his being my father. What details did he give?"

"Why don't you ask him yourself?"

"I would but he's gone."

"Gone?"

"Early this morning. What did he tell you?"

"Not all that much, just that he fished your mother out of the Vistula on the day Warsaw fell and the Praga bridge burned." Does that corroborate your mother's view?"

"No, but it supports *your* mother's story. What else?"

"That he, his mother, and grandfather took her in and nursed her back to health. And . . . that he came to love your mother. . . . "

"Oh, Michał," she cried, blue fire in her eyes, "he *is* my father!"

Iza instinctively moved toward Michał, who wanted to reach out to her but didn't dare. Several moments passed. Michał spoke at last to dispel an odd awkwardness: "Did you tell your mother about his claim?"

"I did."

"How did she react?"

"She denied it but I saw a change come over her, Michał. Her face belied her words."

"I see." Michał was not surprised. "Iza, did Jerzy speak to anyone before he left?"

"Not that I know of—but he left a note for you." Iza withdrew the closed note from her skirts. "Here!"

Michał broke the seal and silently read the short message.

"Well?"

"He merely thanks me for the hospitality and that he has urgent business to attend."

"No word that he'll be in touch? That he'll see you—me—again?" The eyes, like blue pools glistened tears. "After all the wondering, after all the years, is he to disappear from my life? Oh, Michał!" Iza started to tremble, then shake. Her hands covered her face. "To think he came to see me at the convent! Again and again. He cared!"

Michał stepped closer, gently pried her hands away, and encased her in his arms and held her to him. "If he cared to do that much, Iza, he's not likely to disappear." His heart went out to this fragile soul. Her breasts pressed against his coat, and he thought he could feel the beat of her heart. He wanted to suggest they move from the hallway to the reception room but was unwilling to break the moment.

Iza moved her head back slightly, looking up. An invitation, Michał thought. There was no awkwardness now. Michał was about to kiss her when they heard someone entering the hall from the rear of the house. They turned, their arms dropping away from each other.

It was Zofia, who looked as if she had been about to speak, perhaps to say hello, but she clearly had made her own assessment of the situation and so said nothing. Dark, slivered eyes flashing her displeasure, she passed them and moved toward her bedchamber.

Michał and Iza were so taken by surprise and embarrassment that they, too, said nothing. The moment of intimacy had been stolen.

II

VIKTOR SLOWLY MADE HIS WAY to the Third Department headquarters. He would have to see Novosiltsev today and he didn't relish the idea. He had nothing new to report. Their mole had proven worthless and that stratagem was abandoned. Neither had his interview with his brother-in-law Józef yielded anything. The boy had to know something. But he was too clever to be caught up in verbal traps. Viktor had the distinct disadvantage of having to pretend a mere passing interest in the idea of a rising. He wondered now whether threats would have worked. Or a little corporal punishment? He could not administer either, of course. His connection to the Third Department was to remain covert at all costs, especially as it related to his in-laws. And Novosiltsev had forbidden that such methods be employed on the sons of the nobility, those who, if well-motivated, could still make trouble for the Imperial Commissioner. In addition to the Grand Duke's often pro-Polish stance, the Poles still maintained their Sejm, a congress that was largely impotent, but one that could be vocal if prompted.

Viktor was only two doors down from headquarters when he halted, blinking in surprise. There coming out of headquarters was his mother-in-law, Lady Anna Stelnicka. *Good god, what is she doing here?* He instantly recalled her determination to find out her husband's whereabouts.

Viktor ducked behind a peddler's cart and closely watched her. She paused for a moment, pulling the hood of her long dark blue cloak over her head and fastening the garment's clasp at her throat. Putting her head down against the wind, she set off in the opposite direction.

Her expression had seemed one of self-satisfaction. *Odd, very odd.* Certainly she had found no satisfaction here. What did she learn to bolster her spirits? Viktor drew in a long breath and he trembled at the next thought. Had she been looking for *him*? Why? What could it mean? What had she been told? God help any employee who had stupidly provided classified information about him. The thought that she might have discovered his true occupation with Novosiltsev turned his stomach.

As Lady Stelnicka moved off in the other direction, Viktor hurried along the side of the building toward his usual entrance, disregarding any stares his limp caused.

Once in his office, he had no time to recover from seeing his mother-in-law at his place of work, for General Novosiltsev had sent word down that he was to report to him at once.

The subsequent berating Viktor had to endure from Novosiltsev was worse than he had imagined. How could this be? the Imperial Commissioner railed. How could something major be broiling at a cadets academy full of boys still wet behind the ears—with the preeminent Third Department remaining completely in the dark? Is it a pack of inept fools downstairs parading as professionals? And if we're not in the dark, then speak up! The mole was useless? Your brother-in-law the cadet useless, too? And nothing yet on the other one—Michał, with his connection to Czartoryski? And this Jerzy Lesiak, seen leaving the Gronska home, is a member of a secret society—one of the damn clubs. And this from one of my other sources. So many pieces to the puzzle here—and we have nothing. Nothing!

And so it went for more than half an hour of grilling and abuse. Viktor was coming to hate Novosiltsev more and more.

The tirade slowed, like a tiring tempest, and Viktor knew he was about to be dismissed from the office. Now was the moment for his question. "Sir," he began, "I know that my mother-in-law was in the building earlier today. She didn't—"

"Come to see me? She did."

Viktor swallowed hard. "What could she possibly want from you?"

"Not what, Viktor. Whom!"

"Sir?"

"Lady Anna Stelnicka, for her years, is a beautiful and intelligent woman. And I'm guessing she's as clever as the men in her family."

"Sir—"

"What she wants, Viktor, is to have her husband returned from Russia. Or at least to know his location."

"Ah, that was my thought exactly."

Novosiltsev allowed the moment to hang fire. He was deliberately taunting him.

Viktor gave a little cough and attempted faux nonchalance. "And . . . and you gave no concession, of course. But perhaps we *could* supply her with an address. My wife tells me she has a hundred letters written, all without an address. It might keep her quiet. Even if it is a false address."

"An address will be unnecessary, Viktor."

"He's dead? But her expression as she left was—"

"Happy, of course. No, he's not dead although I'm certain that would suit you. And he's not in Russia."

Viktor, always so reserved in front of this man, could not help but gasp. "Where—where is he?"

"At this moment, in a coach, a rather uncomfortable one, I imagine, but one that will reach Warsaw in a matter of days."

"He's . . . he's been released?"

"He has."

Viktor couldn't make out whether Novosiltsev's expression was a smile or a sneer. "How can that be? Did you give clearance?"

"It seems, Viktor, that Prince Adam Czartoryski has a bit more influence with Konstantin than I would have thought. It was the Grand Duke himself who signed the release some time ago, perhaps one of the results of the prince's visit to the Stelnickis last May." Novosiltsev sighed. "The verbal picture I have for years meticulously painted of Czartoryski as the devil incarnate evidently has fallen on Konstantin's deaf ears."

"How long have you known this?"

"A week or more."

"You should have told me, sir."

"I have bigger concerns, Viktor. As do you."

Viktor sat motionless, the blood still draining from his face as the significance of this event thundered home. At last he drew breath to speak. "But—but he's sure to recognize me as his chief interrogator."

"Then that is your dilemna. Ah, family problems! Very vexing sometimes, yes? Very vexing. But you are on Third Department time now. See what you can do right concerning those damn cadets. Do that, will you?"

Perspiration was beading on Józef's forehead. His questioning was held in a small basement room, dirty and musty. He sat at a square table, his superiors on either side. They were Second-Lieutenant Piotr

Wysocki on the left, Colonel Józef Zaliwski on the
right. These were the architects of the coming armed
rising, known by a limited few as Project C. Józef
knew nothing more than that.

"What did you tell him?" Zaliwski asked.

"Who?"

"You know very well who!"

"Viktor Baklanov?" Józef asked and held his
breath, afraid that they really meant Michał, afraid
that they had somehow found out about the illegal
meeting he had engineered. They would consider it
a serious breach, and that would be enough for a
severe punishment—but more than that, they would
assume the clandestine meeting had been arranged
to provide an outsider information about Project C.

Wysocki and Zaliwski looked at each other. "Have
you had *other* visitors?" Wysocki demanded.

"No—no, I have not." Józef prayed that if
questioned, Marcin would hold firm.

"What did he ask you?"

"Mostly we talked about family."

"What else?" Zaliwski demanded.

"In a round-about way he wanted to know about
our activities. He had heard some mission was afoot.
I merely said there were many rumors and that most
of us hoped that the tsar would send us cadets into
service soon."

Zaliwski again. "A clever answer, if he believed it.
That's it?"

"Yes, sir. I would do nothing to endanger the
project."

"Józef, do you know your brother-in-law's

occupation?"

"Yes, he works in some capacity for an attaché at the Imperial Commissioner's. That's all I know."

"You're only partially correct. In point of fact, Viktor Baklanov heads up the Third Department, under the devil Novosiltsev."

It took some moments for this news to penetrate. His pulse raced, not so much at the notion that he had been speaking to the secret police, but at the realization that his sister Barbara had married one of the most accursed Russians in Warsaw.

"This seems to be news to you, Józef," Wysocki said.

Józef could only imagine the shock on his own face. He slowly nodded.

Wysocki and Zaliwski exchanged looks again. "You may go to your quarters now, Stelnicki."

Józef stood, drew his heels together, saluted. "Sirs, I do have a request."

"And it is?" Wysocki asked.

"My only wish is that I might be of some *special* use to Project C. I would be grateful to be implemental somehow."

"Looking for glory, Stelnicki?" Wysocki snapped.

"Not so much as setting things right. You know my father was taken to Siberia in '26 for merely being a member of the Patriotic Society."

"We know that, Stelnicki," Zaliwski said, "and we will keep your request in mind."

Józef thought his tone softened a bit. "Has a date been set, sir?"

"It has," Wysocki interjected, "and you'll know when the time comes. By the way, has Gustaw been in touch with you?"

"No, sir." Only the day before word had spread that Gustaw was missing yet again. "Sir—is he—"

"Dismissed, Stelnicki!"

Józef made his exit, climbing the steps, his mind whirling, thoughts of Gustaw giving way to his request. Had they meant it when they said they would consider him for a key position in the implementation of Project C? He prayed that they had. By all that was good and holy, they would not regret it.

As for Viktor, Józef could not put aside a sense of horror that a member of his family worked within the hated and feared Third Department. That he headed it, for God's sake! It made him sick. Did Barbara know this? She couldn't! Had he managed to keep her in the dark? Was he that masterful at manipulation?

And Michał. No doubt his brother was acting on what he considered the best course for Poland. But the time was coming, the time for independence. The older generation was more hesitant, as Wysocki said so often. Józef had to admit that Michał was of the Old Guard. Change was to come from the young. Rebellion from the young.

Józef felt guilty about lying to his brother concerning Project C. But now he could tell him something. In fact, he felt compelled to tell him. Michał must be very careful of Viktor.

Marcin was not in their room, but he had placed on Józef's desk lines of verse from a French poet, Kazimierz Delavugne, a supporter of France's new revolution. The new poem, "La Varsovienne," was a call to arms for Poland.

Józef scanned the first two stanzas and refrains. They were very fine, but for him the message rang loud and strident in the final lines:

Sound the trumpets! Poles to your ranks!
Follow your eagles through the fire as you advance.
Liberty sounds the charge at the double,
And victory stands at the point of your lance.
All hail to the standard that exiles crowned
With the laurels of Austerlitz, with the palms of Idumée!
O beloved Poland! The dead are free already;
And those who live shall win their liberty.
Poles to the bayonet!
That is our chosen cry
Relayed by the roll of the drum.
To arms, to die!
Long live Freedom!

12

25 November 1830

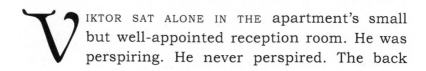

IKTOR SAT ALONE IN THE apartment's small but well-appointed reception room. He was perspiring. He never perspired. The back of his neck was cold, clammy, as were his palms. He knew his world was likely to change irreparably today. For two weeks he had been dreading this day.

"Viktor," Barbara called from the twins' room, "Are you dressed? If you're ready, I could use some help with the boys."

"No, I'm not ready, Barbara," he called.

A few minutes later Barbara appeared in the doorway. "Viktor! You have yet to change. . . . What is it? You look funny. You're not unwell?"

This was his chance. He could plead illness. "No," he said. What if he did stay home? He would merely be postponing the inevitable. There was no escape. "I'm fine."

"Well, please do hurry. You know what this means to me." Barbara pivoted and went back to the twins' room.

He did know what it meant to her. Basia seemed always ebullient, but he had never seen her quite so vibrant as today, so alive, the green eyes glinting with excitement and life.

Nothing like a homecoming, one of the sweetest events in life. Nothing like witnessing someone recalled to life. Nothing like seeing someone return from Siberia. For a day there had been hope. The arrival had been delayed. Word had come that Stelnicki had become too ill to travel, lifting Viktor's hope that fate might intervene so that he would never have to face his father-in-law.

That was but a wish now. Viktor's fists clenched of their own will. Who, for God's sake, comes back from Siberia? No one. Perhaps there was a God. Perhaps it was the one the Stelnickis so devoutly worshipped. And perhaps their God was having his little joke on the Russian interloper within the family.

Would Jan Stelnicki recognize him? Of course, he would. Viktor had stood often enough at the window of the prisoner's cubicle overseeing the questioning; he had done so long before he installed the lacework curtain to protect his identity from the prisoners. What then? With his position known, his career in the Third Department would likely come to an end. He could expect to have what he had already, self-disparagingly, told Barbara he had—a fourth-rate job as an assistant to an attaché's secretary. Ironic, wasn't it? And what of his marriage? The Stelnickis, so stolidly bourgeois in their love, in their patriotism, would be aghast. They would form a frontline offensive. Could Barbara's love for him survive what he had done to her father, to her family, to her? He had no hope that it would, no hope at all.

Viktor thought back to the day they shipped the three minor nobles off to Siberia. Somehow the families had learned the day and time. These Poles became masters at intrigue when pressed, but in day-to-day life they were too guileless for their own good. Dawn hadn't broken yet, but Castle Square was filled with the mothers, fathers, sons, and daughters of the three families there to bid goodbye. But there were others, too, lining the streets that fed into the square, many hundreds who had gotten wind of the day and time of the exile. The ubiquitous and virulent underground patriotic groups in Poland never lost an opportunity to stoke the fires of discontent. Oh, these people were not about to rise up. Not that group. Not that day. But the seeds were being sown . . . Viktor's attention had been drawn then to a young Polish woman—scarcely more than a girl—tearfully bidding goodbye to her father. She was beautiful, perfect, the morning sun catching reddish highlights in her blond hair. All in blue she was, dress and capelike robe, like the Madonna. Now he remembered thinking even then, at that moment, that this woman-child was meant for him. How otherwise? As it happened she never noticed him that day. Her green eyes, gleaming tears, were set on her father only. It was a lucky stroke for Viktor that she had not seen him.

Viktor wasn't in the Third Department for nothing; in the days following, he searched her out, had her followed, checked her background, followed her himself. And then came the seemingly happenstance introduction at a café and subsequent carefully prearranged accidental meetings. That he was Russian put her off at first; he could see that. He had expected as much. But that is where his looks and charm came in. Courting was new to him, so used was he to simple seduction, but he took to it and surprised himself, not so much with his success at making her fall in love—as with the increasing depth and power of his own feelings for her. Was this what they called love?

Larissa had been furious at his sudden lack of interest, of course, but he cared little for that. He had arranged to get her here from Petersburg, pulled strings to get her a job that paid well, too well for what she did. Few women, in fact, had jobs such as hers. She should feel fortunate she wasn't scrubbing floors or taking in laundry, occupations she had held in Russia. He had taken her away from that kind of existence. But now their time was over. He knew that, even if she didn't, or couldn't accept it. After the breakup, he had helped her find a place to live. And it was serendipitous for all involved when Novosiltsev suddenly needed a secretary upstairs, making her no longer ever-present in the Third Department. She wasn't so quick to forgive and forget, he could sense that in their every interaction, but what of it? Some women are that way. She never lived up to her veiled threats anyway.

"Viktor!"

"Almost ready!" he lied, pushing himself up from the chair. He would go. He was many things—but no coward. He looked at the clock on the mantel. One hour. In one hour the homecoming celebration at the Gronska town house would commence. One hour and his life would change.

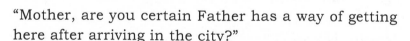

"Mother, are you certain Father has a way of getting here after arriving in the city?"

"Don't worry so, Michał," Anna said, "the Prince said everything would be handled."

"Worry? Mother, you're the one pacing the floor."

Anna swung around, facing him now, her hands moving from her silver green gown to the amber combs in her hair and back again. "Do I look all right? Oh, Michał, it's been four *years*. What will he think?"

Smiling, Michał rose from his chair and took his mother's hands in his. "Father will think you are as beautiful as ever. He will think God has blessed him with a miracle."

It was a miracle, indeed, Michał thought. He was nearly as excited as his mother. And astonished—he had doubted they would ever see him again. Word had it that few people survived Siberia; none returned.

"Sweet Jesus, why isn't he here yet?" Anna withdrew from Michał. So as not to create wrinkles in her gown, Anna carefully lowered herself into an uncomfortable straight-backed chair, one of the extras that had been brought in from the dining hall. "And where is Barbara? She should be here before his arrival. Why must your sister always be late?"

"She has more to think about these days." Michał sat again.

"Oh! The twins—he has yet to see his own grandchildren! What a day this is, Michał, what a day! It's a shame Józef won't be here for the homecoming."

A fortnight had gone by since Michał had met with Józef. The Monday visiting days had been summarily canceled, and he was not to be released from the academy for this occasion—or under any circumstances. Michał recalled the letter—note, really—that Józef had somehow managed to get to him early that morning. *Give Papa my love*, he wrote. It had been addressed to Michał and there was a further message for his eyes only. *Michał, while I was unable to provide you with your requested information, I do have news of an urgent nature. Viktor Baklanov is not who he seems. He is heading the Third Department under Novosiltsev. Whether Barbara is aware her husband is one of the secret police, I don't know.*

Considering the nature of your inquiry, I must caution you to be careful.

"By the breath of Satan," Michał had said aloud upon reading it that morning, and since then he had given little thought to anything—other than the unmasking of Viktor. Emotion overpowered intellect. He had to deal with his intense feelings of hatred and disgust that such a creature as Viktor had wormed his way into the family. The bile that rose within his throat made him think of little else. Now, however, he gave further notice to the interpretation of his brother's written words. How had Józef come upon this information? It had to come from his superiors Wysocki and Zaliwski. It was an easy scenario to figure: their knowledge of Viktor's position and his visit there led to Józef's ban from attending the homecoming. They didn't want Viktor questioning Józef again. All of which led Michał to suspect— believe—that Józef *did* know something about the insurgency plans. He had known and—brother or no brother—he had not shared the information with his older brother, someone of a different mind. And yet Michał could not harbor anger against Józef and his passion for a free and independent Poland. He was a Stelnicki through and through.

The question now was, would Viktor show himself today? His agency no doubt had a hand in sending the three members of the Patriotic Society to Siberia in '26. Had Viktor played any role in the operation? Had he recognized prisoner Jan Stelnicki as Barbara's father? The chronology played out in Michał's head. No, it seemed unlikely that he could have recognized him at the time, for it was some months after the exile that Barbara introduced Viktor to the family. He remembered her speaking of an accidental meeting.

Nonetheless, the secret of his identity was out now. Only Viktor didn't know that his guise had fallen away, that his two brothers-in-law knew his real position under the Imperial Commissioner. So what would keep him away? Would his father recognize him? That would do it. Otherwise, he would show. The thought of him here—eating, drinking, toasting— during such a sweet celebration set Michał's teeth on edge. It was all he could do not to curse his sister for bringing a viper into the family.

The front door opened and Michał and Anna rose from their seats as Wanda and Elzbieta went running. Anna reached for Michał's hand. Hers was trembling. A few seconds later Zofia minced into the room. Michał watched as Anna braced herself a bit, covering her disappointment.

"Still no guest of honor?" Zofia asked.

"Not yet," Anna answered, excusing herself from the room.

"Oh, Anna, if you're going upstairs, tell Iza to come down. I expect she's still fussing about her dress. One day she could care less and the next—oh, I'll never figure her out." Zofia turned and approached Michał. "Jerzy Lesiak was here earlier today, Michał. You were out."

"You saw him?" This was news, indeed. How had that meeting between her and Jerzy gone? Did she deny knowing him to his face? Or—

"Yes," she said simply, her beautiful face smooth and placid. There was a puzzling sort of calm about her. "And he waited about for you a while. When you didn't come, he left this note he had dictated to someone. He can't write himself, you know. I said I would give it to you."

Michał took the sealed note from her. "You—you talked with him?"

"Yes, dear," she said, her expression enigmatic, "we talked."

Michał was fishing for another way to open up this mysterious subject of Zofia and Jerzy when a commotion arose in the front hall, and they turned to see the servants—as well as Iza and Anna—running past, moving toward the front door.

After an absence of four years, Jan Stelnicki had come home.

In the reception room, Iza watched Jan and Anna from a little distance. How they wore their emotions on their sleeves! It warmed her heart to see their happiness. And Michał—he was clearly thrilled to have his father back and to witness life suddenly transform his mother, like the blooming of a long dormant flower. Dressed in a green satin gown that set off her amber-flecked emerald eyes, Cousin Anna fairly glowed as she sat on the sofa with her husband holding her hand, patient with his slow forming answers to questions, so many questions. He was avoiding sober answers to serious questions about his treatment, choosing instead to make little asides and jokes. His captors had done nothing to damage his spirit.

But beneath the joy on Anna's face Iza could read also the surprise and shock. The very sight of Jan Stelnicki touched everyone. It was not the drab brown of the frayed frock coat and trousers that were surely someone else's castoffs. It was that he had aged so, many years beyond the four he had spent as a Russian captive. He went away a hearty, sturdy fellow, a horseman with the swagger of a longtime soldier still in his blood. And he was returned to Anna a ghost of a man, thin and pale, like a chalk drawing left in the rain. The sandy-gray hair was white now, the facial handsomeness still present though the translucent skin scarcely covered the bone structure. His vision had clearly deteriorated, for he seemed unable to focus exactly at first upon the person addressing him. Iza wondered if the daily exposure to bright sunlight on snow and ice hadn't done damage. The oddest thing was, however, that he had not removed his gloves and when Anna suggested he do so, he put her off, saying something about still being cold through and through from the trip.

He took the news that Barbara had married a Russian with a long, silent stare and a nod of the head—but in no time he was joking about his being a *dziadek* and had everyone laughing at his grandfather jokes. Iza realized now why Barbara had managed to be late in arriving: the news of her marriage had to be broken to him first. Anna lighted up, delighting her husband with tales of little Dimitri and Konrad.

Odysseus had come home to his Penelope, Iza thought. This was no less of a homecoming, no less of a love story. She prayed now that Jan and Anna, having spent so many years apart, would still have many more together, that only death—long into the future—would ever separate them again.

Half an hour passed without Barbara's appearance. Michał absently put his hand in his pocket, finding the folded and sealed note from Jerzy that Zofia had given him. In all the excitement he had forgotten it.

He rose now, excused himself and went down the hall to a little room Zofia used to attend to her mail. Closing the door behind him, he took out the letter and broke the seal. It read:

Be advised, Michał, that my comrades have come across information you have been seeking. The firebrands Wysocki and Zaliwski have moved up their little conspiracy. The recent student arrests and disappearance of several cadets precipitates this move. Our sources say that the plan is for the university students to take to the streets, inciting Warsaw's citizens to action. The cadets' objective will be to overtake the Russian garrison and arsenal. At the same time a small group of cadets are to overrun Belweder Palace with the goal of taking hostage the Grand Duke Konstantin. It is a bolder move than we had expected. We think we have a less than a week before the attempt.

Jerzy

"Blood of Christ," Michał muttered aloud, "an uprising and abduction of the tsar's brother?" He had little time to think about it, for a great commotion arose then out in the front hall, and he heard the high-piercing shrieks of little boys. Barbara and the twins had arrived at last.

Had Viktor come with them?

Viktor stood in the hall removing his greatcoat and hat. The boys had rushed ahead and Barbara followed in pursuit. Everyone was in the reception room, it seemed. One of the maids—the younger one—took Viktor's coat and hat and he made his way toward the double doors, slowly, as if he were going to his own execution. He stood on the threshold for a full minute watching the scene, his wife talking to her father, clasping his hand, her mother watching, smiling like a matriarch of a family at last reunited. There were tears all around, excepting the boys and Jan Stelnicki, who was smiling at the twins, dry-eyed.

At that moment, having come from another room, Michał presented himself in the doorway at Viktor's side, and offered a politely stiff hello. Viktor followed his cue, thinking Michał seemed almost surprised to see him there.

"Viktor, come in," Barbara called.

Viktor produced a smile, drew in a breath and advanced.

Later he would not remember the stilted pleasantries of welcoming Jan Stelnicki home and Jan's welcoming him into the family in return. Viktor was struck by the changes in Jan Stelnicki. He was so much older, so frail, so thin. As he reached for his hand, he prepared himself for the moment of recognition. It didn't come—at least he was certain the man didn't recognize him. His blue eyes, somehow paler, seemed not to find him at first and when they did—well, Viktor had the feeling that the man couldn't quite make out his new son-in-law. Dared he hope that he would escape exposure?

At supper Viktor felt fortunate that he was at Anna's end of the table, a good little distance from Jan at the other end. It would have been disturbing to have his father-in-law studying him. When the meal commenced, he noticed that Jan had removed the glove from his left hand, leaving the other glove on. Soup spoon in hand, Jan proceeded to eat his dill pickle soup using his left hand. Even though he was right-handed. Viktor felt a heat come into his face. He knew what Jan was up to. He was taking precautions against calling attention to the gloved hand, the one with the missing index finger.

Sitting directly across from Viktor, Michał watched him with great interest.

And loathing. Viktor had remained very quiet in the reception room, his body stiff, eyes always moving, but at the table he had taken a second glass of wine and started to join in the conversation on a number of mundane subjects. He was well-informed on weather across the continent, particular crops in nearly every nation. Everyone seemed to know not to bring up the politics of those nations. Michał saw him glance—surreptitiously, it seemed—down the table at his father-in-law, a strange intensity in his eyes. He had to have known about the three men

sentenced to Siberia in '26. Had he been heading up
the Third Department then or was he merely one of
many? Perhaps his climb to power occurred later. Jan
Stelnicki betrayed no recognition of him whatsoever
and, true to form, had put aside his shock at finding a
Russian son-in-law, speaking to him quite cordially.
For Barbara's sake, of course. And no doubt, too, for
his grandsons' benefit.

Barbara—was it possible she knew of her
husband's activity in the Third Department? Michał
snuffed the thought immediately. It just wasn't
conceivable. But she must be told. She must be told
soon. He would catch her alone later, before they left.

He glanced down the table, past the twin boys
sitting on the mammoth books, to his sister, who had
hardly eaten at all, had hardly taken her eyes from
their father. On second thought, she was too happy
to spoil it for her. Not tonight.

Part Three

Don't stir Fire with a Sword
—POLISH PROVERB

13

JÓZEF AWOKE TO A VIOLENT shaking. He opened his eyes to see Marcin's contorted face leaning over him. "Józef, wake up! Something's going on. They're rousing the whole floor!"

Józef bolted upright. "What time is it?"

"It's not yet light out."

At that moment the door to their quarters burst open. It was Piotr Wysocki himself. "Your moment's come, Stelnicki! You too, Niemczyk. Most of the others up here are to assemble in the mess hall. You two are to come to my quarters in half an hour. Understood?"

"Project C? " Marcin asked.

Wysocki shot him a look meant to melt. "Thirty minutes!" he shouted and slammed the door behind him.

Józef and Marcin looked at each other.

"Holy Christ, what did I say?" Marcin asked, humiliated.

"Don't worry about it." Józef pulled himself out of bed.

"Well, it could be just a drill."

"Could be," Józef said, "but we haven't had one start this way. And when did you last see Wysocki deign to climb up to our floor? I think it's the real thing."

"Holy Christ." The oath this time was expelled softly and slowly.

As they dressed, Józef replayed in his mind Wysocki's words: *Your moment's come, Stelnicki!* Could it be that his wish has come true—that he was to have some special role in the operation? It seemed so. Why else would he and Marcin be ordered not to the mess hall but to Wysocki's quarters?

By the time he was fully uniformed, currents of excitement and anticipation coursed through his veins. He had been born to do something. Be something. He knew it, had always known it. To hell with music—and Fryderyk Chopin with it! And if his role had to do with the emergence of a free Poland, what better cause could there be? He would gladly die for it. Whatever the outcome, his parents would honor his decision. Hadn't each of them in years gone by risked life and limb for Poland's sake?

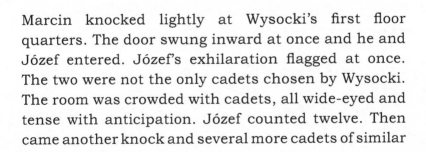

Marcin knocked lightly at Wysocki's first floor quarters. The door swung inward at once and he and Józef entered. Józef's exhilaration flagged at once. The two were not the only cadets chosen by Wysocki. The room was crowded with cadets, all wide-eyed and tense with anticipation. Józef counted twelve. Then came another knock and several more cadets of similar disposition scurried in, Józef's disappointment and irritation increasing with each newcomer.

Wysocki surveyed the silent room, counting heads, it seemed. "All here, I see, and this may be the first time I have not had to call attention."

Quiet laughter. Nervous laughter.

"We have good reason to accelerate our plans. I can assure you this is not a practice, gentleman," Wysocki announced, suddenly serious. "This is the real thing. Project C. And there will be no questions until I've laid it all out. Understood?"

Silence. Nods all around.

"Good! You are eighteen in all, specially chosen."

Only later would Józef learn twenty had been the original number and what had precipitated the early deployment. The two missing cadets had been among six arrested the night before. News, too, would come back that Gustaw's mutilated body had washed up down river. Given time—very little time—the Third Department would paralyze the plans of Wysocki and Zaliwski. They would find things out. Punishment would be brutal. It would likely be the end of the academy. The end of a Polish military. The stakes were enormous.

"You are men—and you are Poles to the heart, yes?"

The response came in one roar: "Yes, sir!"

And so the plan for taking back Warsaw—and Poland—from the Russians was laid out. Wysocki unfurled a large map of the capital and placed it like a carpet in the middle of the floor.

The signal for the commencement of the revolution was to come at seven in the evening. That very evening. A deserted brewery, a wooden structure on Szulec Street, near the Vistula, would be set afire, providing a beacon for those involved at various locations throughout the capital and thus igniting the insurgency. More than 100 students gathered on the south end of the city would ride through the streets calling on the citizens of the capital to rise up. Simultaneously, Wysocki and Zaliwski would lead their cadets, numbering 120, to the Russian garrison in the center of the city, take it by force, attach men to the gates, and seize the garrison's arsenal. The city would be in revolutionary hands by midnight, and those conservative Poles who had acquiesced to Russian rule, some of whom may have been waiting for some vague, more propitious time to throw off the yoke of slavery, would be forced to acknowledge and salute the banner of revolution. This revolution. Not tomorrow's. Today's.

"Now, your faces tell me," Wysocki said, his eyes moving from man to man, "that you wish to know your part in this. It is a special part, you can be certain. The eighteen of you are more critical to the success of this revolution than any other citizen, student, cadet, or officer." He paused for dramatic effect. "For weeks you have been guessing the significance of Project C, yes? Well, had you studied your Latin and Roman history a bit harder, you might have cracked the code. It wasn't so hard.

Latin, Józef thought.

The room grew quiet.

"Sir!" Józef blurted. "You refer to the Roman emperor Constantinus who lived in the fourth century, yes?"

Wysocki smiled. "Indeed, young Józef!—And?"

"And Konstantin is a derivative of the Latin name Constantinus." Józef spoke quickly so no one could steal his thunder. "So our target is Konstantin!"

"Exactly!" Wysocki snapped. "Bravo, Stelnicki!"

Gasps went in waves about the room as the enormity of the task the cadets were being assigned hit home. Then a murmur of amazement followed.

Józef flushed with pride at the compliment and his earlier pique at being merely one of the cadets chosen for the mission evaporated.

Wysocki allowed a full minute of reaction. Józef sensed a thrill running through his fellow cadets. He could hear Marcin at his side muttering "Holy Christ, Holy Christ."

Surveying the intent faces of everyone, Wysocki explained further. "You eighteen are entrusted with the taking of Belweder Palace and the abduction of the Grand Duke Konstantin. Note this, gentlemen: I said capture, as in *safe capture and detainment* of the duke. Assassination is not the object of this mission and it is not to be considered at any cost. Even at the cost of your own lives. Is that clear?"

The cadets nodded in agreement.

"Good! We Poles are not in the habit of killing princes—and we are not going to begin today."

Wysocki now took out another map and laid it over the one of the capital. Józef looked over Marcin's shoulder and saw that it was a detailed map of Łazienki Park—and Belweder Palace. Home of the Grand Duke.

————— ✺ —————

Józef sat at his desk, the late November sky outside the window darkening. He was stealing a look at his miniature portrait of Emilia Chopin, his childhood love, when Marcin came and stood behind him, staring out into the night. Józef dropped the miniature into its velvet pouch, drew tight the drawstrings, and secreted it in the pocket of his coat.

"It's only 6:30, Marcin. What are you looking for? What's gotten into you? We've got half an hour. . . . Are you nervous?"

"Aren't you, Józef?"

"Maybe, a bit."

"Józef, look there. There's smoke!"

"Where? Near the river?"

"Yes, come, look there!"

Józef, still doubtful, rose and moved to the window. He peered over the rooftops of the city and he saw it, dark smoke thickening in the November dusk. As he stared in disbelief, orange flames suddenly flared up from the chosen location as if feasting on a roof of paper maché. "Good God!" he cried, even as the prearranged bells within the school sounded the call to action. "Half an hour off schedule!"

The two cadets grabbed their weapons and rushed out the door.

"Not a good omen, this," Marcin muttered as they clattered down the stairway. "Holy Christ."

————— ✺ —————

A gentleman downstairs to see you, milord," the maid said, quite out of breath from climbing the four flights.

"Thank you, Wanda," Michał replied. Anna, Zofia and Izabel hadn't taken notice of the exchange, so intent were they on peering out the upper story's window in an attempt to see the glow of what must be a great fire down near the river.

Michał excused himself and raced down the stairs. Jerzy awaited him in the front hall, his face grim. "I've seen it, Jerzy. It's that big warehouse by the river on Szulec Street, isn't it? I was just going to lend a hand. You too?"

"No, Michał it's not just a fire." He took in a breath, as if he were about to deliver a reposte in a duel. "It's the signal from the cadets. God help us, but their little revolution has started. And one of their first actions concerns the Grand Duke."

"God's wounds!" Michał felt blood draining from his face. "What do you know?" Michał's concern that his homeland was on the brink of a new tragedy, a new bloodletting, was immediately superseded by his concern for his young brother.

"The students are already pouring into the streets." Jerzy seemed to read in his face his first concern. "As for the cadets we know there are plans for a contingent to attempt to take the garrison."

"And another the Belweder, I would wager?"

Jerzy nodded. "Yes,"

"There's not much the two of us can do against a mob. Except perhaps protect Józef. I must find him. Good god, he's just a boy, and it will kill my mother if anything happens to him. Will you help, Jerzy?"

"Of course, what do you want me to do?"

Michał was already ushering him to the front door. "Go to the garrison to search him out. I'll go to Belweder."

"Michał, I've not met your brother. I don't even know what he looks like."

"Nothing like me. I've got Tatar blood running through me. He's much lighter. You met my father when you came yesterday to see Iza. Imagine him at seventeen—handsome and blond but eyes not so much blue as blue-green."

They were moving down the stairs now—pausing just long enough for Michał to grab hold of his sword and its carriage—and out into the smoke-filled street. "Michał, he sounds like every other cadet, and I can't go checking all their eyes."

Michał stopped and turned to Jerzy, gripping him at the upper arms. "Do what you can, Jerzy! Ask around if you have the opportunity. Call out his name! And—God forbid—if any cadets have—fallen—check for an identification tag." Michał looked hard into this new friend's eyes. "Please, Jerzy, do this for me." He then released him and began sprinting the great distance toward Łazienki Park and Belweder Palace. Instinctively he had put himself in his brother's place, at his brother's age. Had Józef been allowed any choice in the matter, he would choose the palace mission. What better glory?

Jerzy, older by some years, did not keep up and eventually turned off in direction of the garrison.

Just a boy, he had told Jerzy. *Just a boy.* Seventeen, the same age Tadeusz had been when they followed

Napoleon as if he were the Pied Piper. Little Tadek had not come back. This would not end that way. It could not. And for the first time in years—those years of being lost in the mundane everyday goings-on of an estate, years of shutting out hopes for a better day in Poland—he prayed. For Józef. For their homeland.

Belweder Palace was all but unguarded when Józef and the company of cadets came upon it. Grand Duke Konstantin, so sure of himself in his adopted Polish identity, had cut his staff of soldiers to three within the palace grounds, two of whom were posted at the twin guardhouses on either side of the front gates. It was to be an easy operation, Wysocki had bragged, easy enough that he and Zaliwski would be elsewhere, overseeing the more difficult task of overtaking the Russian garrison and seizing the arsenal. The cadet in charge of the Belweder operation was Ludwik Nabielak.

Upon their arrival at the palace, two cadets casually engaged the two Russian sentinels in conversation while the others soundlessly moved in and took hold of them, leaving them bound, gagged, and folded up like grasshoppers, each within his own narrow guard house. The cadets then moved onto the grounds and to their prearranged stations. It was then that they realized that two of the four-man detail of cadets assigned to the garden entrance were missing, somehow lost in the confusion of the premature ignition of the signal fire. "That leaves only you, Marcin and Józef, to take that post," a pale twenty-one-year-old Ludwik Nabielak said. "Is that all right? Can you handle it?"

Before Józef could react, Marcin blurted, "Holy Christ, yes!" Józef nodded. Later he would wish they had argued with their novice leader for a reapportionment that would give them at least one more cadet. Instead, he and Marcin were soon slithering along the side of the palace, ducking low when passing windows of chambers that were aglow with candlelight. They came to the rear of the building and stood, shrouded in shrubbery.

"What to do now?" Marcin asked in a whisper.

Michał looked at his watch. All teams were synchronized to force entry in precisely five minutes. "We look for the guard. You heard Wysocki. There's only one back here. And there are two of us, yes?"

Eyes wide, Marcin nodded. His expression mirrored Józef's own fear. Hugging the wall, Marcin peered around the corner.

"Is he there?" Józef asked.

"I—no, I don't think so."

"This may be easier than we thought. Let's go."

The two turned the corner, pushing through the shrubs and keeping to the wall. When they came to the flagstone patio near the garden door, they paused behind tall evergreens. They watched and listened.

Józef checked his watch. Three minutes. He had been the one to urge Marcin on, but he felt his own heart hammering in his chest now. The enormity of what they were about to do came over him and he froze for a moment. They were about to abduct a prince of Russia, brother to the tsar. His mouth went dry. What consequences might there be? How he had longed to be a part of history—well, he was that now! But what would be the cost? Cold drops of perspiration were collecting at the nape of his neck. He checked the time again, holding his watch with both hands so that Marcin wouldn't see that he was trembling.

"What time now?" Marcin whispered.

"Two minutes."

"Still no sign of the rear guard. Let's go."

Stepping out from their hiding place, the two cadets drew their pistols and stepped onto the flagstones. They moved to the French doors and took stock. The doors had many panes of glass so that if they did not give at first, they would break the glass and release the bolts from inside. They holstered their pistols and waited for the concerted attack to begin.

Another glance at the watch. "One minute," Józef said. They stood stiff and tense peering into a darkened hallway. It was in this pose that they were approached from behind.

"Were you thinking of robbery, soldiers, or something worse?"

The words—thick with a Russian accent—ran like an electrical current through Józef. He whipped around, as did Marcin.

"Don't draw your toy pistols, soldier-boys!"

Józef and Marcin made no move to do so. Józef cursed himself for not having had the instinct to draw at first word. The guard, it seemed, had come out of the manicured maze behind the gardens. He must have been catching a smoke or relieving himself. The white trim of his red uniform glowed in the night. He stood a few feet back from the cadets, his rifle pointed at Józef, but it would take little adjustment to change its site to Marcin.

14

M ICHAŁ RACED ALONG A DARK forested path of the parkland, quickly approaching Belweder Palace. He had been running for at least a mile and had the distinct sense that there was movement elsewhere in the forest. A deer, he thought. He ignored it. Barring a stumble on some root or branch, he would make it to the clearing near the palace in good time. Time enough, he hoped, to prevent Józef from doing something stupid. Time enough to keep him safe from harm. He was well winded when out of nowhere a shadowy figure loomed up in front of him, stiff and silent as one of the ancient trees. There was no time to veer off. He would have to chance the confrontation.

An internal sigh of relief came when he realized the man was wearing neither a Polish nor Russian uniform. Michał stopped abruptly ten paces away.

The fellow blocking the path spoke. "Ah, Michał Stelnicki," he said.

Before the glow of the moon, flickering hauntingly through the uplifted bare branches, could cast enough light for Michał to recognize the face, the voice came home to him. And a familiar bile rose up within him.

Viktor!

Viktor affected a smile. "What is your destination, Michał?"

Michał caught his breath, his spine stiffening. It came home to him with a jolt that his every move was being monitored by the secret police. "Do you ask in your capacity as a bureaucrat of Novosiltsev—or in your capacity in the Third Department?"

While Viktor relayed no surprise at Michał's appearance in the woods, the fact that Michał was already aware of his occupation in the secret police prompted a sickly pallor visible despite the mottled moonlight.

Viktor ignored the question. "We have the same destination, it seems, only to different ends. You're here for Józef, of course. The question is, are you here in collusion with the cadets' plans? Or are you here to dissuade him from partaking in the insurgency?"

Michał thought the truth served him best here. "I'm here to dissuade the cadets from any insurgency."

Viktor scoffed. "Too late for that, my brother. You know as well as I that it's well underway. There's no going back. Is Józef part of the Belweder team? Part of the assassination squad?"

"Assassination?"

Viktor sneered. "You heard me."

"The Grand Duke? They wouldn't assassinate a prince! Take him prisoner, perhaps, but not kill him."

"They want war, Michał."

"It's not what I want!"

"And Czartoryski?"

"Neither does he want war!" Michał rejoined. "You're wrong in thinking he does."

"Your eyes tell me you don't entirely think so. In any case the *cadets* want war." Viktor thrust two fingers into his mouth and let go a whistle.

A signal? To whom? Michał was not about to stay to find out. He started to move forward on the path, expecting Viktor to stand aside. "I'll find out for myself."

In an instant Viktor did the unexpected—he drew his sword.

Michał stopped, still a few paces away. The weapon glinted menacingly in the diffused light. "You intend to keep me from my brother?"

"I do."

"But if I can do something to prevent harm to the Grand Duke— ? You don't believe that's my intention? I assure you, Viktor, that it is."

"I suspect you are speaking the truth. I do."

Michał's stance relaxed and he took a step.

Viktor's sword came up. "Nonetheless, you aren't going to the palace."

Michał stared for a blank moment. If Viktor did believe there was even the slightest chance for the Grand Duke to be spared abduction or harm, why would he hold him back? Why?

Of course! The likely answer came quickly. With the Grand Duke dead, his brother Nicholas' fist would come down heavily on Poland. The seeds of insurrection would be crushed and the power of the

Third Department—Viktor's power—would become limitless. No sooner had the answer come to Michał than Viktor moved into the *en garde* stance, right leg in front, knees slightly bent.

Michał drew his sword from its scabbard and assumed combat stance opposite. His actions were immediate, inbred from his years in the military so that his mind took a moment to catch up. Was this truly happening? Was he about to duel his sister's husband?

He noted Viktor's expression but in the pale, flickering light could not quite decipher it. It seemed a serious smile. This man was not out for play. Viktor might well smile, Michał thought, if he had any indication of how long it had been since he had used his weapon. Michał could not remember the last time.

Viktor advanced. In lieu of the customary word or sound meant to telegraph an imminent attack, Viktor growled, "Poland—Russia's vassal!" as if it were a mean-spirited toast. With that, he effected a wide sweep of his sword over Michał's head.

The action communicated to Michał that his brother-in-law was a show-fighter, one puffed up with his own prowess. In his younger days Michał had dealt with swaggering swains, including fearsome Cossacks, and he had won out over the showiest. But that was years ago and in the bloom of youth. Now, with the hilt in his right hand, his knuckles at 3 o'clock to the blade, he felt the old comfort and a semblance of the old stirring of the blood. The question was, would the strength, the quickness, and the stamina return? Would they sustain him?

These thoughts shot through him like comets with no time to dwell on them, for Viktor lunged at Michał, who stepped back and to the side, a dodge that provided Viktor a moment of preparation for the next attack.

Viktor advanced, his sword coming against Michał's in a beat and then a sequence of beats, sounds foreign to the forest. Michał managed to parry with each strike, searching all the while for an opening to make a proper riposte.

Viktor's attacks continued, lunges and downward chopping cuts against Michał's sword. Michał dodged the lunges and met the downward cuts with the rigid flat of his blade. He felt himself tiring at the worst possible moment—just as he sensed Viktor's confidence, expertise, and energy on the rise.

Did this man intend him harm? Did this man wish to wound him—or worse?

"Like dogs, Poles will bow to Russia!" Viktor said between clenched teeth, his sword striking at Michał's foible, the top third and weakest part of the sword.

The words struck deep into Michał's spleen. A roiling in his blood set him moving, tapping some previously unplumbed reserve of energy. Thoughts of Viktor as Barbara's husband dissipated. Michał thought of Viktor only as Russia incarnate, eternally eager to keep Poland in chains. He sprang into action, and instead of rigid blocking with the flat of his blade or taking the strike with the edge his own sword—both so detrimental to the well-being of his sword—he took to counter-attacking. Energy flowed up from his middle and into the arm that wielded the weapon.

Michał's parries now were followed by bold ripostes. The old methods of parrying were revived, methods learned so long ago. Michał cut off Viktor's attacks with an occasional horizontal sideways blow, as well as with downward cuts, raising his sword from a low position and crossing Viktor's.

Viktor held his ground, but at the corners of his mouth the veneer of sanctimony began to crack.

The beats continued, Michał sharing offensive moves with Viktor as they moved in circular fashion on the forest floor, the swords clanging upon impact and zinging upon caress, providing a contrast to the rustling and crunch of fall leaves underfoot.

When their swords separated, Viktor seized the opportunity to step back, the lame leg dragging a bit as he pivoted to his left, and to pitch forward, executing in a wide swipe a reverse upper cut. Michał drew back his head, suffering only the whining whirr of the blade. Viktor's penchant for show undid him now, for he allowed Michał time and opportunity to bring up his sword at 6 o'clock with such force that Viktor's sword was flung to the ground.

Michał held the point of his sword beneath his brother-in-law's chin. "Don't move a muscle, Viktor. You meant to kill me, yes? Why should I spare you?"

"No—no, truly Michał. I just couldn't allow you to interfere."

"And why is that?" Michał shouted. He was so intent upon vindicating his theory as to why the Third Department would allow a Polish insurgency against Grand Duke Konstantin that he didn't hear the stir and soft crunch of footsteps in the leaves nearby. At his back.

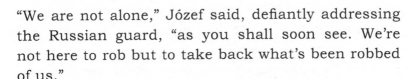

"We are not alone," Józef said, defiantly addressing the Russian guard, "as you shall soon see. We're not here to rob but to take back what's been robbed of us."

"Our country," Marcin interjected.

"Ha!" the Russian laughed. Without taking his eyes, or the aim of his rifle, off Józef, he spit at their feet.

"There are two of us, fellow soldier," Józef said. "You may very well kill one with your rifle, but before you can advance with the bayonet the other will kill you."

"Clever Pole, what would you advise? Release you?" He laughed again, but he was clearly thinking his next move.

"I'd advise you to flee," Marcin said.

"Fool!" the Russian guffawed and spat again. "Carefully take and drop your pistols! Now!"

At that moment a great commotion of shouts and shots arose at the front of the palace. The time had come.

The Russian's eyes grew large and his focus went from Józef to the mullioned door. Perhaps he was seeing some activity through the front windows at the far end of the hall, Józef thought later, but for now the diversion afforded the cadets their opportunity. Józef drew his pistol and fired. The ball entered the Russian's chest jettisoning him back three feet. His rifle slipped away, clattering on to the flagstones. He stayed upright—unsteadily so—staring in dumb shock.

Marcin had his pistol at the ready, but it was clear to all three it would not be necessary. The Russian's feet went out from under him and he sank to the flagstones in a contorted position, his face and eyes visible in the moonlight. Józef witnessed for the first time life leaving one's body. With the swaggering and soldierly attitude gone, the Russian looked to be no older than he. Beneath the bravado he was merely a boy.

Viktor emerged from the trees to see the gates of the Belweder Palace open and unguarded. In striking Michał from behind, Sergei had finally done something right. Viktor had left him at the edge of the park with orders to stay hidden. The less he knew about his real intentions regarding the Grand Duke, the better. On the front portico a scuffle was taking place between cadets and a man he could not identify. It was fully dark now. Did they already have the Grand Duke? Catching the briefest glimpse of their quarry's face in the light shed from a torch held by a cadet, he thought not. They had taken the wrong man.

Viktor could not afford to be seen by one of Konstantin's guards or even by a servant. They were likely to recognize him, and his appearance and intent here had to be known to no one. He dashed toward the right side of the building and cautiously made his way toward the rear, pistol drawn. As he came to the corner of the building, he halted and slowly inched his head around the corner.

A cadet had just left the rear of the palace and was moving in his direction, pushing back shrubbery as he went. Blond hair and serious expression. A boy. For the briefest moment he thought it was Józef, but just as he saw that it was not Józef, he realized that he knew the cadet. It was Józef's roommate, the one who had admitted him to their room and then gone to fetch Józef. The boy would no doubt remember him. Not good.

Viktor drew back and waited.

By the time Jerzy Lesiak came upon the Russian barracks, more than a hundred Polish cadets were already seeking forcible access to the several gates. He watched as the cadets stormed the gates, plying them with shoulders and weapons while calling out "Poland forever!" From inside came the sounds of horses balking and baying amidst the tumult of Russian cries. The cadets fired a few rounds, pressed forward, calling out their hurrahs, and the gates gave way. The structure was surrounded by a wide moat so that the bridges at each gate—now besieged by dozens of Poles—provided only the most difficult egress for the panicking Russian cavalry, cuirassers, uhlans, and hussars. Inside confusion and disorder reigned as each Russian seemed intent on only his own safety.

Jerzy watched as scores of Russians fled across the bridges, dozens brought down by ball and bayonet, others falling into the wide and deep moat, and many more seeking refuge in nearby houses and stables. Jerzy had stood transfixed as the sight unfolded, astounded that the insurrection was truly happening, but now he caught himself, as if waking suddenly, and his first thought was that he wished he had a weapon himself. Then he remembered his promise to Jan Michał.

Jerzy took himself down from the knoll that had been his vantage point and moved quickly toward the meleé. He had one gate in sight. What was he to do, call out Józef Stelnicki's name? He attempted to do so once, but his voice was hopelessly lost amidst the cacophonous cries and clamor. How was he to recognize Józef? He had never met him. It seemed an impossible task.

He caught one cadet by the sleeve. The boy turned toward him, pistol in hand. "I'm searching for a cadet," Jerzy said quickly, allaying the soldier's concern. "Józef Stelnicki, do you know him? Have you seen him?"

The cadet shrugged, shook his head and moved away. The same scenario played out with four more cadets. Finally, a husky fellow recognized the name. "Yes," he said. "Josef is on my floor at the academy."

"Do you know where he is? Is he here?"

"No, he's not. He was one of the ones chosen to go to Belweder Palace. Lucky bastard!"

"To take the Grand Duke?"

The cadet considered Jerzy skeptically, as if considering whether he should provide information. "Yes, sir. And God willing, they did." He gave a little nod and turned away.

Jerzy took stock of the chaotic scene playing about him. There were Russian bodies aplenty—forty or fifty—but he spied not a single cadet laid out. The cadets, fully successful in routing hundreds of surprised and unprepared Russians and in a position to take many of them prisoners, were instead abandoning the barracks and moving down into the city, where Jerzy guessed the student revolutionaries were calling the citizens to action.

It took all he could do to smother his desire to follow the cadets and to focus instead on Józef and the Belweder Palace. Turning about, he started running. Had Michał located his brother?

Józef stood in the main hallway at the rear of the palace. From there he could see that the front doors remained secure. There was a great deal of activity and shots fired in the front of the building, but as yet cadets had not entered. Only he and Marcin had gained entrance, but Marcin had left his pistol with Józef and gone out the back and along the side of the palace to reconnoiter just what was happening at the front. And so Józef stood alone, Marcin's pistol primed and at the ready, his heart hammering to think he was in the home of the Grand Duke with his abduction his mission. Where is Marcin? he worried. He should be back by now. What could be keeping him? And just what is taking place on the front portico and grounds? Had Marcin been drawn into it?

At last he heard footsteps coming in through the garden doors he and Marcin had forced. "It's about time, Marcin, I—"

But as he turned to upbraid his friend, he saw that the person entering was not a cadet. Nor was he in Russian uniform.

"Viktor!"

Viktor showed no surprise. He remained perfectly calm. "Józef, I know what you're here for. Has the Grand Duke shown himself?"

Józef shook his head. Words would not come. What in God's name was Viktor doing here—and seemingly unsurprised and untroubled to find his brother-in-law at the heart of the break-in of the Grand Duke Konstantin's palace.

"Your fellows have the wrong man out there on the portico."

Józef collected himself. "Viktor—we're not here to do any harm to Konstantin. That's the truth."

"But you should, Józef. You must!"

"What?"

"Listen to me, Józef. You want an independent Poland, yes?"

Józef's head swam with conflicting thoughts. He nodded.

"Then if you want a true break with Russia, one that lasts, you must make certain Konstantin doesn't leave here alive."

"You mean for me to kill him?"

"Exactly."

"Why should you—"

"Wish a final break? I've lived here years now. I've

married into your family. I want what's best for your sister. For you. For everyone."

"We're merely to abduct the Grand Duke. That's all."

"To what good end? Listen to me, Józef. Did you kill the Duke's sentinel out there on the flagstones?"

Józef felt a heat coming into his face. "Yes," he said, shunting aside a threatening sense of shame but taking no pride in the killing, either.

"You can't stop there, Józef. Not now. The best thing you can do for your country is kill the duke. One day Adam Mickiewicz will write a poem about you. You'll be a hero. Isn't that what you want?"

"I want a free Poland!"

"Exactly."

Józef heard a door open a great distance down the hall. Quick as lightning Viktor drew Józef into an alcove, out of sight. Viktor stood behind him, gripping him tightly at the shoulders. "That" he hissed, "is the door to chapel of the duke's wife." They listened silently as the footfalls moved away from the fracas at the front portico—and toward them. Viktor peeked down the hall, then drew back at once. "And that is the Grand Duke himself," Viktor whispered, his breath hot on Józef's neck. "This is your moment, Józef. You won't have another. He will bleed as freely as that guard did. Kill him. Do as I say. Kill him for your country, your precious Commonwealth. Do it now!"

By the time Józef drew in a deep, deep breath, Viktor's words ringing in his ears, he realized that his brother-in-law no longer stood behind him. Like a specter he had vanished. But the words reverberated in Józef's head. *Kill him.*

The footsteps were very close now, coming quickly and in time to the thump of Józef's heart.

15

MICHAŁ AWOKE IN A TUMBLE of November leaves. He was alone. He thought his head had been split open. He reached back to the source of pain at the back of his head. It came away with a smudge of blood. It could have been worse, he thought. He sat up. How much time had passed? Minutes? An hour? He had no idea. He stood, intent on getting to the Belweder Palace and to Józef. Dizziness overcame him and he fell to the ground. Slowly, he pulled himself up into a sitting position. He waited for his head to clear. He saw his sword glinting in the leaves, reached for it and employed it to help himself up. Upright at last and with the dizziness receding, he started limping along the path that would take him to the palace of the Grand Duke, praying all the while he would get there in time.

———————⁂———————

Józef stepped out of the alcove and into the path of the man Viktor had assured him to be Grand Duke Konstantin. Although the man's face was already

washed white, Józef, pistol in hand, clearly startled
him and he stopped at once. He was unarmed. Józef
had never seen the Grand Duke and so he quickly
took in this hatless, harried man. The uniform
with its gold epaulettes and many medals was
disheveled as if he had dressed hurriedly. His face
was rather flat and plain as paper but for the graying
muttonchop whiskers. The age did match that of the
duke's—about fifty.

Still, Józef had to make certain. "Your Imperial
Highness," he stammered. The half-statement, half-
question, seemed to have come from someone else.
Addressing him in this fashion sounded ludicrous to
his own ears.

"And you, my young soldier, my young Pole, are
you here to protect me—or to do mischief?" The
Grand Duke's Polish was so perfect it almost made
Józef second guess himself as to the man's identity.
"I can assure you, that I have long been only a friend
to your country. I suggest to you that you help me to
safety . . ."

Józef's would-be captive continued for several
minutes in Polish underscoring for Józef his love
for Poland, its culture, its history, mentioning, too,
his Polish wife. His manner of speech was calm and
deliberate, as if bedlam were not unfolding in front
of the palace, as if there were no pistol pointed at his
heart. The moment felt surreal, as if they were newly
introduced at a reception.

As the Grand Duke droned on, Józef could think
only of Viktor's words. *Kill him*, he had said. It was
not unlike an order. Time seemed to slow but his

thoughts raced faster than words. *Was* it possible that Viktor had Poland's best interest in mind, as he said? He was right in thinking an assassination would preclude a full break with Russia. There was logic in that. It had to be considered. *Kill him.* Even the slow-to-act older generations of Poles would have to respond. They would be drawn into the war effort, like it or not. Józef had asked for a special task in the great effort to break the chains, and God or the fates had delivered him to this place and this time. When he had chosen the military over the music, he could not have imagined himself coming to the very vortex of history in which he now stood. But he was here, gun in hand, the personification of Russia three paces away, a perfect target. He could say to himself that he had no intention of wishing himself the hero Viktor had conjured, but was the claim sincere? Didn't every fellow cadet he knew imagine himself his country's champion?

The duke was studying Józef. "If you're not here to kill me, soldier," he said, "let me pass. And if you are, you have one shot. Do your worst."

This is your moment, Viktor had said. Józef's finger tightened on the trigger. *Viktor*, Józef thought. *Viktor!* His brother-in-law could not know that the secret about his position in the Third Department was a secret no longer—at least not to either of his Polish brothers-in-law. So why would the head of the Russian secret police be urging a Pole to assassinate the Russian Grand Duke? Why? No answer was forthcoming. It was a mystery. But somehow such an outcome would have to work to the Russian advantage. Or Viktor's. *What am I to do?* It was Lieutenant Wysocki's words from early morning that came back to him now: *We Poles are not in the habit of killing princes and we are not going to begin today.*

The Grand Duke had fallen silent. Józef made his decision. "I will not hurt you, Imperial Highness, but you are to come with me. We are to take you into safe custody."

"Custody, my young cadet? What custody could be safe?"

Józef kept the gun pointed at him, motioning for the duke to move. "I can assure you—" Józef stopped in mid-sentence. It was the expression on the man's face that gave him pause. Color had come back into the duke's face during the span of his little discourse, but it was the slightest rise of his bushy right eyebrow and the hint of a curling smile that caught Józef's attention.

And then—too late—Józef realized the man's faded blue eyes had fastened on something other than the gun. Other than Józef.

Something behind Józef.

"Close that window at once, Izabel!" Zofia ordered upon coming into Iza's first floor sitting room at the front of the house. "And the shutters, as well. Are you out of your mind?"

"Mother, there's a crowd coming this way, moving toward the Castle Square."

"A mob is more like it. Do as I say. You're liable to be shot."

"No, come look, Mother. They're students and cadets and a great many citizens, too. Even women. Is it possible we are truly evicting our oppressors?"

"Not likely," Zofia answered, moving toward the casement windows, her intention to close them written on her face. "Don't think a friendly bullet couldn't find your pretty face up here."

Iza turned to plead her case when she realized Anna had entered close upon Zofia's heels.

"Wait, Zofia," Anna said, "I want a look, too."

"It's dangerous, Anna," Zofia said. "To what purpose?"

Anna didn't answer as she stepped to the double casement window, but Iza—and surely her mother—read the concern in Anna's face for her youngest son Józef. Her emerald green eyes moved like searchlights over the crowd. Might he be one of those faces down there? Iza could not read others' hearts, but for herself, she worried also, for Jerzy, the man who claimed to be her father—and for Jan Michał. Where were they in all of this? Certainly not standing immobile at a window. *If only I were a man . . .*

Zofia conceded the argument with a great sigh, and in moments the three were aligned in the window much like patrons in an opera box. Neighbors, too, could be seen at their windows across the narrow street, many cheering their countrymen on. Night had fallen but a number of the crowd carried torches that sent light and shadows playing against the buildings.

"No doubt they're coming to take the Praga Bridge from the Russians," Anna said. "It's essential they hold that point of entry from Russian reinforcements from the East."

"Or from Russians escaping," Zofia added.

The crowd was moving closer, a great chorus of hurrahs echoing off the town houses and the stone façade of St. Martin's Church. It was near the front of the Gronska town house that the masses stopped. An eerie silence ensued.

"Look!" Iza said, her line of vision now directed in the opposite direction, toward the River Vistula and the Castle Square. She drew in a deep breath as Zofia and Anna took in the sight.

What had quelled the crowd were two companies of light cavalry, armed to their visors, their horses breast to breast the width of the street and head to haunches as far as could be seen. They no doubt thickened the surface of the Castle Square like blades of grass.

"They're Polish soldiers." The male voice came from behind the women at the casement. The three turned to see Jan sidling up to Anna now, his face gaunt but glinting with a new energy. "In Russian service, of course."

"I thought you were sleeping, Jan," Anna said.

"Sleep through an insurrection? Not likely."

"Look!" Iza's tone was sharp. She pointed toward the Castle Square. "Two generals from the Polish companies are riding forward to address the crowd."

"They don't look pleased," Zofia said. "I think they're going to try to disperse the crowd."

A murmur ran through the multitude, front to back, as one told the next what was happening. Iza could sense palpable tension. Violence was in the air, thick as the fog from the river.

"Do you recognize them, Jan?" Anna asked. "Are they men you campaigned with?"

"I do. One is Trembicki and the other Potocki. Good men both in days gone by, but I fear they carry water for Konstantin now."

"Stanisław Potocki?" Anna asked, her hand going to her heart.

"The same," her husband said.

"Oh, sweet Madonna, you're right." Anna said.

Iza recalled now that the general and his wife Anusia were dear friends of Anna.

"Their moment of truth has come not on the battlefield," Jan was saying, "but on this very street, Anna."

The two generals drew reins now, some yards from the vanguard of the crowd. "Citizens, students, and soldiers," General Trembicki called. "This insurrection is hereby put down. You are ordered back to your homes, your dormitories, and your barracks. You are to disperse at once if you are to save life and limb and avoid certain arrest."

A discordant muttering grew in volume and ran like the current of a rumbling earthquake through the crowd. Someone in their midst shouted back, "The prisons have been opened. We have freed our own. All unjustly imprisoned!"

"No doubt," Jan whispered to his smaller audience. Iza recognized the poignancy of his remark, and it came as no small surprise that it seemed free of bitterness for his lost years.

"We'll not take their places!" a cadet yelled.

Trembicki stiffened in his saddle. "You are fools to persist in this. Hear me! It is madness. Madness! Those responsible will have to submit to the mercy of the Grand Duke." As Trembicki continued in his reproaches, the crowd grew more and more unsettled and hostile. Demurring voices of men and women alike were prompted to call out reminders of past grievances against Russia and the duke in particular. And those impatient souls at the rear seemed to be pushing the multitude forward.

The speech had not gone well for Trembicki. General Potocki saw fit to speak now. "Halt, now, my good citizens!" he called. "You know me, General Stanisław Potocki. You know that in the past I have fought for independence for our great nation. I have gone gray in the service of our country. Like you, I would like nothing better than to return to the years of our Constitution." As the general detailed his years in service of his country, the crowd stopped their forward movement and gave him their attention.

"But, listen to me, patriots! Listen! It cannot be done in this ragtag fashion. Your venture is doomed. Your chances of success in this are non-existent. The day for freedom will come, but it is not today." These were not words to assuage the crowd and the people set to pushing restlessly forward again. More than a few shouted their disapproval of the general's prediction. Soon the catcalls were going up all around the generals. One man spat upon the ground very near to General Potocki.

Two cadets came to the fore of the crowd. "We know you, General Potocki," one of them said. "Your heart is with us if you listen to it. Say the word and you shall be Commander of the Army! Allow us to join the companies of the men behind you and we shall take the bridge to Praga."

Trembicki scoffed and cursed. Potocki was more sensitive in his reaction but negative nonetheless. Other cadets moved forward and urged Potocki to take command.

"Do it, Stanisław," Jan said through clenched teeth. "Take the chance and weigh not the odds."

Potocki was silent for some seconds, as if considering. The crowd paused, too, as the question hung fire.

"I cannot consider such an offer," he said then. "My duty as a soldier of honor is placed with the Grand Duke."

As these cadets implored Potocki to demonstrate his patriotism, other cadets and citizens became impatient and began calling to the light cavalry behind the generals. "Join us, Patriots," they called. "Will you arrest and kill your brothers? Throw off the Russian bear! Let the white eagle soar once again!"

Such calls grew in intensity. Several cadets bragged of witnessing successes that night against the Russians at different city locations. The generals loudly discounted such boasts but, Iza thought, if they were true, Poland might yet succeed and evict the Russians. She could no longer hear the exchange between the generals and the spokesmen for the cadets. Her attention and that of everyone at the casement window turned to the two companies of light cavalry who seemed to be responding to the cadets with war whoops of enthusiasm. They had made their decision, it seemed, a decision that went against their generals. The soldiers beckoned the people forward, toward Castle Square. The crowd, quickly becoming giddy at the offer, responded with full strides forward.

"Is it a trick?" Zofia asked. "Are they being led to their arrest—or worse?"

"I pray not," Anna said.

"I don't think so," Jan offered. "Look at the faces of the generals. They have lost control of their men. They know it. And I suspect they've been warned by those young cadets down there of what their own refusal to join the revolutionaries will mean to them."

The four at the window fell silent as they watched the crowd press forward. Men and women were so close to the officers' horses that the generals could not maneuver a turnabout and return to their men. Neither could they proceed forward down Piwna Street. The multitude had become a mob.

And then the inevitable occurred. Unruly citizens reached up and pulled Trembicki and Potocki from their horses. Anna gasped, but no one said a word as Zofia shooed everyone back from the window. She had only just closed the shutters when there came the sounds of several shots. Now her arms reached out to either side and she pulled tight the casement windows, latching them securely.

Michał arrived breathless at Belweder Palace. He moved past the open gates and the two narrow guardhouses that stood empty. He paused for a moment. There was no motion to be seen, no sounds to be heard. All was dark but for the pale moonlight that lent a ghostly illumination to the whiteness of the building.

His heart sank. He was too late. What had happened here? He saw a form lying prone and face down on the portico. He hurried toward it and was relieved to see the body belonged to a Russian officer. Kneeling down he turned the body over and recognized the bloodied man at once.

It was General Gendre, a Russian general notorious in reputation. He had been dismissed by the late Tsar Aleksander for graft and other impositions, but Grand Duke Konstantin had taken in the outcast, making him Master of Horse, then general, and finally aid-de-camp to the Duke. All Warsaw—nobles, merchants, nearly everyone—knew him and his wife to be the boldest of swindlers. *Just desserts*, Michał could not help but think, wondering if the cadets knew whom they were killing. Had they mistaken him for the Grand Duke himself? There was a resemblance. Was it murder they had in mind for Konstantin? The outright murder of a Russian prince would tarnish Poland's honor—and bring upon it unrelenting revenge from the his brother, the Tsar.

Michał noticed now that the wounds in the body were many. More than a dozen. Clearly, he realized, the cadets knew their man, knew his reputation and had made a Julius Caesar of him, bayonet blades substituting for daggars.

This was the first violent death he had observed since Waterloo and it made him shudder for a moment.

For him this was the true start of revolution. Where would it lead? Where would it end? He stood and went to the broken front doors. Where was Józef? No one was in evidence anywhere, but he would not leave without investigating. Perhaps a servant remained who might provide information.

Michał walked the long hall, checking the rooms to the right and left. His heels on marble echoed eerily in the empty palace. At the rear, he noticed that the doors to the garden stood open and that one of the glass panes had been broken to facilitate entry. Nothing else looked askew. He decided to walk the entire perimeter of the building before leaving the site, choosing first the left side. It revealed no hint of the attack. He found himself in front again and moved quickly past the body of Gendre and around to the right side of the palace.

He had taken no more than twenty steps when he stopped, his heart accelerating. Another body lay on the ground. He knew by the uniform at once it was that of a cadet. He slowly moved toward it. The boy lay face down. He had received a lethal blow to the head. His czapek lay to the side so that his bloodied blond hair was visible. *Blond hair.* Was this his brother? *Is this Józef?* Tears formed at once in his eyes. His heart tightening, his entire body trembling, he knelt next to the boy, breathed a prayer that it was not his brother, and turned the body over.

Relief flooded through him. It was not Józef. "Thank God," Michał said aloud, "Thank God."

But as he stared at the boy's regular Polish features, obscured at first by the death mask of pain, he did recognize the cadet. It was Józef's roommate. He fought to recall the name. Marek, was it? No, not that. Marceli? No—Marcin, yes, that was it.

His heart went out to Marcin, but his next thought was for his brother. If Marcin had been in on the conspiracy to confront the Grand Duke, he was certain his gut had been right all along: Józef *had* been here at the palace.

He said the briefest of prayers for Marcin even as he stood, determining to return to the garden entrance and move through the building a final time before abandoning the site. On his third step into the dark interior, the toe of his boot struck something, sending it skittering several feet ahead. He halted at once and got down on his knees, his hands sweeping the floor as he crawled along. He found the small item and he ran his fingers over it, much like a blind man would inspect a foreign object.

Michał clutched it in his hand as he stood and hurried toward the front of the palace where the moonlight would allow him to view it. But he already knew what the little treasure was.

On the front portico he opened his hand, exposing his find to the dim light.

Opening the drawstrings and withdrawing the treasure from the blue velvet pouch, he found himself staring at the little portrait on ivory of a startlingly beautiful girl. Emilia Chopin. The little masterpiece was no doubt Józef's most prized possession.

But where was Józef?

16

IZA COULD SIT NO LONGER and left the reception room where her mother, Jan, and Anna sat in near silence, the tension thick as August heat. It was as if they were set upon staying there the night through, mourning a loved one laid out in a casket, as custom dictated. And although she had no doubt many had died this night, there was no body in their town house over which to toast, pray, and sing hymns. She quickly and quietly took the stairs, hurrying once again to her room. Going to the double casement windows, she unlatched them, pulled them open, and threw back the shutters.

The street was empty of souls, Polish or Russian. She could hear the rumble of a crowd calling out their affirmations one moment, their disavowals the next, as one might hear the cheers and jeers coming from an amphitheater. She gauged the gathering to be a few streets away. She looked up now and saw the flickering glow of fire, a newly lighted fire meant as a beacon to beckon people. Turning, she grabbed up her cloak and left her room.

Iza had nearly made it to the front door when she heard her mother behind her. "Izabel, where are you off to? I demand to know."

Iza turned around slowly. Her mother was the only one to ever call her Izabel. "I can't stand merely sitting about. We can't just wait for the morning *Journal* to find out what's happened. What's happening as we sit, stupid and idle, afraid to talk, afraid to know!"

"Izabel!"

"There's a great gathering, Mother. Not a battle but a gathering. A huge fire was set to draw everyone to it."

"Like moths to a flame, no doubt. It's dangerous to be out and about tonight. I won't let you go."

"I'm of a certain age now, Mother, as you've reminded me from time to time."

"Don't be impertinent."

"What is it?" The question came from Anna, who had trailed Zofia into the front hall. "Have you learned something, Iza?"

"Only that there's a great multitude converging, Cousin Anna, and I want to see for myself."

"Where?"

"A few streets away. On Długa, I think."

Anna blinked at the news, the concern for her sons glistening in the green eyes. "Wait a moment, will you, and I'll fetch my cloak. I'll meet you on the portico."

"Anna!" Zofia exclaimed. "Must you always conspire with my daughter against me? Have you both gone daft?"

"Oh, come now, Zofia, what's become of that woman who sent me off across the bridge to escape the Russian lancers?" Anna had paused and focused on her cousin, but as she turned and moved away, she tossed off a deceivingly casual comment. "And you, Zofia, I might add, seated high in the saddle of a Russian lancer's horse."

"What?" Iza blurted, giving no hint to her mother that she had heard the full story from Anna.

"What's this?"

Anna had disappeared, leaving behind a cousin going red in the face. "Nonsense," Zofia said, her voice faltering, "nonsense is what it is."

Having no reason to probe further, Iza smiled and moved out the front door and on to the portico. The sky was aglow with the fire and every so often a cheer went up. What did it portend?

Iza did not have to wait long. When she heard the door open and movements of feet behind her, she turned to see a cloaked Anna along with Jan in his greatcoat. That Jan was coming was a surprise because—although in mind he had grown steadier by the day—he was still a bit unsteady physically. Iza's attention to Jan, however, was eclipsed by another figure who now appeared in the doorway that commanded attention and no little astonishment.

"I'm not to be left behind like some scullery maid," Zofia said, advancing in her shimmering black silk cape as if she were going to a ball at the Royal Castle, as in the old days.

The four moved away from the town house and started for Długa Street.

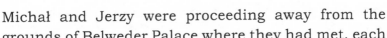

Michał and Jerzy were proceeding away from the grounds of Belweder Palace where they had met, each with his own disappointing news regarding Józef. Their destination was a contained conflagration that seemed to light the core of the city.

They heard the heavy hoof beats of a horse behind them and for caution's sake drew to the side. When they sighted the Polish uniform of a cadet, they were quick to hail him in good Polish so as to let him drop his guard and halt.

"What's happening?" Michał asked.

"We've just about taken the city!" the cadet exulted.

A thrill ran through Michał. Was it possible?

"Just about?" Jerzy asked. "Be more specific, lad."

"The latest news you can hear yourselves down there on Długa Street," the cadet said, nodding toward the glow in the sky. "But what I do know is this: My company has routed the Russian barracks of Sapieha to great success. Other battalions have taken the Stanisław Barracks and Aleksander Barracks. The Russians foolish enough to give fight fell as our soldiers and even some of our citizens descended on them, all crying out, "Hurrah, hurrah!"

Here was a cadet caught up in the bloodlust of his first battle, Michał thought. He had so much to learn, should he survive the next, and the next.

"Polish generals," the cadet went on, "who did not come over and who stood by the Grand Duke were the most foolish of all—and they paid the price."

"What of the Grand Duke?" Michał asked. Only later would he learn that, along with Trembicki and Potocki, who were killed nearly on the doorstep of the Gronska town house, Generals Hauke, Siemiontkowski, and Blummer had all been dispatched as instruments of Russia. "What of Konstantin?"

The cadet shrugged. "Not sure. There were just a few assigned to take him. At first cadets came riding from the palace saying they had slain the duke, but then others claimed he had not been found and that it was the rogue bastard General Gendre who had been killed."

The cadet's epithet for Gendre served to underscore the fact that the cadets indeed knew who it was they were bloodying their many blades on.

"How was he to be taken, as you say?" Jerzy questioned.

"Into custody, sir. Without harm. That was the order. But I've not heard anything." The cadet adjusted his dented czapka on his head. "Now I need to make haste. I daresay every citizen in Warsaw has come out of their homes to hear the news and to celebrate. I can offer the more curious of you a ride if you wish, but I can spare no more time, if you please, sirs."

Neither Michał nor Jerzy considered the offer. They would find their way together on foot.

The cadet made ready to give spur when Michał called, "Wait! Can you tell me if you know my brother? He's a cadet, too—Józef Stelnicki."

The boy paused but a moment before shaking his head. "No, sir. I've heard the name, but that's all. Sorry." Another pause and then he gave spur to his horse.

Michał and Jerzy set off in long strides toward the city center, neither speaking for a while. Michał was thinking of that young cadet, that boy so fired with zeal. In him he saw himself so many years ago when he was one of the Young Guard accompanying Napoleon Bonaparte to Russia. All the cadets had worshipped the little corporal for his acumen in battle and had blindly followed him east across the steppes, confident that his implicit promise to regain for

Poland its independence was legal tender, and quick to cry out at every opportunity, *"Vive l'Empereur!"*

There were battles along the march to Moscow, though bloody and not without significant losses, that served to nourish the young Poles set on excitement, glory, and heroism. It seemed to Michał now, in retrospect, that the issue of independence had been more important to the Polish Old Guard than to the cadets. For the young, the glory superseded everything.

It was after Moscow had been taken that Napoleon revealed himself as incompetent when it came to strategic planning. Oh, he was a great opportunist, especially on the battlefield, where he was the shrewdest of tacticians, but after taking Moscow, with winter coming on and several massive Russian armies loosened and roaming like lionesses eager to protect the pride, what was he to do? He had faltered at strategy and hesitated too many weeks before choosing to abandon Moscow, a choice he refused to call a retreat.

It was then that the Young Guard truly learned what war was. It was more than fighting impossible odds—Russians, Cossacks, lawless peasants—it was sleeplessly nursing wounds, holding back hunger, battling cholera and a half dozen other illnesses that could put you into the earth in a day's time, all the while struggling with an impervious winter there on the frozen, wind-battered steppes of Eastern Europe. War was all of that and it was losing the cadet who rode and fought next to you. It was losing your comrade. And in Michał's case, it was losing his brother Tadek. Where was the glory in that?

And now, in what he saw in tonight's events, in the cadet's demeanor, it was all happening again. Would his father, who had fought to retain Poland's independence more than thirty-five years earlier, harbor—despite renewed hopes—similar misgivings?

Michał knew Jerzy had fought in the infantry years before and considered asking him about it, then thought better of doing so. Not now, he figured, but another time when his thoughts were more settled, when he had had time to consider the wisdom of this insurrection.

He broke the silence with a question on a different matter altogether. "Jerzy, you loved Zofia once, did you not?"

Jerzy turned toward Michał, breaking stride a bit, his facial expression barely discernable in the dimness. Michał couldn't decipher a frown from a smile. When Jerzy didn't answer, he said, "I'm sorry, of course it's none of my business."

Jerzy spoke now as if he hadn't heard Michał's apology.

"Zofia was a woman like none I had ever encountered. The River Vistula washed her up near Kosumce, my village on the right bank. Grandfather and I had come down to the marshy bank to witness a terrible sight—lifeless bodies among charred and broken bridge planks and beams floating by. It was All Souls Day, a fitting day you might say, the day the Russians attempted to invade Warsaw by way of the Praga Bridge. Zofia somehow survived a fall from the bridge, and as the Vistula's current took her for those twenty miles, she held on for dear life to the corpse of a Russian soldier. It was a miracle. Grandfather and I took her home where he and Mother attended her for weeks—until she was well."

"I see."

"Everyone in our village is light-skinned and blond. She was like a goddess with her olive skin, dark hair, and dark Tatar eyes. And she had such life, Michał. She glittered with life. I carved figures from linden wood and she took a liking to them. Called me an artist. That made me feel so proud. Like I mattered. To have a beautiful noblewoman compliment me so."

"She was older?"

Jerzy waved his hand dismissively. "A bit."

"You were smitten."

"She had me teach her how to carve."

"You were both smitten."

I would have given anything for her to stay, but it wasn't in the cards. She had been used to a life so contrary to mine. I was—am—a peasant. I had nothing to offer her."

"And you never saw her again—until the other day."

"Oh, but I did, years ago. When I was a young soldier I searched her out here in Warsaw." Jerzy paused, as if savoring the memory. "Zosia—"

"Zosia? She lets no one use that diminutive."

Another dismissive wave. "She allowed me. On that occasion she also allowed me—how shall I put it?—a soldier's sendoff."

Michał gave a conspiratorial little laugh.

"But it was bittersweet because she made me promise not to attempt to see her again."

"You stayed true to that?"

"I did—but . . ."

"But?"

"When we met the other day, alone, she told me that some years later she had come to the village to see me. To tell me she hadn't forgotten." Jerzy's voice weakened now. "She had been in a closed carriage and as it approached my cottage, she heard my cousin call to her daughter, Zosia. She assumed I had married and that little Zosia was mine."

"Another Zosia?"

"Yes. Ah, the little pranks life plays on us, Michał. Fortune's wheel is ever turning. Zofia had the carriage turn around and go back to Warsaw."

"Sweet Maryia and Józef."

Jerzy abruptly stopped and turned to Michał. "I can remember the day. My cousin and her child were visiting, and when I came around to the front, they were mesmerized by a nobleman's coach that had stopped. It was raining. A nobleman's coach did not come to our village often, I can tell you. I thought perhaps it was stuck in the road, but as I ran toward it in the increasing rain, it lurched forward and began to move quickly away. I stopped and through the rain I—I saw a face at the window. It was blurred by the raindrops, and it was there but a moment before the shade came down. I didn't guess . . . if only . . ."

"You didn't know it was—"

"No, curse the devil! How could I? Fortune is a giver and taker." Jerzy started to walk again.

They went a full street in silence. Michał felt very awkward now for himself and this new friend. "You never married—after?"

"No."

"You loved her very much."

They were close enough to Długa Street now so that a cheer punctuating someone's speech nearly drowned out Jerzy's barely voiced reply. Michał was nearly certain that he said, "I do, still."

17

GUN IN HAND, VIKTOR STOOD in the Imperial Commissioner's office looking down on Kanonia Square. There was no General Nikolai Novosiltsev to berate him now. He had vanished at the first scent of trouble —most likely from the capital, most likely from Poland. In making the slow, jarring climb to the top floor —his last climb—Viktor did not have to face being humiliated about his lameness, for every floor of the five-storied headquarters building seemed deserted. Viktor had just come up from the Third Department headquarters in the cellar where he had dismissed his men. He suggested that they find Konstantin's forces and align themselves with the Grand Duke. This suggestion came easily off the tongue even though he could not be certain Konstantin was even alive. Had Józef—or some other cadet—killed him? He prayed so. The mystery would be answered in short order. He cursed himself now for not having waited at the Belweder for the outcome, but he had run the danger of being recognized by Konstantin or one of his men—or being challenged by other cadets. He could not hope to kill them all, as he had Józef's roommate.

Kanonia Square below was aglow with torches borne by people streaming towards Długa Street. Events had moved fast, much faster than he had imagined. The people had joined the cadets' insurgency with unexpected enthusiasm and resolve. Russians had always underrated the Poles, just as the Turks had at the Battle of Vienna. Here was more modern proof. He wondered if his men would find the Russian forces. Their chances of getting out of the city otherwise were dicey, indeed. Chances were that by morning the city would be in Polish control, run by a mob, and sealed up like a tomb.

Viktor turned from the window and caught his reflection in the tall wall mirror behind Novosiltsev's massive desk. *What am I to do?* Whether the Grand Duke was dead or not, Viktor had not prepared himself for this. He could not stay in the city while it was under Polish rebel control. It would be too dangerous, for his position in the Secret Police had been found out. He should have killed Michał, but his brother-in-law had somehow already known about his occupation. How had that transpired? Had Józef known, too? How? Yes, he could have killed Michał, but if found out, any chance of holding on to Barbara and the boys would be destroyed.

He could spend no more time with conjectures and regrets. He must consider the options now. They were few, he realized. It would not be long before the insurgents—informed by some former captive or even one of his own spies turning coat to save himself— swarmed into the building to free the prisoners in the makeshift dungeon below, looking thoroughly, too, for their Russian captors and inquisitors.

Focus, he told himself. *Focus!* He had come up here to search for the file Novosiltsev kept on him. It was incriminating stuff and in the wrong hands would mean certain execution. He set the gun down on the desk and began rifling through the drawers looking for the folder he had seen one day in the Imperial Commissioner's hands. He knew that it existed, and yet it was not here! At that moment he came across the folder on General Aleksander Rozniecki, and an idea began to form in his mind. It could be useful. Very useful. He held on to it.

Viktor expelled a sigh of frustration. *Where the hell is my file?* Was there time to restart his search? He had no choice. At that moment something caught his ear and his head jerked up, his every nerve on alert. A faint metallic noise pushed all thoughts away. Viktor stared—unblinking—at the office door. The doorknob was slowly turning. Viktor swallowed hard. There was no other exit to the room. He dropped the Rozniecki folder on the desk and retrieved his pistol. He leveled it at the door. He waited.

A long moment passed. The person entering was taking great care. In moments he became aware that the visitant was a woman in a red cloak and red hat. And then he realized it was Larissa, his one-time mistress. The woman who had come to Poland because of him. The woman he had abandoned after falling in love with Barbara.

She looked up, surprised to find someone in her superior's office, and surprise transitioned quickly into alarm when she saw—in silhouette against the window—someone with a pistol aimed at her. She screamed.

"Quiet!" Viktor commanded.

"You!"

"I could say the same, Larissa." He placed the pistol on the desk next to the Rozniecki file. "You didn't go with Nikolai?"

Larissa stared at the desk a beat before returning her gaze to him. She shook her head.

"Why not?"

"He didn't offer," she spat out distastefully, "that's why."

"He thought only of himself?"

"He's a man, no?"

"What brought you here at this hour?"

Larissa nodded toward the desk. "He keeps a wooden box in his top right hand drawer."

A lift of Viktor's eyebrow posed the obvious question.

"Petty cash," she replied, at once embarrassed and defiant.

"Ah, I see. And what are you clutching so tightly?"

"A satchel from my office—a few of my personal items along with paper, pens, and ink." And then in a rush of words: "And you? What are you here for?"

"My file," Viktor said. "I can't find it. You must know where it is, Larissa, yes?"

"I'm not certain he kept one on you, Viktor, in

keeping with your desire to be anonymous. Are you still being anonymous?" Larissa's smile harbored a sneer. "What's the matter—afraid of being fingered by the insurgents, Viktor?"

"It's something you should think about, too." Was she lying about the file? As the commissioner's secretary wouldn't she know about all the files? Larissa could be a cool liar.

"I expect I'll manage. And you—your Polish wife will see that you are well protected, yes?"

Larissa's comment cut him before he could muster a masked expression.

His pause raised a second suspicion. "What is it?" she asked, "something wrong with your wife? . . . Oh, my God, she doesn't know about you, does she?" And then, in a near scream: "Does she?"

Viktor scoffed and pulled up from bedrock his deepest voice: "Of course, she does!"

"Liar! She does not. And now you're in quite a pickle, yes? I imagine she probably comes from a household full of likely insurgents."

The truth in her statement cut to the quick. Viktor angrily pulled open the desk drawer and withdrew the hand carved box from the Tatras. He held it out to Larissa. "Take it," he said.

Larissa did not hesitate to move forward and take it from him. She fitted it into the arm that clutched the satchel, her eyes searching his. "An unlikely end, this. Isn't it, Viktor?"

"It's hardly an end, Larissa. Hardly that. The Poles are a lost race."

"You don't understand, do you? What is it with

men? I meant *us*."

"Oh," Viktor said, although he had known exactly what she meant. "Take care, Larissa."

"I will." Larissa's chin came up a bit. She paused, as if assessing him. "You don't think you love her, do you?"

Viktor stared, too angry to speak.

Larissa waited two beats, turned, and moved toward the door. Suddenly, she halted and pivoted, facing him, her red lips a crooked line of contempt. "Viktor, you aren't capable of loving someone." She turned away again.

"Larissa," Viktor called, even before he knew for certain what he was going to say or do next. He picked up the pistol, his finger pressing lightly against the trigger.

Larissa whirled around, a blur in red, her expression hard and questioning. Her steel gray eyes darted to the gun. A shadow passed over her face.

Viktor paused. He heard her take in a deep breath. It would take but seconds for him to lift it and take aim.

"Well?" She had sensed his temptation—and his indecisiveness.

"I'm sorry, Larissa."

Larissa had not so much as blinked. "Don't worry, Viktor. I'll manage just fine. I hope you do, too." She forced a smile, spun about and passed through the doorway.

Viktor forced her from his mind at once. She had been right: he was in a hell of a pickle. What was he to do? He could have killed her there and then, he thought, knowing Larissa might well relish telling Barbara about his position in the Third Department. But for tonight, at least, self-preservation was her main objective. Besides, Barbara's brothers would probably beat her to the punch. How they would enjoy exposing him as a leader in the Third Department!

Focus! It was unlikely that Michał would have the chance to see his sister this night. Viktor knew that he should be the one to break the news himself. His stomach tightened. A simple apology would not wash with Barbara. He girded himself for a scene. A terrible scene.

Focus! If he was to stay in Warsaw and wait out this foolish—and no doubt ill-fated—insurrection, he knew he would have to do it in hiding.

He picked up General Rozniecki's file. This would be his ticket to a short term underground existence. The folder held everything he needed to claim sanctuary with Rozniecki, the Polish Chief of Police—Chief of Spies!—who had been acting in collusion with Russia's Third Department for years. Viktor had never liked Rozniecki, but what did that matter? He would be his ally—even if he had to coerce him with a file full of the most ghastly material.

As for his own file, he had no choice but to abandon the quest. He turned to exit the office, pausing now a moment to check the status of the square below. There were fewer people now moving through the square and toward a torch-lit Długa Street, where some major gathering was taking place. Leaving the building should pose no problem. As he started to turn away, a flash of red below caught his eye. Larissa's full-length red cloak and red bonnet stood out like bloodstains on the square, even amidst the activity. She was not moving. She had stopped to speak—in a very animated manner—to a small group of Polish cadets. They listened intently as she spoke, gesticulating now toward the building that housed the Office of the Imperial Commissioner. *This building!* She kept pointing down and Viktor knew at once she was telling the Poles of the prisoners that awaited delivery from the cellar dungeon.

"Damn her," Viktor cursed. "God damn her to hell!"

And suddenly he could see her face upturned, her hand moving up, too, finger extended, as she pointed at the very windows of General Nikolai Novosiltsev's office. The cadets glanced up now. Viktor felt as if her finger had sent a bolt to his heart. Here was a woman who held a grudge and knew how to bide her time before venting it. He backed away from the window and into the wall so suddenly that he dislodged the huge mirror which fell forward onto the desk, crashing and breaking into hundreds of shards and fragments.

Viktor took in a deep breath. He knew instinctively that momentarily the cadets—and perhaps some citizens, too—would be rushing into the ground level. And Larissa would be walking slowly away, a smug look on her face. Perhaps across the square she would find a vantage point from which to watch his arrest. That is, if he wasn't executed on the spot.

Clutching the file and the pistol, Viktor limped from the room. Logically, the cadets would be using the stairway at the front. He made his way through a series of rooms now, praying that she had failed to mention there was a rear servant's stairwell that dated back to when the building was a single residence for the priests of Saint Jan's Cathedral.

Damn, Viktor cursed as he painfully made his way down the stairs. *My first impulse was the correct one. Apology be damned. I should have shot her!*

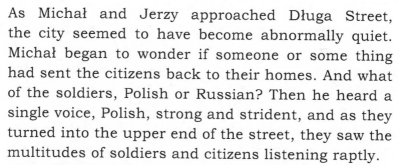

As Michał and Jerzy approached Długa Street, the city seemed to have become abnormally quiet. Michał began to wonder if someone or some thing had sent the citizens back to their homes. And what of the soldiers, Polish or Russian? Then he heard a single voice, Polish, strong and strident, and as they turned into the upper end of the street, they saw the multitudes of soldiers and citizens listening raptly.

A white-haired general was detailing military details as he knew them. The city had been taken, he assured the masses, all but for a small section in the southern part of the city where fighting with Russian soldiers still went on. Intent on finding Józef, Michał pushed on through the crowd, choosing the small pockets where he observed cadet uniforms. Jerzy followed, occasionally pulling at Michał's sleeve to point out some blond cadet who fit Józef's description. Michał would look, shake his head, and they would move on.

Michał noticed that the citizens were well armed. No doubt the city's arsenal had fallen. The general began talking about how certain Polish officers had seemed to know little of the cadets' plans and had sided with the Russians, thus forfeiting their own lives. A young man then took over as speaker, tearfully telling of how he had witnessed prisoners freed from the Franciscan prison. A prisoner himself who had been freed from the Carmelite prison spoke, too, and so it went, with speakers changing every few minutes. That holy places had been taken over by the Russians recently for such evil purposes incensed Michał, but another realization was slowly forming in his mind: that no one speaker seemed to have taken control of the occasion, this historic insurrection. That—and the apparent ignorance of good Polish officers regarding the plot—spawned worry that this insurrection had not been fully thought out. Not carefully enough, at least.

Praying he was wrong, he put off such thoughts and concentrated on finding Józef. They came to the far edge of the crowd without a sighting of his brother.

"Look," Jerzy said suddenly, "across the way! It's Iza and Zofia."

Michał's eyes followed the direction of Jerzy's finger. Iza and Zofia stood some twenty yards away, their eyes sweeping the crowd. And then he saw, a little behind them, his parents. His heart dropped within his chest. What was he to tell his parents about Józef? His father was pale but he seemed caught up in the speaker's plan to wrest from Praga the contents of the arsenal there. He saw now that his mother's eyes were constantly moving, searching, like those of an eagle watching for the return of her fledglings.

Jerzy started to forge a path through the crowd when Michał's hand gripped Jerzy's upper arm.

"Come, Jerzy. Let's go." The two retreated in the direction they had come.

When they were clearly out of range, Michał turned back to Jerzy. "Please help me search further. There was fighting in Bankowa Square. Let's try there. I can't face my mother without news of Józef. Even if it's bad news."

"But I don't understand, Viktor," Barbara said. "What is it you're doing?"

Viktor had his back to his wife, who stood in the open doorway of the bedchamber. He was rifling through drawers and tossing things helter-skelter into a valise. He paused momentarily, drew in a long breath, attempting patience. He would not raise his voice. The last thing he needed was for the twins to wake up. "I explained to you, Barbara Anna, that there's a little revolution going on out there and it's gotten out of hand, more than anyone expected."

"I knew that before you arrived. There was fighting just below on the street. But why must you leave? This I don't understand."

Viktor placed his extra pistol on top of the clothing and snapped closed the bag. Turning, he approached Barbara. "It's very likely that the Grand Duke has been assassinated and that will incite the Poles to more violence. It's already dangerous for me. Truly dangerous."

"Why is that? Your job at the Imperial Commissioner's?"

"Exactly. Most likely Novosiltsev is already close

to Russian soil."

"So? Surely you cannot be blamed for your work on his accounts, can you?"

Viktor's eyes met Barbara's, transmitting a truth he had not intended.

"What is it, Viktor?" Barbara pressed. "You're more than an accountant, is that it?"

"It matters little now."

"What is your position that makes things dangerous for you? I've wondered how we could afford an apartment such as this. You must be quite high up, yes? Tell me. I demand to know."

"The less you know, the better. There will be men looking for me. If you have no information, you can't tell them anything."

"Oh, but they'll tell me something about you, won't they? What will they say? Have you swindled money? Is that it?"

Viktor set down his valise. Of course, she was right. It would be cowardly not to say something himself. "They will tell you . . ."

"What, Viktor? What?"

"They will tell that I have worked for the Secret Police." There—the long hidden truth was out.

Barbara took several seconds for his statement to register. "You're not one of them, are you?" She smiled oddly, as if at a humorless joke, for the thought was too ridiculous. However, her face reflected a mind quick enough to assemble a hundred hints from their past life together that lent it credence. She was taking in his face, too, and his intensely serious expression made for the coup de grace. Her hand went to her mouth. "Oh, my God in Heaven!"

"Don't go off on one of your ravings. Not now. It's my job and it's put food on your table and provided nice things for you and the boys."

"But the Secret Police—my God! How they have tortured us Poles! How many have they sent to dungeons or to die in the cold North? How many have they killed outright? And you, Viktor, you are part of this?"

"I am not like that," Viktor said.

"What are you like, then? You are not the husband I thought you were, the one who would hold me in the mornings. My God, who are you?"

"I'm your husband, Barbara Anna and father to our children. I love you and the boys, you know that."

"And yet you leave each morning and go about persecuting my neighbors, my countrymen? How can this be?"

He shrugged. "I must go, Barbara. There is a good deal of money in the top drawer of the dresser."

"Money! What do I care for money when I find that my life has been a sham!"

"Nevertheless, you will need it. I'll send more when I can. This little revolution will be short-lived. I will return when order is restored." Viktor picked up his valise and moved past Barbara and out of the bedroom.

"What makes you think we will still be here?" Barbara called.

Viktor paused and turned about. "Ah, actually, I think it would be best if you take the boys and stay with your parents at the Gronska town house."

"I'll go where I like and take the boys with me."

Viktor was at the door. "Keep them safe, Basia."

"Ha! Oh, and don't worry about the safety of your precious Grand Duke!"

Viktor turned about. "What do you mean? Why did you say that?"

"Because he escaped the assassination attempt, that's why. His bodyguards paraded him right down this street and he's no doubt out of the city by now. Good news for you, yes, that your fellow Russian scoundrel lives?"

Viktor closed the door behind him without a final goodbye.

Fear was a new emotion for Viktor and he didn't like it. As long as he was on the street, he ran the risk of being confronted by cadets or any of the populace that had been roused to take up arms. He moved as quickly as he dared without appearing suspicious. At last he came to the correct avenue.

Limping, Viktor lugged his valise through a street dark as pitch and made his way up the front stairs of General Rozniecki's city mansion, lifted the brass knocker and brought it down hard against the oak door several times so that the sound reverberated within. He waited, knocked again. He put his ear to the door. He could hear someone moving about. He pounded now at the heavy oak. He heard a faint metallic sound and suddenly became aware of a glint of light at a peephole in the door. An eyeball.

He stood back from the door so that he might be seen. "I am Viktor Baklanov," he shouted. "I demand that you open at once."

A long pause ensued. At last he heard the sounds of bolts being unloosed. The door opened slightly and a face appeared. Viktor pushed open the door and entered, forcefully knocking aside the man who had opened it. A single candle at a nearby side table did little to light the interior. The place looked and resonated like a vault.

"Where's General Rozniecki?"

"Gone," the man said, closing the door, but not without a wary glance at the street.

"Gone where?"

The man turned to Viktor, who recognized him as Bartosz, the general's most trusted servant. It was Bartosz, a Pole and the go-between who supplied the payroll for Viktor and his men. He was a tall, sturdy man in his forties. The forehead of his roundish face had suffered a wound that extended up into the balding front of his head. "He escaped."

"Escaped?"

Bartosz nodded. "From a gang of hoodlums—soldiers and students mostly. They came in knocking things about and looking for the general."

It made sense, Viktor thought. The man was anything but discreet about his darker dealings as Chief of Police. Pole or not, he would be a prime target. "How did he manage to get away? I see that you did not."

"He took to his hiding place and when they left, he commandeered a coach and bribed the driver to allow him to drive. As far as I know he escaped wearing the coachman's cloak.—Has the whole city been given over to the young revolutionaries?"

"Much of it has. But some of those fools rising up are old fools. At any rate, it should not last long. The Grand Duke has escaped and he will no doubt rally his forces to suppress it."

"I see."

The comment showed no bias and Viktor could only wonder whether Bartosz might sympathize with the rising. "You didn't run?"

"No, I would have nowhere to go."

"I don't intend to run, either. Tell me, Bartosz , where is this hiding place the general had?"

Viktor was led to a small room at the east end of the sprawling mansion. As Bartosz lighted several tapers, Viktor took note of a large desk with a cushioned leather chair behind it and a considerably simpler and less comfortable wooden chair in front. The only other thing of consequence was a very large tapestry of peacocks in a garden setting. It was framed in gold-painted bamboo and took up much of the wall that in most rooms would have housed the fireplace. Viktor recognized General Rozniecki's utilitarian purposes here. He had no doubt that this room was where the general received reports from his own spies and interviewed suspicious characters. It was best to keep them in a cold place and on a hard chair. And no doubt the oversized peacocks—with the eye-shaped markings on their feathers reminiscent of the evil eye—lent an unsettling aura to the room.

Bartosz approached the tapestry, knelt, and adjusted something at the bottom of the bamboo frame. Viktor heard a faint click and watched as the frame moved forward on vertical hinges. Behind the frame the gray stucco wall seemed quite ordinary— until another adjustment beneath a floorboard and a gentle push from Bartosz caused a stuccoed door to push open, revealing another room. The servant took two tapers, handed one to Viktor and led the way. Stooping to make his way through the doorway, Viktor followed, passing through the brick fittings of what had once been the fireplace for the office. Inside he stood to his full height, took stock, and whistled as he perused the amenities. Although it was windowless, the large room housed a bed, several chairs, a table with silver candelabras, and a well-stocked bookcase situated near a wine cupboard, equally well-stocked.

"Your master is a cautious man, it seems, Bartosz. Clever and cautious. So the room finally served its purpose."

"Oh, it's been doing that for years," Bartosz muttered.

"What do you mean?" Looking around now, the room and its contents—a mussed bed, empty bottles, dirty plates, open books—did appear to have been used often.

Bartosz cast his dark eyes on Viktor, his expression indicative that he may have said too much. But he thought for a moment, gave a little shrug as if to allay his second thoughts, and moved back to the door, motioning Viktor forward. He pulled closed the framed tapestry, then pushed the door closed. He opened now a small hinged window in the door. Viktor had failed to notice it before. Bartosz pulled a nearby chair over. "If you take a seat, you will understand, my lord."

Viktor sat. He looked through the window and realized he could see into the other room through two peepholes.

"You are looking through the center eyes of two of the peacock feathers."

Another whistle. He shot a questioning glance at Bartosz.

"One can also hear fairly well what goes on in that room," Bartosz said. "The general had Macrot, his secretary of spies, sit exactly where you are sitting. He would transcribe the conversations that were carried on in the other room."

"Ah, so walls do have ears. And if someone incriminated himself, it became a matter of record."

Bartosz began to pile the dirty plates on the table. "While that no doubt happened, my lord, the primary use of this little arrangement was to cheat his own spies. You see, when his mercenary spies came to him with information, he would have Macrot here record the content of the reports. Then, when the spy would be led to another room for libation, the secretary would emerge from behind the tapestry and provide the general with the document, one that he had predated, of course."

Viktor looked at Bartosz with undisguised astonishment. "Then the general would use that to prove to the spy that the information was old news— stale and worthless, yes?"

"Exactly. I believe he took great enjoyment in cheating his own spies."

Viktor remembered several instances when his

men had come back to him with just such a story of Rozniecki and his mysterious spies. An intense—but impotent—anger simmered inside him.

Bartosz took notice. "No honor among thieves, as they say, my lord."

"Or among spies apparently, my friend. What's become of Macrot?"

Bartosz stood with a pile of dishes. "When the rebel patrol came in to find the general and take his personal papers and files, Macrot and several of his satellites fired upon them. It was a stupid thing to do and they paid for it. Shot dead they were."

Viktor noted the off-handedness of the remark and could make nothing of it. Did Bartosz harbor some sense of allegiance to the Polish cause? He moved to a more comfortable chair and sat thinking after Bartosz had carried the dishes out of the hidden chamber.

General Aleksander Rozniecki, as Chief of Police, had been his superior, of course, but Viktor had considered himself lucky to report directly to the Imperial Commissioner, General Nikolai Novosiltsev. As despicable as Novosiltsev was, at least he had not turned coat on his own country. Rozniecki had served in the Polish army forty years, even commanding a brigade under Napoleon—supposedly with honor— but under the imposed Russian government of recent years he had been corrupted into a tool of tyranny, one who became known for swindles, bribery, extortion. Those who dared oppose him found themselves in prison. Viktor recalled an accusation of poisoning, but the proceedings were somehow obviated. No little wonder there. After all, the general was a close friend of Grand Duke Konstantin.

Viktor took in his surroundings. This will do, he thought. This will have to do. After all, the little cadet insurrection could not last long. A few days? A week? Sooner than would have been the case had the Grand Duke been killed, for the news would have to reach the tsar before retaliation could take place. With Konstantin alive, he would no doubt move swiftly with his Russian soldiers and those Polish soldiers who knew their own interest and stayed true to him. In the meantime, he would be safe here.

He thought about Barbara and the boys. He hoped she had the good sense to get them to Zofia's. He sighed heavily at the thought that they were to be separated, however long it might be. Somehow, he would win back her heart and have his family again.

He could hear Bartosz returning now. He could manipulate the servant, make him provide his meals, discourage any would-be intruders. He would bully him if need be.

Viktor watched Bartosz closely as he stepped into the hidden chamber. The question was, could he trust this Pole?

18

30 November 1830

ICHAŁ CAME TO STAND IN the reception room of the Gronska town house. Dawn had broken. A terrible mixture of fear and hope were on the faces that turned toward him now, the image of Józef emblazoned on every one of them: Jan, who had already lost one son in the Napoleonic debacle; Anna, Józef's mother, who had taken a sacred vow to hold her son back from the military; Iza, whose face showed both concern for young Józef and compassion for his parents.

Michał cleared his throat, wishing he could bring these faces to life, knowing that he could not. "We— Jerzy and I—have searched through the night . It has come to naught.—Józef is missing."

"Missing?" The word was little more than a breath from Anna.

"You found nothing?" Jan asked, his gloved hand tightening on his wife's hand. "Nothing?"

Michał nodded. "We know that he was one of the detail that made the attempt at the Grand Duke's."

"Sweet Jesus," Anna hissed.

"He was to kill him?" Jan demanded.

"We don't know that, Father." Michał had called Jan *Father* for years without a second thought. After all, Jan had adopted him, treated him as his own, loved him unconditionally. But the old pain of having to face him after losing Tadeusz—Jan's natural son—on the trek back from Moscow rose up in force. It was a guilt he had tried to put to rest, and yet here he was forced to deliver bad news about Jan's youngest son, a mere boy.

"What do you know?" Jan asked. "What of his comrades? The others?

"His roommate, Marcin . . ."

"Yes? You found him?"

Michał couldn't get the words out. His expression, he knew, told the story.

Iza moved from her chair to sit at Anna's feet. Anna's free hand reached for hers. "What of the hospitals?" Anna asked.

"We've checked, Mother. We'll check again later." Michał moved toward Anna and stood awkwardly before her. "You're not to think the worst, Mother. You must not. He is a Stelnicki, you know."

"So was Tadeusz," she said, "my little Tadek."

Michał's heart tore at the profound sadness in her voice.

Anna's head came up at once now and she gave it a little shake, the silver in the fading auburn glinting in the new light coming in from the window. "No, I won't think the worst, Michał." She brushed back at an unshed tear and attempted a smile. The voice became stronger, too. "None of us will, do you hear?"

Jan squeezed her hand even as he looked up at Michał. "Michałek," he asked, "how goes it in the city?"

His stepfather used his diminutive and for that Michał could have kissed him. For now at least, the pain and guilt ebbed away.

Michał pulled up a chair, collected himself, and spoke of the events of the previous night as he had witnessed them, taking care not to mention his finding Józef's miniature portrait of Emilia Chopin on the floor of the Grand Duke's Palace. Neither did he mention his altercation with Viktor Baklanov—the revelation of his brother-in-law's true identity would keep for another time.

"We heard something from the speakers on Długa Street," Jan said. "But how do we stand now?"

"Plans have been put into place for the defense of the city. Detachments now hold the garrison at the bridge, not far away, and wagons have crossed the bridge to Praga to carry back ammunition from the great armory there. The Russians guarding it were forced to retire not only by our infantry but by a significant segment of the populace of Praga."

"The people are ripe for this, it seems," Iza said. "And in the city itself, Michał?"

"The enemy occupies the northern quarter of the city to the barrier of Powazko as well as part of the southern part."

"And the Grand Duke?" Jan asked.

They think he is with the largest force at the Powazko Barrier."

"Has he retained Polish soldiers, as well as Russian?"

"He has."

"That will be a dicey thing for him," Jan said, "once he chooses to put down the insurrection, as he surely will. Will Pole fight Pole?"

Anna suddenly stirred. She had been following the conversation closer than Michał had thought. "And the leaders of this rising, Michał, have they given consideration as to the direction this thing will take—how we will govern, *who* will govern?"

Michał could only give a little shrug. He had no answer for the very question he had posed to himself earlier that night. He had, however, amazement that his mother had cut to the quick of the matter, the one unknown that would spell liberty or defeat in the coming days.

In any case the genie promising the ever elusive independence was out of the bottle—and no one would be able to cork him up again.

Ten minutes later, with the servants busy in the kitchen preparing the morning meal, Iza opened the door to come face-to-face with Jerzy Lesiak. Her heart accelerated. She stared. Here was the man who claimed to be her father. Was it possible? Or had her mother been telling the truth all along? So few details, other than her father was long dead, a nameless lord killed at the Praga ramparts while defending Warsaw in 1794. She stared, looking for some piece of herself in Jerzy's strong, handsome face.

"Are you going to ask me in?" Jerzy said.

"What—Oh!" Iza cried, stepping aside.

Jerzy stepped in. "Thank you."

"Everyone's in the reception room."

"Your mother, too?"

"No, she's gone on to bed."

"I see." He looked to the reception room where a muted conversation could be heard. "Is there someplace where we may talk?'

Iza nodded, swallowing hard and feigning nonchalance. "In here." She led the way to the music room.

Jerzy waited for Iza to sit before doing so himself. Suddenly, however, he seemed tongue-tied.

"You say that you are my father?" Iza blurted, stunned by her own nerve. The mystery had gone on too many years.

Jerzy seemed surprised and somehow relieved. He nodded. "Yes, Izabela, I say so because it's true. You are mine. Mine and Zofia's. God's wounds, it's time for you to know it."

"Mother says it's not true. She says—"

Jerzy raised his voice. "I don't think she will deny it any longer. She would dare not tell any such thing to my face. You see, we've spoken—your mother and I."

"You have?" The question came as a kind of gasp. Iza sat back into the heavily cushioned chair. "Will you tell me about . . . about you and my mother, Lord Lesiak?"

"I will, but I must begin by saying I am no lord. I am a mere farmer, Izabela. I hope that is not too much of a disappointment to you."

"Oh no, my lord." The appellation fell off her tongue before she realized the blunder. She stopped, blushing at her foolishness, then realized that amusement had given chase to his serious expression.

They both laughed. "And you must call me *Iza*.

Only my mother calls me *Izabela*."

Jerzy nodded. It was then that he told her of his first meeting with Zofia. Even now, so many years later, Iza could tell how her mother had mesmerized and captivated a young Jerzy. The man was now well into his fifties and yet he remembered with astonishing clarity the day that he, at seventeen, had come upon the seemingly lifeless form of Zofia in the River Vistula. It was All Souls Day in 1794. His story coincided with Cousin Anna's account of that day when the Russians had come down on Praga in a killing rampage, sending hundreds off of a burnt and broken bridge into the cold waters. Miles to the east, Jerzy and his grandfather had pulled her from a watery grave. In the days following, as his mother and grandfather nursed the beautiful dark-haired girl back to health, Jerzy, helplessly nervous as a mouse, watched in awe and admiration—and then, when she showed him attention, even asking him to teach her his artistry at carving figures out of linden wood, the feelings for her deepened to love.

In speaking of her mother, Iza watched Jerzy's face come alive and glow with the memories. So many years, and yet it was clear to her that his love for her mother had never died. How had she turned away from such a good and loyal man—to live alone so many years?

"Do you believe me?" Jerzy asked, leaning forward, attempting to bridge the chasm of years and untruths. His forehead was rippled in concern.

Iza fought to hold back tears. "Yes," she said. "Yes, I do."

Great droplets appeared now in Jerzy's eyes. Embarrassed, he brushed at them.

Iza wanted to rise, move toward him, embrace him. And yet the great reserve natural to her—inculcated by a mother slow to show her demonstrative warmth and further nourished in the convent—made her hold back.

An awkwardness ensued.

"Perhaps," Jerzy said at last, standing and managing a smile, "we should go in to the others now?"

Iza stood, too, thinking how this man—her father—could possess such childlike anxiousness. Impulsively, she went up on her toes and kissed him on the cheek.

He was at once surprised and touched. "I've waited years for that kiss, Izabel—Iza."

"As have I," Iza said.

They entered the reception room, and Michał had only just made a formal introduction of Jerzy to his parents when a knock came at the door. A few minutes later Elzbieta came into the room to announce the arrival of Lady Barbara Anna Baklanov.

Sleepy-eyed and still in their little white night-shirts, the twins were urged forward by their mother. Their grandparents greeted them as if a dawn visit in night clothes were quite routine.

Presently Barbara called the maid and had the boys taken upstairs. Once they were away and out of earshot, Barbara's façade of equanimity fell away. Iza had always thought Barbara so very strong emotionally, but pale and unsteady now, she seemed on the brink of collapse.

Michał stood and helped her to sit next to

her mother.

Anna took Barbara's hand in hers. "Basia, dearest," she said, "what is it?"

Barbara choked back her tears, the green eyes moving about the room, taking in every face. "Józef?" she asked.

"We don't know," Anna whispered. "But about you—"

"Where's Viktor?" her father interjected, his left hand moving over the gloved hand, as if to hide it.

Barbara bit her lower lip. "He's gone."

Anna squeezed her hand. "Because of his Russian background, dear? It was to be expected, I suppose. No matter the outcome of this night, I'm sure you'll be reunited. You must take heart. Jan and I have been through many separations because of war. You know that."

"Yes," Barbara said, "yes, but—"

"There's more," Anna pressed. "What is it, Basia?"

"Viktor is targeted by Poles in retribution."

"Targeted?"

Barbara nodded. "You see—I only just found out—that Viktor's position is with the secret police."

Iza drew in a very long breath at the news. Viktor Baklanov was a piece of a puzzle that had not fit well into the Stelnicki family. For love of Barbara and her love for her husband, Iza and the other family members had tried to welcome him into the clan at best and tolerated him at worst. But the thought that he was working against Polish citizens in perhaps terrible ways—everyone knew the ways of the secret police—made Iza ill at her stomach.

The shock that Iza felt was mirrored in Anna's face. Iza's line of vision moved to Jan and then to Jan Michał. Here was another jolt. Neither father nor son seemed even mildly surprised. Had they known Viktor was in the secret police? How?

The maid stepped into the room now, her voice as drained and tired as her expression. No one—but for Zofia—had gotten any sleep this night. In Zofia's absence, she addressed Iza: "Are there any instructions for the breakfast, Mademoiselle?"

"Use your judgment, Wanda."

The maid nodded but stood motionless.

"Yes," Iza asked, "what is it, Wanda? Something else?"

The maid nodded toward Barbara. "Lady Baklanov's trunk has arrived, milady."

Barbara and the twins had come to stay.

At eight in the morning, Michał joined Jerzy and Iza in the reception room after the three had taken a modest breakfast. His parents and Barbara had retired before the meal. Zofia had yet to emerge from her bedchamber; she had retired in the early morning hours and it seemed intermittent cries, calls, and songs out in the streets or the comings and goings within her own town house little disturbed her rest. His mother had told him that Zofia slept with an eyemask and ears stuffed with cotton. He smiled to himself, wondering at her reaction when she finds out that Barbara and the rambunctious twins had moved in, trunk and all. She had little use for children. And if Jerzy were still here when she arose—what then? How would she treat him? He could not help but wonder what went on between them the other day when they met.

"Are you about ready?" Michał asked Jerzy.

"I'm at your disposal and chomping at the bit, as they say."

"Where are you to go?" Iza asked. "To look for Józef?" She stood. "Allow me to quickly change so that I might—"

Jerzy rose at once. His demur came a beat earlier than Michał's. "No, Iza."

"Why not? I insist. I am as worried as anyone over Józef."

"Of course you are, Iza," Michał said, rising, "but we don't know what we will find out there. There may still be neighborhoods controlled by the Russians. There may still be fighting going on."

"That's fine by me. This is historic!"

"You haven't slept all night, Iza," Michał said. "You need your rest."

"Neither have you two slept," Iza said. "I couldn't possibly sleep."

"It's dangerous," Jerzy said. "Too dangerous."

Michał saw that Jerzy had caught her by the wrist as she attempted to exit the room and the touch seemed to send a current through each of them. They stood as statues for a moment. Then Iza glanced down at the hand that had somehow moved so that Jerzy held her hand in his. Was this the first touch—awkward and tender—between father and daughter?

A kind of embarrassment ensued now and their

hands fell away.

A knocking at the front door broke the spell.

A flustered Elzbieta came in moments later, announcing in an excited tone: "Prince Adam Czartoryski!"

Michał's own amazement was reflected in the faces of Iza and Jerzy. The three turned to greet the prince. Introductions were quick and lacking in small talk. "I'll get right to the point, Michał," the prince said. "For the most part, the city of Warsaw is under Polish control. This morning we formed a provisional government."

"We?" Michał asked.

"A number of us. Quite a few from the Administrative Council."

Michał was taken by surprise. He knew that the Administrative Council was largely a body of older men, more or less content with things as they were. "But what about the conspirators?"

"Most inept, you can be sure. They lit the fuse but had no idea how to lead afterwards. It's our feeling that a direct confrontation with Russia is to be avoided at all costs. If we don't step in, rule will go to the masses and chaos will abound."

"But we're not to give up?" Jerzy cried.

The prince turned to Jerzy. "No, not that. But cool heads are needed to end rebellion and reach some accommodation with the tsar."

"Excuse me, your grace," Jerzy said, "but how is that not giving up?"

The prince forced a smile. "We cannot afford to incite the full brunt of Russia to come down on

Poland, as in '94. We must deal very carefully with the Grand Duke and his brother the tsar. We have made gains and perhaps—just perhaps—this volatile situation can be used to our advantage."

"But not to gain full independence?" Michał asked.

Surprising even herself, Iza suddenly insinuated herself into this male conversation. "And the restoration of the *full* kingdom? The Commonwealth of Poland and Lithuania?"

"Ah, Iza," the prince said. "Full restoration is a pipe dream, I'm afraid.—I'm sorry, but in our hurried introductions, I did not catch your family name."

"Gronska,"

"Of course, you are related to the Lady Zofia?"

"She is my mother, your grace. We met before— you and I—quite a few years ago now."

"Really?" he said, rubbing his chin. Michał remembered Iza's story of how Zofia had tried to mastermind a romance and marriage between Iza and the prince—and this only after having tried to land him herself, years earlier. Michał watched as the prince—usually the quintessence of equipoise— clearly recalling Zofia's unbidden overtures, slowly colored and shifted his footing. "Of course, my dear. Of course."

Michał came to his rescue. "How can I be of service, your grace?" Another prince might have felt nothing, shown nothing, at such a delicate moment, but Michał knew this prince well enough already to call him princely.

The prince granted him a thankful smile. "I am here to deputize you, Jan Michał Stelnicki. You, along with Prince Drucki-Lubecki and Joachim Lelewel, are to go to meet with Grand Duke Konstantin. He and his forces—both Russian and Polish, I might add—are camped within the city limits at Mokotów."

"I?" Michał knew he must look as dumbstruck as he felt. He heard Iza, too, draw in a breath of astonishment.

"I have two reasons, Michał. First, you have seen war firsthand, time and again. You are no longer a slave to glory and a stranger to violent death. You will not be carried away like some young cadet. Your sense and equanimity will help you in the role of arbiter between Druck-Lubecki and Lelewell, who do not often see eye to eye. Neither have you been shy of telling me your honest thoughts. I assume you can do so with these two. If they go into a meeting with the Grand Duke already at odds themselves, we're doomed."

"I see." Michał did a quick calculation. While Prince Franciszek Drucki-Lubecki, a Russian in his early fifties, was Minister of the Treasury—Joachim Lelewell, in his middle forties, had been a Polish professor of European History at Wilno until the Governor ousted him at the bequest of the Grand Duke, who was intent on fostering the Russian point of view in education. No doubt the very identities of Druck-Lubecki and Lelewell made them polar opposites. "You're saying, your grace, that my person is to stand between two mountains and coax them together without my getting crushed in the bargain?"

The prince gave a lively and genuine laugh.

"And the goal? What outcome do we wish to

attain—from *your* point of view?

"I would like to see the rebellion end. Enough have died already. You are to determine whether the Grand Duke is inclined to come against the city. You should caution him that such a decision—given the mind of the general populace—is most unwise. For both sides. It would be best if he departs, and if he agrees to do so he may safely take a prescribed route. Accommodations would be made for him along the way. I would even have my mother receive him honorably at Puławy, my family estate. When enough time has passed, I hope that we can gain some constitutional concessions from Russia."

"In return for encouraging an end to the rebellion?" Michał asked.

"Yes. An odd situation, I know. But see here, Michał, the Grand Duke took a Polish bride and considers himself Polish. I'm convinced he won't wish to inflict harm on Poland. Now, my boy, will you do this in my stead? I have much to do here to try to put the lid on this boiling cauldron."

"Yes, your grace."

"Excellent! You must get your things together. There are carriages outside."

"I'll take my horse, if you don't mind."

"Fine."

Michał felt Jerzy nudge him in the side. "Your grace, would you mind if Jerzy accompanies me?"

"What? No, I guess not."

"Just what is going on here, may I ask?" The mellifluous but slightly tart question preceded the arrival of Zofia in her reception room. Her hair and makeup were perfect and the morning dress of light blue showed off her figure to advantage.

Michał sorely wished he had a painting of her expression when she recognized Prince Adam Czartoryski. Her eyes went wide as moons and he gauged her scalp as pulling back at least an inch. "Your grace!" she cried, dropping into a curtsey.

"Countess Zofia Gronska," the prince said. "How is it the years take their toll on everyone but you? Look at you! If I didn't know better I would deny the fact that Iza here is your daughter. You are more like sisters."

"Thank you, your grace."

That Zofia did not contradict him made Michał chuckle to himself.

"What is the reason for this call?" Zofia's almond-shaped black eyes sparkled. "Why didn't someone come fetch me? I've been awake and at my toilette for a good hour or more."

The prince took and kissed Zofia's hand. "I must take my leave, Lady Zofia. Your daughter can relay the meat of the meeting. Michał and Jerzy are to accompany me."

Jerzy's name brought Zofia up short. She drew back her hand from the prince and spun about to face Jerzy. The look she gave him—so sudden and unplanned—resonated an honesty she had no artifice to camouflage. Her breathing came in short gasps while her mind must have been spinning.

Jerzy stepped toward her, bowed, and kissed her hand. His head came up now and she looked into his eyes. Her mouth fell open a bit as if to speak, but she could not. Instead of words, she gave a slow nod of her brilliantly coiffed head.

It was a nod, Michał thought, that acknowledged her relationship with Jerzy so many years before and a nod that brought a supremely happy smile to Iza's face. For the first time in her life, Iza had both parents.

The prince seemed lost amidst the heaviness of the moment, for he had no way of knowing the significance of the situation. "Well," he said in a halting manner, "I—rather, we—must be off. Michał, you are to meet Druck-Lubecki and Lelewell at Bankowa Square. Hurry. And—thank you." He turned and started moving out of the room.

"Wait, your grace," Michał called.

The prince turned, his face questioning.

"Forgive me, but you said—when you arrived, that is—you said you were asking me to take this mission to the Grand Duke for two reasons. And—well, did I somehow miss hearing the second?"

"Oh, Good God, no, Michał! I had been saving the best for last. You know the fruit to the feast, as they say. And then I forgot altogether!" The prince moved back into the room so that he completed a circle of curious faces.

"A young man by the name of Ludwik Nabielak came to see me and others of the Administrative Council early this morning. This young cadet was in charge of those who attacked the Grand Duke's palace last night. He had a report to make. And he wanted to put to rest rumors that the cadets had planned an assassination rather than an abduction."

Michał felt his heart thumping in his chest. Dared he hope . . . "Did he—did he have news of Józef?"

The prince nodded. "He was last seen alive, Michał. There is hope."

"God's bones! Where was he seen?"

"On a westbound avenue. On a horse, his hands tied in back. He was a prisoner in the company of the Grand Duke himself as his forces made their way toward the barriers of Mokotów, where the Konstantin and some 8,000 men are now encamped in the fields beyond."

19

Mokotów, Warsaw

JÓZEF AWOKE TO A JOSTLING and several light slaps across his face. "Up, cadet, up!"

More humiliation, Józef thought. So much for the glory of rebellion against Russia. So much for the plan to abduct Grand Duke Konstantin. And the questioning: upon arriving at the Mokotów barriers, he had been questioned for hours as to the motives of the rebel leaders and, more especially, the intent concerning the Grand Duke. Józef was able to speak truthfully: he knew nothing of the leaders' plans other than his own part in it. Further, he could in good conscience deny that their objective was assassination, this in spite of being dealt head and body blows. Over and over, he told them they were merely to abduct the Grand Duke. His interrogators did not believe him. He may very well have looked guilty, too, for—at Viktor Baklanov's urging—he *had* thought of killing Konstantin.

"Come along, get up," the soldier said, nudging him. Through his foggy and sluggish brain came the realization that the soldier's voice was a Polish voice. Józef's first thought was that he was being freed, that the Polish forces had overcome the Grand Duke's forces.

The soldier pulled at Józef's upper body so that he sat cross-legged on the hard ground. His hands remained bound. The night before, he had been thrown to the floor of the tent even before it had been fully erected. Somehow, despite the cold of the night and discomfort of his bonds, he had fallen asleep.

Unconscious was a better descriptor, he thought. For how long? A few hours? Outside, the sun was high enough to throw silhouettes of soldiers against the tent sides. Guards for his little portable prison? Freedom might be elusive.

"Hurry him up!" A second soldier at the opening flap called in an accent unmistakably Russian. Only now did Józef realize that both soldiers wore red uniforms. Freedom fully dissipated.

"I'm going to cut your bonds," the Pole told Józef. "Do nothing stupid."

"There are still Poles like you loyal to the Grand

Duke?" Józef asked.

"Of course. You cadets truly went astray. Fools—did you think you could succeed at something like this?"

Józef's mouth went dry. "The rebellion has been put down?"

"Nearly so."

This could not be true, Józef thought. "Or so you've been told."

The soldier shrugged. "No reason to believe otherwise. The city will be locked down in no time and the Grand Duke will be back at his comfortable little palace."

"And me?"

After freeing Józef's hands, the soldier pulled him to his feet, bringing them face to face. "I would not trade places with you, cadet." His breath was sour. "Not for the prettiest whore in Warsaw. Oh, the Grand Duke has taken a special interest in you. You'll likely hang, my boy."

Józef had no time to react, for he was being pushed from the tent. Upon exiting, he was bookended by the Russian and the Pole. He blinked, realizing a detail of four additional soldiers stood ready as an escort detail. "Where am I being taken?"

"To the firing squad," the Russian soldier said matter-of-factly. "Move along."

So much for my military career of distinction, Józef thought, fighting off fear. His hand moved into his jacket in search of Emilia's miniature. It was gone. He had lost it. He grew dizzy.

And his mother—who had so fought against his

entering the military—what would she think? Hadn't she made enough sacrifices for Poland? He thought of breaking free and making a run for it, but to be shot in the back would be a worse fate than bravely climbing some hastily made gallows.

They had walked some fifty paces when the Pole turned to him and seemed to read the pain on his face. "Don't worry, cadet" he said. "Konstantin is notoriously indecisive and slow to act. We're to take you to him. It's probably just a little reprieve, but you might create a good story for him. I hear he can sometimes be quite gullible.—Maybe you'll need to take a piss first?"

At Mokotów, Michał waited impatiently for the Grand Duke to return from his personal tent where he was drawing up a proclamation that he and the two council members sitting across from him at the collapsible wooden table would carry back to the city proper. Joachim Lelewell—sharp nose and droopy eyes offset by the new windswept fashion of hair—sat like the quiet academician that he was, while Prince Franciszek Drucki-Lubecki—moon-faced with three main strands of hair tortured up from the sides and back and pasted across the shining dome of a head— fidgeted on the uncomfortable folding stool, pulling now and then at the high collar that provided no evidence of a neck. While not an official member of the party, Jerzy waited outside the tent.

The presentation the Prince and Lelewell had made to the Grand Duke had been concise and well thought out. Michał had made small contributions previous to their audience, but Czartoryski's intention of Michał's acting as arbiter had not quite played out. With serious faces and an occasional nervous smile, the two council members asked the Grand Duke his intentions. Did he mean to attack the city? Had he requested help from the garrison at Lithuania? Or did he mean to depart?

Their argument: to attack would bring down untold violence, for the Polish army had already come over to the side of the people, except for the several companies of grenadiers of the footguard and a regiment of chasseurs of the guard that remained with the Grand Duke. The nation—which the Grand Duke claimed to love—would suffer, as would he and his army. On the other hand, should he choose to depart for Russia, the insurrection would end and he would not only be allowed to do so peaceably, but he would also be provided with first rate accommodations along the way. Peaceful negotiations between Poland and Russia could then follow.

Before leaving the tent for his own, the Grand Duke had turned about, his face flushing. "You must be honest with me, gentleman. Was it not my assassination that the rebel cadets intended? My death!"

Both the prince and Lelewell faltered at first in their denials. Michał kept his powder dry until their rather overwrought assurances that death was not the aim, based on mere opinion or gossip, played out to little effect.

"Your Royal Highness," Michał said, catching

Konstantin's attention before he could exit the tent.

The Grand Duke turned to Michał, his expression one of curiosity.

Michał spoke now of what he had heard directly from a cadet and with all the conviction he could muster: "I can tell you that the leaders of the cadets cautioned them that your life was not to be endangered. They told the cadets that Poles do not kill princes. And that is the case. That is our history."

The Grand Duke paused then, his small beadlike eyes boring into Michał. He was giving Michał's statement a weightier consideration than he had afforded to those of the other two.

The shadow of an odd—perhaps ironic—smile played on Konstantin's thin lips. "There was," he said, "one young fellow who did give it some consideration." And without speaking further, he turned and took his leave.

He was taking good time, Michał thought now, shifting in his seat and continuing to fight off his exhaustion. The Grand Duke had left them a good hour before without an indication of his answer. Of what was to come. That was the trait of indecisive men, Michał thought, you never know where they stand—or for how long.

And then there was Michał's personal concern: Józef. The conference with the Grand Duke had not as yet afforded mention of his brother. Michał knew he could not leave the tent without asking about him. Was he safe? Was he here? What was to be done with him? Might the Grand Duke listen to a plea for his life? How was Michał to bring up the subject? And how might the volatile Konstantin react?

Michał suddenly recalled the *young fellow* the Grand Duke had spoken of, the cadet who had come close to killing one of Russia's grand dukes. Had he meant Jozef? Was that the reason for the odd smile?

And then the most treacherous thought dared come to the fore: What if Józef had already been dealt with? What if . . .

The tent flap was thrown open now and the Grand Duke entered, a formal proclamation in his hand. Michał realized Konstantin had no real facial profile; his face, while puffy, was the flattest Michał had ever seen. The military coat, however, with its overpowering epaulettes, medals, and gold buttons cascading down a stomach long enhanced by his love of Polish dumplings and pastry distracted one from his visage.

The Grand Duke came to the table, sat on his stool, one higher than theirs, and read it aloud like some schoolmaster. In it he said he did not intend to attack Warsaw, and if he did deem it necessary at some point, he would give the city forty-eight hours notice. He denied that he had sent for the Russian force garrisoned in Lithuania. Moreover, he would write to his brother the tsar—and King of Poland— asking for amnesty for those involved in the uprising. Lastly, he suggested the exchange of prisoners.

Michał watched the reactions of Prince Drucki-Lubecki and Lelewell. No nods. No smiles. They saw the same problems with this treaty as did he: the Grand Duke did not say he would withdraw; further, he seemed to allow for a future attack on the city, a two-day warning notwithstanding.

Lelewell seemed the least pleased and was about to speak when the Grand Duke rose, motioned the others to also rise, and made a point of handing the proclamation to Lelewell. Clearly, the meeting was at an end. The two council members, their faces drawn down in disappointment, read the signs and prepared to leave the tent.

Michał felt the blood rising to his face. He had to say something. By now he was certain that Prince Adam had sent him along with the other two for the primary reason of making a plea for Józef. If only he was not too late to do so.

"Your Royal Highness," Michał said, "if I may have a further moment of your time?"

"Yes—Michał is it not?"

"Yes. You . . . you noted that you are in favor of amnesty."

A royal nod.

"And you are in favor of exchanging prisoners. Yes?"

"Did I not just read to you the proclamation, Michał? Did I not say these things?"

Michał's heart beat erratically. He was certain he had angered the Grand Duke. He fought for words that would assuage a volatile disposition. "Your Royal Highness, I was only . . . that is, it was my intention—"

The Grand Duke raised his hand, silencing Michał at once.

Here was failure, Michał knew. The Grand Duke was about to leave. This was the end of the meeting. He would not be allowed another word.

Instead, however, Konstantin's head lowered, his

fleshy neck folding into ripples, his eyes somehow dancing, somehow laughing. "My dear Lord Stelnicki, did you not realize that when I heard your name at the start of the meeting I would guess why you had come. You are related to one of the abductors, yes? The cadet Józef Stelnicki, yes?"

Stunned, Michał nodded. "Yes, your highness."

"He is your son, yes?"

Michał shook his head. "Brother."

"Ah, younger by many years."

"Yes."

"And you are here to plead for his life?"

Michał drew in a deep, deep breath. "Yes."

December 1830, Warsaw

VIKTOR PACED ACROSS THE HUGE reception room of the mansion, the lame foot dragging and scraping on the oak boards. He had ventured to slip out of the hidden room. Staying there for any length of time was enough to drive one insane. Besides, he needed physical exercise. Just the walking felt good. The room had saved his life on at least two occasions when deputies from the rebel government had called, checking and double-checking that General Rozniecki was not in residence. No neck like a traitor's neck, Viktor thought.

Viktor promised himself he would dare to explore the city one day soon, if only to catch a fleeting sight of Barbara and the boys. He would chance it. Not today, however; since mid-morning he had been aware of much noise and hubbub in the quarter, this despite the cold and the previous night's heavy snow.

He was losing track of days. When Bartosz returned he would ask him to find a calendar. How long have I been here? he wondered, stopping for a moment. Three weeks? Damn—more! Nearly four. Christmas had just passed—what was it, three days ago? Caroling had gone on at all hours of the day and night. What had these Poles to celebrate? Didn't they realize the hammer would fall in short order?

Through a slight vertical opening where the curtain panels met, Viktor saw that it was snowing again. Bartosz was out marketing. Remarkably, the city had come back to a normal sort of life within a few days of the insurrection. A Polish National Guard had been established, giving protection to the bank and the treasury, as well as establishing order throughout Warsaw. Shops were open and business was being conducted. Well, let the fool Poles be lulled into a state of ordinariness and contentment. They will pay handsomely one day soon. The sooner the better.

Outside, the tumult seemed to be gaining in intensity. He could hear a group running past the mansion. He dared not draw back the curtains. Where is that idiot servant? What did this disturbance mean?

At last, Viktor folded himself into an armchair near the bay window, throwing his feet up on the window seat, ever so carefully using his boots to part the curtains where they met, just enough so that he might see Bartosz ascend the stairs of the portico upon his return.

He sighed. No, to give the devil his due: Bartosz was not an idiot, and that was precisely the reason why Viktor did not quite trust him yet. Oh, Bartosz had handled the deputies of the interim government quite professionally, effectively brushing them off with nothing more that a cursory look at the room with the peacocks tapestry, the tapestry behind which Viktor had sweated a good deal. And in these past few weeks he had been his lifeline to the happenings in the city, gleaning and dispensing a wealth of information.

First, a surprise: the Poles had been able to take control of most of the city as well as Praga. A hastily-formed provisional government made some demands of Grand Duke Konstantin while he was encamped in the fields of Mokotów. When he did not say he was leaving—or that he would not attack the city, the dissatisfied Poles sent another deputation making it clear that they would attack him if he did not withdraw from Poland. Here, in Viktor's opinion, they made a blunder that would cost them: they gave Konstantin not only permission to leave, but also assured him safe passage to Russia, and fancy lodgings along the way into the bargain. Such stupidity. But as if not to be outdone, the Grand Duke provided his own one-two punch of idiocy. He did not attack the city at a critical moment—before order and organization settled in—when he would have triumphed. And then, before leaving Mokotów on 3 December, he cut loose any of his Polish soldiers who wished to leave and return to the city. Up to that point, their Polish generals had been deliberately misleading them, assuring them that the insurgency was small and in collapse. Upon hearing Konstantin decree their freedom to choose, the Poles' cries of "Liberty" went up in one voice as his six companies of grenadiers of the foot guard moved out of the fields, and an entire regiment of chasseurs of the guard left him with a royal view of horses' asses. No Pole remained with him, not even his closest aide. Did the imbecile think that they would not now take up arms against him? Viktor conjectured that Konstantin's Polish wife and his immersion into Polish culture had proven his Achilles heel. Grand Duke Konstantin was a disgrace to Russia. *If only Józef had killed him.*

The Sejm opened its session on 18 December. The new government was to be called The National Government of the Kingdom of Poland. Lithuanian Prince Radziwill was named Generalissimo of the Army. Particularly irritating to Viktor was the news that the person Michał had entertained in Sochaczew back in May—Prince Adam Czartoryski—was nominated president of the national government. Viktor had spit outright when he heard that. The Third Department should have taken care of him long ago.

The Sejm proposed that Tsar Nicholas would remain King of Poland while ambassadors were sent to St Petersburg requesting that the tsar withdraw all Russian troops from the kingdom, that the Constitution be observed to the letter and, like his predecessor Aleksander had promised, that all the old Commonwealth provinces now designated part of Russia should be liberated and allowed to partake in the Constitution. Simple enough, Viktor snickered, picking at his overlong fingernails. The ambassadors were to invite Nicholas to Warsaw for the opening of the Sejm. He laughed aloud, thinking that this was the apple in their apple cake, a cake that the tsar would smear in their faces. Or so Viktor hoped. He prayed for the tsar to loose all hell on the Poles. Successful arbitration would do nothing for *his* future. But in a defeated Poland, Viktor would rise like a phoenix.

General Józef Chlopicki was named Dictator by the Poles, replacing the provisional government. Viktor knew he was well respected, worshipped even, for he had entered the army at fourteen and fought heroically under Kościuszko in 1794, as well with the French campaigns in Italy under Dąbrowski, in the Spain Campaign, and in Russia under Napoleon. In 1814 Tsar Aleksander had made him a general in the newly-formed Polish Army under the auspices of Russia, but Chlopicki somehow displeased the moody Konstantin who took away his commission. Now, to hear Bartosz tell it, though, the people's confidence in the aging hero's dictatorship was already eroding, for the augmentation of the army was slow and inconsistent, and as a result, fortifications were being ignored. More in the way of barricades and mines was being done by volunteer citizens than by any orders from Dictator Chlopicki. This was good news indeed to Viktor. The more divided the Poles, the better.

Suddenly Viktor heard a noise out front and through the vertical slit in the drapes he could see Bartosz arriving on the platform of the snow-laden portico. Viktor was in the process of jumping up to go to the door in order to inquire about the uproar when his peripheral vision caught a second figure ascending the few stairs. His first thought: Bartosz had given him away! How much would someone pay for him to turn in Nikolai Novosiltsev's deputy in charge of the Secret Police? A tidy amount, no doubt. That Bartosz would turn on him one day haunted him at night. But then he caught the voice of the figure, a woman's voice. He dared to tug slightly on the curtains for a better view. She wore a cloak, the hood of which covered her profile.

Viktor thought now that Barbara Anna had somehow found him. But how? And why? Had she had a change of heart? Later he would admit to himself that despite the complications his wife's appearance would create, his heart had momentarily swelled with pleasure.

He made for the front door at once, his lame leg in tow. From the peep hole he would be able to see her, face forward. But even as he moved he made the decision that he would not—could not—give himself away, even to his wife. Even to Barbara Anna.

At the door he pulled back the tiny hinged cover of the peephole and brought his eye flush to the door. All he could see was the back of Bartosz' hatted head. *Damn the fellow*, he cursed to himself. He heard his name now and froze.

Bartosz was clearly trying to send the woman on her way. He took a step to his left, and at that moment Viktor got a clear view of the woman.

Larissa. Only now did he recognize that the snow covered red bonnet and cloak were the same she had worn when she had stood in the square, pointing him out to Polish cadets.

His heart came to a stop. He blinked, as if doing so could make her disappear. *What in Satan's hell is she doing here?* How did she know? Was it a guess? A bullet in the dark?

And then he recalled something else from his last visit to the office of the Imperial Commissioner. Just moments before Larissa arrived in the room, he had pulled General Rozniecki's file from Novosiltsev's drawer and placed it on the desk. Later, he had placed his gun next to the file. Had she taken note of the file? Likely so. Might she have guessed his motive in singling it out?

And what did she want? She had already done what she could to see him ruined—to see him dead. He must keep her at a good distance.

He listened closely. In low tones Bartosz was attempting to conclude their little encounter. "I assure you again, Mademoiselle, that he is not here."

"Has he been here?" Larissa asked. Her eyes became fastened to the door behind Bartosz, riveted like search lanterns. Viktor quickly took his eye from the peephole.

"I'm afraid that I don't know the man."

"Don't give me that."

"It is true, Mademoiselle. In any case, no one is here."

"Would you allow me in?"

"I have no authority to do so, Mademoiselle."

The conversation continued for a longer while than Viktor would have expected, growing quieter, more muddled. He could not make out the words and he dared not put his ear to the peephole. And so it went until he heard her voice receding. He sighed in relief, and yet he wondered if she had seen his eye in the peephole.

The door opened and Bartosz slipped in, startled at first by Viktor's presence and then by his intense demeanor, but his characteristic flippancy won out. "A friend of yours?"

"No friend of mine," Viktor snapped. "What did she want?"

"You," Bartosz said, giving a shrug. He started toward the rear of the house, tossing off some comment about women scorned.

Viktor pulled him up short and spun him about. A package of meat fell to the floor with a thud. "Tell me!"

Bartosz' eyes widened. "She's looking for you. Didn't say why."

"What took so long out there? Damn you, what did you tell her?"

Bartosz tilted his head as if humoring a child. "I told her I didn't know you. Had never heard of you. That you have never been here."

"And?"

"She doesn't convince easily. But she went away, did she not?" Bartosz bent to retrieve the package. "Venison stew tonight?" he asked, in that irritatingly too familiar tone he had taken of late with Viktor. No "sir," no title of any kind. And he didn't expect an answer, it seemed, for he started to move toward the kitchen.

"Wait a minute, Bartosz!"

The servant turned about. "Yes?"

"What in Hades is going on in the city? It sounds

as if everyone has turned out of their houses ready to fight."

"Exactly that. The rebels have heard back from the tsar. Nicholas' proclamation arrived from Moscow and has been posted in the squares. And the people are at arms about it. 'To battle! To battle!' they are crying. They are convinced war is the only way now."

"Let me guess the content of the proclamation. Nicholas condemns the criminality of the rebels and demands that armaments be turned over and all things be returned to the way of life before 29 November. It's only in this way that Poland can be saved from self-destruction."

"A close enough summary. You must have gypsy blood."

Viktor ignored Bartosz' impertinence. "Further, I would go so far as to say he has no intention of coming to Poland."

"And best for him if he doesn't."

"What do you mean?"

"Well, the people are incensed and ready now to take to the field, but they are being urged to wait for the convocation of the Seym on 17 January. It's expected that your tsar will be deposed as King of Poland."

"Foolish Poles," Viktor muttered. "So it is to be war—full scale war." He had begun to expect as much, but it still came as a shock.

"War is an old friend of Poland," Bartosz called back as he moved toward the kitchen at the rear of the mansion.

Viktor returned to his lair behind the tapestry of

peacocks where he would await the venison stew. He sat. He had hoped that Józef or one of the cadets would kill the Grand Duke so that the reign of fire from Russia would be immediate, uncompromising, and decisive. No great war would be necessary. And in the aftermath of tighter Russian control he would ascend the ladder. There would be promotions, recognition. In due course a title and an estate. But the entire affair had been bungled by both the Poles and the Russians. The Russians had waited too long already for this to be an easy thing. How could Nicholas not know the Polish temperament, the Polish spirit? His proclamation brought a full cauldron to the boiling point and there was no telling the consequences.

How long am I to live in this non-existence? In his imagination the days and months stretched out like an uncharted, horizonless prairie.

Viktor's thoughts came back to Larissa. *She doesn't convince easily,* Bartosz had said. He had that right. And neither does she give up, it seemed. *What does she want?* What would she try next? She would not give up on Bartosz. Even if she hadn't noticed an eye in the peephole, she hadn't believed him. She must know that—contrary to what Bartosz told her— the man who carried the Chief of Police's payroll to Novosiltsev's office would be aware of the identity of the Deputy Chief of Police. She must know that he was lying. She would bide her time. She would coerce him in some way for information. Bribe him—with what? Money? Herself?

And, Viktor wondered, if he had to stay hidden for months, would Bartosz maintain his confidence?

Perhaps he had tired already of Viktor's domineering manner and irritability. Perhaps he had tired of preparing an interloper's meals. Indeed, how easy it would be to stir poison into the stew—or to add the wrong sort of mushrooms to it. Deathcaps were the most deadly and not uncommon in Warsaw forests. Or—Bartosz could merely turn him over to the Poles.

Bartosz brought in the venison stew a little later. By then Viktor had come to the conclusion that the man's' usefulness had reached its limit. And his recent thoughts caused him to taste the stew with some hesitancy. After all, no manor house was without arsenic as a remedy for rats.

Like most of Bartosz' dishes, however, it was quite good.

Part Four

It Happens in an Hour that
Comes not in an Age
—POLISH PROVERB

20

12 February 1831, Warsaw

"ARE YOU COMING, MOTHER?—MOTHER?"

The voice jolted Anna from her thoughts. She had been standing at the window of the sitting room of her little suite atop the Gronska town house, vacantly watching unusually thick streams of Saturday worshippers converge on the snowy steps of St. Martin's, then disappear beyond the doors. At dusk, it seemed to her that the bells of every church belfry had gone mad with the recent news: the first engagement of the enemy had taken place.

Anna's eyes focused. Blurrily reflected on the window glass was the image of her daughter's face. Behind her, Barbara Anna stood in the doorway, her blonde hair covered by the hood of her cloak.

"Mother?—Are you coming to Mass?"

"No," Anna said, without turning about.

"Are you all right, Mother?"

A long pause, then: "Yes, dear. You go on."

"The boys will be disappointed."

"And so they will learn. They will learn disappointment."

Barbara turned to go, then paused. "They say it was a Pole who fired the first shot."

"A cadet?"

"Why—yes."

A few moments passed. The door closed then and Anna placed her cheek against the cool glass. How had it come to this? War. Yet again.

Anna Stelnicka's heart was coming apart, like a favorite garment worn to shreds. For the third time in her life her Poland was struggling to push back the enemy, to release her chains, to reclaim independence. What were the chances now? And now—again—the callous winds of war had hurled loved ones far from her.

The thought was well punctuated by a second round of tolling from St, Martin's heavy brass bells. The perimeters of the window panes had been sealed with wax against the winter winds, but the glass vibrated nonetheless in time with the deep clanging. Anna kept her cheek pressed against the glass.

The bells had rung crazily that morning, too. She had gone outside to watch the strangest funeral procession she had ever witnessed. The dead person, Anna learned from some placards the mourners carried, was Jan Kiliński, the bootmaker and acclaimed patriot from the years of the Third of May Constitution. What made the cortege so odd was that Kiliński had died some years before, in 1819. The purpose of this mock funeral, an observer told her, was to agitate the citizenry against Tsar Nicholas and Russian domination. The organizers were hoping for the rise of a new Jan Kiliński.

Jan Kiliński indeed! She could tell them a few things she had witnessed firsthand about Jan Kiliński. The memories came back in a dizzying wave. In 1794, he had led a secret insurrection within Warsaw against the occupying Prussians and Russians. Anna didn't doubt his patriotism then or now, but the little group of patriots to which she had belonged all those years ago was convinced that any attempt by Kiliński prior to Tadeusz Kościuszko's impending arrival would provoke a bloodbath—one that Russia's Catherine would avenge a thousand fold—and so they engaged Anna to warn the king of the intended uprising so that he might convince Kiliński to hold off and wait for the level-headed Kościuszko and his troops. Anna's attempt to see the king was foiled at first try, so she had had to impersonate Zofia—flamboyantly dressing and acting the part—to effectively gain an audience with King Stanisław, who had once had a dalliance with Zofia. The masquerade was a success, and the king appreciated Anna's derring-do but seemed not to have any real influence over the rebels, who charged ahead with the rising. The occupiers were evicted from the capital but, as feared, the streets flowed thick and red with blood. And the prediction about Catherine materialized: she sent her most merciless general, Suworow, to take back Warsaw. He and his lancers came down on the suburb of Praga, massacring some 12,000 innocents before Warsaw capitulated. The king surprised Anna for her patriotic effort—however useless it proved in the end—by endowing her with the title of princess. The king had no power to do so according to Polish law—his power came, ironically, under the auspices of Catherine. Anna shook her head at the thought. A title given by a Russian Tsarina? It meant nothing to her.

As for Kiliński—a hero? Perhaps, but one with more courage than cleverness.

And now, years later, what of the cadets and their two leaders? Were they not made of the same cloth as Kiliński? Firebrands? What had they reaped?

The Polish forces, some 50,000, had left Warsaw at the opening of the month, marching proudly through the capital's avenues while lines of the senators and deputies of the National Government stood on either side. Cheering them on, too, was the entire citizenry, it seemed: man, woman, and child, both szlachta and peasant. It took little coaxing from a single firm male tenor to set the crowds singing their beloved national hymns, so long forbidden.

Each day brought momentous news. The Dictator—General Chlopicki—had already been forced from his post for failing to ready the country for war in good time. People said he thought an end to differences between Poland and Russia would come only through negotiations. Nicholas' proclamation in December refuted that notion, but while talking a good game, Chlopicki was doing precious little to build fortifications and to call up and train the large forces that would be needed. Time was lost because he had little hope for Poland's besting the giant Russia. Now, since Chlopicki's resignation, things certainly were happening with lightning speed. Prince Czartoryski had opened the Seym on 19 January, whereupon the senators and deputies made short work of creating the manifesto that deprived the Romanov family of Poland's crown, absolved all Poles of their oath of loyalty to Russia, and proclaimed the sovereignty of the Polish nation.

Anna thought now of young Józef's homecoming in December. How bittersweet it was. "Mother!" he had called from the front entryway as he took his battered cadet's czapka from his blond head. Michał, who had seen Józef home fresh from the grasp of Grand Duke Konstantin, stood proudly beside him. It was a miracle to see her youngest, alive and tearfully smiling at her. Had he run to her, or she to him? She couldn't remember now.

Another mother might have thought that that would be the end of things military for a son barely escaping execution. But not Anna. When he was called up again within a week, he was chomping at the bit. No, she was not surprised. He was now part of a battalion in Southeast Poland, somewhere between the Rivers Bug and Narew. It was a dangerous mission, she knew. The further east, the closer to Russia, the earlier that battalion would see action. Each morning she got down on her knees and prayed for his safety.

Neither was she surprised when Michał rejoined the cavalry after so many years of civilian life—albeit a restless life. He had put in for a commission that would allow him to keep an eye on Józef, but it was not to be. Michał's lancer unit had been assigned to the Modlin Fortress, north of Warsaw. It may be for the best, she thought now. Józef was on his own quest many more miles east of Warsaw. He had to rise or fall on his own. In any event, her sons were gone again. She could not help but think about Tadeusz, the one who had not come home. Somehow she felt confident that Michał would survive the coming storm—perhaps because he had survived so much already—but nonetheless he was there in her prayers along with Józef, for whom she had no such confidence. He was an artist, not a soldier. For that, she herself could bear the blame—or blessing.

And the words of the gypsy woman Mira still managed to tunnel back to her through the years: *The boy will one day bait the Russian bear.*

What did surprise Anna, however, shaking her to bedrock, was her husband Jan. She had never entertained the faintest idea that the man who had returned a white-haired ghost from the camps in Siberia would be strong enough to take up arms yet again. Oh, he had gained a little in weight and in strength—and mind—but he still seemed a shadow of his youth. His spirit was large, however, and he would not be held back. Having fought with Kościuszko in '94, in the Italian campaign, and years later with Napoleon, and seeing his sons now take up the banner for independence, how could he not do so, he had asked her, his cobalt blue eyes brimming. He did ask Anna for her blessing. Could she refuse this man his final campaign? No more than she could try to douse the intentions of Józef or Michał. She sent him off as she had them: with no tears, until the door had closed behind him. Ironically, he was being sent the further: all the way to Zamość in Southeastern

Poland, 154 miles from Warsaw. The reason for his assignment, he said, was his knowledge of the area, for he had relatives there and knew the terrain.

Anna caught the thin, high sound of the twins' voices now. She wiped away the condensation from the pane she had been breathing on, and from her vantage point she watched below as Barbara Anna and Iza shepherded the boys across the street, toward the church. What was it the one held in his hand? A little figure. Anna recognized it as one of the set of wooden toy soldiers her own sons had played with years before. Unexpected tears came to her eyes.

A little while later, Zofia knocked and stepped in without waiting for an invitation. "Hello, Anna," she said, moving up to stand behind her at the window. "You aren't going?"

"No.—Nor you, it seems."

Zofia gave a little laugh. "For the protection of the many within the church. I'm certain the roof would fall in. Or the statues' faces would freeze into frowns."

Anna attempted a laugh of her own.

The two cousins stood as sentinels at the casement. Several minutes passed. "All gone," Zofia said at last. Her sigh was real, no stagecraft here. "Jan and Jan Michał and Józef and Jurek."

Jurek—Zofia used the diminutive for Jerzy. Jerzy! Of course, he had gone, too. Iza's father. In the weeks before he left, he and his daughter Iza had spent no little time getting to know one another. It clearly meant so much to both of them. Observing this newly-formed relationship, Zofia had gone from denial to disdain to indifference. But now—for Zofia to add Jerzy's name to the litany of family patriots and to use his diminutive—Anna could not fathom its meaning.

"Basia," Iza said, coming into the reception room where Barbara sat, having just put the twins to bed. "There's a woman here to see you."

"A woman?"

"Yes—a Russian woman. She didn't give her name."

Barbara rose slowly from her chair. She was clearly tired from the day. "Whatever does she want?"

"She wouldn't say that, either. She insists on seeing you."

"Ask her in then, will you?"

Iza walked back to the woman waiting near the front entrance. "This way, please." The woman's red cloak was of a fine material but rumpled, soiled, and showing wear. She carried a brown satchel.

Iza watched Barbara's face upon the woman's entry into the reception room. Plainly, Barbara did not recognize the woman. Iza nodded and prepared to leave, but a quick glance from Barbara held her.

The woman who had seemed confident and prepossessing at the door paused now, her glance moving from Barbara to Iza and back again. "I—I am Larissa. I worked with your husband."

"I see."

"What I have to say is rather—personal."

Barbara took her meaning and spoke before Iza could react. "Iza, please stay." Then to Larissa: "You may say what you came to say in front of Iza. She is my closest friend."

Larissa nodded unhappily. "Very well." She drew in a deep breath. "I'm afraid you did not know the—particulars of your husband's occupation."

"At the Imperial Commissioner's? You're wrong. I do know. He worked within the Third Department."

The woman was taken aback, Iza could tell. She drew herself up. "Do you know in what capacity?"

Barbara was silent and seemed to be bracing herself.

The woman went on: "Under Nikolai Novosiltsev he was deputized to *lead* the Third Department. As such he made many decisions—"

"He *led* the department?"

"He did."

"Why are you telling me this?"

"I feel you should know— "

"Know what? Just what is your interest in telling me *anything*?"

The woman seemed about to say something, then her mouth closed, her lips flattening into a thin line. She stepped forward and took a portfolio from the satchel. She handed it to Barbara. "I think this will speak for me, Madame Baklanov. Can you read Russian?"

"I can."

Iza wondered at this, for it was years ago that both she and Barbara had taken classroom Russian in convent school.

The woman handed the portfolio to Barbara, then pivoted to effect her exit.

Iza followed her and wordlessly saw her to the door. When she returned to the reception room,

Barbara was seated and rifling through the several file folders she had withdrawn from the portfolio. "What are they, Basia?"

"They seem to be documents on the various persons Viktor interrogated at the Third Department headquarters. Good God! The Russians document everything. I don't dare read them. I'm certain Viktor did terrible things as part of his job. I won't give her the satisfaction of reading them." Barbara looked up at Iza. "Did she say anything more to you at the door?"

"No, she slipped like a thief into the night. I can't imagine what her purpose was in coming here."

Barbara's flashing green eyes caught and held Iza's. "Oh, yes, you can. You're in the convent no longer, Iza. You needn't pretend on my account. She's very pretty, is she not?"

Iza had no answer. Yes, they both had taken the same reading of her: she had been—or was still—Viktor's lover.

"I won't read these," Barbara said, her gaze falling again on the folders. "They belong in the fireplace. Whatever Viktor did as part of his occupation is in the past. I must remember that. He is still the father of the twins. And, Iza, he is still my husband." She looked up at Iza, as if in appeal.

"He is." Iza wished she could say more in support of Viktor so as to comfort her childhood friend, but words dried up. From the first she had had an aversion to Viktor Baklanov.

"Here," Barbara said, "take these and throw them onto the grate."

But as Iza moved forward, Barbara's eyes became

transfixed on the label of a particular folder. "God's teeth!" Barbara called out in a piercing shriek.

"What is it, Basia?—What?"

Turning her head to the wall, Barbara thrust a file at Iza. "Here!"

Iza could scarcely believe what she saw neatly written—and easily translatable—on the label of the file:

Deposition of Jan Stelnicki, 1826
Interrogator Viktor Baklanov.

Michał worried over Józef, who had been restored to his unit of cadets by one of the two architects of the insurrection: Piotr Wysocki had come personally to the Gronska town house to collect him. Oh, he longed to go, but that did not alter the pain—and fear—registered on their mother's face. Michał felt more responsible for Józef now than he ever had. He had promised to look after him for his parents' sake—especially his mother's. And he had promised himself to do so in memory of his brother Tadeusz. But now new feelings toward Józef stirred.

Upon retrieving him from the grasp of the Grand Duke, Michał had asked him exactly what had gone on at the Grand Duke's palace. They stood in the dimly lit Gronska stable prior to entering the town house.

"Marcin and I were part of the team that was to abduct Konstantin," Józef had said, "but everything went haywire from the first. The setting of the fire near the river was to be the signal, but it was ignited too soon. Somehow, two of the cadets who were to be with Marcin and me at the rear entrance didn't show. And then a guard took us by surprise, and I—I—"

"You killed him?" Michał saw his brother fighting back the tears and thought of the first soldier he himself had killed.

"Yes. And then Viktor appears out of nowhere and tells me I must kill Konstantin. That it was best for Poland. He did make me think about it. I was frightened yet somehow emboldened. To think that Poland might be free again! Oh, he said I would be a hero, and I'm probably vain enough to have let that cloud my thoughts, too. But suddenly Viktor was gone and the Grand Duke was moving in my direction. I had my pistol aimed at his heart and could have done it! Yet I asked myself why Viktor would be goading me into such a thing. It didn't make sense."

"You can bet that he would somehow rise in the Russian bureaucracy if you had killed Konstantin and his brother the tsar came down on us with full force and no mercy. Viktor could *own* this city."

Józef digested this thought, then said: "At the moment of my decision the words of Piotr Wysocki came back. He said to us that Poles do not kill princes."

"And so you let the moment pass?"

"I did. And then suddenly I was knocked unconscious only to wake up as a prisoner myself."

Michał chuckled. "There was much knocking about the brains that night."

"What, you too?"

"Yes, but that's a story I'll save for later."

"Michał . . ."

"What, Józef?"

"Did I do wrong?"

Michał flung his arm around Józef. "God's mercy, Józef, you did right! We do not kill princes. Neither do we kill unarmed men, noble or not." They were both silent for a full minute. At last, Michał said, "I have something for you."

"What, Michał—what?"

"Something I found the other night at Belweder Palace." Michał took from his coat pocket the blue velvet pouch containing the little portrait of Emilia Chopin. "Here."

Józef 's tuquoise eyes lighted up. With trembling fingers, Józef slowly withdrew the miniature and stared at the portrait as if he could not comprehend. He looked up at Michał. And then the tears came in a rush.

It was at that moment, Michał remembered now, that something became as important—more important!—than protecting his brother and that was *loving* his brother. He extended his arms and drew Józef into his embrace. As they stood there, both trembling, a life-long chasm between them closed.

Days later, Michał had signed on to the military also, just as every able boy and man was doing, including—to everyone's complete shock—his father.

But it was Józef whom he had sworn to protect. He had promised his mother—and he had promised himself—not to come home from war without this brother. But they had been placed in different units: Józef was a good distance away with Piotr Wysocki's battalion at Siedlce, about 56 miles east of Warsaw, while he had been assigned to a lancer squadron that was about to leave Warsaw for the Modlin Fortress, about 30 miles north of the capital. He had to think of something. But what?

21

14 February 1831, Warsaw

IZA WAS COMING DOWN THE stairs when she heard a hubbub of activity at the front door. Barbara and the twins were just arriving home after an afternoon out.

"Take the boys to their room," she was telling Wanda.

The twins hailed Iza excitedly as they passed, but the servant spared no time in herding them toward the stairs.

Iza's attention was now drawn to Barbara, who was hanging her cloak on the hall tree. She appeared pale and distracted. "My God, Basia, you look as if you have seen a ghost!"

"I—I suppose that I have."

Iza grasped hold of Barbara's hand. It seemed abnormally cold, the weather notwithstanding. "Viktor?"

"Yes," she whispered. "Viktor."

"Where?"

"We were in the square. He was following us."

"To what purpose?"

"I don't know."

"Did the boys see him?"

"No, that would have caused a stir on the street and I don't suppose that kind of attention would be a good thing for him. As it is, he was running the risk of being arrested on the spot."

"But he knew that you were aware of his presence? How did you react?"

"I became nervous. I don't know, I came all apart inside. After reading that file, Iza, I want nothing to do with him. Nothing! And yet—"

"He's their father."

Barbara's green eyes, so much like Anna's but lacking the amber specks, locked onto Iza's. "Exactly. He sets great store by them. What am I to do?"

Iza was at a loss for an answer. "Come in now. There's company for supper."

Barbara held her back. "Iza, it's not just the boys. How—how do you stop loving someone?" Her large eyes pooled. "Even if they've done terrible things?"

Iza hugged her now. She remembered Armand, whose family had torn him from her because of her mother's resistance and, she heard later, reputation. She had tried to stop loving him. *Had* she? And there was her mother—she had tried to stop loving her, too. It was hard to love her, but harder to stop. She felt Barbara trembling against her. "I don't know, Basia. I don't know." Both were silent for what seemed a very long time.

When at last a commotion was heard coming from the reception room, Barbara gently pulled away. "What company did you say?"

"Michał is here for a brief conference with Prince Adam Czartoryski. Military matters."

At that moment the double doors to the reception room opened and Michał and the prince emerged.

At table Iza sat across from Michał and his mother. The meal was a simple one of mushroom soup, trout, potato pancakes, and beetroot salad. Conversation was of slight matters, but as the meal went on, the dormant subject of politics surfaced.

"Had it been left to me," Prince Adam Czartoyski said in answer to a question by Anna, "I would have worked for the re-establishment of Poland through Russia herself." He sat at the head of the table—Zofia at the foot—while Wanda and her daughter Elzbieta nervously went about the business of serving the courses.

"Rather than through war—open rebellion?" Anna asked.

"Exactly. But as it is, our youths have been impatient and anxious to act. One cannot blame them, but my dream has been crushed. It was to see the guarantee of Poland's nationality as decreed by the Treaty of Vienna realized by slowly working away at Russia's will regarding our national independence."

"And now there are many at Tsar Nicholas' court," Michał added, "that will welcome this insurrection as a perfect reason and opportunity to void the very existence of Poland and come down on us with an iron boot."

"So everything is at risk," Iza said.

"Is there no hope of reconciliation?" Zofia asked.

The prince shook his head. "As you know, on the ninth of this month the first shot was fired by Piotr Wysocki's battalion. It was to hold off the Russian advance, so it was a necessary shot but one that could not keep them at bay for very long."

Iza could not help but notice Anna pale and draw herself up at the mention of Józef's battalion. The fear for her youngest was evident, but so too was pride.

"We will need some victories early on," the prince continued, "if we hope to bring Nicholas to the table."

"Your grace," Anna asked, "how badly outnumbered are we?"

"Our main force is about 50,000 and although the Russians claim 200,000—"

"Two hundred thousand!" Anna said with a gasp.

"Actually, Lady Anna, we believe that number is inflated and that it's more like 150,000."

"Still . . ." Anna said.

"We should not risk our full armies against theirs," the prince explained. "We should attack when the numbers are in our favor and when it will be a surprise. Smaller attacks, smaller skirmishes, in other words."

More talk in this vein led Iza to wonder why it was that the prince had not been made Generalissimo of the Army. He seemed to have the experience and the mind for it.

"Is there no hope that other nations will come to

our aid?" Zofia asked.

"Those hopes have been dashed," the prince said. "Not Austria, Prussia, England, or Sweden. I've spent months trying to enlist them. Even our friend France is only too glad to see Russia engaged with us rather than interfering in *their* interests in points west."

"Your grace," Anna asked, "are you able to tell us where things stand now?"

"Well, Lady Anna, I can tell you that the Russians have crossed our boundaries in three places . . . and that they seem to have the suburb of Praga in their sights as their access to the capital itself."

The table went silent for several moments.

"Like in 1794 when we lost everything," Zofia said, at last. "Dog's Blood!—oh, excuse me, your grace, but it's a good thing I never rebuilt our town house on the Praga escarpment."

The prince afforded a tight smile. His eyes were trained on Zofia, Iza noted. They reflected—what? Surprise? Embarrassment? Disapproval? As for herself, Iza burned with shame—not for the oath her mother had made—but to think that she could voice such a selfish sentiment when the lives of so many and the future of Poland herself swayed in the balance.

Momentarily, the maids came in to serve dessert, a poppy seed roll. The faces they encountered, however, seemed little inclined to smile at a favorite sweet.

After Prince Czartoryski's departure, Iza watched Michał pull on his military greatcoat. Seeing him in

uniform again after so many years conjured up days
of their youth, and it came to her with a jolt that she
must have loved him even then. "You're to leave then,
too?" Iza asked.

"I've got another appointment to keep at the
artillery garrison—about Józef."

"Is he all right, Michał?"

"As far as I know. The Siedlce region is quite a
distance. I worry for him."

"I see that you do." Iza reached up with both hands
to lay flat his collar. "A good and faithful brother, as
it should be. . . . And who's to worry for you, Michał?"

Michał caught the break in her voice and held her
gaze. "You?"

"Yes, Michał." His brown eyes held hers. "Oh, yes."

Michał took her hands in his as they came away
from his collar and held them. Neither spoke.

Finally, Iza said, "Do you return to the
fortress tonight?"

"No, Iza, not tonight. The morning will be soon
enough. . . .Will you . . . will you wait up?"

Iza felt a foreign sensation, a kind of hammering
in her heart. "Yes, Michał, I will."

Michał dropped her hands and reached around
her, pulling her to him now, crushing her against the
buttons of his military jacket as he leaned down and
kissed her with abandon.

In a hard, uncomfortable chair Michał sat waiting for
General Sowiński, Minister of War, in a small office
of the Warsaw Arsenal Garrison headquarters. He

had guided his horse at a slow trot toward the village of Wielka Wola, situated on the western outskirts of Warsaw, slowing and stopping often for other evening traffic in the streets. For the duration of the ride, and even now, thoughts of Józef had been superseded by thoughts of Iza. Her concern for him had been so very clear in her expression and in her voice. To find someone now, at this age in life . . . and in wartime . . . gave him pause. Was there somehow still a chance for them?

"Well, well, soldier, what might I do for you?" A deep but musical voice pulled Michał into the present. General Józef Sowiński entered the room with a decided limp. "I don't have a lot of time to spare, you know."

Michał stood and saluted at once. He suddenly became flustered. What had given him the nerve to request a meeting with the Minister of War? "I . . . appreciate any time you can spare, General."

"Your father is Jan Stelnicki, yes?" The general was taking measure of Michał.

"Yes." That the general knew his father bolstered his self-confidence.

"How is he? Good God, so few come back from Siberia! That was some news." The general painstakingly moved around his desk and sat.

"Truth to be told, it was an unexpected miracle, General. And he's good enough to have reenlisted."

"I'm not surprised. He'll make the Ruski regret their uncharacteristic clemency. Sit down, soldier. You're not here about him, are you?"

Michał sat. "No, I'm here about my younger brother."

The general stared silently, his fingers drumming the desk.

Michał suddenly felt nervous. Had this been the right thing to do? "Well, you see, General Sowiński, he's with Piotr Wysocki's battalion in Siedlce, and . . . and I was hoping you would use your influence . . .

The general sat stone-faced.

"That is, I would like to request that he be reassigned to Wielka Wola, here at your command."

"He's hurt? Has be been wounded?"

"No, sir, not that I know of."

"Well then, what reason have you for what I have to say is a highly unorthodox request? One I am unlikely to grant, I can tell you."

"It's for his safety, sir, and for the well-being of his—my mother. She's already lost one son."

The general's eyes narrowed in appraisal. "There are mothers, Michał, who have given Poland their only sons, plenty of them, and there are mothers who have given all of their sons."

"I know that, General. But Mother still cherishes great hopes for Józef. You see, he plays piano and composes. He's good, too, and has a future. I'm no expert but Fryderyk Chopin's own father says so."

The general harrumphed. "The other son—?"

"Tadek."

"How did he die?"

"He and I were in the retreat from Moscow. What with the Russians, angry citizens, and the Cossocks, it was hell. In a skirmish he took shot to his leg and we couldn't get to a proper doctor before poison set in. He was buried in the snowy ice-hard ground of the Eastern steppes."

"Nasty business, that. The whole Napoleon affair. I know—I was there. I had a little problem with a leg, too. Russia—1812." The general took a letter opener and tapped his leg with it.

Michał realized it was his wooden leg. He had for the moment forgotten the general's well-known disability. Now he could find no words.

General Sowiński let out a long sigh. "You know Marzanna can come for him here, too. "

"Yes, sir," Michał said, the image of Goddess Death as clear in his mind as when he was a child imagining the folk deity in her white dress coming for him, her scythe moving in a wide arc. "It's just that Wysocki is a bit of a . . . a—"

"A hothead?"

Michał nodded. "General, I realize my brother could die here as easily as in Siedlce, or anywhere. But if he meets his fate here, at least his mother could see him buried. Something she could not do for Tadek."

"And what is this brother's name?"

"Józef, after Józef Poniatowski."

"A fine name Józef," the general said with a laugh. "Now had you said *I* was his namesake, I might do something for the boy."

Michał gave a little laugh, too, a nervous one. Words failed him. The general stared at Michał a long time. The moment hung fire.

Then, suddenly, the general rose and came around from behind the desk to Michał, his wooden leg dragging slightly.

Michał stood.

"Very well, Stelnicki, I will give your request every consideration."

Every consideration, Michał thought as he rode back toward the city's center and Piwna Street. He supposed it was the best answer he could have expected; generals were loath to immediately yield to a subordinate's request. Would the general ultimately grant the request? If so, would Józef despise him for interfering? That is, if he somehow were to find out. Prince Czartoryski had described Piotr Wysocki as a firebrand, one who had doubly burnished that title with the cadets' rising and more recently by seeing to it that the first shot fired between Poland and Russia came from his battalion at Siedlce. Michał recalled now how his mother spoke of a gypsy who had predicted that Józef would one day bait the Russian bear. Blood of vipers! The woman who had assisted at his brother's birth had not been far off from the truth. Józef had been present both at the heart of the attempted abduction of the Grand Duke and on the field when the first shot was fired on the Russian army.

To give Piotr Wysocki his due, however, the Siedlce action prevented—for the time being—Russian General Grigorij from crossing the River Liviec, the single obstacle that could impede his army's progress toward Praga.

Michał had to admit that General Sowiński was correct in saying Death could come for Józef or any soldier, no matter his assignment. And yet, Michał thought, close quarters with Piotr Wysocki would only increase the risk. No, he did not regret interfering by requesting that Józef be transferred.

Her mind preoccupied, Barbara Anna left the Gronska town house and made her way up the street. She, along with her mother and Iza, had joined a society under the presidency of Madame Hoffman-Tanska, renowned for her literary productions but more respected now for organizing women of all ranks—genteel or not, city or country—whose focus was the care of the ill and wounded. She walked unaccompanied now. Anna and Iza had left earlier that morning for Gniński Palace on the escarpment above the Vistula. For a decade the palace had served as a military field hospital. As of late Barbara had taken to accompanying her mother and Iza to the palace where they visited the sick and prepared an abundance of bandages for the battles that seemed certain to wend their noisy, bloody ways to Warsaw. Today, however, one of the twins, little Dimitri, had become choleric with a cold and so Barbara had stayed behind until he fell asleep.

It was on Avenue Krakowskie Przedmieście that she became aware of footsteps close behind. Thoughts of her children vanished and she was instantly alerted to—what? Danger? Except for today, she had made it a rule not take to the streets alone anymore; she went out in the company of others and certainly did not allow the twins to tag along, not since . . . but this wide, well travelled thoroughfare was safe, she told herself.

"Basia!"

Hearing her diminutive sent a chill up her back and nearly halted her in her tracks, but she put aside the temptation to stop and turn around. She increased her speed. Surely her name was common enough and there were enough people on the street this mid-morning—

"Basia!" The voice was louder, more insistent—and recognizable.

She turned about to face him. It was useless to run. "What do you want, Viktor?"

He was dressed in the most unassuming greatcoat of dark wool. Underneath his fur hat—a beaver one, not his ostentatiously tall spotted leopard one—his pale blue eyes were trying to assess her. He smiled, still confident in his ability to charm. "To speak to you, Basia."

They stood near the Holy Cross Church, and he reached out his hand to hers in order to draw her to the side of the building, away from footpath traffic. She withdrew her hand immediately but followed him. There was no use in postponing their meeting.

"I've missed you, Basia. The boys, too."

"You may be my husband, Viktor, and you are the father of my boys, but I don't know you any longer." She avoided his eye contact. "I don't want to know you at all."

Viktor drew in a long breath. "Do you know this church has a lower church down in the vaults? The architecture is extraordinary."

"I am not sightseeing today, Viktor."

"We can talk there."

Barbara shook her head. "I have another destination."

"The hospital, yes? Whatever you women do there can wait."

It came home to her now that Viktor was well apprised of her movements when she ventured outside the house. She felt a kind of compression at her heart. He—or his minions—had been spying on her, stalking her.

"Listen to me, Barbara Anna," he was saying, "we can reconcile our differences."

"Can we? I think not. You were less than forthcoming. You were not just some bureaucrat in the Imperial Commissioner's office. Viktor, you were, in effect, the head of the Secret Police and answerable only to Novosiltsev."

"How do you know these things? Your brother Michał?"

"What does it matter? I know what the Third Department has done to people. I know what *you've* done to people. . . . I know what you've done to my father!"

Viktor turned white as the limestone of the church façade behind him. "Who told you that?"

Barbara did not reply. Were not the subject so dark and her heart so rent, she might have taken pleasure in playing turnabout at his game of espionage.

"Barbara Anna, I regret that. I could not have known at the time that I would marry his daughter."

"Is *that* how you became aware of me? Through my father's trial and exile? And all those happenstance meetings—they were hardly serendipitous, were they, Viktor?"

Viktor's back stiffened. "No, of course not! Basia, I arranged them. You see, I loved you from the first."

"You mean to say you wanted to possess me. You were dishonest from the first."

"We can get past this. This insurrection will be over soon—"

"Do you think so?" Barbara interrupted. "And you expect your fellow countrymen to return triumphantly and that life will return to what it was? Ha! You'll go on plaguing us Poles."

"It won't be like that, I promise. I won't deny whatever your father told you about me—"

"My father is too good a man to have shed light on your dark deeds, Viktor Baklanov. Too good a man!"

Once again the color drained from Viktor's face. His eyes widened. "Then, who? Who?"

"Someone to whom you have no doubt been dishonest, as well. Tell me, Viktor, has she been your mistress all this time?"

"Larissa?" It was scarcely more than a breath. Then in full voice: "God damn her! She came to you?"

"With your file. You Russians are meticulous record keepers."

"I was not unfaithful to you. I ended things with Larissa after I met you. You must know that, Basia. We were happy—you, me, and the boys. You would have felt it had it been otherwise."

Barbara paused assessing this, accepting it as the probable truth. "It doesn't matter now, Viktor. Our lives are moving in different directions. It's too late."

"No, when order is restored—"

"By order, you mean *Russian* order?"

"Yes, of course. Let me speak, Basia. Things will get very bad here for those who partook in this. Things will be bad for your family. Your parents will lose their Sochaczew estate as surely as Zofia will lose her holdings. And Siberia—"

"Siberia!" The thought ripped through Barbara like a knife.

"Your family will be on shifting, dangerous ground. But I will be in a position to make things safe for them and their homes. I'm certain of it."

Barbara thought she would be ill right there at the church's foundation. Siberia! *Was* that a possibility? Oh, she could not be certain of a Polish victory. Who could? They were so out-manned and out-gunned.

As if reading her thoughts, Viktor said, "Tsar Nicholas is no friend of the Poles. He is not like his father, Aleksander. And he is no Konstantin, either, dithering about whether to take back what he had. He is a vindictive tyrant and he will take down Warsaw to its foundation, and any gentry foolish enough to stay around will find themselves in the ground or in Siberia wishing they were in the ground."

Barbara took this in, then drew herself up. "I'm a Pole and will remain so. Neither I nor my family will accept help from you, Viktor Baklanov. Whatever may come." Barbara started to turn away.

"Your children—*our* children—are half Russian."

Barbara paused for a moment, her heart beating hard, her eyes averted. She lifted her head, then met his gaze. "We Poles have lived with bigger and heavier crosses."

Viktor's arm shot out in an effort to stop her, but she was too quick in her pivot and made her way to the street.

Michał lay on his cot, restless as the ticking clock nearby, his thoughts on Józef.

News of a key operation at Dobre, just 30 miles east of Warsaw came with a joyful jolt to Michał's camp at Modlin Fortress. Under General Skyzynecki, eight thousand Poles resisted an arm of the Russian army—Rosen's—four times its number. Many of the Poles performed their first service in arms, enthusiastically driving back the enemy at the point of the bayonet. Estimated Russian losses were 6000 men killed, wounded, or captured; Polish losses did not exceed 800. Michał heard of the celebrations in Warsaw, enlivened no doubt by the word of prisoners that Grand Duke Konstantin had been there in the flesh to witness the humiliation, but he knew that in the end Skyzynecki would have to yield the ground they had held so bravely, allowing Russians a little bit closer to Warsaw, Poland's heart.

The Russian master plan seemed clear. Various commanders under Field Marshal Hans Karl von Diebitsch had already crossed into Poland at four different points, covering an expanse of 96 miles. In a Napoleonic-like strategy, Diebitsch would come at the center of Polish forces, at Siedlce while his other commanders outflank the defenders, allowing the combined Russian forces to march directly to Warsaw, ending the war in one fell swoop.

Word among the Old Guard was that the Poles would slowly retire toward the Warsaw suburb of Praga. There on the eastern side of the River Vistula the various corps would remain parallel to one another, taking on the Russians in skirmishes rather than allowing Diebitsch's plan for an immediate frontal assault on the capital. Oh, there would be a major decisive battle, but it would be waged only after the Russians had been incrementally weakened.

Michał wondered if Sowiński had transferred Józef, wondered if he should have interfered. Like his father, he was not much for formal prayers, but sometimes in the matter of war there was little else upon which to grasp. If in making its web, a spider could hurl out into space its flimsy filaments and find the attempt rewarded, might prayers, too—for Józef, their father, and Jerzy—be answered?

Where were these three in this game of war that men played? And then, just before sleep, his thoughts settled upon Iza and the memory of the night he had returned to her after meeting with Sowiński. He remembered most her face, pale as the pillow and a contrast to the crown of her black hair, and her dancing, loving eyes of blue, cornflower blue.

If nothing else, they—he and Iza—had had that night.

22

AT THE TOP FLOOR OF the Gronska town house, Anna stood at the window facing east. Thunderous booms of distant cannonades from towns as far off as Milosna and Okuniew could be heard in Warsaw as fighting inched closer. Movement of the conflict was encroaching on the environs of Praga, where only the River Vistula separated that suburb from the walled capital of Warsaw. For two days currents of fear and tension had been running through the capital and its citizens like a thousand lightning strikes.

It was merely dusk now, but the guns that usually continued to the point of full darkness had ceased. *Peculiar*, Anna thought. What did it portend? She looked down at the street. Those few people present moved along in small groups, their voices hushed, as if in tune with her eerie presentiment that something significant had happened—or was about to happen.

Within a few minutes a crier came running up the center of the bricked street, signaling something of immediate import. What was it? Anna struggled to open the casement window that had not been opened all winter, but when it finally gave way, she heard merely muffled shouts on the chilled air. The crier had already passed out of sight and hearing. People were flocking out of their houses amidst a tumult of noise and confusion. They were heading in one direction: toward Castle Square.

Barbara Anna entered the room now after a quick knock.

"Basia—where is everyone going?"

"Across the bridge to Praga—that's where. Mother, you must make ready! There's been a short term armistice."

"An armistice?" The idea seemed inconceivable. She took a moment to take it in. "Does this mean our men are in rout?"

"No, a three-hour truce has been called to bury the dead."

Barbara's statement was a knife with two edges. *Three hours. Bury the dead.* But there was no time for questions. No time to think of the dead. It was for the living that Madame Hoffman-Tanska had formed her group of women. Plans for such a situation as this had been formulated in great detail. Within half of an hour her army of women and the hospital wagons laden with food and medical supplies would be filling the streets, moving toward the bridge to Praga.

Anna quickly dressed in the prescribed dark blue and met Barbara and Iza on the little portico. Within minutes they sighted a hospital wagon led by a single white horse. They worked their way through the crush of people, gave greeting to the driver and woman in the pilot seat, placed their right hands upon the side of the wagon, and fell into the slow movement of the masses. "It's like a great exodus!" Iza called out above the din.

Anna prayed that it was not an exodus and that these thousands of good people—all hoping to aid the soldiers and see their loved ones—would be able to return to their homes when the three hours came to an end. She had learned that nothing in war was to be trusted.

Slowly, the makeshift caravan of eclectic vehicles and souls moved through the Castle Square, past the column supporting the bronze figure of King Zygmunt—a cross in one hand sword in the other—snaking down then, toward the bridge.

When the carriage rumbled onto the wooden planks of the structure, the scene about Anna fell away like scenery from a stage and a memory of a bygone bridge on the same site transported her. The indelible memories of November 1794 played out in astonishing detail: how she and Zofia and a thousand other souls were attempting to escape wave after wave of Russian soldiers who came into Praga from the east, cutting down men, women, and children with lances, swords, cutlasses. Were it not for Zofia's brazenness—and sacrifice—Anna would not have made it to the Warsaw side before the collapse of the bridge.

A voice near her bolted her back to the present. "It's a miracle that the bridge is still in one piece." Barbara's statement—ironic in light of Anna's trance-like memory—served to clear her mind. Night had fallen but the moon and a parade of moving torches held back the dark.

"I just hope it can bear this kind of weight!" Iza shouted above the din of the crowd.

It wasn't fire that that they had to worry about, as it had been in 1794. Often by now—mid-February—the Vistula had started its magnificent thaw, one that often damaged or completely broke up the bridge. During the course of each spring, many repairs had to be done to make it once again serviceable.

Three hours, Anna thought. She would remember the bittersweet sights and sounds of those three hours for the rest of her days. Eager to meet their defenders, the population of Warsaw flowed through the center of Praga and out onto the fields where the various Polish armies were coalescing. These were the fields of glory upon which in the days to come Poland's future would be decided. But for now, parents sought out sons, wives their husbands, children their fathers. Tearful, joyful reunions went on about them as snatches of hymns came from one quarter only to be echoed in another. Some citizens failed in finding their loved ones and had to hear from commanders or read from posted lists the names of their fallen, but Anna witnessed how they came to grips with their grief, knowing the cause for which their heroes had valiantly died. She wondered if she could be as brave.

Miraculously, no sooner had the wagon been stopped at an open-air field hospital and the dispersal of provisions and medical aid begun than Michał appeared, embracing Anna first, then Barbara, then Iza. Anna noticed the joy on the faces of Michał and Iza, confirming in her mind what had been merely a suspicion: that a very special bond had bloomed between them.

Michał turned to her now. "Mother, Józef has been transferred. I've only just heard. He's stationed here, at the Warsaw Artillery Arsenal."

Anna's face brightened. "He's safe and well?"

"He is. General Józef Sowiński has taken him under his wing."

"Thank God. And your father?"

"He's still in the Zamość area, I was told by a reliable source. His knowledge of that area is invaluable. So, you see, everyone is accounted for."

"Indeed," Anna said, relieved and as happy as possible amidst such uncertainty. The major battle for Warsaw was perhaps just hours away. "Have there been many dead, Michał?"

"We may have lost 6,000, but I can tell you far fewer Poles than Russians. Our call for an armistice to bury the dead was but a ruse. We're waiting for reinforcements. And besides, we've probably gained as many peasants as the number of the fallen. Armed with pitchforks and the like, they've come."

"Ah, the people," Anna said, "they seldom disappoint."

"I must move on to my own duties now, ladies," Michał announced, bowing and doffing his czapka in an exaggerated fashion. It was almost as if he were saying his farewell at a dance or some such social occasion even though Anna suspected that his duties had to do with the burials.

It was an hour later, with the wagon nearly empty of food and medical supplies, that Barbara cried out, "Mother, isn't that Cousin Zofia over there, accompanying one of the coroner's wagons?"

Iza looked up, her eyes narrowing and following the direction Barbara indicated. "It is," she said, without a scintilla of surprise in her voice.

"She's . . . she's—"

"You're surprised, Basia," Iza said, a twinkle in her eye. "I can't blame you. When did you ever see my mother go out of her way for someone else? And yet, she joined Madame Hoffman-Tanska's legion of women a few weeks ago."

"That's where she's been going?"

"Indeed and without fanfare." Iza turned and called out: "Mother!"

Anna could see that Barbara was thinking *all the more wonder,* but she would not say it aloud.

"Who can say what goes on in my mother's head?" Iza said.

Zofia was disengaging herself from the coroner's wagon and starting to cross toward them, so Anna, whose own surprise was mild, spoke up. "Politics and national boundaries mean little to Zofia, but when her home and loved ones are threatened, you can expect her to move like a mother bear."

Zofia wore the plain blue dress advanced by Madame Hoffman-Tanska, but over it she had one of her most luxurious capes, one of black silk and white fur. At least for the moment, the contrast seemed to define her very character.

Zofia kissed each of them, making small talk as she did so. This was no social gathering, however, and presently she made ready to return to her duties— duties that clearly had to do with readying the dead for burial—but in an abrupt move, she pulled her daughter aside and whispered something in her ear. Iza's face darkened, her eyes suddenly gleamed with tears, and she slowly shook her head.

With Zofia gone, Barbara dared to ask, "What's wrong, Iza?"

"Mother wanted to know," Iza said, her words catching in her throat, "if I had heard anything of Jerzy, my father." She wiped at a tear before it could fall, her eyes vividly blue in torchlight, going from Barbara to Anna. She drew in a breath before answering the unvoiced question on Barbara's face. "He's not here and neither is he on the lists."

Anna was dumbstruck on two counts. First, she had agreed with Michał that everyone was accounted for. That was not the case. Iza's newly found father was not accounted for, and Anna burned with shame to think she had been so remiss as not to think of him—or Iza, who had kept her worries about him a secret. Even more striking than that, however, was the surprise Anna felt now in recalling the pain and concern on Zofia's face. Zofia's feelings for her lover of more than thirty years ago were genuine—and full of a fire rekindled.

Wielka Wola

JÓZEF WIPED AT HIS FOREHEAD. He had worked up a sweat brushing down his horse, Tad, a fine Polish Arabian. The color of chestnuts, it had eyes that

seemed to look into one's soul. He had named him
for his brother Tadeusz. He wrote nothing of this in
a letter he had sent to his mother from Siedlce. He
meant only to establish a bond with the brother he
never knew, but would she think it disrespectful?
Perhaps not, but neither did she need a reminder
about her long-ago loss. Józef finished his brushing
with several long strokes. "There, how's that, my
friend?" he asked, as if the horse might answer.
"Miss the country, don't you, Tad? I do, too. Maybe
tomorrow I'll take you out for an airing better than
today's. We'll go far from the city!" Józef tossed the
brush up onto a shelf. He lifted a months-old limp
carrot to the grateful mouth and exited the stall
without a backward glance. "Count on it!" he called
back. Fastidiously caring for Tad had always soothed
him as much as it had the horse. But not today. Oh,
he was thankful for having been able to keep Tad upon
being transferred to the Warsaw Artillery Garrison
although his work here had not as yet required use
of a horse. Truth told, there was little else about his
new position to give him cheer.

The transfer had come out of the sky, like a bolt
from the gods. No other cadets of his class that had
been with him under Piotr Wysocki at Siedlce had
been moved. Why had he been singled out? Here
he knew no one. He had not yet even encountered
another cadet. They were all artillery men, as one
would expect. What would a cadet planning a
lancer career be doing among artillery men? It was
a mistake. It had to be. But no one above him in
authority had listened to him. If only he could catch

sight of General Sowiński . . .

Józef brushed straw from his blue uniform, then kicked at the gravel as he left the stable area and made his way into the courtyard of the garrison. He placed his red czapka on his head. The day was cold but the sun was bright. Why here, for God's sake? Here on Długa Steet and within a short distance of the Gronska town house? Not that he was about to visit his mother even if she was still at Cousin Zofia's. The mere thought was a humiliation. He should be in the field. He should be at Siedlce with Wysocki and his fellow cadets. Why, during the recent three-hour armistice he hadn't even been allowed to go out onto the plains of Praga with most of Warsaw's citizenry to meet and help the soldiers who had been giving battle on the outskirts of Praga. He had been needed to man the garrison, he was told, as well as clean the inner workings of cannons. He spit on the ground.

He thought of Siedlce now and he brightened for a moment. Actually, the action had begun at Mendzyrzec, a little town near Siedlce. He was with one of two new regiments of light cavalry. Cossacks had been sighted at dusk by a scout the night before, so a skirmish was expected by dawn. A squadron of the Old Guard would take the lead and one of the old-timers, Tomasz, suggested the Young Guard draw lots to choose the first to fire against the Cossacks. "Fortune favors the young!" he had cried, his volume brazened by a bit of brandy. The cadets gathered around excitedly, anxious for their first action, their first trial on the field, and so it was that Józef drew the single long straw. The memory brought a warm flush of pleasure to his cheeks.

It went much as Tomasz had forecast. At first light, two regiments of Cossacks appeared upon a little ridge and moved stealthily down toward Mendzyrzec, confident they were taking the camp by surprise.

At a given signal, the Polish forces—Józef in the middle of the Old Guard—moved out from a forest of ash trees, calling out their "hurrahs," lances and carbines at the ready. It was the Cossack force that was surprised and confusion reigned as the width of their line had to turn toward the attack coming from their right.

The attack commenced with the Old and Young Guard pouncing, giving no time for the enemy to pull their horses and weapons into a semblance of order.

"Now, little Józef!" Tomasz shouted when the Cossacks came into range. Józef aimed his carbine at a white-suited Cossack and fired. While he missed his mark, the skirmish had begun. Józef, well protected by the Old Guard, did manage to wield his lance effectively, wounding and knocking a Russian soldier from his horse. It was a little victory managed with help, he knew, but a victory nonetheless that sent his pulses running like the cold February wind that whipped around the plain. In short order the Poles were dealing blows among the startled Cossacks, dispersing them. Fifteen were killed and a squadron and six officers were taken prisoner.

Later in the day the cavalry retired to the environs of Siedlce. Word came back within two days that the conflict that day had been the first skirmish of the Rising, excluding the day of the insurrection the

November previous. And it was he, Józef thought now—remembering the toast of wine raised that night to him and the cause of independence—who had fired the first shot of the Rising.

The proud thought, however, was tempered by the current sight about him: the massive walls and buildings of the Warsaw Artillery Garrison. What had brought him here to Wielka Wola on the western outskirts of the capital? To him this was a prison.

"You're the Stelnicki boy, are you not?" The voice came from behind.

Józef bristled at the epithet. "Cadet," he said, still walking, face forward.

"Ah, cadet, of course. Forgive me, Cadet Stelnicki."

Józef pivoted, thinking it was Karol, the old ostler, who must have followed him out of the barn. It was not. He recognized General Józef Sowiński at once. He had a long face, made to seem even longer by the gray muttonchop whiskers extending from a surprisingly healthy head of hair that curled forward at mid forehead—or was it a wig? It was a kind face. Józef saluted. He knew he should apologize, do a bit of groveling, but the words wouldn't come. He hadn't asked to be here.

"Walking toward the mess hall, cadet?"

"I had no goal in mind, sir."

"We all have goals, my . . . er, young cadet. Or we should have. Mind if I walk with you?"

Józef nodded uncertainly. The two started walking. Józef's pace slowed a bit to accommodate conversation and the slower stride incumbent upon the general's wooden leg, about which stories abounded. His heart, however, raced. Would he have the nerve to question his assignment now that he had the opportunity?

"Have you gotten acquainted with the garrison, Józef?"

Why was the commander of the garrison—much less the Minister of War—taking such an interest in him? Józef could not imagine. "Well enough, sir."

"Good, good!"

"Yes, sir."

"But you're less than happy, Józef?"

"Cadets don't complain, sir."

"But you'd like to, I think. Yes?"

Józef did not respond.

"You were at Siedlce for the first attack? The opening volley."

"Yes, sir."

The general inquired now about the particulars of the skirmish, requiring details when Józef became too taciturn in the telling.

After the story was told to his satisfaction, the general halted and put his hand on Józef's shoulder. "Fate had placed you at the nexus of history, my friend. And now you think you will be missing action, cooped up in an artillery garrison. That's it, isn't it, Cadet Stelnicki?"

Józef looked head-on into the older man's face, the piercing eyes made more so by the blue of his double-breasted uniform. He felt blood rushing to his own face.

"Cadet?"

Józef straightened a bit, screwing up his courage.

"Sir, I don't know why I've been transferred here. I think it's a mistake, but I can't make anyone realize that."

"You're here because there was a need, Stelnicki. Soldiers obey. Don't worry, you'll not be bored."

"The action here in Warsaw, General Sowiński, if I may say so, took place last November." Later, he would wonder where he had conjured up the nerve to counter the Minister of War.

"Indeed, indeed." Evidently amused by Józef's pluck, the general could not mask a solicitous smile. "But don't think we won't see action again, Józef. Warsaw has always been the flashpoint for our little quibbles with Mother Russia."

Józef knew not to argue further.

"I knew your father, Józef. Met him in both the Kościusko and Bonaparte campaigns. Good man. How is he?"

"He's rejoined as a staff officer, General."

"One is never too old to come to the defense of our country."

That the general registered no surprise seemed odd. How could he have known? "He was in Zamość last I heard," Józef said.

"Indeed. I'll leave you here, then, my young cadet. You are your father's very image, Józef. The very image, whereas your brother . . ." General Sowiński's voice stuttered to a close without a finish to the sentence.

Józef was left to stare after him, noting the uneven gait, the sun glinting off his gold epaulettes. The man had tried to be clever and supportive, but he had recognized his mistake at the last. He said more than he had planned. Józef knew now the general had met with Michał and that his brother had somehow manipulated this transfer to the garrison.

Damn Jan Michał!

Viktor paced the reception room, back and forth. He became anxious every time Bartosz left the house to do the marketing or attend to some other errand. While he had ultimately decided that Bartosz was worth too much to him and his everyday needs to take the most drastic measures, the man still occasionally unnerved him, making him question his own judgment—and security. But then, too, Bartosz always came back able to supply him with the news of the day. It was the one thing that kept Viktor sane.

Today he had been gone over two hours, and the usual visions of the man revealing everything to his fellow Poles played in Viktor's head. He had thought it out a dozen times: on the one hand, Bartosz would be well rewarded by the rebels for denouncing a Russian official in the Third Department but, on the other hand, surely he wouldn't think that people would really forget that *he* had been the servant and willing instrument of the Polish turncoat General Rozniecki? To date, Viktor had no solid reason to distrust Bartosz, but he paced nervously, nonetheless, his eyes moving every few minutes to the mantel clock.

He walked now to the window facing the street and drew back a curtain panel. There in the snowy street a woman stood observing the mansion.

He didn't recognize her at once because she had changed so in fewer than three months. He thought for a moment she was a street vendor—or whore. She had an unkempt look about her—tousled hair beneath a shapeless bonnet and a long black cloak, rumpled and equally sad. The face seemed lifeless, pale and haggard, eyes deep in hollows. Viktor stood so amazed at the sight of Larissa dressed in funereal fashion that he held the curtain back a beat too long. Her head turned, eyes darting in his direction. Her peripheral vision had caught some movement—or perhaps she felt someone's gaze upon her.

He drew back and allowed the folds to fall back into place. He was confident she could not have seen him, but he also knew she could not have missed the motion of the drapery. She would know someone was at home. He didn't even have time to draw in a breath before she made it to the door and began pulling at the bell. Then came the sound of the brass knocker against the oak door, insistent and increasing in volume.

Viktor stood frozen to the floor. After a while the noise ceased. He could almost sense her coming to stand near the window again. He knew a retaining wall there kept her a few feet at bay; still, he hardly moved a muscle—until he heard Bartosz' key in the lock some thirty minutes later.

No, Bartosz told him, he had not seen her. Larissa had disappeared. Would she stay away? Not likely, he told himself. Viktor retired to the hidden room and sat. Larissa's appearance had been deeply unsettling. Judging by her clothes and thinness, he surmised she must have been evicted from her rooms—or she had chosen to give them up. Had her money given out? Or had a Polish landlord taken exception to a Russian under his roof, pretty or not? Being Russian in the capital was no advantage these days and her accent was strong enough to give her away immediately. Was she living on the streets? More importantly, what was driving her to continue her search for him? Did she think he still cared for her? She was misled if that was the case. Did she merely hope to gain help from him? He could provide that, if he chose to do so. Rozniecki had left in such a hurry as to leave behind a significant cache of gold ducats hidden beneath the floorboards there in the hidden room. Blood money, no doubt, of which Bartosz was unaware. Yes, he could pay her, but could he dare to trust her?

Bartosz' finely-spiced goulash did little to cheer Viktor, who slept little that night, until the early hours of the morning when exhaustion overcame him.

He came awake some hours later, after night had fallen. The candles had guttered and gone out, making the windowless room dark as a cave. It seemed he had been drawn from a deep sleep—but by what? A dream? He had no recollection of having dreamt, but then again, he seldom remembered details of his dreams.

It was then that he heard the voices on the other side of the door. The pulse at his temple throbbed. There were several people in the room Rozniecki had once used to cheat his own spies. Slowly, noiselessly, he arose from the narrow bed and made his way in the darkness to the door. He knelt, hands searching for the hinged window in the door that would allow him to see and hear fairly well what went on in the Rozniecki office.

But he found he could see little, for someone with dark breeches was standing directly in front of the peacock painting and the two tiny holes in the center of two of the tail feathers.

He detected four voices. Four men, one of whom was Bartosz. It seemed an ordinary discussion at first. But as the volume rose, it became clear that Bartosz was being questioned—no, interrogated. He could understand some of the words although sometimes the Polish ran too fast for him. The situation became quite clear: they were insisting others were living in the house. In a steady, confident voice, Bartosz denied it. He had lived there alone, he said, since Rozniecki had fled. He spoke of the general in the most negative way, calling him a scurrilous scoundrel, so as to distance himself from his former employer and ingratiate himself to the Polish rebels. He sounded sincere, but would they believe him? Perhaps they would take him away? Torture him? Force him to reveal the hidden room?

They were moving now, exiting the room. Distant, echoing noises indicated a thorough search was being made of the mansion. In short order Viktor heard footfalls above him. He prayed none of the Poles was quick enough to notice that the room above was so much larger than the office fronting the hidden room. He found himself holding his breath as the footfalls retreated and silence fell.

Then several of the men reentered the office. He

could not hear Bartosz' voice. Viktor's heart beat erratically. He took in a deep breath and dared not bend to peek out through the peepholes. Had he given him away? Were these men about to discover the secret of the peacocks painting?

The heavy boots moved about the perimeter of the room. One man stopped very near by. Viktor could hear him slightly wheezing. He was certain he was standing very near the painting. He heard the man say, "Dog's blood, these peacocks are unlucky creatures. Didn't the scoundrel Rozniecki know that?"

Moments later the men left the room. *Not so unlucky*, Viktor thought, *not for me*. He did not move even when he thought he heard the front door close.

A long hour passed.

Then came footfalls in the next room again—and the sounds of a single man approaching the painting. Now he heard the faint squeek of hinges followed by the lifting of the plank of wood and the click of the mechanism that allowed the door in the stucco wall to open.

The door opened and a man stood before Viktor, who was still kneeling, his hand on a pistol, another at the ready. Viktor blinked at the lantern that shone down on him, making a silhouette of the man. He stood now and exited the hidden chamber.

"The woman," Bartosz said.

It was all he needed to say.

23

April 1831, Modlin Fortress

IN THE DAYS FOLLOWING HIS brief reunion with his family on the field of Praga, Michał had little time to savor the memory of that moment. In General Skrzynecki's division of the Grand Army, days were spent in preparing for battle, instructing new cadets in the uses of the lance, carbine, and sword, reconnaissance, digging trenches, throwing up ramparts, and doing battle at Wawre, Grochów, Kawęczyn and a dozen other villages. He recognized and thought it strange that his part in war so absorbed him that the entire day could pass without thought of home and family. It was as if he had two lives and each was fully separate of the other. At night the fact that he had another life came as a little shock each time. At the midnight hour he would fall so exhausted onto his pallet that thoughts of his brother's safety—or even thoughts of Iza—were brief and blurred by immediate sleep.

Russian prisoners vindicated the Polish Old Guard's contention that the Field Marshall Diebitsch's strategy was a full frontal assault at Praga. It was, however, a strategy that was failing so that Poles had reason to be optimistic. The Poles' counter-strategy of engaging his armies separately in small and large skirmishes was having its effect on the war effort—as well as on a deflated Diebitsch, who had taken to leading the columns to the fire himself, but to no greater success. It was reported, too, that Grand Duke Konstantin stayed close to the Diebitsch forces, but his royal presence did little to incite Russian victories. Michał imagined that the average Russian fought mainly to stay alive.

Michał did not relish taking the lives of Russians, many as young as Józef. But he at least had the advantage of knowing why he and his men were fighting. They were in a holy contest, fighting for liberty and for freedom from despots. Did these young Russians know why they had been sent to fight and die? He recalled the old proverb often used when Poland and Lithuania had been a flourishing commonwealth: "In Russia do as one must; in Poland as one will."

Despite the numbers' being stacked in favor of Diebitsch, major Polish victories were celebrated in March and April, one inflicting ten thousand casualties, another harvesting as many prisoners. In addition, successful raids were conducted into Lithuania and Volhynia. These feats had thrilled Michał and fed his hopes. And Michał was still with General Skrzynecki's forces on 10 April when they arrived at Iganie, a village just west of the huge Russian munitions depot at Siedlce, to find Polish forces had taken the village, killed 3,000 men and taken 1,500 prisoners while losing fewer than 500 of their own forces. Michał assumed General Skrzynecki as Commander-in-Chief would order pursuit of the withdrawing Russian army. Inexplicably, he did not.

And then came days and days of quiet and inaction. Michał worried. Why were they giving Diebitsch time to recoup and strategize? Doing so went against everything he had ever studied at the Officer Cadets School or witnessed on the field. You follow and exhaust the enemy, giving him no time to think or regroup. Was this not battle sense? Common sense? Already men were calling Skrzynecki "The Delayer."

Wielka Wola

THE DOOR TO GENERAL SOWIŃSKI's office was closed. Józef approached it warily, his courage flagging and heart at a canter. He stopped in his tracks. His anger over his brother's unwanted intervention regarding this reassignment had put him out of sorts and had built and built for days until he thought he would explode. It reminded him of a boil on his forefinger he had once had as a child. The thing grew larger and more painful by the day— until one day his mother deemed it time and lanced it, spilling out the infection.

How had Michał dared? *Dog's blood!* News had come from Siedlce of the Russian rout, news that kindled and ignited deep discontent within Józef. Without his brother's interference, Józef would have been there as witness and participant. Thus, only this morning he had decided to speak with the general and beg to be returned to Wysocki's battalion. He

knew doing so went against every rule instilled in
him as a cadet. Obedience was all. But it was either
speak up or be driven mad with frustration. He was
miserable here, each day longer than the one before.
The general seemed a reasonable man. Would he
listen? He had once been a cadet, Józef thought, his
hope on the rise—until he realized that the similarity
cut two ways. Most likely, as a cadet the general had
never gone to his superior with a request like Józef's.
He removed his czapka and gave his head a shake
as if to dispel his doubts. Whatever the general's
reaction, Józef would have had his say and that
in itself would provide some relief from his anger,
just as the lancing had relieved the pain from his
inflamed finger.

Józef drew himself up now, screwing up his
courage and stepping to the door. He had come this
far. *God's bones*, he would do it!

He knocked. What seemed an eternity passed. He
knocked again.

"Come in." General Sowiński had a rather
musical voice. Józef had noted as much at their first
meeting. The voice that came from beyond the door
was obviously his, but the dulcet tones bespoke a
yawn in progress. *Damn!* Józef had awakened the
general. The meeting, the request, was doomed.
Józef thought of hightailing it out of there in hopes
of finding the general at another time—when he was
alert and receptive.

But before he knew it his hand was on the bronze
door knob.

The room had been darkened, its two windows

shuttered. Józef entered, trepidation filling him like liquid an empty vessel.

"Who is it, then?" The voice came from behind the desk.

"Cadet Józef Stelnicki, General Sowiński." Józef peered through the gloom and the general's white shirt began to materialize. His hands cupped the back of his head as he lay back against the desk chair, his right leg propped up on the desk. Józef felt blood coming into his cheeks. He swallowed hard. He had awakened the Minister of War. A bad omen. What else could go haywire?

"Come in, come in, my boy." His tone was surprisingly welcoming. "It's Józef, yes? Couldn't forget that now, could I? My father used the diminutive *Józefek* when he was angry at me. I never liked it. How about you?"

Józef dared to take a few steps, then halted. "I—I prefer *Józef*."

"Indeed, indeed. Well, well, to what do I owe this visit, my young cadet? Would you first open the shutters?"

Józef stepped to the two windows that fronted the garrison courtyard and slid open the shutters, allowing the midday light to flood the room.

When he turned to face the general at this new angle, he saw at once that the general's wooden leg stood against the wall behind and to the right of the desk chair. Józef's gaze moved involuntarily to the seat of the general's chair. The left thigh, smaller than the right, came to the edge of the chair, allowing the dark blue material of his empty trouser leg to loosely hang.

Józef's heart contracted. "I'm intruding, General Sowiński. I should go."

"What? Nonsense. Come, sit there."

Józef obeyed. The chair to which the general motioned was at the side of the desk so that it would be nearly impossible for Józef to ignore the disability.

"How's that horse of yours? From my window there I'm seeing you ride out and return, seems like every day. A fine animal, that. Polish Arabian, of course."

"Yes, sir." Józef found himself staring at the general's face in order to avoid looking at the empty trouser leg, but when he shifted his gaze it fell on the oddest device that was the general's wooden leg at rest. His discomfort heightened.

"Had my favorite animal blown right out from under me."

"Sir?"

"My Arabian. Rabbit, I called him, for he could race the wind. It was at the Battle of Mozhaysk, not so very far from Moscow. The cannonball took the horse as well as my left leg. My wife blamed Bonaparte for going against common sense and allowing us to get caught in Russia during winter." The general shrugged. "But such is the game, my boy."

A game? Józef considered. His brother Tadeusz had been left buried in frigid ground during that same campaign. That same *game*.

"Will you make a career of it, young Józef?"

"I hope to, sir."

"What about your music?"

Józef felt a heat coming into his face. Here was

further evidence of Jan Michał's interference. "You are well informed, sir," he said, sarcasm in the words if not in the tone.

The general shrugged and a hint of a smile played on his mouth. He was well aware he had given himself—and Michał's meddling—away at their last meeting. "Your music, lad?"

"It's not as important as independence for Poland, sir."

"Mmm, indeed. How old would you say I am?" The general pushed back his well-curled hair. "Don't let the gray fool you, boy."

This was strange and treacherous terrain. Józef assumed the general was past sixty but he was not so foolish as to hazard a guess of any kind.

"Put you on the spot, have I? I'm fifty-three and I imagine I look much older."

Józef struggled to hide his surprise.

"I stood at Praga's ramparts in 1794 when the Russians came down on us. I was about your age, just seventeen. After the dismemberment of our country, my regiment was taken into the Prussian army—lock, stock, and barrel. Then, like so many, I returned to Polish service and to follow Napoleon who promised us much. I've lost count of the battles. Then came some quiet years, that is, until you cadets took a sturdy stick to the Russian hornets' nest. Now I'm Minister of War." He let out a great sigh. "You can't escape your fate, can you? You told me you saw action at Siedlce, yes?"

"Yes, sir. I was allowed first shot."

"Indeed? Impressive."

"Yes, sir, I guess so. I was lucky."

Then the general mumbled a proverb Józef had heard before but he could not decipher the intent. He said: "Each age has its own follies."

The general went to grasp his wooden leg but found it just out of reach.

Józef's good sense and manners told him he should jump to assistance, and yet he found that he had no wish to touch the object. He sat unmoving, paralyzed.

The general began pulling at the loose trouser leg, hiking it up. "Józef, would you mind handing me my peg? There's a good lad."

Józef had no other recourse. Torn between shame at his reticence and a strange repulsion, he stood, moved toward the device, lifted it. It was lighter than he had imagined. Turning to the general, he saw that by now the trouser had been hiked part way above the thigh so that the stump was exposed. He felt a nausea wash over him.

"A right clever contraption this," the general said, taking the leg. "Look here, the upper portion is boxwood that's been hollowed out to receive my thigh. See here, I had a good surgeon. You notice where the skin is folded under? I have no feeling there at the end. Of course, the surgeon insisted I wear the leg eight months so as to make certain the stump was fully wasted."

Józef had no choice but to watch as the general pulled the leg onto the thigh, securing it then to his pelvis with a strap.

"Ah, there!" The general extended the leg. "Now if you would do the honors and give a tug to my trouser leg."

Józef took the hem of the garment in hand and pulled it over the boxwood where it fit with some snugness, then down to where the leg tapered and held in place the peg, surprisingly small in circumference. The folds of the trouser leg fell then to the floor, masking the slight flare of the peg at the bottom.

The general sighed. "Ah, complete again, so to speak. Sit, my boy."

Józef obeyed, waiting to be asked again for the purpose of his visit.

General Sowiński sat forward in his chair, his hand moving on his desk toward some object. He picked it up and tossed it to Józef.

The action was unexpected but Józef managed a clumsy catch. He stared at the ten-pointed silver badge attached to a red ribbon. It was the French Legion of Honor medal. His eyes widened at the sight. He had never seen one.

"The little man gave me that himself, Józef. Strangely, Napoleon appeared short, but in person his height matched that of his tallest man. Such was his presence."

Józef looked up from the badge just in time to catch another item from the general. The catch was smoother this time. Józef drew in a deep breath. Another medal, one that was attached to a blue and black ribbon and one that he recognized. It was the golden cross of the Polish Virtuti Militari. His eyes moved from one to the other, one cupped in one hand, one in the other.

"Had to dust them off, my boy. They've been in a trunk. Couldn't exactly wear them while I served Konstantin now, could I? Maybe you'll help me attach them before you leave?" The general nodded to his formal military jacket that hung on a hook near the window. It was deep blue, of course, and double breasted. The buttons, like the impressive epaulettes, were gold. "For now I can wear those again. And for the future—who knows? You know, I suspect my wife would have had me trade the whole costume for that of a professor or even a farmer. An old soldier—now dead—once told me that only one in five soldiers is a real warrior and the rest are soldiers by circumstance. But I've found that it's more like one in twenty that are true warriors who thrive on the sword and battle and blood-letting and death. In time I found I was not one in twenty. Too late, alas.—Do you have a girl, Józef?"

"No, sir." The question—bizarrely off topic, Józef thought—tore at his heart. His right hand instinctively moved up toward his jacket's inside pocket that held Emilia's miniature. Realizing that hand held the Virtuti Militari, he aborted the move. He could not help but think what a strange turn this visit had taken.

"Ah, well, it won't be long, I'm certain, a handsome lad like you, in or out of uniform.—Do you know, after I have you help me with my medals, I'd like to see your horse. How does that sound?"

Stranger still. "Fine, sir."

"Good! When this is all over, Cadet Stelnicki, I hope you go back to your music." The general was already up from his chair and moving toward his jacket, the peg of the wooden leg punctuating every other step.

At the stable the two talked at some length of the Polish Arabian line of horses. Half an hour later, the general left him alone with Tad without any further inquiry as to why Józef had gone to see him.

Józef lay in bed that night, the visit and the general's comments replaying in his mind. The general was a clever man. He had known what Józef wanted and somehow the words, the medals, the wooden leg had impacted Józef in such a way, inexplicable even to him as he lay there fully wake, that the issue had been closed.

The boil had been lanced. Obedience was all.

Only later—much later—would he come to understand the lesson about glory and war—and that General Sowiński had brought him to a place where two paths met.

June 1831, Warsaw

"COME HERE, WILL YOU?" VIKTOR called to Bartosz, who had just arrived home from marketing.

Bartosz stepped into the Rozniecki office, where Viktor spent a good deal of his time, having grown bolder with the weeks and tired of the restraints of the stuffy, hidden room.

"Yes, sir?"

"What news today?"

Bartosz gave a little shrug. Like so many harnessed into household service, he was a serious man but he seemed even more so today.

"What is it, Bartosz? Why are you so tight-lipped?"

"My mind was elsewhere. There's talk of a setback, sir."

"A setback? For whom? For God's sake, man, put down your packages and tell me!"

Bartosz spilled his six or seven packages on a table near the door but moved no closer to Viktor. "The Poles. It was not unexpected."

Viktor had become used to hearing of miraculous minor victories on the part of the insurgents so that this news *was* news. It was no setback in his eyes. "When and where, Bartosz? What is the talk?"

"End of last month at Ostrołęka. It's about seventy-five miles northeast."

"I *know* where it is! Get on with it, man."

"Well, no one has heard the story first hand yet, but what is known is that the Poles were stubbornly fighting to hold the town and keep General Diebitsch from crossing the River Narew. The fighting was intense and while the Russians lost plenty, the Poles lost the best of their infantry, thousands, they say, along with hundreds of officers and two generals."

"Two generals? Was Skrzynecki one?"

"I did not hear his name mentioned." Bartosz turned to retrieve his packages. Evidently he had revealed all he had heard.

"One can hope, Bartosz. One can hope." Viktor longed to hear that the usually adroit General

Skrzynecki was among the killed. But what about Bartosz? What were his hopes? He had delivered earlier reports with a seeming objectivity. And yet, at first coming into the room, he had seemed downcast. Did this man who had worked, quite willingly and profitably, for a Pole who was employed by Russia as a spy truly lack—like Rozniecki himself—a vested interest in his own country?

It was a point to ponder . . . later, for now there came a knocking at the front door and both Viktor and Bartosz came to attention.

"Go see who it is, Bartosz."

Even before he could fully secrete himself in the hidden room, Bartosz hurried back into the office. "It's the woman, sir!"

"Larissa?" Viktor found himself saying her name even though he knew it could be no other. "The same one from before, you mean?"

Bartosz nodded, his face paling.

"You know the plan, Bartosz. Are you prepared to follow through on it?"

Another nod.

"Good man. Now let her in."

Viktor remained in the office. He carefully closed the door to the hidden room and moved the huge painting of peacocks into place.

"Peacocks, indeed!" The voice behind him was Larissa's. "How befitting."

Viktor had expected her to return weeks ago and had since begun to think he was well rid of her so that when he said, "What a surprise this is, Larissa," he was speaking the truth. He turned away from the painting to face her, wondering if she had seen him swing it into place over the doorway to the hidden room, then deeming that possibility of no matter. Not now.

Larissa wore a beige dress he had seen before when he took her to a ball—before he had been bewitched by Basia. The garment was soiled and fraying in places—ruined finery. Her hair was unkempt, her face gaunt, the gray eyes somehow dulled.

"Don't worry, Viktor, I've not come to ask you to take me back now that you are without your loving wife."

Viktor bristled at the mention of Barbara and the memory of Larissa's meeting with her. "It is a temporary separation—until Russia regains control of Warsaw."

Viktor made a show of calling to Bartosz to bring two glasses of wine, good wine from the cellar.

"You are an optimist, Viktor—about your wife, I mean."

"Sit, won't you?" Viktor motioned to the chair in front of the desk. He moved around to the desk chair. "And you, Larissa," he said, taking his seat, "have loose lips."

Her eyes widened slightly. She took his meaning at once.

"You've done your worst in trying to alienate my wife. To no avail," he lied. "Now tell me what you want."

"You're a fool if you think she still loves you and twice the fool if you think you ever loved her."

Viktor tasted bile rising in his throat. "What do you *want*?"

"Money, Viktor," Larissa sniffed. "I've been

put out of two pensions and refused housing at a dozen others. I want enough money to live on until such a time when there are safe carriages again to St. Petersburg."

Under the guise of concern, Viktor plied her with questions about her experiences of the last few months, even suggesting two places that might take her in.

Bartosz entered now with two glasses of red wine. Viktor stood and offered one to Larissa, who took it and drank, rather greedily. As for himself he took the crystal goblet with the slight chip on the rim.

"About the money," Viktor stated after Bartosz had left the room, "had you asked me a few months ago, Larissa, I did have a good deal of money. But no more. It's quite costly keeping house, I'm finding. While the shops are open, the best meats and fish are to be found on the black market at exorbitant prices." He continued in this vein, speaking the truth, watching her eyes slowly glaze over as the poison did its work.

When they closed, he called for Bartosz.

In her bedchamber Iza drew on her nurse's blue dress in preparation to take up her shift at the hospital. News of the disaster at Ostrołęka had been the subject for days in Warsaw. After a good many victories, it had come as a shock. Lists of the dead and wounded had yet to arrive. What of Michał? He had been there under General Skyzynecki's command. She prayed that he was not one of the 300 officers who had been—no, she wouldn't even voice it to herself. He was safe. He had to be. And what of her father, Jerzy? No one knew where he was.

Iza heard the sounds of marching in the street below and went to the window. The soldiers had already passed. Just soldiers assigned to the city, she assumed. She wished she could do more than she was doing. She was still relatively young and strong. If only the Polish Sejm had not vetoed Madame Hoffman-Tanska's proposal for their women's aid group. She had suggested that there be three companies of women: the first to stay behind the lines of battle in order to carry off the wounded; the second to attend to the wounded in the vehicles that carried the wounded; and the third to help with the many provisions needed, such as bandages and wrappings of cotton and wool. If the all-male Sejm had not been so obstinate as to reject the idea, Iza would have chosen the first group.

On the ground floor she discovered her mother in the reception room.

"Izabel, come in here. There's been some news."

Iza grew faint, her mouth falling slack. She hurried in. "What? What is it, Mother?"

"Anna's had a letter."

"From whom?" She felt her heart pounding in her chest. "*About* whom?"

"It is from Jan."

"Jan Michał?"

"No, Izabel, Anna's husband Jan."

"Oh. He's still at Zamość? And safe?"

"He is—and he tells Anna that Jerzy is there,

as well."

"Thank God. I'm so relieved to hear it. You would think he'd have gotten word to us before this."

"Izabel, you must know where he comes from, that little village on the River Vistula. Child, he can't write."

Iza was thunderstruck. Jerzy was well-spoken and always neatly dressed, but he had little formal education and was a simple man at heart. She felt her face burning with embarrassment.

"Ironic, isn't it?—Anna's husband there with my . . . your father. All these years later."

There was a strangeness to it, but Iza couldn't quite bring the irony into clear focus. "Mother, did you once love Jan?"

Zofia flinched. "Why would you ask that, Izabel?"

"Just little things I picked up over the years from Cousin Anna and Basia—and you."

"Ah, a lifetime ago I thought to marry him. I admit it. But he became smitten with Anna. And I—I saw marriage to him as a way of avoiding the arranged marriage my parents had planned. But no, I didn't love him. I came between Jan and Anna. It was a terrible thing I did."

What her mother didn't say was that Anna had been pressured into marrying Zofia's intended and that it ended badly. There was more to the story of the two cousins, Iza could tell, but for now she pursued the subject of her father. "And Jerzy?"

"Oh, Izabel, Jerzy and I come from different worlds." Zofia turned her back to Iza. "There was no future for Jerzy and me."

"Did you love him?"

"Love? It was not for us." Zofia turned to face Iza, a smile somehow more bitter than sweet. "And you, Izabel, have you found love?"

How easily her mother could turn the tables. "Yes, Mother," Iza said, her voice catching.

Zofia was clearly waiting for her to say more, but Iza—heart and mind on Michał—pivoted and swept from the room, moving quickly for the door lest her mother see the tears already spilling down her cheeks.

24

July 1831, Zamość, Poland

HAVING RIDDEN SEVERAL MILES NORTHEAST of the Zamość Fortress, Jerzy Lesiak and two other soldiers were reconnoitering the area for sign of enemy movement.

"We'll ride to that ridge," Lieutenant Albin Klimek called and the three rode on, taking the long, gently sloping way, Klimek in the lead with Jerzy and a cadet, Kazimierz, flanking him. A perfect lookout point. It was an easy order, Jerzy thought, a predictable one. And one *he* would have given—had he been born into the szlachta, been educated as one of the minor nobility and completed studies at the Officer Cadets School. Had that been the case, he would not have left the army years before and he might be a general this day, not taking the lead from a twenty-five-year-old lieutenant.

Once, in the advance on Russia, he had saved the life of an aide-de-camp of Napoleon. Word had gotten to the little Corsican himself and Napoleon made a point of congratulating him in public and was about to promote him to major. It took Jerzy's poor French and a good deal of crudely spontaneous sign language for Jerzy to convey to l'Emperor that he could not read and write—French or Polish—and, as such, was unsuited for promotion.

Jerzy shrugged off these inequities. They seldom bothered him anymore. Fate goes as it must. On the battlefield he was equal to every man at his side. But there were other differences having to do with his birth that stung as deeply today as in the past. Were it not for his birth, he might have married the young woman he had drawn from the river so many years ago. Zofia . . . she had been his for such a short time. Were it not for his birth, he would have been the father to Iza he had wanted to be. And there might have been other children, too.

The three soldiers came to the top of the ridge and looked out over the prairie below that extended less than a mile, ending at the cusp of a thick birch forest. It was a perfect summer day, the trees standing like bleached sentinels against the cloudless sky, the thick grasses below dotted with wildflowers of white, yellow, and blue, bending and stirring gracefully with the wind. On such a day Jerzy wondered how it was that country fought country, man fought man.

It seemed that the three simultaneously sighted the figure on horseback.

"One of ours," Lieutenant Klimek whispered.

Unless, Jerzy thought, not without sarcasm, the Russians were now wearing czapkas and blue uniforms trimmed with crimson.

"What does he think he's doing?" Klimek hissed.

"Scouting," Kazimierz said.

Jerzy was remarking to himself that the cadet had more sense than Klimek when something about the figure caught his attention. He watched him closely. It was an officer—and one whose posture betrayed the fact that he was not so very young. As if sensing their presence, or hearing Klimek's rambling complaints— rising in volume—that he had no business scouting out *his* area, the officer looked up, caught sight of them and gave a little wave. He then directed his horse closer to the forest.

"The old fool!" Klimek muttered.

"He knows the area, lieutenant," Jerzy said.

"You know him?"

"I do. He's Major Jan Stelnicki."

"Well, he may have done his last reconnoitering, Jerzy. Look there!"

Jerzy looked due north and fell silent.

"Cossacks!" the cadet cried.

There were five of them coming over the horizon, all robed in white, their massive warhorses leaving behind them not a wake of dust, but a path of beaten grasses and flying clods of earth.

"Jan!" Jerzy called out the alarm.

Jan turned in his saddle and took notice. The Cossack warriors had seen him and were bearing down on him like hounds on a hare.

"His Polish Arabian can outrun those monster destriers," Klimek said, "but he best get moving."

Jerzy's worst fear was realized as he watched Jan turn his horse—to face his attackers.

The cadet's mouth fell slack. "He's going to take them on!"

"He's a dead man!" Klimek said.

"Sweet Jesus in Heaven!" Jerzy cried. Jan was well into his sixties. What was he thinking—to stand his ground, mad as Don Quixote?

Jerzy gave rein to his horse, giving spur so hard it surely drew blood. He ignored Klimek's order to halt. He was flying down the ridge now, couldn't stop if he wanted to, dirt and stones flying, praying not for himself but for the stability of his own Polish Arabian's legs on the rocky, nearly vertical cliff.

Jan had used just the pressure of his knees to direct the well-trained horse's turnabout because his hands were already busy with weapons. He drew himself up in the saddle now, his mind filling with a sense of destiny coming for him, destiny coupled with a sense of déjà vous, for many years before he had given good fight to just such a gang of Cossacks, the same white robes, the same massive warhorses heaving and snorting. He well knew the difference between that time and this. Even then he had been no match against their numbers despite being young and strong and determined.

"God's teeth!" Jan cursed aloud as he watched one of the Cossacks pull away from the others, his dark stallion's hoofs loudly pounding the plains. He wanted to be first to engage Jan, and his guttural warrior whoop made it evident that—in contrast to that other meeting—there would be no prisoners taken this time.

If only he had his lance at point, he would make short work of the angry zealot. But the lance rest was empty. What good were lances on a reconnaissance mission?

"Come, Jadwiga," Jan whispered, withdrawing his longtime sword from her scabbard. "By God, be true as ever, Jadwiga." His hand on her handle, he felt the old war-joy pumping through his heart now, returning to his veins. Youth was gone, strength diminished, but determination—determination abounded.

The steel coruscated in the sunlight, so Jan knew the Cossack would be prepared. But his plan was for Jadwiga to dance with the second arrival, for he kept his loaded carbine out of sight, a sudden surprise for the most impetuous of the suitors. As for the third, fourth, and fifth Cossack callers . . . who could say?

About halfway down the perilously steep incline, Jerzy heard another horse behind him. Somehow he knew at once it was Kazimierz and not Klimek.

But the day was not through with providing surprises. By the time Jerzy's horse stumbled onto the prairie grass, he could hear not one, but two, horses thumping down behind him. Klimek was not allowing them to go into battle alone. Later, Jerzy would ruminate over the truth that it often takes circumstances—or fate—to coerce some men to heroism. So it was for Klimek— a reluctant hero who fell under a Cossack's sword that day.

Warsaw

ANNA AWOKE IN A SWEAT. She could not believe she had fallen asleep. She had come home tired after a long morning shift at the hospital that began at 4 A.M. After the significant loss at Ostrołęka, the main body of the Polish army had retreated to Praga, just across the river, so that all the hospitals were overflowing with men, Polish soldiers and Russian prisoners. Sitting up at the side of the bed, she gave a slight shake of her head. Her intention had been merely to lie down and rest her eyes. Focusing on the window facing the street, she saw that the afternoon sun was still strong outside. The clock on the mantel told her she had lost a full hour.

She had dreamt of Jan again, that first fateful meeting in the meadow at Halicz replaying in her mind. How handsome he had been—and how incorrigible in his teasing of her. A smile forced itself upon her—until she remembered that something had jarred her awake. What was it? She listened carefully. The house was silent as a well. Was it in the dream, some sense of unease? Anna found herself second guessing her part in allowing him to go off to war yet again—and at his age. However, she came to the conclusion, as always, that she would not have kept him home. Was he safe there at Zamość?

There had been little good news of late. Anna went to the window. These days the faces passing the town house to and from St. Martin's were always serious, so serious. Women prayed while the men too old to go off and fight argued in the streets and squares about the tactics employed by certain inept Polish generals. News had come that General Diebitsch had died of the cholera the month before so that was a topic of great concern. No one knew what to make of it. Who would the Russians send next and what difference would the replacement make? And the rumor that cholera was spreading among both armies rang like an alarm bell through the city and especially in the hospitals.

Viktor sat at the great oak Rozniecki desk, the secret door open across the room, the peacocks painting ajar in case some danger of exposure arose. Larissa had been buried in the grounds in the rear of the mansion and posed no threat, but what if she had spoken of him to someone? What if someone came looking for her? It paid to be cautious.

He wondered if he was being cautious enough regarding Bartosz. Oh, the man had played his part well enough in the matter of Larissa, but he seemed increasingly hard to read. Viktor had thought he sensed for the moment—when the servant had come back from marketing with the news of the drubbing the Poles had taken at Ostrołęka—a fleeting resentment in his dark eyes against the Russian he was sheltering. Did this man who for years had abetted a notorious Polish traitor still harbor a sense of patriotism?

Viktor pushed aside the Polish journals. *The Monitor* had resumed its publication and depending on its availability Bartosz would bring copies home. A more militant journal, *New Poland*, had been introduced, too. Certain important details were to be found in these, but Viktor trusted Bartosz's reports more. The word of the people on the street and in the squares made for a truer picture of events than newspapers that were likely tools of propaganda.

Viktor looked down at his own journal, an old account book of Rozniecki's that had detailed—he imagined—a thorough record of the swindler's doings. Viktor had torn out the used pages and, ignoring the vertical lines meant for numerical figuring, he regularly sketched in Bartosz' nearly daily briefings, enumerating the events on the field and in the capital that had occurred since Ostrołęka, nearly all in favor of the Russians. At each recitation Viktor watched every muscle and line in Bartosz' face, listened to every tonal shift in his delivery, analyzed each word choice. No, there was nothing more to indict the man. In fact, he recounted the Polish setbacks with an extraordinary indifference.

And the setbacks for the Poles were many.

Recently, word had come that Prussia was no longer pretending neutrality, that its government was openly aiding Russian troops. But Lithuania was a more important story. Early on in the insurrection, Lithuania had voiced its enthusiastic desire to join the Poles, yet the Polish military leaders dallied at the offer for so long that Russia had been given the time to entrench their forces in that part of the Commonwealth.

Too bad for the Poles, Viktor had written in the journal. Things in the city, too, were becoming more and more chaotic. The various factions in the Sejm had become polarized. A bill to distribute land to peasants and soldiers in return for service infuriated the conservatives. The Patriotic Society exerted a strong influence, calling for the freedom of serfs and a more concentrated war plan. Russia had replaced Diebitsch with General Ivan Paszkiewicz, who was each day enlarging and strengthening his stance, currently in the northern Vistula valley. Word coming back from the warfront had Sejm members calling for replacing General Skrzynecki, whose epithet *The Delayer* was heard daily in the Sejm. Not even Prince Adam Czartoryski escaped tongue lashings for his months spent on vain attempts to recruit other nations to Poland's side. Unrest was decidedly heating up. Viktor would wait for the boil.

Viktor wrote now in the journal. *Things are in a ferment here in Warsaw, becoming more chaotic with each day. I know that if I bide my time, when the Russian takeover occurs, I will find a way to ingratiate myself to those in charge, perhaps to Paszkiewicz himself. And so I wait. One day, too, I will have to make a decision about Bartosz.*

So absorbed was Viktor in his journal that he failed to hear the front door or approaching footsteps until they were very close by. Startled, he closed the book and shoved it into the side desk drawer. When he looked up, he tried to mask the relief he felt when he saw it was merely Bartosz returning from Market Square.

"I took you by surprise," Bartosz said through the open door.

"What? No, not at all." Viktor attempted a smile, wondering if Bartosz had seen the book, then setting aside the concern. Why, he doubted the man could even read Russian.

"Come in, Bartosz. What news bring you today? Anything?" The servant's eyes were wide, uncharacteristically so. "Come and sit."

Bartosz drew up a chair to the front of the desk. He had a strange sort of look of amazement on his face. "The capital is abuzz with the news."

"Tell me, damn it!" That Bartosz failed to address him as "sir" or "my lord" was a constant source of irritation.

"It's the Grand Duke Konstantin."

"What about him?"

"He's dead."

"What? How? Surely not on the field? The Poles?"

"Oh, no. It was the cholera. Died very quick-like in Minsk a couple of days ago."

Viktor realized now that Bartosz was taking the measure of his reaction to the tsar's brother's death as a guide to his own reaction. "Just desserts," Viktor said and he meant it. "He handled the crisis of his life here at Warsaw like a fool. He should have attacked the city at once, not shrink away into the night, as he did. The insurrection could have been put down in a heartbeat. What is of concern, however, is that cholera is on the rise. Is that the case?"

Bartosz nodded. "In both armies."

"A level field, as they say.—There's something else. I can see it on your face. What is it?"

"Well, my lord, a marvel of sorts—have you heard of the Russian Count Orloff?"

"Yes, I've heard of him." Viktor was deliberately cryptic.

"He was visiting the Grand Duke after having been to Prussia on a mission from the tsar meant to secure even more overt help for Russia's war effort. What's unusual is that the story goes that the Grand Duke died suddenly the day after Count Orloff departed."

"So?"

"The very day after!" Bartosz cried. "People are naturally suspicious."

"Of a plot? It's the cholera, for God's sake. If anything it's God's plot." Viktor could not help but wish that Konstantin's death had come earlier—at the hands of Józef. Russia would have struck at Poland immediately and with decision. *And I would not be in hiding.*

"But back in June," Bartosz was saying, "Count Orloff was sent to meet with General Diebitsch."

"Yes?"

"The general died the day after Orloff left.

Again, unexpectedly."

"Ah, so the gossips have a conspiracy theory, one that traces back to St. Petersburg?"

Bartosz was paling. "They say it's a poison that done it."

"Do they indeed? One as clever as yours? What did you call it?"

"Belladonna."

"Ah, well the truth will out, I expect." Viktor wished he had bitten his tongue or uttered gibberish rather than bring up the subject of Larissa, for Bartosz' wrinkled forehead and downturned mouth advertised his divided sensitivity at having participated in the killing of a woman.

After Bartosz managed an awkward exit, Viktor considered the coincidence of the deaths of a general and a grand duke. He knew, more than did Bartosz, that conspiracy was commonplace in St. Petersburg. Would Tsar Nicholas wish Diebitsch dead? He could have merely had him recalled. As for Grand Duke Konstantin, would the tsar have his own brother murdered? Murders within families were not unheard of in Russia, but Konstantin's position had so devolved as to leave him without a power base, and therefore of little threat, so Viktor deemed murder as unlikely. No doubt there were other men who might wish Diebitsch and Konstantin dead. For one, he could imagine his own superior Nikolai Novosiltsev as harboring grudges—and he was more than capable of treason. Where was he since he had fled Warsaw?

Viktor's thoughts came back to Count Orloff. Viktor knew quite a few things about the man, things he had kept from Bartosz. The count's title *Harbinger of Death* was well known to the Russian people. It was an inheritance from his father, as well as from his grandfather. The latter had become an intimate of Empress Catherine through his part in poisoning and strangling of her husband Peter, while Orloff's father had played a role in the undoing of Paul, the current tsar's father. *Harbinger of death*—it was a family business, Viktor thought and laughed aloud. In light of his own miserable existence of late, it was at least something he could laugh at.

The memory of Bartosz' face and demeanor, however, cut short his humor. Here was a man who seemed to have the poisoning of Larissa weighing on his conscience. And Viktor, who considered himself an expert in interrogation, now knew that—in the event of an inquiry into the missing Larissa—Bartosz would not withstand even the most rudimentary questioning. More importantly, might this delayed regret over the poisoning presage a similar reaction regarding Barosz' divided political loyalty?

25

Modlin Fortress

ICHAŁ CLIMBED TO THE VERY highest battlements of the fortress. He looked out into the night, struggling to hold off depression. While General Skyzynecki and the Grand Army had come and gone, he had orders to stay at the fortress mentoring the Young Guards and even the peasants armed on their arrival with merely scythes from their farms. It was important work, he knew, and he did manage to insert himself into patrols that got caught up in skirmishes with Russians. The action kept him sharp, but less than satisfied.

His wish that the Russians would coalesce here at the little village of Modlin was just that, he thought in more sober moments, a wish. The longest citadel in Poland and perhaps all of Europe, Modlin Fortress sat at the confluence of the Rivers Vistula, Bug, Narew—and even the Wrka, a tributary of the Narew. It would be a hard nut for Paszkiewicz to crack. Warsaw, on the other hand, had the advantage of the Vistula that afforded considerable protection to the east, but its boundaries to the west were expansive and vulnerable. And Warsaw was the prize. It took no gypsy to predict that the real battles would occur at the capital. Paszkiewicz was being allowed days to assemble west of the Vistula and to bring in other armies. *God rot him!* It was enough to drive one mad! What was the reason for this inaction by Poles? How the Russian general had been allowed passage across the Vistula was a comedy of errors worthy of the history books one day. And each day word came back that Warsaw was in a state of near rebellion. No one was happy with the way the war was being waged, not the people, the military leaders, the members of the Sejm. And reports had it that Joachim Lelewel, one of the men Michał had accompanied to try to reason with the Grand Duke months ago, was now head of the radicalized Patriotic Society and beyond reason himself. The sum of these things would all work to the advantage of Paszkiewicz. The showdown would be at Warsaw, 30 miles to the south. Michał was convinced of it. And he would not be there.

It was a bitter irony, Michał thought, his notion of having Józef transferred to the Artillery Garrison at Wielka Wola—a little village that was no more than a suburb of Warsaw—for safety. In so doing he had placed his young brother in the direct line of attack. Well, he would see the action he craved, God help him.

Michał wondered about his father. Was he still in the south, at Zamość? A recent letter from his mother expressed her concern. Jerzy had been there, too, she wrote, but she had had no word of them even though she knew of other letters that had come through from Zamość.

And—other than Józef—what of the safety of his loved ones in Warsaw? His mother, Barbara and the twins, Zofia?

Michał stared up into the night sky searching in vain now for the North Star. His mind's eye, however, mutinied, countering with a vision of Iza's eyes of blue, beautiful cornflower blue. "Iza," he said aloud. "Iza." The two words were as serious a prayer as he had ever prayed.

August 1831, Warsaw

AT NOON VIKTOR WAS STANDING tucked into the shadows of the narrow alleyway between the town houses across from the Gronska home. He had been there since before dawn, waiting to broach Barbara. At first light he had seen Anna Stelnicka leave, dressed in her hospital blues. Then Iza had left at mid-morning in similar apparel.

Iza. He remembered standing just where he was now some months ago, having followed Iza home. It had been a foolish impulse. At the Chopin concert he had happened to notice that she was refusing a ride home from Zofia's driver and so he had followed her. He thought it curious and wondered if she was about to meet up with Michał, in whom he and the Third Department were very interested. He remembered telling himself as much that night—and that he was seeing to her safety on the nighttime streets—but the truth was, he had found her quite attractive that evening, innocent and vulnerable. It was good fortune for both of them that she moved quickly, allowing him no time to catch up to her, to yield to temptation. He had been completely faithful to Barbara since their marriage. But for a moment that night he had dared fate . . .

Now, the great bronze bell in St. Martin's bell tower blasted the first trio of consecutive strokes, calling people to pray the noon Angeles. It was deafening, but more than that, the bell was cracked, rendering the pealing cacophonous. Viktor started to curse, but when he noticed that the front door of the Gronska town house had opened, the oath fell away. He waited. No one emerged.

Then came the next three tolls, reverberating up and down Piwna Street, causing children to hold their ears. Of course! Just as people stopped in the street in prayer, so too had the person who opened the door. She stood in shadow.

Viktor waited patiently for the final three crashes of the clapper. They came in a timely fashion, augmented by the tolls of countless other churches, near and far.

When the tolling ceased and people resumed motion once again, Viktor saw the woman step onto the portico, broom in hand. It was Elzbieta, the young maid.

Damn! Viktor cursed.

The waiting continued.

Two hours later, a young man—probably a university student—came to stop on the street and happened to glance down the little alley, taking note of Viktor. Viktor turned away immediately, shielding his face and adjusting his stance so that it would appear as if he were relieving himself. He waited, half expecting the man to challenge him in some way. His hand went to and held the sheathed knife in the breast pocket of his frock coat.

Two minutes later he turned back to the street. The man was gone. It was a dangerous chance he was taking, especially these last two days. To his amazement, in the midst of war, a recent Military Sejm had been convened and Gereralissimo Skyzynecki had failed to win a vote of confidence from his commanders and had been relieved of his duty. Agreement on a successor was not so easy. Several generals had refused the post. All hell was breaking out in the capital. The Patriotic Society had become even more radical. Without the influence of Skyzynecki and the presence of Czartoryski, who had left the city, the Patriotic Society had seen to it that alleged turncoat officers, spies, demagogues, political critics and the like were put on trial. Late, two nights earlier, prisons had been forced and thirty-four men were killed, including four generals. Order was restored just before dawn, the mob leaders were executed, and the Patriotic Society was dissolved. One particular group of three had been found halfway to the Russian camp with a letter to General Paszkiewicz, detailing the capital's current weakness. It was an engraved invitation had they managed its delivery. The traitors were hanged at once from the nearest lamp post.

It was that gruesome little story that provided the seed of an idea to take root in Viktor's mind.

But for now—after nearly three hours of waiting—

Barbara appeared on the portico. She said something to the maid, took the three steps to the street and began to move toward Castle Square.

Viktor allowed her to move some fifteen or twenty yards before he followed her. He took care to put his hand to his hat and cover his face so that should Elzbieta look up, she would not recognize him.

It took some doing, but he caught up to Barbara in the square. She turned when he called to her, a shadow passing over her face at the sight of him. Her face hardened. "What is it?"

"I want to talk with you."

Her mouth pursed a bit, the chin lifting. "Talk?"

"Yes, I want us to come to an arrangement, some agreement."

The green of Barbara's eyes seemed to darken in the way that he noticed her mother's had when they told her of their engagement. "There will be no arrangement, as you say, Viktor."

"You're angry about my secrecy. I can't blame—"

"If only that were all."

"Listen, what I said to you in the winter about the danger to you and your family will come to pass. And I suspect it will be more extreme than anything I imagined then—before this insurrection took such an ugly turn."

"Ugly, yes. But perhaps it's you that's in danger now. If I were to call out now, here in the square, your life would be forfeit. Are you aware of what has been going on?"

"The hangings? I know. Listen to me, Basia, General Paszkiewicz is just outside the city, biding his time. When he makes his move, the capital will fall. Your Poland will fall. And it will not go easy on you Poles. It won't be like last time or the time before that. This is Nicholas in charge, not Aleksander. Nobles from Czartoryski on down will be dispossessed. Your parents, everyone you know. Participants and sympathizers will be hanged or sent to work camps. Your father knows first hand of such places."

"Thanks to you!"

Viktor cursed himself for bringing up her father. Her eyes had begun to brim with tears, but when he alluded to her father's incarceration, she stiffened, steeling herself. "I ask you to forgive me for any harm I caused your father. Had I known—"

"Had you known he would be your father-in-law, you would have spared him. Of course! But what about the next Pole over whom you held such power? Not so lucky for him, yes?"

Viktor's voice dropped to a whisper. "We meant so much to one another, Basia."

"You were masquerading, Viktor. I was a fool."

Viktor drew in a long breath. "What about the boys?"

"What about them?"

"Would you see them sent to the hinterlands to grow up in a work camp? Could you bear to be separated from them?"

"I would kill myself and them first!"

"A modern Medea?" He scoffed. But, for the moment at least, he read the determination in her eyes and he believed her. "Basia, it need not come to that. I can make it up to you for what I've done.

I will have a position here once again. A position of importance. I will see that you and the Stelnicki and Gronska families are protected. I can do that."

Barbara paused for what seemed a long time. Would she listen to common sense? Did she wish that she, her children, and family members survive what was coming?

Barbara drew herself up now and spoke clearly and deliberately. "I refuse any help from you, Viktor. Do you hear me? And I won't yield one more minute to you." She turned her back to him.

"I can *take* the boys, Barbara," he said before she could put her feet in motion.

Barbara spun around. He had gotten her attention. "You would do that?"

Viktor answered her with silence. He saw her eyes flash green hatred, then be taken by something behind him.

"There are three soldiers about thirty paces behind you." She spoke softly but with resolve. "Don't turn around, Viktor. They are walking this way. If I were to call those patriots over right now, you would have no life, whether Warsaw falls or we hold out against a despot. I imagine a lamp post would be your home well before nightfall."

"You're not serious. Basia, I—"

A finger to her lips silenced him. "You have not more twenty seconds to move quickly away from me. If you are still standing here when they go to pass us, I will stop them."

"You wouldn't."

"How badly do you wish to find out?"

From behind, Viktor could hear the boots moving

toward them. He knew he had fewer than ten seconds.

He tipped the wide-brimmed hat to her and moved off toward Podwale Street, exiting the square just as the three o'clock Angeles began clanging from any number of churches, reverberating throughout the square loud as the bells on doomsday. Others stopped to pray. He did not.

The Rozniecki mansion was silent as a monastery upon his return. He suspected Bartosz was still making his rounds of marketing.

Viktor went directly to the kitchen, propelled by a vortex of emotions: shock, damaged pride, deep, deep anger—and only later would he admit, heartbreak.

He had a task here and tried to focus on that, only that.

From the cabinet below he carefully lifted the clear glass container of a grayish substance. He noted a mark on its side meant to designate the volume after its last use. Should he remove some, Bartosz would know it. Drawing down a clean, clear glass, he spooned out and into the glass what he gauged a half cup of the substance. Setting that aside, he drew down from the shelf the cannister of flour. He spooned out the same amount of flour into the clear glass container, taking care to thoroughly mix the gray and white substances and leave the mixture at the previous marking—in the event that Bartosz was as suspicious as he. He returned the cannister and the glass container to their respective places.

He was left now with his glass of the gray

substance, no one the wiser. He proceeded to the door leading down to the cellar cold room. He quickly found the large pot of bigos that Bartosz had made the day before. Lifting the lid he dropped the dustlike gray substance into the thick stew, found a long spoon, stirred the concoction of broth, herbs, veal, pork, sausage, onions, tomatoes, sauerkraut—and now, arsenic.

The arsenic was an accessible item. Bartosz had not disclosed to him where he had gotten the belladonna, nor where he might have stored any left over, and naturally, Viktor could not now raise suspicions by asking about it. Arsenic would have to do. Would it have the same quick-acting effects?

Before he left the cold room, he cut for himself a large piece of cheese. Stopping in the kitchen long enough to saw off a hunk of bread, he hurried to his room. Thoughts of Barbara were not far away, but for now he had much to think about.

By the time Bartosz arrived an hour later, Viktor had decided to bait him before proceeding with his plan, telling him that he would need different clothes, nondescript and dark clothing of Polish tailoring—and that he planned to find his way to the Paszkiewicz camp at Raszyn, a town southwest of the capital. In the telling Viktor watched the servant with eagle's eyes. Of course, without being explicitly told, Bartosz would know that Viktor was attempting that which had gotten three Russian sympathizers hanged just the day before: providing the Russians with the word that the chaos in the city, combined with the fact that most of the Polish forces had crossed from Warsaw to Praga in order to deal with a small Russian force there. Now was the most advantageous time for Paszkiewicz to make his move on Warsaw at Wielka Wola.

"There's a grave danger to that, sir," Bartosz said. The man did understand.

It was the first time Viktor could remember his having called him *sir*. There was something in that. And there was something in a very minor muscle tic beneath his right eye. Together these little things betrayed him. Viktor had been an interrogator too long not to take notice of such things. Oh, Bartosz might lack enough of a conscience to work for a traitor like Rozniecki and wink at things that went on in front of him, but in the end he was too much a Pole and not to be trusted.

"There's a danger in merely breathing, Bartosz. Now I am looking forward to that national dish of yours—what is it called?"

"Bigos."

"Ah, yes. I think we shall both feast on it tonight. We have wine, yes?"

"The bigos is to simmer three days, sir. It needs one more day."

Viktor held his composure. "Nonsense, man. It will be delicious."

"But—"

"I insist, Bartosz."

The servant nodded, recognizing an order.

The plate of bigos set to the side, Viktor sat working

at his bread and cheese, relishing little of it. He glanced over at the boots, breeches, and greatcoat—all black—that Bartosz had provided. There was, too, a lump of coal that would darken his face and hands.

When he was dressed he left the hidden room and went, slowly, to the kitchen. The poison had had time to work. The swinging door was open. Inside he did not find a dead or even prostrate Bartosz.

The servant sat at his small table fully alert, expectant even. The plate of bigos had been moved to the side. Viktor's attention was drawn to the glass that sat directly in front of him. The sides of the glass were coated with a filmy residue. *Holy Christ!* He knew at once that that was the glass he had used earlier for the poison. He had been found out.

Viktor's stomach pitched. He had meant to wash out the glass and return it to its place, but he had stupidly left it in the cold room. Viktor swallowed hard. What now?

Bartosz read his mind. "Oh, I did eat some," he said, "before I discovered the glass." The attempt to smile ended in a grimace, and came home to Viktor now that the poison was working after all. "Ah, Viktor, arsenic is a slow-working poison, nothing like the belladonna. Why, some folks even survive it." A hardness came into Bartosz' dark eyes now. "Poisonings—by you Ruski," he said, alluding to the suspicions around Count Orloff, "a cowardly way to kill your enemy, no?"

Viktor had no time to process the damning accusation because in the next moment he saw something move slightly behind the glass: a small pistol.

Bartosz raised the gun, aimed it at Viktor.

But he hesitated as if to say something.

His mistake! Viktor pulled his own pistol—already primed—from the greatcoat. He aimed for the chest and fired.

The impact at the shoulder forced Bartosz's upper body back against the chair, the hand that held the gun flagging. Bartosz tried to steady his arm, took aim and fired. The bullet wisked above Viktor's head.

Viktor cursed himself for his own aim. In an instant, he withdrew his second pistol, fired and the bullet this time flew true, straight to the heart.

16 August 1831, Wielka Wola

IT WAS NOT YET DAWN. Józef had fed his horse and worked now at brushing him down but his mind was still on the letter he had had from Michał who—reading between the lines—sounded restless at the Modlin Fortress. Like everyone he was concerned about the amassing Russian army. He was worried, too, about their father. Neither he nor his mother had word from him in many weeks—or from Jerzy, for that matter. Józef knew that mail from outposts could be a dicey thing; after all, he received Michał's letter only because General Sowiński's aide-de-camp had made a trip to Modlin Fortress and, hearing about the courier's presence there, Michał had prevailed upon him to carry the letter back.

Michał, of course, wanted to know how he was getting on. The resentment and anger Józef had harbored against his brother had dissipated as he became more and more comfortable with his current duties, and the time came when he was at peace with the overtures Michał had made to secure for him a safer post. The general, meanwhile, had taken Józef under his wing, going so far as calling him *son* on occasion. And he was told by officer and cadet alike that the time for the decisive action was coming. Besides, Piotr Wysocki and many of Józef's fellow cadets at Siedlce had been reassigned here to help bolster Warsaw defenses. He chuckled to himself, thinking that perhaps *he* would see action and not Jan Michał.

"How's that young Arabian stallion doing, Józef?"

Polish Arabian, Józef thought, turning to see General Sowiński closing the stable door behind him. While he had made it a habit to stop by in the mid-afternoons, after Józef was finished with his usual duties maintaining weapons of every imaginable type, he had never been seen up and about this early. Józef saluted. "Tadek's a bit edgy this morning, General."

"As are we all, my boy. As are we all."

Józef thought little of the comment.

The general harrumphed. "Your letter, no bad news from your brother, I hope."

"No, sir."

"Good!" The general smiled.

"I'll write him back tomorrow. Sooner, if you think you may have someone going to Modlin."

"Not likely, Józef. Not likely. Too dangerous. We have the Modlin and Zamość fortresses in our control, but the rest of the nation is a hunting ground for the Ruski."

Józef thought now how his family had a stake at both fortresses: Michał at Modlin; his father and Jerzy at Zamość.

For the moment their conversation reverted to the horse and small talk, but Józef became convinced the general had a purpose in coming in at such an early hour. A serious purpose.

When Józef went to place the saddle on Tadek, the general's hand stopped him. "No riding today, Józef. Not today."

Their relationship had developed to the stage whereby Józef felt he could dare to question a statement such as this. "But, sir, I take him out only around the perimeter of the garrison. Since the Russians are parked out on the plains, I wouldn't dare go further."

"You won't dare leave the garrison, Józef."

"What is it, sir? What's happened?"

General Sowiński's eyes shone like blue fire. "Two guards were murdered last night and a third injured. Someone—and I pray it was no Pole—got past us despite our precautions and made his way to the Paszkiewicz camp. God damn him to hell! By now they know just how weak we stand, so outnumbered and what with the majority of our forces elsewhere. And with citizens in an uproar and a Military Sejm changing the leadership, no less! God's bones! The Paszkiewicz forces have taken our supply depot at Łowicz in their march from the west. Our ammunition and our provisions are nearly depleted and in the meantime the Ruski move toward us from every quarter."

"Are things so bad, sir?"

"We have but one chance."

"Sir?"

"To funnel pell mell all our resources here to the capital and take a stand for our freedom! And when they come down upon us, my Józef, Wielka Wola will be the key position."

If only there were time, Józef thought, time for Polish forces to coalesce. He looked for hope in the general's face, watching the general's long, flaring whiskers that would draw back like curtains at his characteristic smile. But there was no such movement now.

26

21 August 1831, Wielka Wola

"GENERAL IVAN PASZKIEWICZ IS LIKE a lion who sits on his hands while his jackals draw attention elsewhere, waiting, waiting for the dirty work to be done and the timing just so. It

is then that he will pounce." Second-lieutenant Piotr
Wysocki was addressing his cadets in the yard of
the garrison. "Our military and civic leaders are in
disarray, but I warrant you, we are not!"

Wysocki went on in that vein while Józef listened.
He was certainly correct in what he said. Joachim
Lelewel and his Patriotic Society had brought such
a state of unrest—some said anarchy—to the capital
that Prince Czartoryski, in order to disassociate
himself with Lelewel, had made a motion to the
Sejm calling for the dissolution of the provisional
government. It passed. General Jan Krukowiecki
seized the moment and usurped the presidency.

Wysocki would not say as much, but the word
among the troops was that Krukowiecki already
viewed the insurrection as a catastrophe—that it was
lost—and that he meant to retain his power through
the negotiations and beyond.

Inexplicably, when needed most at the capital, one
corps had been sent northwest to Plock to take on
one of Paszkiewicz' armies while another corps had
moved east toward another Russian force at Podlasie,
accompanied by Prince Czartoryski, who had traded
the comfort of diplomacy for the roughness of the
roads and poorly appointed camps. Warsaw was left
in a precarious situation.

Józef watched Piotr Wysocki, noting some
difference in the man from the day he had called
Józef and Marcin down to the rooms he shared with
Colonel Józef Zaliwski to inform them of their part in
the November Rising. For the moment he wondered
where the tide of events had taken Zaliwski, but he

soon came back to his study of Wysocki. He seemed
older, still committed to his beliefs, but what was
to be read in his face, in his voice? Had he become
jaded? No doubt he had seen terrible things at
Siedlce, done terrible things, violence that had left
its mark, despite the words he used now to raise the
spirits of the cadets.

Here was the man, Józef realized anew,
who—almost single-handedly—had initiated the
insurrection that had gone on for nearly a year. And
with that realization came another: that he himself
had no small part in the attempted abduction of
Grand Duke Konstantin. He felt different from the
person who had stepped onto the grounds of the
Grand Duke's palace; in no small way that difference
had come through General Sowiński, whose easy
nature and wisdom shone through despite the sights
he had witnessed in Kosciuśzko's army, the Prussian
service, Napoleon's mad campaign—and now this. He
carried more than a wooden leg, the one to which
Józef had lost his aversion; he carried the weight
of those war years, years signified by the highest
medals and ribbons. But these medals and ribbons—
emblematic of the glory Józef, Marcin, and the other
cadets sought—were sometimes open for display and
at others put away to become tarnished and dusty in
a drawer.

What endured was the desire for independence,
not the need for glory.

Józef looked at the faces all about him. Most
seemed familiar to him; a few had been friends.
However, Marcin and so many others—friends

and fellow cadets—were missing, devoured by the machine called war. He wondered if they had learned what he had.

He wondered how many would survive what was to come.

22 August 1831, Warsaw

NEVER ONE TO SHOW SURPRISE, Mother Abbess Teodora looked up from her desk with unblinking dark eyes as the former Sister Izabel was ushered into her office. "These are perilous times for you to be out and about—"

"Iza . . . I'm called Iza now, Mother Abbess."

The abbess smiled."Take a chair . . . Iza."

Iza obeyed, settling into the hard chair she had occupied two years before when she had been informed that she could not take her final vows, that she could not remain a Carmelite. Today she had worn her most modest day dress, a gown of deep blue with sleeves that tied at the wrists with light blue ribbons. Still, she felt self-conscious. "I've come to ask a favor, Mother Abbess."

"Oh, child, you don't—"

Iza had read the nun's reaction. "Oh no, nothing like that. You were quite right. I had fooled myself into thinking I had a vocation."

"Ah, praise God!" The two laughed. "And how have you been these many months?"

Iza thought. "Happy, Mother Abbess," she blurted, "and unhappy."

"So it goes with the world out there as well as within cloistered walls. But when you said *happy* in the way you did, I suspected at once that you have found love, yes?"

A heated flush rose into Iza's face. "Yes, Mother Abbess."

The abbess' expression darkened suddenly. "Not with that fellow who tried to romance you in the garden?"

"Mother Abbess, that was my father."

The abbess could be taken by surprise, Iza realized, for the eyes—brown as the Carmelite scapular—widened and the starched white wimple on her forehead perceptibly retracted.

Iza explained now the unraveling of the mystery of her birth without going into great detail, for she had another purpose on her mind.

"It sounds like an episode out of one of those books you would read. You know, those forbidden romances?"

Iza laughed.

"He's a younger man, I suppose? Than the man in the garden—your father, I mean?"

"Yes, just a few years older than I."

"And in the service of his country, I imagine. That makes for the *unhappy* element."

Iza nodded.

"Saints preserve us, every one!" the Abbess cried. "Look at your nails!"

In a motion that reflected an ease that had begun to come over her, Iza had placed her interlocked hands on the edge of the abbess' desk. She looked now at her hands and nails. She had washed them but in her rush, she had not scrubbed them nearly well enough. She could feel the blood pulsing at her temples. She felt like a novice again.

"No doubt you still garden, Izabel, but those are the hands of a field worker."

"I've been helping with the fortifications, Mother Abbess."

"Fortifications!"

"Yes. Oh, I work at the hospital, too, ordinary sort of women's work—consoling patients, helping doctors, creating bandages and the like—but I wanted to do more. Help was needed to fortify the city against the Russians at our gates. There are too few soldiers here in the capital to do it. Men, women, nobles, peasants, clergy are all turning out to build the ramparts around the city."

"You're building ramparts, Izabel?"

"I've been helping with the lunettes."

"Lunettes? Dare I ask?"

"Lunettes are earthen, detached fortifications, half-moon shaped."

"Thus, the name, I see. As well as the reason for the dirt under your nails. You amaze me, Izabel."

"It's little enough. I would like to do much more. I would like to ride and fight!"

"Izabel! Have you gone mad?"

"No, Mother Abbess, it's been done."

The abbess sat silent, waiting for Iza's elaboration.

Here was another subject far from the crux of today's interview with Abbess Teodora—but one that evoked Iza's enthusiasm. "There's a young countess who's gone to war and whom I'd like to emulate had I the skills and the bravery. People are talking about her and the journals tell of her exploits."

"A Polish Joan of Arc?"

"Lithuanian, actually. Her name is Emilia Plater and she had the advantages of being an excellent horsewoman and marksman. Initially she formed her own partisan unit and managed to seize a town from the Russians!"

"She fights, then?"

"Oh, yes. She became commanding officer of the Polish First Lithuanian Infantry Regiment. She's been promoted to *captain!*"

"An amazing story. A heroine for our times. But I'm certain your hospital work and building these *lunettes* make for heroism enough, Iza."

"It's what I can do."

"Indeed. Now, my dear, it's time you told me why you've come."

Iza chose the direct route. "Mother Abbess, I've come to ask that my dowry be returned to me."

"I see." The abbess' head moved back a bit, her expression unchanging. "When you left us two years ago, you said nothing of it. Why this interest now?"

"I didn't know then I would have a use for it." The money and estate had been left in Iza's name by her mother's best friend, Princess Charlotte Sic, so that it would not be squandered by Zofia. And so it was that at the time of Iza's return to life on Piwna

Street she had the fear that her mother would be too interested in the monies and estate. Perhaps more interested in those things than in the return of her daughter to the world. To her mother's credit, she asked Iza about the dowry once and did not seem overly concerned when Iza intimated that it was left to be used at the discretion of the convent.

"And now it will somehow be useful?"

"Yes."

"Having to do with your young man?"

"Yes, as well as all of my family."

The abbess sat in silence, clearly expecting more of an explanation.

"Mother Abbess, General Paszkiewicz is preparing his invasion. It may come tomorrow."

"As soon as that? They're across the river, at Praga, if I may venture a guess?"

"No, though that would be more defensible. His main forces are at Raszyn to the west of the city. They'll come in at Wielka Wola. Mother Abbess, if the Russians take the capital, they take Poland. Things will become very difficult for families of those who served."

"The money will provide bribes?"

"No, the word is that with this tsar no bribe will keep the magnates, szlachta, and patriots from execution—or from the work camps in the far north."

The abbess' clenched hand beat her breast three times. "Siberia?"

Iza nodded.

"Have things truly come to this?" A brief silence ensued, then the abbess asked, "How would you use the money—and the estate in France, I suppose you would sell that?"

"No, Mother Abbess, I would not. You see, it is very possible that we will need that estate, that we will be forced to emigrate."

"Indeed, indeed.—Are people preparing for such an outcome?"

"Yes."

The abbess let out a long breath. "Well, if nothing else, we taught you that readiness is all, whether it's for emigration or salvation."

Iza did not know how to respond to the abbess' comment. After a silence, she said, "Of course, I would expect the convent to retain funds in payment for the years that I lived here."

The hooded brown eyes studied Iza as if for the first time while Iza waited for her decision.

27

6 September 1831, Wielka Wola

"GOD'S ARSE!" JÓZEF CRIED, HIS heart pounding against his chest.

Amidst the violent chaos that Wielka Wola had become, he forgot that the chamber of his pistol had already been emptied—with success—and so it proved useless against the Russian infantryman who was hurling himself toward him, bayonet gleaming in the noon sun. Józef feinted a move to the left but went right as the bayonet ripped into his uniform coat at his left side. There would be pain later, but now he felt only the need to strike and brought his sword crashing down on the collarbone of the soldier, the sounds of the crack and the cry coming simultaneously. A second strike severed the artery at the neck and silenced the man, his body awash in crimson. Józef knew that to exult in triumph was to invite defeat. He looked up to see what seemed hordes sweeping over the plains and coming—like this man had—into the village of Wielka Wola. There must be twenty battalions, he figured. Later, the Russians themselves would attest to thirty.

His gaze moved down now to his superior, Piotr Wysocki, co-architect of the insurrection, who lay sprawled a few feet away, his chest wound clearly a mortal one. Józef had not been quick enough to save him from the Russian he had just killed. He went to Wysocki now and tried to lift him from under the shoulders so as to drag him to the little church some yards away. At least he would die without a contorted Russian face hovering over him. Would the enemy respect sanctuary? And then—as for himself—what?

"No!" Wysocki called out—in pain, yes—but in his starkest commanding tone. "Leave me! There's no use. Watch for yourself. And for the general! He just entered the churchyard there."

Józef gently released Wysocki's upper body to the

blood-soaked ground, nodded, and turned to go. He had advanced no more than ten feet when he heard Wysocki say, "Thank you, Józef." His last words.

Józef did not look back. He was running now in his search of another Józef, General Sowiński.

The Paszkiewicz forces had vacated the town of Raszyn the day before and moved the six miles northeast to the plain of Wielka Wola, so when the attack on Warsaw commenced at five o'clock in the morning it came as no surprise. The onslaught began with at least a 90-gun battery attacking two lunettes situated on the outskirts of Wielka Wola. Józef and his company occupied a lunette manning four cannon while the lunette to the left had two companies manning five cannon. These crescent-shaped earthen bulwarks had been built in haste by the citizens and were not strong enough to sustain such fire power as they were receiving; in addition, they were situated too far from the village for the garrison guns to provide cover so that within an hour the lunette on the left had been scaled and the guns rendered useless. The surviving Polish infantrymen took up positions within the lunette on the right. One of these cadets told Józef of a Polish officer who had killed outright two of his own men who were preparing to ask the enemy for quarter.

Józef's lunette resisted the onslaught, manning the cannons and fighting hand-to-hand the five Russian regiments determined to overtake it. Fellow Poles, comrades and friends, fell to his left and to his right, and within a second hour Józef imagined there were no more that ten or eleven of them still standing. It was at that moment—amidst the noise of guns, swordplay, and warcries—that Lieutenant Novosielski ordered those few out of the lunette, whereupon he set fire to a powder magazine, sacrificing himself to blow up the lunette and a dozen Russians with it. The massive explosion occurred as Józef and the others fell back toward the village, and for the moment the field rained down body parts and shreds of Russian uniforms.

It was a small enough loss for the enemy who came into Wielka Wola itself now with the strength of thirty battalions. The third hour of the battle saw slaughter on a massive scale and, despite the brave dispute of every foot of ground, the silencing of the garrison's eight cannon.

Józef hurried into the small churchyard. Here, too, there was little space of ground that did not hold a body, Pole and Russian alike. For the moment there was no movement, but then he caught sight of General Sowiński who stood near an ammunition wagon, busily loading musket after musket.

"General!" Józef called.

The general turned, ready to take aim, recognized Józef, and called him over. Considering the excesses of the past few hours where blood and bullets and death reigned, the general's face—dirtied and bloodied as it was—shone with calm and resolve.

"Help me, Józef. We can load a few more of these.

That's a good lad."

Józef didn't know what to do, what to say. Dare he tell the commander in charge that the fight was lost? "General Sowiński—"

"Hop to it, cadet!" The general turned to Józef, read his mind. "I'll not surrender, my boy. This was my lot. I've always known it, I think. The wheel of fortune has turned for me. But for you—I told your brother I'd watch out for you—you must accept quarter if it's being offered. You have your life before you. Mine is behind. And don't think for a moment this is glory. I've taught you better."

Józef was about to argue when a call came from the churchyard entrance. He recognized the Russian word for *general* and knew the intent. The fall of the Warsaw Artillery Garrison would be complete with the capture—or death—of General Sowiński.

Józef knew only a smattering of words in Russian and as the officer moved in toward them, he recognized the word for *quarter*. To his side he heard the general bellow, "No quarter!" Then came the explosion near to his right ear and the Russian officer fell dead. The general bawled out the national motto "Conquer or die!"

By now the yard was filling with Russian uniforms. The general turned to gather up another musket, but he found that swiveling to and from the wagon behind him a clumsy movement because of his wooden leg. Moments were lost.

Another soldier was rushing them. Józef took up a musket at once and took aim. Pivoting, the general pushed the barrel of Józef's musket into the air and the ball went heavenward. He shoved Józef aside now, calling out in Russian that the cadet deserved quarter and yet managing to get off one more shot that took the life of the second Russian. And then the third Russian was upon him and the general took a bayonet to his midsection. The Russians swarmed around them.

Józef managed to turn to the carriage to take up another musket. It was upon turning back that he was struck beneath the chin with the butt of a rifle. He fell at once to the ground. He was unconscious only momentarily, it seemed. He lifted his head now and through a blur saw multiple bayonets jettisoned into the general's body. Only on the sixth or seventh strike did the general's head nod and life go out of his eyes. Amazingly, his body remained standing, supported by the wagon behind him and the rigidity of his wooden leg.

As Józef was pulled to his feet, he prepared himself to die. He reconciled himself with God and put his hand over the breast pocket that held Emilia Chopin's miniature. He did not call for quarter. He would not. He would die as bravely as had General Józef Sowiński. *Forgive me, Mother.*

His arms were being held by two soldiers as he watched their superior move toward him, bayonet at the ready. He closed his eyes. He would not allow the enemy the satisfaction of seeing his life slip away.

A long silence ensued. His heart thumped like a drum gone wild. Opening his eyes, he saw that the soldier's face was not more that a foot away from his, a great, menacingly happy smile on his face. The Russian said something, but the only thing Józef understood was the name of the Grand Duke Konstantin.

And then he remembered the soldier. He had been the guard at Mokotów when he had been placed under arrest for his part in the attempted abduction. He had been the sadistic one who had lied, telling him he was to be executed.

The Russian was talking excitedly now to those around him. Józef realized he was being treated as a special prisoner, one that perhaps the tsar himself would want to see. The wheel had turned for him, too, and he knew he could look forward to a public execution.

Józef closed his eyes, wishing his life had been taken there, in battle.

28

27 September 1831, Warsaw

"ARRESTED?" ANNA ASKED.

Michał nodded, peering down into the emerald hurt of his mother's eyes, preferring the battlefield to what he saw there. "Three weeks ago."

The two stood in the reception room of the Gronska town house, the semi-circle of Barbara, Zofia, and Iza forming their audience.

"Then he's alive!" His mother blinked back tears. "And he's been given quarter. He's a prisoner like any other?"

Before Michał could answer, his sister took a step forward. "Will he be sent away, Michał? They say the soldiers will be sent across the steppes into—"

"He's not being held as a soldier, Barbara." His sister had always been too quick to speak her thoughts and now he had followed suit. He immediately cursed himself for a bluntness that he knew now would lead to the truth.

"Then—how?" Anna asked.

Michał drew in a deep breath. There was no going back, no dressing it up. "Józef is being held on charges of treason in one of the convent prisons for his part in the attempted murder of Grand Duke Konstantin. There's to be a tribunal."

The women gasped. Each knew the likely outcome of such a trial. A Russian tribunal was all for show and no one was ever acquitted.

Zofia spoke up now. "But you yourself said, Michał, that it was merely an abduction, that the cadets had orders not to harm Konstantin."

"While that's true, the fact that his aide-de-camp was killed on the steps of the palace will go hard against that argument, especially when they will want to believe otherwise."

"But Konstanin himself released him," Anna said.

"He did at that," Michał said.

No one voiced the fact that Konstantin was dead though Michał saw it engraved on the faces around him. There would be no mercy from his brother, the tsar.

Anna's eyes fixed on Michał's. "And yet you came here this morning to tell me—us—to pack our things so that we can go to Paris? Michał, what's come over you? You would expect me to leave Poland without any word from your father—and with your brother to go on trial?"

"You must, Mother," Michał said, unused to giving orders to his mother. "For your safety and for the safety of everyone here."

"Never!"

"I intend to stay through the trial, Mother, and to find out about Father—and Jerzy. But I shall have to do it in hiding."

"You must leave, Anna," Zofia said. She sidled up to her cousin and placed her hand around her waist. "Michał will send us word of Jan and Jerzy." Michał recognized in her voice and choice of words an unspoken fatalism regarding the two who had not been heard from in months.

"Mother's right, Cousin Anna," Iza said. "You must go, as must Barbara and the twins."

Did she mean to exclude herself? Michał saw Zofia's dark eyes narrow at her daughter's comment and knew she—like him—expected as much.

Barbara's silence bespoke a tacit agreement with the others. Anna stared in disbelief at the anarchy around her.

"You *all* must go—or risk everything!" Michał said.

"Everything?" Zofia scoffed. "After our Constitution was put down by Catherine in 1794, I lost the estate at Halicz and our town house on the escarpment of Praga was burned to the ground before my mother's body could be properly buried. Now you say that your parents' home in Sochaczew has been sequestered and that this town house will face the same fate? Anna here has lost her young Tadeusz and only God knows the whereabouts of Jan and Jerzy! Michał, how short of *everything* is that?" She drew herself up, not in the showy way Michał might have expected, but in a way that reflected resolve. "And now you say we are to give up our homeland? Is that not everything?"

Coming at the end of Zofia's litany was the last thing Michał expected from her: a statement of patriotism.

Iza turned to Zofia. "Mother, I—"

"You must go, too, Izabel," Zofia interrupted, putting her forefinger to Iza's lips. "You, too."

Michał knew that that would not be the end of the argument, that Iza would want to stay with him, that he must convince her otherwise.

Michał was left alone in the reception room. The twins had been awakened and the excitement of packing for a journey was evident in their voices.

He had been careful not to use the word *emigrate*, but he knew that that was what he was insisting his mother and the others do.

He allowed himself to fall back into a high-backed cushioned chair. It didn't have to end this way, he thought. Of course, in their zeal the cadets had impulsively baited the great Russian bear, and in sheer numbers of soldiers and weaponry they had been outnumbered, but had other decisions been made by both political and military leaders, the ending could have been different.

While the fall of Warsaw certainly presaged the fall of Poland, the fighting had continued. Michał knew of at least five generals in command of significant forces who were left now without word from the capital and precious little inter-communication among themselves. At Modlin Fortress Michał had witnessed what remained of the Warsaw soldiers—tired, hungry, and often barefooted—march into the fortress. He had seen little action by that point so that when the opportunity to join General Karol Różycki in the area of Lublin, he was happy to go. A second motivation involved location. Rumor had it that Różycki would combine forces with those at Zamość and in that event he would be able to find out the circumstances of his father and Jerzy Lesiak. He had not yet learned of Józef's fate.

It had been at Zawichost, southeast of Lublin, that Michał's small company had joined Różycki. Two days later Prince Czartoryski himself caught up with Różycki, engengering within the forces a great renewed enthusiasm. The prince was elated at seeing Michał again; however, the news he brought was disheartening. The Czartoryski estate, Puławy, had been confiscated, its national treasures of art and books taken to Russia. Worse, the prince had been with General Ramorino who, with his 11,000 men and 40 cannon, had staged a final battle against an estimated 35,000 and untold number of cannon. When their ammunition was depleted, the Russian cannonading continued for another hour or more, even as the survivors crossed over into Austria and laid down their arms. Rather than surrender, the prince sought to fight another day with Różycki, who had had recent successes.

With Romorino no longer a target, the Russian Generals Rosen and Rudiger combined forces to come against Różycki. And so it was that Michał fought his last battle side by side with Prince Czartoryski. With but 6,000 men they fought the entire day against overwhelming odds and wave upon wave of Russian reinforcements. The time came at last for the survivors to enter Austria and lay down their arms. The prince and Michał found a spot near an unusual semi-circle of birch trees—a configuration they pledged to remember—and dug deeply with their hands. In the long, narrow hole they placed their swords, the hilts facing Poland, Michał bidding a silent farewell to his longtime blade, Jadwiga, both men vowing to reclaim them one day. Having replaced the earth, they tamped it down with their boots then stood looking at each other. Both were close to tears. The prince uttered then the oft-used phrase: "Poland is not lost while we yet live."

Not long afterwards they went their separate ways, Michał to Warsaw, and the prince to France and without delay, for his execution had already been ordered by Nicholas.

"Michał."

Michał was startled from his thoughts. He had not heard Iza come into the reception room. Outside, dusk was coming on. He stood now, taking in her face as if it were for the last time. How many times he had wondered whether he would see those blue eyes, the color of cornflowers, startlingly set off by the porcelain complexion and dark, dark hair.

"Michał!"

"Yes, Iza?"

"You said Józef was being held in one of the convent prisons. Which one?"

"The one on Wolska Street."

"You mean the Carmelite convent—where you accompanied me once."

"Why, yes! I had forgotten. The same."

Iza took his hand in hers. "Michał," she said again.

"Yes?"

"I have an idea."

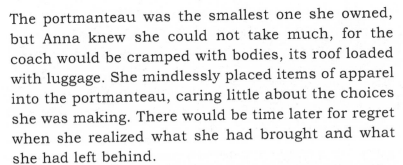

The portmanteau was the smallest one she owned, but Anna knew she could not take much, for the coach would be cramped with bodies, its roof loaded with luggage. She mindlessly placed items of apparel into the portmanteau, caring little about the choices she was making. There would be time later for regret when she realized what she had brought and what she had left behind.

All was lost—that reality had started slowly, the way a tide might begin, by playing tag with a sleeper's toes, then imperceptibly growing bolder, encroaching further, deepening, threatening, taking.

Topolostan, her familial estate at Sochaczew, was gone, taken by the tide of Russians. The estate manager Jacob and his wife Emma had already fled to France, sending word where they were and that any monies they had been able to muster would be kept there for safekeeping. Was she never again to see her childhood home, pray at the graves of her parents and infant brother?

Leaving Poland—it was inconceivable. How had it come to this so quickly, in less than one year? And leaving Józef—what was to happen to him? Treason. The implications of the word brought on lightheadedness. She dropped into the chair near the window facing Piwna Street. The verdict would be a foregone conclusion. It would be a show trial that would result in an immediate execution or exile to a work camp in Siberia. What would she choose for her son? Had it been she, she would embrace death.

Anna stared vacantly at a small pile of Jan's clothing on the bed next to the portmanteau. Where was he in this aftermath? Was she about to pack the clothes of a dead man? She cursed him for leaving her to this fate, then cursed herself for allowing a sixty-five-year old man to go off to war.

And yet . . . and yet he had come home after countless campaigns. She closed her eyes, retreating into the good years, the optimistic years, the years with him at home. Anna wrapped herself in the warm bliss of family, recalling the times between the war years when nations and politics left the stage to family. There had been moments right there at Topolostan when she felt as if she had had her own little Arkadia, the renowned Radziwill gardens at Nieborow, so close to Sochaczew.

A knock came at the door followed by Iza's voice: "Mother says you should come downstairs, Cousin Anna."

"What is it?"

"She says to come down."

Anna seldom knew Iza to be evasive. "Very well." Using the arms of the chair she pushed herself up. Everything seemed an effort.

By the time she went to the door Iza was gone. Anna stepped out into the hall and listened. There were voices rising from the reception room. She heard Zofia's voice, high and excited, and a male voice, too, even though Michał had gone to confirm the plans for the morrow's carriage and drivers. She moved down slowly, her back hugging the wall, her heart catching.

Anna came to stand in the doorway of the reception room. The tall man in the filthy and ragged uniform had his back to her. It was not Jan, but she recognized him even before he realized she was behind him and turned to greet her.

"Jerzy," she said, at once happy—and disappointed that it wasn't Jan. Zofia and Iza stood nearby, their eyes brimming. She smiled. She could be happy for them.

Jerzy stepped forward and kissed her hand. A long moment passed, as if neither could find the words.

Her lips trembling and her legs threatening to go out from under her, Anna managed one word, one whispered word: "Jan?" *Where is my husband?*

Jerzy kissed her hand again and Anna thought

the worst. But then he took hold of her arm and he pivoted back to his original position so that they now stood side by side, facing the interior of the room.

Anna realized someone sat on the far sofa, a thin man with white hair and cobalt blue eyes. Her legs did give out now. The room moved vertiginously—and were it not for Jerzy's hold on her—she would have fallen to the floor.

"Anna Maria," Jan said, as she moved toward him. His voice was small and raspy. "My little Ania, forgive me for not rising."

"You've been ill, Jan."

"A touch," he said.

"A touch?" Zofia asked. "The cholera is no *touch*."

Anna gasped. "Cholera?"

Jan smiled. "Come sit, my love. It could kill General Diebitsch and it could kill the Grand Duke Konstantin, Anna, but it could not kill me." He winked. "I told you I would come back."

Anna settled into the sofa, into his embrace. "You always have." Oblivious to everyone else, she kissed him then.

And then, as Zofia and Iza served refreshments—for the servants had been given final payment and allowed to go to the safe-homes of friends or families—the story came out: how shortly after Jerzy and two others had come to Jan's defense against Cossacks and soundly beaten them, Jan had come down with the cholera; how Jerzy had stayed by him, nursing him through the often fatal illness; how they had been allowed to pass through a dozen Russian barricades on their long trek home—and here they both laughed—by merely casually mentioning the word *cholera*. Jerzy's eyes twinkled. "The Ruskis were quick to put dirty handkerchiefs to their noses and wave us forward."

Jan finished the story, making little of the bloodletting, Anna knew, for the benefit of the audience. Her smile faded now as a dark thought would not be kept at bay any longer. She turned to her husband. "Have they—have they told you about Józef?"

Jan took and squeezed her hand. "Yes, Ania, they have."

Viktor Baklanov sat at the the massive desk. It was his now. General Aleksander Rozniecki, the corrupt Polish turncoat, was not likely to return. Neither would Nikolai Novosiltsev, he was told. Their careers had been exposed and they would be marked men by the Poles. Not so Viktor. He was heir apparent to head up the Third Department—and without having to answer to Novosiltsev.

The door to the hidden room had been unused for days now, the peacocks painting in its place. The room might very well serve Viktor's purpose one day and so for now he kept it secret from Sergei, who, along with a few others, had managed to find him. He and Luka had been in hiding all these months— until Luka had gotten quite drunk and belligerent with several patriots who had hanged him from a lamp post during those days of chaos in the middle of August.

Viktor leaned back in his chair, lighting his pipe and luxuriating in the knowledge that he would be the one to reinstitute the Secret Police in the city. Paszkiewicz had been generous with him for the information he had provided and had sent praise back to St. Petersburg. Viktor's specific information regarding the extent of the chaos among the Poles themselves had made the strike against the capital a timely one, indeed, and while it had not fallen like a house of cards—these damn Poles were stubborn souls—it had fallen. And the fortresses at Modlin and Zamość not so very long afterward.

His thoughts came back to Barbara now. He was tempted to force another meeting, but what good would that do? The stubborn streak seemed especially strong in her. Sergei and another agent were watching the Gronska town house so that he might at least know the comings and goings of his wife and children. But . . . to what end? He stared into the lighted chamber of his pipe as a gypsy might study tea leaves. Was it possible to *make* someone love you?

29

I ZA REACHED BACK INTO THE wardrobe and withdrew one of the two Carmelite habits she had pilfered on the day she had left the convent. Over a plain day dress of the thinnest Indian cotton, she drew on the dark wool tunic, her extended arms avoiding the pockets and double sleeves. She poked her head through the aperture in the scapular next, arranging the long woolen panels that swept the floor. She took the coif, bringing it down on her head in a front to back movement, making sure to tuck in all of her dark hair. The white starched crown band came next to be followed by veil and the myriad pins that it took to hold the headgear together. Iza paused as she reflected on the two veils, the black and the white. In the convent she had worn only the novice's veil. If just for today, she decided, she would wear the black. The belt, stockings, and sandals, all black, and the oversized wooden rosary beads completed her masquerade.

Iza glanced at the clock on her mantel. Four in the morning. The carriage that was to take the family to France was to arrive at six o'clock and they were to be gone well before 6:30.

She moved stealthily into the dim hall, turning her back to noiselessly close the door.

"Iza?"

The whispered voice startled her, but when she turned to face Barbara in her nightshift, it was Barbara who was dealt a shock.

"Shhh," Iza whispered.

"What in God's name—?"

"Indeed," Iza intoned, pulling Barbara back into the bedchamber.

"What's going on, Iza? Are you going back to—"

"No, I'm not, Basia. And I don't have time for long

explanations. Michał is waiting downstairs."

"Michał?—Oh, this has to do with the convent, doesn't it?—And Józef!"

"We're going to get him out of there and take him to France with us."

Barbara's eyes grew large. "How will that be possible?"

"Actually, we haven't worked it all out yet. We'll tell you afterwards. Now—"

"Not so fast! I'm going with you."

"You can't Basia. It's dangerous."

"He's *my* brother! I will go."

Iza looked to the clock and let out a great sigh.

Waiting at the front door, the hall lighted by one guttering candle, Michał saw two robed figures silently descending the steps, and he would have thought he was seeing double except that the second figure wore a white veil instead of black.

"Barbara?" he whispered, his mind racing at this complication.

"Do you think I've missed my calling, Michałek? The white veil is for novices. Did you know that? Now, don't glower at me so. I'll be a help to you."

Michał knew the minutes were ticking and since their plan was one of the moment, perhaps there would be a part for his sister to play. He wordlessly waved them through the front door. They would walk the several streets to Wolska Street.

Mother Abbess Teodora herself opened the door, blinking incredulously at Iza in habit as well as another woman in novice garb.

Iza affected a smile. "May we come, in Mother Abbess?"

The nun scarcely noticed Michał until she nodded and motioned for them to enter, and as they did so her eyes moved right and left up and down the street. Times were dangerous.

"Speak softly," she warned once they stood in her office, "there is one crusty old guard that walks this floor."

"We've come about Józef, Mother Abbess," Iza said. "Józef Stelnicki."

The abbess gasped. "Is he the young man you've gotten yourself mixed up with?"

"No," Iza said, fending off a laugh, "Józef is their brother." Iza now introduced her to Michał and Barbara.

The abbess smiled, nodding at Michał. "Then *this* must be he, yes?"

Iza's face went scarlet, causing the abbess to laugh at the confirmation. She turned toward Michał. "You wish to visit with him, of course."

"More than that," Michał said, "we wish to take him with us to France."

The white crown band on the abbess' forehead perceptibly moved back. "*Take* him? Are you all serious? How?"

"The plan is in development," Michał volunteered when the other two fell silent.

"And you expect me to stand by?"

"Oh no, Mother Abbess," Barbara said, "we need your *help*."

"And you, it seems, need a plan?" The abbess drew in a long breath, assessing the faces around her, her gaze falling last on Iza. "Well, if this one here can make lunettes, I imagine an old nun can do something, too."

"Thank you, Mother Abbess," Iza said. "We should be able to think of something."

The abbess was suddenly all business. "Other than myself, there are only the old and infirm here. I've sent most everyone else away, especially the younger nuns. The Russians have either been stretched thin or they are very trusting. There is the one guard up here and several downstairs where the prisoners are. Yes, we will come up with something, Sister—I mean Iza."

Iza would always wonder whether the little faux pas had been meant as a joke.

Ten minutes later Michał left by way of the front entrance—a male's presence would be suspicious, threatening even—and the other three took a back stairway to avoid the attention of the ground floor guard and proceeded to the cellar.

"I was going to write to you, Iza," the abbess whispered as they moved down the stone steps. "I've seen to it that your assets—all of them—have been placed with our convent in France. You need only to go there and identify yourself."

"Thank you, Mother Abbess," Iza whispered.

"I wish you good luck, something we're all going to need momentarily. Now let me do the talking."

Arriving in the cellar, they moved down the hall to the center intersection, a guard at a desk warily watching as they approached.

"These good sisters," Mother Abbess announced with authority even before they came to his station, "have come to see the Stelnicki prisoner."

"No visitors!"

"Ah, but these are his sisters, and their mother has just died. They wish to tell him as much. I assure you they will be no trouble. It will take no more than a few minutes."

The guard harrumphed. "I'll tell him as much." He gave a crooked smile and coughed out a laugh. "No prisoners!"

"Oh, Yuri," the abbess crooned, "we can allow them that much. Imagine if your sister came bringing such news. Just imagine."

Yuri shrugged, victim of a religious siren.

"Let's just give them a few minutes alone with the prisoner. While they are visiting I will see if I can't find a bottle of wine that has been spared yesterday's break-in of the wine cellar by the other guards. I have my own hiding place. I'm sure I could find something."

She should be on the stage, Iza thought.

In minutes they arrived at the cell door. Yuri drew his pistol, unlocked the door and motioned Iza and Barbara in. As Iza passed by, the abbess gave her a knowing nod. Iza's hand tightened on the iron key that the abbess had retained, unbeknownst to the Russian officials, when the convent had been taken over.

Józef stood, blinked, and stared in disbelief at his two visitors in masquerade. The door clanged shut behind them and the turnkey locked them in. "Ten minutes," he growled.

"How in Hades did you manage this stunt?" Józef asked. He was thin, dirty, his uniform torn and caked with dry blood.

"You look terrible!" Barbara said.

"Christ! Had I known two angels of the lord were coming I would have conjured up a monk's robe."

"Never mind that, we're here to get you out," Iza said.

Józef's lower jaw dropped. "What?"

"We have only those ten minutes and two are gone by now," Iza continued. She showed him the key. "This will get us out of this door and out of the upstairs door and into the garden. From there we head to a secret door in the garden wall where Michał will be waiting on the street side. The abbess said the lock is broken so that only a latch secures it."

"Michał?—And then?"

"The family is leaving for France in little more than an hour."

"Good God!"

Barbara already had the cell door open and they slipped noiselessly out into the hall, Iza leading the way. They came to the deserted desk at the intersection and moved toward the staircase that would take them up to the courtyard door. If there were other guards in the cellar, it seemed, they were sleeping or throwing dice somewhere else in what had always seemed to Iza like a labyrinth of catacombs.

In climbing the stone stairs, Barbara tripped on the front panel of her scapular but caught herself in time. At the top, Barbara unlocked the courtyard door and the three slipped out, closing the door and keeping their backs pinned to the building. As planned, Barbara tossed the key into an acacia bush closeby for the abbess to find later. Iza turned to Józef. "Barbara and I will walk nonchalantly to the far wall there. Any number of eyes may be watching from the building. You're to wait here until until we reach into the ivy and unlatch the gate. Then come to us double time."

Józef smiled. "Don't worry, it will be triple time!"

As the two costumed nuns moved out into the garden, passing the snow-covered patches of herbs Iza used to cultivate, Iza suddenly felt something was wrong—but what? So far . . . all to the good. She put aside her fears, thinking she would never be able to thank the abbess enough for her part in the escape. The nun would probably have to answer for it, too, unless she could draw even further on her acting skills.

They reached the ivy-covered wall and it took some time for Iza to find the exact location. Valuable minutes ticked by. Dare they motion to Józef before the door was found and opened? It was only when they heard Michał lightly tapping that they found the outline of the door in the wall—and finally the hook and eye latch. It took the work of three of them to swing the never-used door inward, breaking the branches of ivy as they did so.

Iza turned to wave Józef forward. Her heart sickened at once.

He had been discovered. A tall guard was wrestling with him and in moments there were two overpowering him.

"Go on!" Józef called. "Go!"

His face stricken, Michał stepped into the garden to assess the situation.

"There are four of us," Iza said impulsively. "I've brought a mallet." She pulled the tool from her double sleeve. Amazed at her derring-do, Michał nonetheless put his hand on her arm to restrain her just as a third figure stepped from the doorway into the garden. Dressed rather finely and clearly not a guard, he held himself with authority as he issued orders to the two men, who— with some trouble— brought Józef down to the ground. The man stood looking now—at them.

"God's Bones!" Michał cursed. In case they were stopped by a Russian patrol, he had not brought sword or pistol, merely a dagger. He would use it in an eyeblink, too, but for the fact that he had two women in his care. He dared not attempt force. He knew in his gut it would end badly. "We need to leave," he said. "Now!" He reached out to take Iza and Barbara by the arms, but Barbara resisted and pulled free.

"Oh, my God!" Barbara cried, stepping further into the garden, her green eyes flashing horror and anger in the direction of the man standing over Józef.

Iza stepped up to her. "You heard Michał. We've failed, Basia, we can't afford arrest. Think of the others at home—the plan to leave the capital will fail!"

It was as if Barbara were deaf. She took another step—and then ripped the white veil from her head as if to reveal her identity to the Russians.

"For God's sake, what are you doing?" Michał rushed forward and grabbed Barbara's elbows now and forced her back. In moments the three were on the other side of the wall. Michał pulled closed the door, turned, and hurried them down the street.

Barbara was hysterically crying now. "Did you see?" she yelled aloud as they ran. "Did you see?"

"I did," Michał answered.

They were running as fast as the heavy robes would allow.

"See what?" Iza asked.

Michał turned to her and mouthed the word: *Viktor*. The third man had been Viktor Baklanov.

When they turned down Piwna Street, the coach was there—a Godsend—in front of the Gronska town house, the two hired men lashing several portmanteaux to the roof. This was a welcome sight to Iza but did not lessen her trepidation. According to insiders the szlachta who had participated in the effort against the tsar had no more than two days to execute plans to leave their homeland. It was no mercy on the Russians' part; it was more a matter of manpower and getting the wheels of bureaucracy to budge—and roll. No one truly knew the future. In the current climate even many of those who had remained neutral had chosen emigration.

But Iza knew they did not have the luxury of

any time at all. Viktor's timely appearance could be no coincidence. There had been a spy. No doubt the Gronska town house was under night and day observation with all activities reported to Viktor. Iza felt a hammering at her heart. She knew he would use whatever resources he had—and no doubt they were many now that he sat atop Fortune's wheel—to see their attempt to flee Poland thwarted. They might have only minutes to get away and even then would he not give chase?

Even as they reached the carriage—Iza praying everyone else was already seated within it and that it was ready to depart—she kept glancing back, expecting at any moment to see Viktor at the head of a secret police detail riding toward them.

The door to the coach was open. Jan and the twin boys were seated on one bench, Dimitri on his lap, Konrad leaning into him, both asleep.

Iza turned to Barbara and brushed at her tears. "You must get in now and say nothing to your father about what just occurred. You must be strong this day, Basia, stronger than you have ever been. Here, put your veil back on and tell your father we are dressed as we are to make clearing the gates and border easier. Do you hear me?"

Barbara looked at her a long moment, nodded, the harrowing knowledge that her brother's life was in Viktor's hands unspoken. She replaced the white veil and allowed Michał to help her up into the coach.

One glance at Michał told Iza he was as nervous as she. Like quicksilver he had gathered weapons from the house. He stood now, pistol in hand, his eyes straying again and again to the top of the street.

Iza turned to see Anna stepping down from the portico to the street. She went to her immediately. "Cousin Anna, you must hurry now. Where is my mother?"

"Ah, Zofia," Anna said with a sigh and an odd look at Iza's appearance. "She's still packing a trunk—I do hope there's room for it—and she is talking with Jerzy."

Jerzy! She had nearly forgotten her father. Her heart lurched. She had had such little time to get to know him. And now she would be saying goodbye to him. "A trunk, you say?" Iza was incredulous. "My God, we don't have time. Get into the coach. I'm going in to hurry her up."

Anna put her hand on Iza to restrain her. "No, don't do that, Iza. I suspect Zofia and Jerzy are having a conversation many years in the making. Now, tell me why you are dressed as you are."

Iza could not tell Anna of the failed plot to free her son even if she had time to do so, and so provided instead the convenient story—which might prove true—about the habits possibly allowing them to more easily pass through the city gates and at Poland's border.

Anna walked over to the coach and Iza watched as Michał saw her safely stowed, at the same time providing some excuse for his absence earlier in the morning, his eyes always reverting to the far end of the street.

Iza was sorely tempted to search out her mother and Jerzy. She waited. One minute. Then, two.

"Go get your mother, Iza," Michał ordered. "Christ's wounds! Hurry! We can't wait any longer!"

Iza turned toward the portico and took a few steps. The door opened now and Zofia and Jerzy came out, descending the portico steps as if all the time in the world belonged to them. "Mother, hurry! Where in Hades is your trunk?" She turned to Michał. "Do go get my mother's trunk, Michał."

A motion from Zofia stopped Michał at once. "I have something to tell you, Izabel."

"What is it, Mother? You don't understand that we must leave *now*!"

Zofia moved toward the coach. "Anna must hear this, too," she pronounced.

Anna leaned out one coach window, Barbara the other.

"Much as I've always wanted to see Paris, Anna," Zofia said, "I'm not going with you."

The statement drew protests all around. Only Jerzy remained silent as a monk. "Mother," Iza said, "you can't stay here. They will take your home and then they will take *you*!"

"I am staying with Jurek," Zofia said. Jerzy's diminutive fell lightly from her lips, like a breeze. She reached out and drew Jerzy's hand to her, held it there. "He's to take me to his village, Kosumce, on the Vistula. I was safe there once and so I will be again. I'll not leave Poland. I'll not leave Jurek. Not again."

The protests died at once. It took a long moment for reality to register with Iza—the reality that her parents were in love, that they would be together after so many years of living in different worlds. And the reality that she would be leaving them both behind. "Then I—I shall stay, as well."

"You will not!" Zofia's command was sharp. "Your place is with Michał. His place is with his family as they forge this . . . this new life. You must go, Izabel."

Iza turned to look at Michał, but he was staring at the other end of Piwna Street.

Michał did not contradict Zofia, but he had already decided that he would not be going to France. Not now. He would stay and work out another plan to free Józef. He would not leave him, though staying behind could very well cost him his own happiness with Iza—and his life. And he would kill Viktor, no matter the cost. No matter the family relationship. Credible political gossip had it that an unnamed leader of the Third Department had been the one who had stolen through Polish lines in order to tell General Paszkiewicz of the chaos in the capital and that the time was right to strike. His gut told him that man had been Viktor. He recalled that he had gotten the best of Viktor in their duel in the parkland near Belweder Palace. How he wished now that his concern for Barbara had not held held him back from killing him then and there!

He thought the old war joy he had felt in battle was part of the past, but it bubbled up within him now, buoyant and strong, zinging through his blood at the thought of killing his brother-in-law.

Michał saw the two men on horseback as soon

as they made the turn into Piwna Street, taking good time. Riding with Viktor Baklanov was a man in Russian uniform. Either they had a good many following behind or they had supreme confidence in their own ability. Undue confidence. Michał withdrew his pistol, keeping it pointed down at the cobblestones, and had his sword at the ready. His heart beat fast. Could he kill Viktor right there in the street—with Barbara steps away in the coach? And the twins, Viktor's children? An ugly situation. The decision came with little thought and less indecision. He would shoot the soldier first, then take on Viktor in a duel—unless Viktor had a pistol and could prove himself a good shot. If other Russians were on their way, then all would be lost—except that Viktor Baklanov would have had his due.

Michał stepped out into the street, raised the pistol, pointed it at Viktor even though he meant to kill the Russian soldier first. "We mean to leave, Viktor," he called out.

Viktor sat stiff in his saddle, proud, unperturbed. Michał could see no other way of getting the coach to roll out of Piwna Street without killing them both. He had killed a good many in his time. What were another two? He shifted his aim to the Russian soldier and prepared to fire. After today, he vowed, the killing would stop.

Viktor said something to the soldier now, simultaneously holding an upturned hand to Michał, who held his fire another moment.

The soldier removed the Russian helmet from his head. The action nearly prompted Michał to fire, but in an instant he realized that this soldier with the white-blond hair was no Russian soldier. The turquoise of his eyes was visible even at that distance.

"No need for that, Michał," Viktor said.

"Józef!" Anna cried from the coach window.

Taking hold of the reins of the other horse, Viktor said something and Józef slid from his horse. "He's yours," Viktor announced, his face hard.

What is his game? Behind him, Michał heard Barbara say something. He turned to see her make an attempt to exit the coach, her green eyes wet. His mother put a hand on her arm and she was stayed.

A long, long moment passed.

"See to the boys, Basia!" Viktor called. "Raise them well!" He swung his horse around and began moving back up the street, the other horse in tow. "Do not delay!" he called.

It was a warning. They had to escape Warsaw with all possible speed. Michał knew that Viktor was putting his own career and even his life in jeopardy by releasing an important prisoner, one who had attempted to abduct a Grand Duke of Russia. He watched Viktor urge the horses into a canter. Michał let out a long breath, the war joy going with it. He lowered his pistol now, looked from one amazed face to the next, saw his mother stepping down and embracing her youngest son. Was Viktor—this man who had perpetrated such evil—capable of sacrifice? Or was it merely a show of love, one meant to fool Barbara, perhaps even Viktor himself? On Barbara's face, though, he saw something more than amazement. Love for Viktor? Yes, he was certain of it. The pain in her face, the tears, told all. And heartbreak.

Józef's father had jumped from the carriage and now came forward. He had not missed a moment of the drama. "What did he say to you, Józef, there on the horses?" Jan asked.

"Very little, Father, just that he envied me my family."

"Rightfully so," Jan said, "rightfully so."

"My mother," Zofia said now, "used to say that before there are nations there are families."

Now came the goodbyes, travellers crowding into the coach, Michał hoisting himself above so as to sit with the hired men, Zofia and Jerzy standing on the portico that in short order would belong to someone else, perhaps a Russian bureaucrat. They all called out their goodbyes. Awakened, Dimitri and Konrad lent their high voices to the farewells.

Then, suddenly, Zofia called out. "Do forgive me, Ania." In those words Michał read transgressions against his mother from years ago, transgressions never admitted—until now.

Not two beats went by before Anna replied: "I love you, Zofia." All was forgiven.

"Come back one day, Anna!" Zofia begged.

In the morning sun, now rising crimson in the east, Michał saw something he had never seen before: Zofia's cheeks wet with tears.

Below, Anna answered: "How can I not come back to my beloved Poland?—How can I not? Goodbye, cousin. Live well!" And from his place atop the coach, Michał heard these words and his heart caught, for he realized his mother was choking back her own tears.

Michał knew, as did they, that Anna and Zofia—cousins, adversaries, and friends at last—would never see one another again.

Epilogue

The Stream is always Purest
At its Source
—POLISH PROVERB

3 May 1832

My Dearest Zofia,

At last, Jan has secured the secret means whereby I can get this message to Kosumce. May God guide it along the way so that it does find its path to you. How appropriate~or ironic?~that I should write it on the Third of May, our Constitution Day.

Where to begin? At the end, perhaps, of my time in Poland when we passed through the western gates of Warsaw, trundling along little travelled roads skirting Sochaczew. We dared not stop at Topolostan though I longed to see my familial home~now sequestered~one last time and kneel at the graves of my parents.

You cannot imagine the number of émigrés from Poland that have arrived here~estimates have it as high as nine thousand. As our carriage, one of many in a column, passed through the western German communities, we were buoyed by the incredibly warm and enthusiastic locals. Once in France we were given a friendly welcome and directed to a small town, one of several that served as a depot for the organized reception of the arrivals. There Iza learned the details of the small country estate she had inherited from your dear friend, the French Princess Charlotte Sic, not so very many miles from Paris. Upon Iza's marriage to Jan Michał there at the depot~oh my, perhaps I should have led with the news of the marriage!~the newlyweds departed for the estate.

While all of us had been urged to come live with them, our fates seem to lie within the city of Paris.

Here, we have been reunited with Jacob, our estate manager at Sochaczew and his wife Emma. Jacob had transferred our estate funds to a bank here so that we are better off than many of the émigrés who had to leave everything behind. Here in Paris the undaunted heart of a Poland-in-exile beats with the political and social thought that we hope will one day culminate in our return home. The words of our national anthem have never held more meaning: "Poland has not yet perished while we still live." Prince Adam Czartoryski is here and a circle seems to be forming around him. Jan and Michał see him often, while~to my great joy!~Józef has been reunited with his friend Fryderyk Chopin and has resumed his musical studies here, where artistic and cultural inspiration abounds. Basia and the boys, whose French is par excellence these days, have taken an apartment near ours so we see them often. She is having the hardest time of all of us.

And I? you might ask. Remembering your mother's words, I am trying to be content with my family around me~but for you and Jerzy~

What of you, Zofia? My eyes fill with tears when I think that you have at last allowed yourself happiness. Jerzy is such a fine man. The goodness of the years you have now will make up for the lost years, dearest. Live well, my cousin.

And now~Jan has just brought in the mail and in it is a missive from the country. Iza writes that she and Michał are expecting a child. Ah, I close my eyes and I see you smiling across the miles, your dark eyes dancing. You are to have a new title~Babka Zofia! I am smiling, too.

~~All my love, my dearest cousin~~
Anna

Historical Note

WHILE THE FAILURE OF THE cadets' insurrection against Russian autocracy brought an end to the Polish army, to the Sejm, and to the semi-independence of the Congress Kingdom, Polish nationalism flourished under the new oppression, leading to political and military action within what had been the Commonwealth, as well as among the nine thousand émigrés in France.

Thus, history repeated the collapse of the Polish dream of full independence: in 1794 Princess Anna Maria Berezowska-Stelnicka witnessed the the dissolution of the kingdom by Russia, Prussia, and Austria; in 1813 Poland's infatuation with Napoleon Bonaparte and his dream of an egalitarian Europe ended badly; and then came the cadet's insurrection of 1830. Following these, for the better part of a century, hope and the indefatigable Polish spirit lived on through revolutions and insurrections—until 1918 and the rebirth of Poland and Lithuania. However, World War II would defer the dream again—until the fall of the Iron Curtain and a modern vindication.

Author's Note

KONIEC WIEŃCZY DZIEŁO. THE END crowns the work. Following *Against a Crimson Sky*, *The Warsaw Conspiracy* completes a trilogy begun with *Push Not the River*, a novel based on a diary of a Polish countess. Sending my characters out into the world is both sad and joyous. *Na zdrowie!*

Reading Group Guide Questions

1. How do you interpret the first proverb, "Birth is Much; But Breeding is more"?
2. Discuss the longtime relationship of cousins Anna and Zofia.
3. How is Iza's character illustrated? Does she change?
4. How do Michal's feelings about one brother impact feelings for the other?
5. What does the story demonstrate about Poland's national character?
6. Is Jozef's quest to distinguish himself a universal one? What holds him back? Is he ultimately successful?
7. To what extent does the "outsider" theme play out?
8. What are Viktor's better qualities? Is he a hero is some way(s)?
9. How true is the proverb, "It Happens in an Hour that Comes Not in an Age"?
10. In what ways does Anna's final letter to Zofia complete a circle?

Next from James Conroyd Martin

The Story of the First 9-11

IN JULY OF 1683 VIENNA came under siege by the full brunt of the Ottoman Empire so that by 11 September it stood as the main outpost of Christian Europe. The citizens were starving and the walls of the city were giving way. Vienna was about to fall under the guns and mines of the Ottomans. Its collapse would mean plundered European cities, Christian slaves, and forced conversions. Allied European armies under the supreme command of Polish King Jan III Sobieski arrived not an hour too soon. The King descended the hill, riding at the van of his legendary winged hussars—armed with lances, pistols, and sabres—and an army of 40,000 against 140,000. Reputedly, the sight and sound of the wings of feathers attached to the hussars frightened both man and beast. Panic swept through the enemy and the battle was over within three hours. Europe had been saved from the enemy.

The Boy Who Wanted Wings is the story of a young Tatar boy adopted into a Polish peasant household. Aleksy has a long-held dream of becoming a Polish Hussar, a dream complicated by a forbidden love for a nobleman's daughter. It is only when the Ottomans seek to conquer Europe, coming at Vienna in 1683 for a monumental and decisive battle, that fate intervenes, providing Aleksy with opportunities—and obstacles.

An Excerpt from The Boy Who Wanted Wings

By James Conroyd Martin

DESPITE BEING SOMETIMES LABELED *THE Tatar* by some of his peers, as well as by some adults who snarled at him, Aleksy had been content to stay within the cocoon of Polishness he had come to know. Even though as the years went by and he became less fearful of venturing away from the family that had taken him in, he was afraid that doing so would hurt them. And so he had embraced Christianity and the Polish way of living.

But then there were times like these when he felt removed from every thing and everyone around him. Oh, he knew that the boundaries of class set a count's daughter upon a dais and well out of his reach, but to think now that the fortune of his birth and an appearance that reflected a coloring and visage that reached back to parents and ancestors

made the chasm between him and the girl in yellow
so much deeper and—despite logic—somehow a fault
of his own.

Still, he thought, his acceptance of things Polish
could be providential—should he ever have the
opportunity—slight as it was—of meeting the girl
in yellow.

About halfway up the mountain, he came to a
little clearing that jutted out over a cleared field. He
dismounted. His eyes fastened on the activity below.
This is what he had come for, and so he put the
count's daughter from his mind. Brooding on what
cannot be, he determined, would come to nothing.

The company of hussars on the field seemed larger
today, at least fifty, Aleksy guessed. They were being
mustered into formation now, their lances glinting in
the sun, the black and gold pennants flying. There
would be none of the usual games, it seemed, no
jousting, no running at a ring whereby the lancers
would attempt to wield their lance so precisely as to
catch a small ring that hung from a portable wooden
framework. Today they were forming up for sober and
orderly maneuvers. He wondered at their formality.

Aleksy took note of the multitude of colors below
and the little mystery resolved itself. Whereas on
other occasions the men, some very young and
generally of modest noble birth and means, wore
outer garments of a blue, often cheap material, today
they had been joined by wealthier nobles who could
afford wardrobes rich in the assortment of color and
material. These men—in their silks and brocades
and in their wolf and leopard skins or striped capes—

gathered to the side of the formation to watch and deliver commentary. Some of these were the Old Guard of the Kwarciani, the most elite of Hussars permanently stationed at borderlands east of Halicz to counter raids by Cossacks and Tatars unfriendly to the Commonwealth of Lithuania and Poland. Their reviews would be taken, no doubt, with great solemnity. Every soldier would make every effort to impress them. In recent years the group's numbers had been reduced by massacres and talk had it that they were eager to replenish their manpower. Perhaps a few of the novices below would be chosen to join the Kwarciani.

Some place at his core went cold with jealousy. If only he were allowed to train as a hussar. He could be as good as any of them. *Better.* No one he knew was more skillful at a bow than he. He could show those hussars a thing or two about the makings of an archer—even though he had come to realize fewer and fewer of the lancers bothered to carry a bow and quiver. The majority had come to disparage the art of archery in favor of pistols, relying instead on the lance, a pair of pistols, and a sabre.

Naturally enough, there was no disdain for the lance, the very lifeblood and signature weapon of the hussar army. Aleksy smiled to himself when he thought of his own handcrafted lance. Through his father he had made friends with Count Halicki's old stablemaster, Pawel, who one magical day had allowed him to peruse an old lance once used by the count. Having fashioned his own bow and arrows, he was already an expert in woodcraft when he took the measurements of the lance and carefully replicated it, creating it from a seventeen foot length of wood cut in halves and hollowed out as far as the rounded handguard at the lower end, thus reducing its weight. The shorter section managed by the lancer was left solid wood for leverage purposes. Finding a glue that would bind the two halves together had been a challenge, but an off-hand comment by Borys about a Mongolian recipe using a tar made from birch bark brought success.

Aleksy's thoughts conjured an elation that was only momentary, for he thought now how he had had to hide away his secret project under a pile of hay in the barn—and unless he should happen to be practicing with it one day in the forest when a wayward boar might come his way, he would never be able to use it. The thought of mounting a plow horse like Kastor with it instead of riding atop one of the Polish Arabians strutting below made him burn with—what? Indignation? Embarrassment? Humiliation—yes, he decided, humiliation was the most accurate descriptor.

Inexplicably, the thought of the girl in yellow once again seized him, lifting him, causing his heart to catch. Would he exchange one dream for the other? Life as a hussar for life with her?

He thought he just might risk anything to succumb to her charms.

Connect with the Author

Blog: http://www.jamescmartin.com
Facebook:
http://www.facebook.com/pages/
James-Conroyd-Martin/29546357206O

Made in the USA
San Bernardino, CA
16 August 2015